Mad About The Boy?

MAD ABOUT THE BOY?

Dolores Gordon-Smith

ISIS
LARGE PRINT
Oxford

Copyright © Dolores Gordon-Smith, 2008

First published in Great Britain 2008
by
Constable
an imprint of Constable & Robinson Ltd

Published in Large Print 2009 by ISIS Publishing Ltd.,
7 Centremead, Osney Mead, Oxford OX2 0ES
by arrangement with
Constable & Robinson Ltd

British Library Cataloguing in Publication Data
Gordon-Smith, Dolores
    Mad about the boy?. – Large print ed.
    1. Murder – Investigation – England – Sussex
    – Fiction
    2. World War, 1914–1918 – Veterans – Fiction
    3. Detective and mystery stories
    4. Large type books
    I. Title
    823.9'2 [F]

    ISBN 978–0–7531–8180–5 (hb)
    ISBN 978–0–7531–8181–2 (pb)

Printed and bound in Great Britain by
T. J. International Ltd., Padstow, Cornwall

To my father, Gordon Frederick Whitbread,
who tells such brilliant stories

CHAPTER
ONE

Arthur Stanton stubbed out his cigarette, peering anxiously through the haze of smoke at his reflection in the mirror. A sharp crack sounded outside the open bedroom window and his fingers twitched, pulling his white tie into a creased ribbon. For God's sake, couldn't they stop that *bloody* noise? Fireworks. He drew a deep breath. Take it easy, Arthur, he told himself firmly, it's only fireworks. They're setting up the display for tonight. He threw down the crumpled tie and fumbled for another cigarette. How the hell was he supposed to get ready with all that row going on? Another bang sounded and he shuddered. These weren't even the fireworks proper. The big show was later in the evening and, compared to that, all these odd bangs and cracks would pale into insignificance. He'd enjoyed fireworks at one time. What the devil was the matter with him? All he had to do was put on a tie.

He caught sight of his long, worried face in the mirror and clicked his tongue in disgust. For a grown man to be reduced to a state where he couldn't tie a ruddy tie because of a few mistimed fireworks was crazy. How on earth was he going to cope later on? Why the devil was he here at all?

He knew, he thought gloomily, the answer to that. He was here because he'd been invited to Hesperus for the ball and to stay for a few days afterwards. This, he'd told himself with a surge of hope, was the chance he'd been waiting for. To be with Isabelle in her own home was an opportunity he'd seized with both hands. Yes, of course he knew there'd be other people about — there were always other people about when Isabelle was there — but he'd painted a picture, a rose-coloured, idyllic picture, of just the two of them. He'd spent the previous fortnight sweltering in a London heatwave, longing for this week in Sussex, dreaming of lazy summer days and rich velvet nights. It was just the sort of weather to go boating on the river or for long walks through the woods or maybe picnicking in some secluded spot. It'd have to be, he thought cynically, very secluded indeed to cut out the hordes of friends Isabelle always seemed to be surrounded by.

Fool! He looked at the crumpled tie in his hand. The weather was the only thing in that pipe dream that had matched up to reality. Yes, it was summer. Yes, Isabelle was here at home in Hesperus, and yes, there were rivers, woods, shady lawns and long June nights. But for all the chances he'd had to get Isabelle alone, she might as well be standing in the middle of Piccadilly Circus.

Aunt Alice and Uncle Phil are holding a ball for their Silver Wedding, Jack had said. *Hesperus will be really nice at this time of year. We're having a fireworks display. You'll enjoy it.* Enjoy it! Jack must know how he felt. Jack, of all people, should have guessed how he'd react and why. Stanton paused. Jack really should have known. So why . . . ?

The hazel eyes in the mirror narrowed. There had been a faint question mark at the end of "You'll enjoy it." So Jack had guessed. There had been other questions, too. Bloody marvellous. Stanton's reflected face twisted. He obviously thinks I'm verging on a basket case. The next thing you know I'll be giving the loony bin some business. He stopped, chilled, as his stomach clenched in a heavy lump of fear.

That wasn't funny. He rested his forehead on his hand. Loony bin. *Hospital* . . .

He straightened up. There was one person in this world and one person only who could prevent him going back. He forced himself to look at his reflection squarely. Me. Me. Jack wasn't going to stick him in a . . . a . . . He swallowed. A *hospital* — he forced himself to think the word — again.

A puzzled look came into the mirrored face. Why on earth had he put it like that? Jack wasn't responsible. It wasn't Jack's fault. Jack had met him at King's Cross. It was meant to be over. The . . . the *hospital* had discharged him and he was supposed to be fit for active service once more.

The Euston Road. The pleasure of being with an old friend. Jack's an old friend. Hold on to that. He told me he was a friend. I know he's a friend. But . . . *Traffic. So much traffic.* He's talking about cricket scores. *Can't he hear the noise of the traffic?* He's talking about the weather. *I can't hear what he's saying because of the noise. Can't he see the crowds? He*

3

made me come here. Here, where there are hundreds of people. What's he saying now? A new musical? What? Do I fancy seeing a show? Go to where there are more people? Aren't there enough here? There are hundreds of people jostling, pushing. What about something to eat? *I'll be trapped. He knows I'll be trapped inside a crowded room. Can't he see the faces of the crowd, waiting for me to panic, daring me to run?* There's an Italian restaurant in Soho. *That noise! Oh, God, that noise!*

Everything had gone blank, then Jack was talking to someone, a big man in a blue uniform. "It's all right, don't worry, officer. He was badly shot up at Passchendaele. We thought he was all right." Jack's anxious face, close to his. "Don't worry, Arthur, I'll take care of you." *Liar!*

He'd been taken to . . . to That Place again and Jack had abandoned him.

The strength of the emotion pulled him up sharp. He hadn't been abandoned. Jack *had* helped him. He couldn't possibly have stayed. After all, Jack had to return to his squadron. He'd given up his two precious days of home leave to meet him and all this was so damned unfair. I ought to be bloody well ashamed of myself, thought Stanton. It was just that the inside and the outside of that time had never matched but grated away at the back of his mind. For the first time he wondered what Jack had thought about it all. He'd never mentioned it. It might never have happened for all the difference it seemed to make, but, if only Jack knew, that was difficult as well. Because it had

4

happened and it had been — well, difficult. I might as well call it that as anything, he thought; difficult.

He looked at the crumpled tie again. He couldn't wear that to the ball. Wearily he took a spare from the drawer, wincing as another firework cracked outside the window. I don't care, thought Stanton. I'm going to tie this wretched — damn!

A knock sounded on the door and Stanton guiltily stood up.

Without waiting for an answer, Jack Haldean came in. "Aren't you ready yet, Cinderella? You'll be late for the ball."

Haldean's tie, Stanton noticed with a twinge of irritation, was immaculate, like the rest of his dress clothes. He didn't know how it was, but old Jack somehow always looked more foreign in evening dress than in ordinary things, a bit like a cultured gypsy mixed with some Spanish hidalgo, with his black hair smoothed down and his white shirt emphasizing the Mediterranean darkness of his skin. He looks as if he's about to dance a tango or start the Inquisition or, thought Stanton grumpily, lead some ruddy dance band. Then he met the warm friendliness of those dark eyes and, for the second time in as many minutes, felt ashamed.

Haldean looked round the room curiously. "Where's your valet?"

"He gave notice." Stanton hurriedly knotted his tie. "I haven't had a chance to replace him yet. Didn't I tell you?" He looked in the mirror and frowned. "Will that do, Jack?"

Haldean twitched the recalcitrant cloth into place. "It will now. Come on, everything's about to kick off."

Privately, Haldean was concerned. He'd been unhappy for a while about his old friend. Arthur was naturally a cheerful, kindly sort, sensitive to other people's feelings, who'd go to an awful lot of trouble without making a fuss or even without thinking there was anything to make a fuss about. A dependable bloke, thought Haldean, which sounded virtuous but dull. It wasn't dull; Arthur had mixed it with an amiable goofiness which leavened out the solid worth, and he wasn't perfect. He was forgetful, late for meals and lost things but those weren't really faults. Naturally, after what had happened in the war, he couldn't be expected to be the life and soul of the party, but he'd been getting there. To outward appearances Arthur had come through the war unscathed and looked much the same as he always had; a tall, well-proportioned man with deep hazel eyes, a firm jaw, high forehead and brown hair that would not, despite his best endeavours, stay fashionably sleeked back. And he had been getting over it. Now? Now he looked washed out and nervy. At a guess that was partly the fireworks — the evening had been punctuated by random cracks and bangs — but Haldean had no hesitation in laying the blame for Arthur's nerves squarely on his cousin Isabelle's shoulders, and that, too, was partly due to the war.

If he hadn't been in the army Stanton would have met Isabelle ages ago and would have witnessed her transformation from a leggy schoolgirl with spots into an acknowledged beauty. Quite when the miracle had happened Haldean didn't know, but there was no doubt that Isabelle, with her green eyes, her rich auburn hair and her wicked grin, had a shattering effect on quite a number of young men. Stanton should have been just another name on the list. But Isabelle clearly liked Arthur, liked him very much. Liked him so much, in fact, that Haldean had caught himself thinking how pleasant it would be to have his cousin married to his best friend.

Then Isabelle had met Malcolm Smith-Fennimore and Stanton had been eclipsed. Because Smith-Fennimore, merchant banker, aviator, racing driver, broad-shouldered, blue-eyed and fair-haired, wasn't just some idle rich bloke. He was deeply sincere, troubled by the world around him and obviously hungrily searching for happiness. Isabelle had taken one look and melted. Which left, thought Haldean, poor old Arthur out in the cold and no mistake.

However, no matter how fraught the poor chap's feelings were, they still had to go to the ball. A hum of animated conversation met them as they as they rounded the curve of the stone staircase. The house was thronged with people in evening dress. Isabelle was in the middle of the hall, talking politely to the new arrivals.

She looked up and smiled as she saw them. Haldean heard Stanton's quick intake of breath. It wasn't surprising. Isabelle was lovely anyway but now, dressed for the ball, she was simply beautiful. She rid herself adroitly of a stout woman in satin with pearls and

7

feathers and zigzagged through the crush to the foot of the stairs.

"So there you are," she said in an undertone. "I've been waiting ages. Why on earth everyone doesn't go into the ballroom instead of hanging around in the hall, I don't know. Jack, will you dance with Squeak Robiceux?"

"The terrible twin? Delighted, old thing," said Haldean, taking her arm. The three of them stepped round the edge of the crowd and walked towards the ballroom. "Shall I take on Bubble Robiceux as well? There's a reduction for quantity."

Isabelle shook her head. "Bubble hasn't got a problem. She's as thick as thieves with Tim Preston and that's why Squeak's a bit high and dry."

"I'll gladly dance with Squeak," put in Stanton. "She must feel a bit lost without Bubble."

"She does," said Isabelle. "Thanks, Arthur. That's nice of you. Step in if you see her stranded, won't you, Jack?"

Haldean grinned. "Trust old Uncle Jack. As always, I shall be a willing lamb to the slaughter. I shall hold her hand, glide her round the dance floor and, if necessary, whisk her into the conservatory and whisper sweet somethings into her shell-like ears. All part of the service. Moderate charges and families waited upon daily."

"There's no need to go overdoing it," said Isabelle. "I could imagine you being worryingly magnetic if you really turned on the charm. You might look like South

American Joe, but keep it under wraps, will you? I want her entertained, not heartbroken."

"I shall aim for modified rapture." He nodded to Lawson, the footman, splendid in full livery, who announced them at the top of his stentorian voice, and went into the ballroom, smiling as he caught the eye of Aunt Alice who stood with Uncle Philip, greeting the guests.

Haldean whistled involuntarily. Aunt Alice had really been to town. The last ball at Hesperus had been at Christmas and, despite its size, the room had been snug with Christmas colours of green and red. Now, on this night in high summer, all the french windows stood open and the smells of the garden mixed with the heady scent of the cascades of white roses spilling down the walls. Under the diamond brilliance of the huge chandelier the silver ribbons looped round the walls glistened like threads of frost, reflected in the glassy shine of the deeply polished floor. The orchestra was tuning up and there was a buzz of excitement from the people thronging the room. He smiled at his cousin. "This looks tip-top."

Isabelle looked round the waiting crowd and gave a happy little wriggle of anticipation. "We're going to have a wonderful time."

And they were, thought Haldean. Later on he'd slip up to the balcony to see what it looked like from up there. He grinned. That had been a real childhood treat. He, Isabelle and her brother Greg had been allowed to sit on the balcony and eat ice-cream and watch the dancers below before being packed off to bed. Those had been magical nights, the rich, mingling colours of the women's dresses contrasting with the black and white of the men. It was the smells that whisked him back, a heady mixture of perfumes, warm people and the oil-and-chalk smell of the ballroom. At the far end of the room was the conservatory. Now that had been an unobtainable Mecca when he was a kid. There was a whole room packed with elaborate pastries, rafts of tiny sandwiches, lemonade and gold-topped green bottles in glittering ice. He wished Greg was here to share it all, but Greg was far away from Sussex, sweltering in the tropic heat of Malaya. He had gone out two months ago, working as the assistant manager in a rubber firm, and it was anyone's guess when he'd be home again. Just for a moment Haldean felt a twinge of sadness but shook it off. Hello, things were about to get going.

Uncle Philip stepped up on to the orchestra stand. "I'm not much of a hand at speeches . . ." he said. That was true enough, but his obvious sincerity as he thanked everyone for their company and good wishes was more moving than a polished performance would have been. His broad smile at the enthusiastic applause which greeted his words spoke for itself.

The clapping died down and there was an expectant rustle as the leader of the orchestra announced the first dance.

Stanton coughed. "Er . . . I say, Isabelle, are you engaged for this dance?" His face lit up. "You aren't? I don't suppose you would? Would you?"

Isabelle favoured Stanton with a smile. "Of course I will."

Stanton caught his breath once more and took her arm.

That, thought Haldean, was downright cruel. Dance with poor old Arthur, yes, but was there really any need to gaze at him with that "If You Were the Only Boy in the World" expression? It was a downright shame Greg wasn't here. He'd tell her. But Greg wasn't here. Which meant, thought Haldean glumly, that he'd have to step into the breach. Why on earth couldn't she let him down gently instead of pouring petrol on the flames? As soon as Smith-Fennimore walked into the room Arthur would be dropped with a thud. He really was going to have to tackle Isabelle about it. Arthur couldn't take it. The poor devil had been getting downright twitchy recently. His nerves hadn't skinned over enough for this sort of treatment. Damn it, Belle, stop it, he mentally pleaded as he saw her hand caress his friend's arm. And Arthur should have more sense.

With his good mood well and truly dented, Haldean turned away to go in search of a drink.

What he found was his old friend Tim Preston, marching down the side of the ballroom with a scowl on his normally good-tempered face. "That *bloody* man," he said.

"Who?" asked Haldean.

"Need you ask?" said Preston. "Lyvenden, of course. My esteemed employer. God knows why your uncle invited him. If he knew half of what I know, he wouldn't have him in the house."

"To be honest, Tim, I did wonder about it myself. I can't say I took to him at lunch."

That was an understatement. Even though Uncle Philip could get along with just about anyone on earth — chiefly by assuming everyone was exactly like himself — Haldean had been surprised by his uncle's new acquaintance. Victor, Lord Lyvenden, was a tubby little arms and munitions manufacturer from Birmingham who had promised a firework display. Lord Lyvenden had arrived in state, complete with his wife, Lady Harriet, his wife's companion, Mrs Strachan, his servants and workmen. That he'd also brought his secretary, Tim Preston, who knew both Haldean and Stanton and was a close friend of Malcolm Smith-Fennimore's, was unexpected but welcome.

Haldean had caught the pained expression on Preston's face as Lyvenden held forth to his unenthralled audience over lunch about how he'd helped the war effort and how, undaunted by the fact that there no longer was any war to help, he'd had the Foresight, Enterprise and Initiative to develop the fireworks part of his business, principally, according to him, to aid The Operatives Of The Leading Manufactories Of Our Sadly Depressed Industrial Heartland. The capital letters were clearly audible when Lord Lyvenden spoke. Haldean had to fight the urge to shout "Hear, hear!"

"I suppose he does some sort of good by providing jobs," Haldean said to Preston doubtfully. "Homes fit for heroes, and all that."

Preston leaned forward. "Don't believe a word of it, old man. The only person Old Tubby wants to help is himself. He's as mean as sin and I don't believe he's as successful as he likes to make out, either. There's a lot of cheap arms kicking about nowadays, as you'd expect, and the bottom's dropped out of the market. His peerage cost him a cool fifty thousand and you have to sell a lot of Roman candles to make up that sort of money. I think he's struggling. That's why he was so anxious to get on the board of Malcolm's bank."

"Malcolm's bank?"

"Yes. That was partly my fault. Lyvenden knew I knew Malcolm and made it his business to scrape an acquaintance. Before you could say 'knife', he was on the board. I warned Malcolm what he was like, but he pulled a long face and talked business at me. I suppose Malcolm knows what he's doing, but I wouldn't trust Lyvenden as far as I could throw him. I tell you," said Preston, drawing Haldean away from the swirling dancers, "if I don't get another job soon, I'll go crackers. Every damn time he sees me he has me running up to his blasted room for something. Lady Harriet's forgotten her bag, so guess who has to go and fetch it?"

"You?" suggested Haldean with a grin.

"Abso-ruddy-lutely," replied Preston with feeling. He glanced over his shoulder to make sure they couldn't be overheard. "I've been up and down like the proverbial bride's nightie. He's awful to work for. I wrote three perfectly good letters for him this afternoon, all of which ended up in the waste-paper basket."

"You can't blame him for wanting to get it right," put in Haldean.

Preston snorted. "Can't I though! You don't know what he's like. As if that wasn't enough, I picked up the wrong papers and he went bonkers. He's neurotic about those papers. God knows what he got so worked up about. It was all in some sort of code and I couldn't understand a word of it."

Haldean looked doubtful. "It was in code, you say? To be fair, it might really be important. Doesn't he have government contracts and what-have-you for his munitions works? After all, fireworks are only a sideline. The munitions stuff would have to be confidential."

Preston gave another snort. "Confidential! Let me tell you, Jack," he said, steering him towards the door, "if I had any confidential documents, Old Tubby is the last person I'd trust them with." He cast another quick glance over his shoulder. "D'you know what I found the other day, mixed up with some quotes for cardboard sheeting? A love letter."

"A love letter? From Lady Harriet, you mean?"

Preston gave him a withering look. "No one gets love letters from their wife, Jack. Talk sense. No, this was from his latest armful, so to speak, Mrs Strachan, Lady Harriet's so-called companion." Preston paused. "He pays her very well," he added meaningfully.

Haldean was stunned. "You don't mean the Mrs Strachan who's here, do you?" Preston nodded gleefully. "My God, Tim, he must be mad. If it got out he'd brought a . . ." He hesitated. "I'd better call her

14

his mistress, I suppose, to a house party, he'd be ruined."

"I know." Preston's grin was infectious. "It's not really done to arrive with a ready-made harem, is it? Especially one of the Queen of Hearts, so to speak. Finding someone on the spot's different."

Haldean laughed. "Don't be coarse. Hesperus has never been somewhere to play musical bedrooms, but that's above the odds anywhere. What the blazes is Lyvenden thinking of?"

"God only knows. And look at her. She's no scorcher, is she?"

Haldean glanced across the room to where Mrs Strachan was languidly sipping a glass of champagne. She was wearing a frilly apricot and white dress with ostrich feathers and looked like a dissolving wedding cake. "I hope to God my uncle never finds out. He'd blow a fuse."

Preston smoothed back his sandy hair with a grin. "Shocking, isn't it? She did start off as Lady H's companion, that's kosher enough. Old Tubby can't keep his hands off the domestics — or anything else in a skirt, for that matter. I tell you, Jack, he's not a nice man."

"Poor Lady Harriet."

Preston sniffed. "Save your sympathy. If I were married to her, I'd want some time off myself. She's a complete iceberg, a shocking snob and hates his guts as well. She's the daughter of old Ballavinch, who went half dotty with horses and drink, and he married her off to the highest bidder. The title's pukka, though, and

15

that's what Lyvenden was after. He wanted a posh wife who'd get him into society."

"Watch it!" warned Haldean, catching sight of the red-faced Lord Lyvenden walking ponderously towards them. Preston swore and shot off down the room, leaving Haldean with the irate peer.

"Was that Preston?" puffed Lord Lyvenden. "Eh, boy?"

"It was, sir," said Haldean smoothly. "I must apologize for holding him up."

"Hmm. When I ask for something to be done, I expect it to *be* done." Lord Lyvenden frowned at him. "It's Hutchinson, isn't it?"

"Haldean, Lord Lyvenden. Jack Haldean."

"Ah yes," said Lord Lyvenden with satisfaction. "Rivers was telling me about you. You do murders, don't you?"

"Not exactly," replied Haldean, keeping his face straight with some difficulty. "I write about them, though. I write detective stories."

"Thought as much. I don't read 'em myself. I've far too much to do." A crack of a firework sounded from outside and Lord Lyvenden frowned. "Did you hear that? It's a good job I'm here otherwise it would all be a complete shambles. I've checked every item in that display myself. Every item, sir," he added, as if Haldean had been arguing about it. "You'd think the men would be capable of setting up a firework display but they're not. They'd never get it right if I left them to it. Constant care, that's my motto. Constant care and vigilance. Thank heaven you don't have any responsibilities, boy." He nodded and strode away, the worries of the world heavy on his shoulders.

Haldean turned to find Isabelle at his shoulder.

"Go and dance with Squeak Robiceux," she hissed. "*Now!*"

"I want a drink."

"Not now, Jack. The poor girl's waiting."

Haldean turned to where Squeak Robiceux was standing. She looked lovely, if uncharacteristically nervous. Her fair hair was dressed with a pink ribbon embroidered with pearls that perfectly set off the pearls of her necklace and the pink and cream of her ballgown. She saw his glance and smiled, a quick, rather tentative smile. Haldean's conscience bit him. Poor old Squeak must have spent ages getting ready and it wasn't too much for the girl to expect someone to dance with her. He liked the Robiceux twins. They were old friends of Isabelle's and she'd often told him how the virtually indistinguishable twins had enlivened the dull life of school. And now Squeak was on her own; it must be rotten for her, especially as she'd been so looking forward to the ball.

"Of course I'll dance with Squeak," he said. "It's a pleasure."

"Good-oh." Isabelle turned as a man hovered respectfully beside her. "The next dance, Ronnie? That's spoken for, I'm afraid." She flashed out a melting, if artificial, smile. "You can have the fourth one from now if you like."

Ronnie Hawthorne coloured with pleasure. "I say, that's awfully good of you."

"Not at all." She looked round to find Haldean still there and switched off the smile. "Please, Jack. You promised."

Haldean duly danced.

It was a good three-quarters of an hour afterwards, during which he had Waltzed, Shimmied, Glided, Jog-Trotted and Missouri Walked, that Lady Rivers approached.

"Jack, there's a peculiar-looking man at the door," she said, drawing him away. "He's asking for your Uncle Alfred and I can't find him anywhere. I can't ask Philip to help. He's far too busy and the servants have all got their hands full. Will you take care of this man until we find Alfred? I can't have him wandering all over the house and he didn't seem to understand anything I said to him. He's certainly not English. Goodness knows where Alfred came across him, but he's definitely odd. I left him in the hall."

"I'll see to him, Aunt Alice. Don't worry."

Haldean lit a cigarette and walked out of the brilliant, noisy ballroom into the empty, shadowy house, hearing the music fade behind him. His weak leg, a souvenir of the war, throbbed warningly and it was a relief to stop dancing for a while. He could feel quite grateful to Alfred Charnock's visitor, no matter how odd. Almost by definition, any visitor for Isabelle's Uncle Alfred could be described as odd. Alfred Charnock was Aunt Alice's stepbrother, and, although well over forty, stalked through life like a lean panther with a dark, moody charm which he used to wind otherwise sensible women round his finger. Not only that, it was Charnock who had introduced Lord Lyvenden to Uncle Phil and that was probably his worst offence to date. He had been living at Hesperus for months now, having come to grief, so he said, in the City. And whatever scheme Charnock had been involved in, it was bound to be dodgy, Haldean thought uncharitably. There was a mysterious blank about what he'd done in the war, too. Isabelle had a typically romantic reason for his silence. *Russia! And they're still after him!*

But there might, thought Haldean, pausing at the pillared doorway to the now deserted hall and summing up Charnock's visitor, be some truth in the Russian story after all. For the man slumped on the settle was certainly a Slav. He had high cheekbones and hair so fair it was nearly white, and he wore knee-length boots and a short leather jacket which were obviously foreign. His age might have been anything from twenty-five to well over thirty. Haldean coughed and the man turned a pair of hard, pale blue eyes to his.

"Al-fred Char-nock?" The man picked over the syllables of the name carefully. "You are Al-fred Char-nock, yes?"

Before Haldean could answer, Charnock himself came down the stairs into the hall. He stopped short, then crossed to the settle, snapping out a sentence in a language Haldean didn't understand. Although the meaning was obscure, the emotion was transparent. Charnock was furious. The Slav looked sullenly at the floor, spat, and gestured towards Haldean in the shadow of the doorway.

Charnock whirled, forcing a smile. "Jack! Been here long?"

Haldean shook his head. "I've just arrived. Aunt Alice asked me to take care of your visitor until you could be found."

Charnock cocked his head and rapped out another sentence to the man, receiving a grunted reply. Then he relaxed. "Thanks, Jack. Good of you to bother. I'm going to have to go out for a while." He indicated the Slav. "This is an old friend of mine. I came across him in the war. He's a bit up against it. I'll have to go and see if I can get him a bed for the night. I won't inflict him on Alice. She's got enough to do and I don't want to trouble her. Can you ask Egerton to leave the side door unbolted? I may be some time." Charnock rapidly escorted the man out of the front door, leaving Haldean to close it after him.

And what, thought Haldean, turning back to the ballroom, was all that about? Old friend be blowed. Old friends could be counted on to recognize one another and it was clear the Slav had not known Charnock. So who the devil was he? And why did Charnock want him out of the house so urgently? Giving Aunt Alice any trouble was something which had never bothered Charnock in the past. No. For some reason Charnock had been very anxious that Aunt Alice shouldn't see any more of the man than was necessary. Why?

20

In the ballroom, Arthur Stanton was leaning by the door. He was beginning to enjoy himself. Hesperus reminded him of home before it had all been broken up and sold. He had lived twenty miles up the coast and was touched to find his father's name still affectionately remembered. He took a great delight in the everyday conversations around him. No one had mentioned Flanders or the war or illness, just solid, ordinary things such as the weather and crops and dogs. He had a great yearning to be part of this world once more, with a house and some land and settled, reliable tasks in front of him and all . . . *all that* so firmly behind that he need never think of it again. Then Isabelle walked towards him and, as he saw her smile, contentment changed to delight.

She grinned at him conspiratorially. "Arthur, do you want to save a human life?"

Her smile was exhilarating. "That sounds rather a good idea. Whose?"

"Mine."

Stanton felt a glow of sheer pleasure. "I'll say. What do I have to do?"

She leaned forward. "Meet me by the stone seat at the end of the terrace with some cigarettes and a cocktail. Make sure mine's got plenty of gin in it. I'm going to die if I have to spend another minute in here." She turned as a cry of "Isabelle! My dear!" sounded behind her. "Mrs Gavinthorpe!" she said with every appearance of sincerity. "How lovely to see you again!" She tipped him a wink as she swept away.

She'd chosen *him*. Not Jack or Tim or any of the other dozens of men in the ballroom or even Smith-Fennimore, with whom she'd danced far too often that evening, but *him*! He fetched the drinks, went out on to the terrace and took a deep breath as he saw her shadowy figure come towards him. The light and music of the ball spilling through the open french windows seemed distant and remote, as if they belonged to another world. A brilliant moon chequered the house and gardens in black and silver. A man laughed and the sound was far away.

"Are those the cocktails?" asked Isabelle, unethereally enough. She took a substantial drink and sighed. "Thank God for gin." She looked at his face and laughed. "Oh dear, I've shocked you."

"No, you haven't," said Stanton, nettled. "I've seen you drink cocktails dozens of times."

"Ah yes, but that was in London and what goes on in London, so I've been told, won't do here. Have you got a cigarette? Thanks. I need it."

"Whatever have they been bothering you about?" asked Stanton. He sat beside her and lit her cigarette. "I'm sorry, they're only gaspers. Shall I get you something else?"

She shook her head and put her hand on his arm. "No, don't go. To be honest, I just wanted some time off. I've had to be so nice to so many people, it all got to be a bit of a strain. I've danced with at least three old relics of about ninety-six and been ever so polite, even though one smelt of snuff, one trod on my dress and the other told me about every ball he'd been to since the Crimea. At that point I saw you and thought of gin. I knew you'd be a sport. Goodness knows where Jack's got to and Tim's spent the evening either glued on to Bubble Robiceux or running errands for Lord Lyvenden."

Stanton coughed. "What about Smith-Fennimore?" If there was an edge to his voice, she didn't notice it. Her hand seemed to burn through the cloth of his sleeve.

"Malcolm? I like Malcolm, but . . ." She sipped her drink reflectively. "He's difficult to relax with. I could never imagine being out here with him and simply having a drink and a cigarette." She looked at Stanton affectionately and squeezed his arm. "You're different. You're a very easy person to be with."

There were so many mixed messages in this speech that Stanton baulked at working them out. He let the tangle of thought go and smoked in silence, feeling her warm presence beside him. He was afraid to break the spell and yet . . . An owl hooted in the distance and a rustle close by suggested it would not hunt in vain. Surely this was the moment? She'd said she felt happy with him.

Isabelle stood up and threw away the stub of her cigarette, watching it firefly into darkness. "I'd better be getting back, I suppose."

The moonlight caught the nape of her neck, the skin of her shoulders and the delicate angle of her jaw. Stanton scrambled to his feet and held out his hand. "Please don't go." As she turned to face him, her hand lightly holding his, his stomach turned to water.

"Arthur?" For once she looked absolutely serious and it made him, if possible, love her even more. "Arthur, please don't."

"I've got to," he insisted. "I love you." He'd said it. He'd tried to say it for months. "I love you. There's never been anyone like you, Isabelle. I'm asking you to marry me. You must know I love you." He reached out and touched her face with the palm of his hand. She said nothing, but looked at him with such compassion that he knew what her answer was. He strapped down the numbing feeling of desperation and stroked her cheek gently, pleading with his eyes. Slowly she shook her head and Stanton felt his world start to splinter round him.

"I'm sorry," she said quietly. "We're friends, Arthur. I don't want to hurt you. I never did want to hurt you."

He dropped his hand and drew a deep breath. "No. It's no, isn't it?"

She moved impulsively then was still once more. "I'm sorry."

He met her eyes squarely. "Sorry? You've got nothing to be sorry for." Again she moved towards him but this time he drew back. Then, on an impulse, he took her hand, raised it to his lips and gently kissed her fingertips. "You'd better go."

There was a quick look of concern in her eyes. "You will be all right, won't you?"

He straightened up, put his shoulders back, and made himself smile. "Of course. I'll sit in the garden and eat worms. Off you go, before they send search parties for you."

She gave a smile of relief. "I'm so glad we can still be friends." She walked away, glanced round once, hesitated, and went into the house.

He watched after her, smiling faintly, but as soon as she had gone he collapsed on the stone seat and lowered his head into his hands. For minutes he sat there unmoving, then rubbed the heel of his hand across his eyes. With clumsy, shaking fingers he pulled out his cigarette case and tried to open it. The cigarettes spilled out on to the stone flags. He watched them dully before slamming the case shut with unnecessary violence and thrusting it back in his pocket. "Damn!" he said faintly, then, louder, "Damn!" He got up and strode back to the house.

The noise of the ball assaulted his ears. He couldn't face it. Not yet. He walked along the terrace, into the deserted dining room and so into the hall.

Tim Preston was on the stairs. "Arthur! Would you believe it? Lyvenden's done it *again*! He's forgotten his cigarette case this time and sent me to fetch it. What d'you say to that?"

Stanton, unable to trust his voice, couldn't say anything and nodded a reply. He drifted back to the ballroom and leant against the oak panelling, his eyes automatically searching for Isabelle. He couldn't see her. What did it matter, anyway?

"I was wondering where you'd got to, Arthur." It was Haldean. "We've just got time to get a drink and wedge ourselves in somewhere to see these blessed fireworks."

He took in Stanton's strained face. He couldn't ask *Are you all right?* Stanton obviously wasn't, but he wouldn't be any happier for having it pointed out. "I gather the correct attitude is to stand around in slack-jawed wonder making 'Ooh' noises at appropriate intervals." He knew he was talking to fill up the gaps, but Stanton seemed relieved by the fact that he hadn't, apparently, noticed anything. He steered his friend across the room and out on to the terrace. "That's better. We'll get a decent view from here. Hello, here's the Master of Ceremonies, old Lyvenden himself." More gap-filling. "He looks even redder than usual. Must be rotten, being fat in a crush like this." He was bordering on inanity, but he guessed it was helping. "Oh, God have mercy, he's going to make a speech. We might have known he couldn't resist the opportunity."

The entire party followed Lord Lyvenden and Lady Harriet outside on to the lawn. Haldean wedged himself beside the french windows and gave himself up to the dubious pleasure of listening to Lyvenden's raptures on This Happy Occasion of his hosts' Argent Anniversary.

Haldean grinned in involuntary appreciation and settled back to enjoy the speech. The florid always made him smile and Lord Lyvenden had struck a rich vein. Lord Lyvenden, it appeared, was happy (*great and unalloyed gratification*) to be here. Lord Lyvenden hoped that everyone else was equally happy (*share my jubilation*) and offered his congratulations (*heartfelt felicities*) to Sir Philip and Lady Rivers. He humbly offered, as a small token of his regard, a display of fireworks, or, as he preferred to phrase it, *These*

Polychromatic Pyrotechnics, a phrase that reduced Haldean to discreet hiccups of laughter.

He turned to share the joke with Stanton, but his friend had vanished. Concerned, Haldean tried to see where he had gone, but was hemmed in by the crowd. Lyvenden, in fine fettle, allowed himself a few more orotund flourishes before he abruptly decided to sink the public man in the private. "Harriet, my dear," he boomed at half volume to his wife. "You should not be out here without your shawl. You might take cold."

"Nonsense, Victor," she drawled. "The night is perfectly fine."

"Nevertheless, I shall send for it directly." His eyes roamed over the crowd but for once Preston had managed to stay out of sight. Yvette, Lady Harriet's maid, who was standing with the rest of the servants behind the guests, was dispatched. On the terrace, Lord Lyvenden gave the assembled company the benefit of Some Further Thoughts. Turning, Haldean caught sight of Stanton by the door. Muttering excuses, he pushed his way to the back of the group.

Stanton nodded to him. "Sorry I disappeared, Jack. I couldn't stand the crowd."

"We'll stay here if you like. No need to mix it with hoi polloi."

Lord Lyvenden produced a triumphant and, thankfully, final rhetorical embellishment, then summoned his foreman, who took a length of fuse from his khaki dust-coat and handed it over. Then, with as much ceremony as would attend the launch of a transatlantic liner, Lyvenden lit the fuse and handed it back to his waiting employee. The foreman walked over to the silent display and, on a signal from Lord Lyvenden, lit the touchpapers. There was a terrific crash, rockets zoomed and the sky lit up in a blaze of colour.

"My God," breathed Haldean. "It's like the Somme."

Beside him, Stanton groaned and shielded his eyes. Haldean took one look at his ashen face then grasped him firmly by the arm, shepherding his unresisting friend out of the ballroom and into the drawing room.

Here, at the front of the house, the noise was deadened. Stanton slumped in a chair and breathed a sigh of relief. "Sorry, Jack. Stupid of me. When those fireworks went off I felt as if I'd had all the stuffing knocked out of me. Is that soda water on the sideboard? Could you get me some?"

Haldean gave him a drink and straddled his legs over a chair, watching Stanton fumble for a cigarette. His case was empty. "Here, have one of mine." Stanton took his lighter from his pocket and spun the little wheel for a few moments, unable to get it to light. Haldean struck a match. "Use this. What on earth's the matter, Arthur? Surely it's not just the fireworks?"

"Mind your own bloody business," snarled Stanton, and was immediately contrite at the sight of Haldean's hurt expression. "Sorry. I'm sorry. It's just . . . Oh hell, can't you guess?"

"Isabelle?"

Stanton nodded and drew deeply on his cigarette. "It's all over. Skittled out." He raised his glass. "Here's to Smith-Fennimore. Looks, talent, charm and now the best damn girl in the world. What the hell. I knew I didn't stand a chance." He straightened his shoulders and gave a wobbly smile. "Women, Jack, are the devil. God, listen to me. Trite and clichéd by turns. Irresistible."

"Arthur, don't," begged Haldean. "Go easy on yourself."

Stanton shrugged. "I'll get over it." He took another sip of water. "It's the only thing I can do."

They smoked in silence, listening to the popping of fireworks in the distance. As they faded, Haldean crushed out his second cigarette. "I suppose I'd better be getting back," he said apologetically. "If you want to slope off, I'm sure it'll be all right."

"Slope off?" Stanton shook his head. "I can't do that." The fireworks exploded in a tremendous final crash. There was a long pause, then the music started again. "Let's go. I'll have to face her again sometime."

By an unlucky chance the first couple they saw on the dance floor were Isabelle and Smith-Fennimore. Looking at the physical grace with which they moved, Haldean couldn't help thinking they made a genuinely striking pair. Stanton heaved a deep sigh and was about to walk away when the music stopped and the dancers applauded.

Sir Philip, who had been giving a very creditable account of himself on the dance floor, saw Haldean and walked over to him. "Ah, Jack, m'boy. I've been looking for you, and you, Captain Stanton. You play golf, don't you, Captain? Good. There's a new links a couple of miles down the coast and Alice and I thought we could get up a party for everyone who was staying for a few days."

Isabelle and Smith-Fennimore joined them. "Are you talking about golf, Dad?" She gave Stanton a determinedly level look. "I didn't get a chance to mention it to you, Arthur, but I think it's a lovely idea."

"Yes, I . . ." began Sir Philip, then stopped in surprise.

The butler, Egerton, had come quickly into the room. He looked red and flustered and, when he saw Sir Philip, visibly relieved. "Sir Philip! Sir Philip! Thank goodness I've found you, sir!"

Sir Philip looked at him. "Well, here I am, man. What's the matter? Spit it out."

Egerton actually clutched at Sir Philip's arm. "It's Adamson, sir, Lord Lyvenden's man. He's just been to his master's room to prepare it for the night and he found Mr Preston."

"Well, why shouldn't he find Mr Preston? He's all right, isn't he?"

"No, sir." Egerton could hardly get the words out. "Oh sir . . . He's shot himself!"

CHAPTER
TWO

Haldean followed his uncle and Stanton into Lord Lyvenden's room. No one spoke. It was as if they were afraid of disturbing the man at the desk. He realized he'd hoped that Egerton had made a mistake or that Tim had been playing some sort of silly joke. That would be just like Tim, but the stillness of the body shocked him. Haldean looked at the body sprawled in the absurd angles of death, forcing himself to take in the details.

Preston was slumped in a chair pulled up to the desk. Lord Lyvenden had used his bedroom as his office and Preston lay half on the desk, his right leg stuck out awkwardly by the chair and his arms flung wide. A note, the suicide note, lay by Preston's sprawled left arm. Haldean picked up the note, read it quickly and sighed. So money was behind it all. Poor devil. He knew he was looking at the note so he didn't have to look at Tim. Because Tim wasn't Tim any more, but a lifeless caricature of a man with a pistol in his right hand and a small bloody hole matting the hair behind his right ear. It was such a tiny hole to let out a whole life.

The door opened and Smith-Fennimore walked quietly into the room. He looked at Sir Philip, Haldean and Stanton before his eyes slid reluctantly to Preston.

"I didn't believe it," said Smith-Fennimore softly. His voice trailed off and he reached out to touch Preston's hand. He seemed stupefied. "Why?" he demanded, a break in his voice. "Why did he do it?"

Haldean gave him the note. "He left this. It is his handwriting, I suppose?"

Smith-Fennimore took the note, his face grim. "Yes, that's his writing. I'd know it anywhere." He read the few lines and sighed. "He says it's because of money." He looked up. "Money? What did he need money for? I'd have given him money. Anything he needed." He shook his head, dazed. "Money never mattered. He knew that."

No, thought Haldean, money wouldn't matter to Smith-Fennimore. Tim had mattered, mattered a lot. He'd seen them race together at Brooklands with Tim acting as Smith-Fennimore's riding mechanic. Tim was a brilliant driver but he couldn't afford a car. It took an awful lot of money to keep up with the Brooklands crowd.

Smith-Fennimore put the note back on the desk with a shaky hand. He swallowed, and had to make a couple of attempts to speak. "We were going in for the Isle of Man race again. He was so damn pleased about it." He put the back of his hand to his mouth. "So damn pleased." He shuddered and made an obvious effort to collect his thoughts. "Sir Philip, Isabelle's looking for Dr Speldhurst. He's at the ball somewhere." He stopped and took a deep breath. "As far as I can tell, no one else realizes what's happened."

"I'd better go and help her," said Sir Philip. He looked at Smith-Fennimore. "Will you give me a hand, Commander, to get the body on the bed?"

Smith-Fennimore winced but nodded his head in agreement.

Haldean looked up sharply. "You mustn't do that." His uncle gazed at him. "You mustn't move him," Haldean insisted. "You mustn't move anything until the police arrive."

Sir Philip looked harried. "The police? God damn it, boy, we can't wait for them. He'll be as stiff as a board in a hour or so and we'll never shift him."

"You still mustn't move him," repeated Haldean. "You mustn't touch anything until the police have had a look."

Sir Philip chewed his moustache in vexation, then his face cleared. "The Chief Constable's downstairs. I'll get him to come up here, Jack, if you're determined to do things by the book. Will that satisfy you?"

Haldean nodded. Sir Philip and Smith-Fennimore left the room. Haldean and Stanton stood in silence. There didn't seem much to say.

"Lord Lyvenden will have to move rooms," said Stanton eventually. "Where did Lady Harriet sleep?"

"In the next room. There's a connecting door." Haldean pointed to the double oak door. "You can make it into a suite." A fresh thought struck him and he winced. "What about Bubble Robiceux? She'll be downstairs, waiting for him."

Stanton grimaced. "I suppose we'd better go and tell her."

"One of us should stay here in case someone else comes in."

Stanton nodded. "I'll go and find Bubble. Poor kid. She doesn't deserve this."

"Take her to her room and let her maid look after her. I'll ask the doctor to call and see her afterwards. He can give her something to help her sleep."

Stanton nodded and left. Haldean leant against the mantelpiece, staring unseeingly in front of him. He shook himself then took out his cigarette case. He paused before he opened it. It seemed disrespectful somehow to smoke with Tim in the room, and yet Tim would never have minded when he was alive. ("Chuck me a gasper, old scream, you're sitting there like a man with no arms . . .") Surely the smell of cigarette smoke was no worse than the smell of gunpowder which hung about the room. He really wanted a cigarette.

Footsteps sounded outside and saved him from making a decision. He thrust the cigarette case back into his pocket as Sir Philip, accompanied by Dr Speldhurst and the Chief Constable, Major-General Flint, came into the room.

Haldean recognized the doctor. He usually wore a baggy tweed suit with a sprinkling of cigar ash down the front and he looked out of place in evening clothes, especially as he was carrying his doctor's bag. He had a pair of pince-nez spectacles through which he glared at his patients, as if daring them to get any worse whilst under his care. He was now glaring through them at the wound on Preston's head.

"This is a bad business," the doctor said briskly. "A very bad business indeed." He opened his bag. "It's lucky I had this with me." Haldean had never seen him without it. "Mind you, I like to be prepared. You never know what'll crop up. I wasn't expecting anything of this sort, though. I thought a sprained ankle would be the height of it."

He raised Preston's head and put a thermometer under his neck before picking up his hand and flexing the joints. Taking out the thermometer he held it up to the light. "He's been dead about an hour, give or take ten minutes or so either side. There's powder and burning marks round the wound. That ties in with the revolver being discharged at close quarters." The doctor drew back, returning the thermometer to its case. "It's lucky we can still move him, Sir Philip. With these brain injuries rigor often sets in instantly and we have to crack the joints to move the body."

"Is the body in the position you would expect to find it, Doctor?" asked Haldean.

Dr Speldhurst spun round and subjected Haldean to the full beam from the pince-nez. "And who might you be, young man?" The recognition obviously wasn't mutual.

Sir Philip intervened. "This is my nephew, Major Haldean, Speldhurst. He's staying with us at present."

Dr Speldhurst nodded briefly. "In answer to your question, Major, the body is not positioned exactly as I would have expected, no. It's difficult to predict the effect of sudden trauma but I would have expected the hand holding the gun to have dropped down by his side."

General Flint spoke in a no-nonsense voice. "Do you think he's been moved at all?"

Dr Speldhurst shook his head decisively. "I should say not." He turned his attention to the bullet wound once more. He tilted Preston's head gently and ran his hands over the skull. "No exit wound, but looking at the angle of entry, I should say that the bullet traversed the brain ending up in the frontal lobe. Death would have been instantaneous, of course. Well, gentlemen, that's all I can do here." He looked at Sir Philip. "I'll make arrangements for the removal of the body. Now, I believe I have a couple of patients amongst your servants. They'll need something to help them sleep."

Haldean remembered his promise to Stanton. "Could you take a look at Miss Robiceux, Doctor?" What on earth was Bubble's proper name? "Miss Celia Robiceux." That was it. "She was fond of Tim and I think she'll be pretty cut up about it. And Miss Rivers," he added.

Dr Speldhurst pencilled a note on his shirt cuff and looked critically at Haldean. "What about you, young man? You look a bit green about the gills. Want something to help you sleep? Suffer from nerves? War-strain?"

"No," replied Haldean shortly and not quite truthfully in answer to all three questions.

"Hmm. I'll leave something with Sir Philip just in case." He walked to the door. "Bad business this," he repeated. He looked once more at Preston. "And damned inconsiderate of him, too."

After the doctor had gone, General Flint picked up the note by Preston's hand and read it out loud. "*I regret the action which I have been forced to undertake and any distress which might ensue. The motive for my action is purely financial.* That's clear enough." He put the note back on the desk. "There's nothing much more we can do." He pulled out a gold fob watch. "Just check the time with me, Rivers. I make it ten to eleven — yes? That means the death occurred between twenty to ten and ten o'clock. Let's have a look at the gun."

Haldean winced as the General took the pistol from Preston's hand, casually holding it in his palm.

"This is a pretty little toy of a thing, isn't it, Rivers?" said General Flint. He snapped out the chamber. "One bullet fired, I see. It doesn't look like a real gun and yet it's obviously deadly enough." He held the glittering gun under the light on the desk. "It's got something engraved on the handle. The initials V. L. and what looks like a coat of arms. There's a maker's name too. Sparkbrook."

"That's Lyvenden's firm," said Haldean. "The Sparkbrook Armouries and Munitions Company Limited, to give it its full title. He was telling us about it at lunch. I bet it's his pistol."

"You're probably right," agreed the General. "I imagine he kept it in his desk drawer. I know a lot of businessmen do so. Makes them feel safer, I suppose." He put the gun back on the desk. "We'd better move the body. Perhaps you'd give us a hand, Major?"

Overcoming his reluctance, Haldean took Preston underneath the shoulders and with Sir Philip's help placed the body reverently on the bed. Funnily enough he was conscious of a feeling of relief after doing it. Preston felt like every other dead body he'd had to carry and looked a great deal better than most.

Sir Philip stepped back and sighed. "I'll have to ask Alice which other room we've got free and get it made up for Lyvenden. What happens next, Flint?"

Flint clicked his tongue. "There's nothing much we can do until tomorrow. I'll send one of the local men round to take some statements and after that it's simply a case of waiting for the inquest. There'll have to be an inquest but I wouldn't concern yourself unduly about it, Rivers. It's only a formality. Did he have any family?"

"He had a sister and there was an uncle who acted as his trustee," said Haldean.

General Flint looked at Sir Philip. "You'll have to get in touch with them to see what they want to do about the body."

"Yes, I'll do that." Sir Philip looked horribly tired. "Jack, would you mind staying here until I can get someone to come and get Lyvenden's things?"

"Of course."

"I'd better go and sort something out with Alice. God, what a business!"

Haldean waited until his uncle and General Flint left, then walked over to the desk. He'd had to bite his tongue when General Flint had picked up the gun but really, even if it had been fingerprinted properly, what could he expect it to tell him? It would certainly have

Tim's prints on it as it'd been in Tim's hand, and Lyvenden's too if it was his gun. He looked at the weapon with its silver barrel and mother-of-pearl handle. It was an ostentatious little gun, he thought, just the sort of gun Lyvenden would have.

The door opened and he looked up, expecting to see one of the servants, but it was Malcolm Smith-Fennimore.

"Hello, Haldean. I had to come back. I couldn't credit it was really true."

"How is everyone?" asked Haldean. "How's Bubble Robiceux?"

Smith-Fennimore shrugged. "I don't know." He wandered over to the fireplace and leaned against the mantel, resting his forehead on his hand. "This is a rotten show," he said eventually. "I never dreamed that Tim would pull a stunt like this." He walked over to the bed and sighed. "I can't believe he did it. Shouldn't we put a sheet over him or something?"

Haldean went to stand beside him by the bed. "I suppose we should, really. If the servants have got to come in here, it'll give them a nasty shock. I haven't a clue where the sheets are, but if you can lift him out of the way, I can get the bedspread . . . Thanks, Fennimore." He made to put the cover over the body, but Smith-Fennimore stopped him.

"Wait." He leaned forward and closed Preston's eyes, then stepped back with a grimace. "I never thought I'd have to do that for Tim," he said softly. "What a bloody life! I need a drink. Want to join me?"

Haldean shook his head. "I've got to wait until someone comes for Lyvenden's things."

As he opened the door to leave, the music of the ball sounded loudly up the stairs. Haldean winced. It was all still going on down there. And up here? The ball was over. For Tim it had finished far too soon. All the weary mechanisms of sudden death would have to begin, the inquest, the statements, the questions . . . The ball was well and truly over.

Haldean sat warming his back in the sun on the windowsill of Lord Lyvenden's former bedroom. He looked at Arthur Stanton thoughtfully. It was Sunday morning and nearly everyone else had gone to church. The house was very quiet. He had asked Stanton to stay behind because he badly wanted to talk things over with him. He really wanted to find out what Isabelle thought, but Isabelle, still pale after the tragedy of last night, was devoting all her time to Bubble and Squeak and had gone off to church with them and the others.

Preston's body had been moved to a spare bedroom on the third floor until it could be taken away, for which fact Haldean was sincerely grateful.

Stanton moved restlessly. "Do we really have to be in here, Jack? I can't say I like it much."

Haldean looked at him wryly. "I'm sorry, Arthur. I can't say I like it much either, but I thought it'd be a good chance to talk about things while the house was more or less deserted."

"Talk?" asked Stanton. "What's there to talk about?"

Haldean ran a hand through his hair. "Look, I don't know how you're going to take this, but I've been thinking about last night. Do you honestly believe Tim was suicidal?"

"I suppose I've got to believe it, haven't I?"

"Have you, Arthur? I don't know if I do." He got off the windowsill and wandered round the room, eventually stopping by the bed. The depression made by Preston's body was still visible. "What if Tim didn't commit suicide at all?"

Stanton looked at him with puzzled hazel eyes. "He must have done, Jack. It couldn't have been an accident. He left a note."

Haldean shook his head. "No, it couldn't have been an accident." He spoke very hesitantly. "I was wondering if he'd been murdered."

"*Murdered?*" Stanton half laughed, then stopped as he saw his friend's serious face. He drew a deep breath. "Of course he wasn't murdered," he said patiently. "He committed suicide. The Chief Constable said so."

"And you think Major-General Flint is infallible?"

"He should know what he's talking about." Stanton wriggled in irritation. "After all, Jack, he must have seen dozens of suicides."

Haldean raised his eyebrows. "Dozens? I doubt it."

"All right, perhaps not dozens, then," agreed Stanton, "but he'll have seen enough." He paused, choosing his words with obvious tact. "Look, old man, be honest with yourself. Are you sure you're not thinking of murder because of the sort of stories you write? I mean, they're all about murders and so on, aren't they? You know you love inventing mysteries."

Haldean acknowledged Stanton's point with a rueful smile. "I might be. I thought as much myself, but I think we owe it to Tim to investigate it as best we can."

"I think we owe it to Tim to not monkey around." He looked very uncomfortable. "Drop it, Jack. It's . . . It's . . . Well, it's in pretty poor taste."

Haldean was about to answer when the door opened and Smith-Fennimore came into the room. He looked surprised to see them.

"I heard voices. What are you doing in here? Come to that, how did you get in? I thought this room had been locked up."

"It had, but my key fitted the lock," said Haldean with a smile. "All the locks here are pretty feeble." He took a deep breath. "We're trying to see if we can find anything out of the way. I know this may sound odd, Fennimore, but I find it damn nearly impossible to believe that Tim killed himself."

"What else could have happened?"

Stanton's response had warned Haldean that what seemed so likely to him was far from obvious to anyone else. Besides that, it was one thing talking it over with Arthur, it was quite another bringing it up with Smith-Fennimore. He had been knocked sideways last night and the last thing Haldean wanted to do was make it worse for him. When he spoke his voice was quiet. "He could have been murdered."

Smith-Fennimore's shoulders stiffened and he raised his head. The warning in his eyes made Haldean step

42

back. "Are you playing around with this? Because if you are, Haldean, I'm telling you to stop it now. I'm damned if you're going to use Tim's death as some sort of entertainment. Writing fiction is one thing. This is real."

"I know it's real." Haldean's voice was still quiet. "I cared about Tim, too."

His sincerity carried weight. Smith-Fennimore's shoulders relaxed and the anger in his eyes gave way to bewilderment. "But you can't mean it, man. You just can't. What do you know — what can you know? — that the police and the doctor don't?"

"I knew Tim."

Smith-Fennimore stared at him. "Yes?"

"Well, think," said Haldean impatiently. "Think for yourself. You spoke to Tim last night. We all did. What would you say his mood was?"

"His mood? He must have been feeling awful."

"Forget what happened. I mean from what you saw with your own eyes, how would you describe his mood?"

Smith-Fennimore started to speak then stopped and frowned in concentration. "The trouble was I didn't see much of Tim," he said eventually. "To be honest, he seemed okay. He was pretty down in the mouth a couple of weeks ago, but he was fine the next time I saw him." Stanton moved as if he was about to speak, then motioned for Smith-Fennimore to carry on. "As far as last night goes," continued Smith-Fennimore with a look at Stanton, "he was a bit cheesed off about all the running around he was doing for Lyvenden, but apart from that he was all right." He pulled a face. "He'd been dancing with Bubble Robiceux and we talked about which car we were going to use for the Isle of Man. He was excited about that."

Haldean nodded. "So his mood wasn't depressed. How did he strike you, Arthur?"

Stanton shrugged. "About the same, I suppose. I hardly spoke to him."

"I spoke to him," said Haldean, lighting a cigarette. "I had quite a long conversation with him. He didn't strike me as remotely depressed. He was impatient and annoyed with Lyvenden — as you say, Fennimore, cheesed off — but not depressed. Now that was at the start of the evening, I grant you, but not so very long afterwards we're meant to believe that he became so desperate he scribbled a note, picked up a gun and shot himself. He'd have had to be a bit more than cheesed off to do that, no matter how many errands Lord Lyvenden had sent him on."

Smith-Fennimore sat down on the arm of the chair and rested his chin in his hand. Haldean could see the thought take root in his mind. "His note said he was worried about money," he said slowly. "He'd never said anything to me, but I'd wondered a couple of times if he was all right. I tried to speak to him seriously once or twice but he laughed it off." He looked at Haldean. "I'd like to know if he was stuck for money."

Stanton stirred uneasily. "He was."

Both Haldean and Smith-Fennimore looked at him. "I know he was," said Stanton. "He was up against the wall. What he said in that note was true. He came to see me about a fortnight ago. You said he struck you as down in the mouth, Smith-Fennimore. When he turned up at my flat he was in a hell of a state. He'd run through his allowance and his salary and was up to his ears in debt. He owed about three hundred pounds altogether."

Haldean whistled involuntarily. "My God! What did you tell him to do?"

"I told him to stop running round with the Brooklands crowd. And . . ." He shrugged. "I lent him the money. I didn't expect to get it back."

Haldean's eyebrows rose. "You gave Tim Preston three hundred quid?"

Stanton put his hands wide. "What else could I do? He said it was either that or the river and, God help me, Jack, I honestly thought he meant it. He was grateful, I'll say that for him."

"I should damn well think he was," muttered Haldean. He shook his head thoughtfully. "Maybe I'm wrong. Maybe he did top himself."

"Why?" said Smith-Fennimore in a strained voice. "If Stanton gave him the money, why should he kill himself? After all, even if he got into trouble again he must have known I'd have helped him. I wish he'd talked to me." He looked at Stanton. "Why did he go to you? I'd have made it all right for him. I thought he trusted me."

Haldean shifted, moved to sympathy for the big fair-haired man in front of him, but it was Stanton who spoke.

"He told me why. He thought a great deal too much of you to tell you what a fool he'd been."

Smith-Fennimore drew a deep breath. "Idiot," he murmured. "I couldn't have given a damn." He shook himself and stood up. "Does that change things, Haldean?"

Haldean let out a deep breath. "I don't know. Knowing that Tim really was stuck makes a difference."

"Does it?" Smith-Fennimore stood up restlessly. "Does it really? What made you think of murder in the first place? His sudden change of mood?"

"That's it," said Haldean.

"But that's still as valid as before." He walked to the window and, standing with his back to them, stuck his hands in his pockets. His shoulders were rigid with tension. "Do we tell the police?"

Haldean shook his head. "I'd like to, but we need something a bit more definite to tell them. You see, now General Flint has decided it's suicide, we'll have to have something more concrete than unfounded suspicions to make him investigate the case properly." He blew out a mouthful of smoke in an irritated sigh. "I wish Superintendent Ashley was here but he's on holiday. I got to know him last year. There was a murder over in Breedenbrook."

Smith-Fennimore turned round. "Was that the business the newspapers called The Fortune Teller's Tent Mystery? You were caught up in it, weren't you?"

Haldean nodded. "That's the one. After that, I know Ashley would take me seriously. As it is . . ." He shrugged. "If there's anything to find, we'll have to find it."

"Us?" Smith-Fennimore looked startled. "What do you want us to do? I don't know what to look for. I'm not a detective."

Haldean gave a faint grin. "It's not so very complicated." He walked across the room and propped himself against the mantelpiece. "The first thing we do is to go back to last night. Arthur, when was the last time you saw Tim?"

"Crikey, Jack, I don't know what time it was. I didn't look at my watch."

"Well, how soon before the fireworks was it?"

Stanton frowned. "It can't have been long. I came in from the terrace to the hall and saw Tim going up the stairs. He told me Lyvenden wanted his cigarette case." His face cleared. "That's right. Then I went back to the ballroom, saw you and we stood together to watch the fireworks."

"And neither of us saw him again. Did you see him, Fennimore?"

Smith-Fennimore shook his head. "I saw him earlier in the evening, but I was talking to Sir Philip for quite a while before the fireworks started. I certainly didn't see Tim then. Mind you, I wasn't looking for him especially."

"He didn't watch the fireworks," said Haldean thoughtfully. "Do you remember when Lord Lyvenden was making his speech? He suddenly decided Lady Harriet needed her shawl. He looked round the crowd and I thought he was looking for Tim."

"That's right, Haldean," agreed Smith-Fennimore. "Now you mention it, I thought much the same thing. He sent Lady Harriet's maid, didn't he?"

"That's right. So, as Arthur saw Tim go upstairs just before the fireworks and as he wasn't there during the fireworks, let's assume for the time being that's when it happened. It certainly fits in with what the doctor said. Now, if Tim was murdered, the murderer came into the room with him. Did they leave any traces?"

Smith-Fennimore raised an eyebrow. "Cigar ash and footprints, you mean? This is Sherlock Holmes and no mistake."

"Perhaps it is," said Haldean with a fleeting smile. "Let's look. Incidentally, Fennimore, do you know anything about this gun?" He picked it up from the desk and handed it to him. "General Flint had a good look at it last night so even if there were any useful fingerprints on it, they won't be there now."

Smith-Fennimore reached his hand out for the gun. "It's Lyvenden's," he said. "I've seen it before. He always kept it in his desk." He pulled a face. "I remember Tim commenting on it. The poor beggar knew it was there all right. Doesn't that scupper your murder theory, Haldean?"

"Not necessarily. The gun could have been on the desk or if the drawer was open it could have been visible." He smiled deprecatingly. "There's another fairly obvious explanation but the great thing in this game is not to jump to conclusions too early and to collect what evidence we can." He looked at Stanton and Smith-Fennimore. "Er . . . shall we start?"

The three men began to look round the room.

Stanton stood by the fireplace. For Jack's sake he'd go through with this charade, but it was a charade. He glanced along the mantelpiece. What on earth was he meant to be looking for? Jack might know what he was doing but he certainly didn't. There was a clock, an ashtray, china figures of a shepherd and shepherdess . . . What could he get out of them? Nothing. This was a waste of time. Still, he supposed he'd better look as if he were doing something if Jack was so set on it. He bent down and moved the fire screen surrounding the hearth. There was a scattering of soot in the empty grate. A discarded and charred packet of Goldflake lay to one side. "The chimney needs cleaning," he announced. "Is that significant?"

"I wouldn't have thought so," said Haldean absently. He looked up as Smith-Fennimore gave a stifled exclamation. "What is it?"

Smith-Fennimore was flicking through the papers on the desk. He looked up when Haldean spoke, his mouth set in a grim line. "I can't believe it! This is incredible."

"What've you found?" asked Haldean.

"Files. Confidential files. Lyvenden shouldn't have these papers here." Smith-Fennimore tapped the documents in front of him. "Good God, none of these files should have been taken out of the bank and they certainly shouldn't be left lying around in this casual way."

"What bank?" asked Stanton.

"My bank, Smith, Wilson and Fennimore. Lyvenden's a director. I'll have to have a word with him about this." He picked up three files and put them under his arm. "I'm taking these with me."

"I don't think we should take anything out of the room," said Haldean.

Smith-Fennimore snorted. "These shouldn't have been here in the first place. I'm not having my clients' affairs left for the police to poke into. I'll be happier when I've got them under lock and key. I don't know what the devil Lyvenden was thinking of."

"Tim said he was careless with papers."

"Tim was right. What's that you're looking at?"

"The suicide note," said Haldean thoughtfully. "Does it seem odd to you?"

Smith-Fennimore and Stanton looked at the note critically. "Not really," said Smith-Fennimore in the end. "Apart from the fact it's on a half-sheet of paper."

"Well, that could be just the only paper that was handy," said Haldean. "No, what I mean is that all the writing is at the top of the sheet. The note's only a few lines long. Why cram it all at the top of the paper?"

"Dunno," said Stanton. "I still think it's suicide. Maybe he was going to write more and then couldn't go on."

Haldean put down the note and continued his search, dropping down on his hands and knees to crawl under the desk. "Nothing much here apart from fluff. Waste-paper basket. Empty." He backed out and, standing up, dusted off the knees of his trousers. "There's one thing I want to try. Fennimore, could you play the victim for me? I want you to pretend to shoot yourself."

Smith-Fennimore pulled a face. "Come on, Haldean, that's a bit morbid, isn't it?"

Haldean made a pacifying gesture with his hands. "Will you try it? I just want to see something."

"I suppose so." Smith-Fennimore reluctantly sat down and lifted his fingers to his head. "Bang. Is that what I'm supposed to say? What did that show us?"

Haldean stood back and looked at him critically. "Where did you shoot yourself?"

Smith-Fennimore looked at his fingers and placed them to his head once more. "Here, on my temple."

"So you did. And that would be the natural place to shoot yourself, wouldn't it? But Tim didn't do that. He shot himself here." Taking Smith-Fennimore's hand he moved the fingers round until they were considerably behind the right ear. "Just here, where the bulgy bit of your head goes into the back of your neck. Why should he do that?"

"Maybe he was disturbed," suggested Stanton. "Look, like this. If I could just sit in the chair . . ." Smith-Fennimore got up and let Stanton take his place. "Now, I've got a gun to my head," he said, raising his fingers as Smith-Fennimore had done, "and I'm just about to pull the trigger, when there's a noise. That would make me turn my head — like so — and the bullet would miss my temple but go in behind my ear."

"Brilliant, Arthur," said Haldean. "But what noise?"

"What about the maid in the next room? If she'd come up for Lady Harriet's shawl, maybe Tim heard her and it made him jump." He gave an irritated shake of his head. "As I said, I just don't believe it, Jack. You're barking up the wrong tree. Tim killed himself. The poor devil felt like hell and shot himself. That's all there is to it."

"Is it?" asked Smith-Fennimore suddenly. "Is it?" Haldean caught the note of suppressed anger in his voice. "Look, Haldean, all this stuff about murder. You've done this before. Do you really think there's a possibility that Tim was murdered?"

Haldean hesitated, then nodded his head. "Yes. I do. Obviously the fact that Tim really was stuck for money changes things, but on the other hand, if Arthur had helped him out, then that reason had gone, for the time being at least." He looked at Stanton. "Did Tim have any other debts?"

Stanton shook his head. "I don't think so. When he'd stopped telling me how awful things were, I made him go through everything he owed. I don't think he kept anything back. It amounted to just over three hundred quid. I wrote him a cheque there and then. The trouble is that if he'd continued to hang around with the Brooklands crowd, it wouldn't be long before he was in the same mess again. Maybe that's what made him feel so rotten, knowing that the money I'd given him was just a stop-gap."

"There's some truth in that, Arthur," said Haldean. "He could hardly keep on asking you for the dibs."

"He could have asked me," said Smith-Fennimore quickly. "Bloody hell, if I'd had the slightest idea of what he was up against, I'd have given him a job. Apart from anything else, he was my riding mechanic. He knew how much I relied on him. All he had to do was ask." He gave an impatient shrug of his shoulders. "Come on, Haldean. What do you really think?"

Haldean clicked his tongue in a dissatisfied way. "The official verdict could be correct and I might be making an absolute fool of myself by suggesting anything else. I know that. But last night General Flint made his mind up very quickly. He didn't conduct anything like a proper investigation. I think there are questions to be answered. Tim was my friend and I feel I owe it to him."

"Friend?" said Smith-Fennimore in an undertone. "He was the best friend I had." Haldean could hear the emotion in his voice. "We shared a hell of a lot together. But it can't be murder. Why should anyone want to kill Tim? It's so pointless."

Pointless? thought Haldean. No. If it was murder it wouldn't be pointless . . .

CHAPTER
THREE

The three men came out of Lyvenden's room. The chatter of voices from the hall below told them that the church party was back. "Shall we go down?" asked Haldean.

Smith-Fennimore tapped the files under his arm. "I'm going to put these away safely, then treat myself to a word with Lyvenden."

"Well, for heaven's sake, do it quietly," said Haldean. "I feel really sorry for Aunt Alice and Uncle Phil — Aunt Alice in particular. She was so looking forward to her silver wedding and what happened to Tim has rather taken the shine off it. If you have a row with Lyvenden, it'll just make things worse."

"I'll . . ." Smith-Fennimore looked at him and his face lost its look of mulish obstinacy. "All right. I'll be discreet." He walked off to his own room.

Stanton watched him go. "Do you honestly like him, Jack?"

Haldean nodded. "He's all right. I can understand why you're not crazy about him."

"I could have liked him," said Stanton. "In fact I would have done if things had turned out differently, even if he does think he's the only one who cares about

Tim." He stuck his hands in his pockets. "What the devil does it matter? Come on, let's go downstairs."

There was quite a crowd in the hall. Lady Rivers looked up and smiled as she saw Haldean and Stanton. "There you are." She handed her coat to the waiting Egerton, pulled off her gloves, unpinned her hat and put them on the hall table with a definite air of relief. "Thank goodness that's over. The church was absolutely packed. I don't know how news gets round so fast, but it does. Almost everyone in the village seemed to have heard about poor Mr Preston. Practically all of Stanmore Parry seemed to be there — even the chapel people — simply to look at us. Goodness knows what they expected to get out of it."

"They were expressing their sympathy, Alice," said her husband.

"They were satisfying their curiosity more like, Philip. Did you hear that wretched Daphne Tanner? She was itching to find out exactly what happened last night. Then Mr Freeman, the curate, joined us. I know he's a very pious sort of man, but he does strike me as incredibly self-righteous. Simply because I said I felt sorry for Mr Preston he warned me of the dangers of misdirected compassion, and I do think it was tactless of him to talk about self-destruction as an act of sinful folly. Thank goodness you weren't with us, Jack. You'd have hated it."

Haldean, who usually coped with his urge to kick the sanctimonious Mr Freeman by referring him to his sense of the ridiculous, found his reserves of humour at a very low ebb.

He stepped closer to Isabelle who was standing with Bubble and Squeak Robiceux. They were about the only people in the hall who weren't talking. The Robiceuxs looked uncharacteristically solemn. "It all sounds perfectly septic," he said sympathetically.

"It was putrid, Jack," said Isabelle with a shudder. "Knowing that everyone was looking at us and talking about us. Will there be an inquest?"

"There's bound to be, I'm afraid."

"That'll be even worse. *Why* did it have to happen?"

"That's what I've been thinking," began Haldean, when he was interrupted by Lady Harriet who was approaching the staircase in a determined way. He moved aside to allow her to get past him. Aunt Alice followed.

"Lady Harriet," she called. "As you know, we have had to put your husband in the garden suite on the ground floor. Would you like to change your room so you can be next to him?"

Lady Harriet stopped and looked at her hostess with some surprise. "Change? Whatever for? I am perfectly comfortable, and the fact that there was a death in the next room does not concern me in the slightest." She swept on her way, leaving Lady Rivers biting her lip in irritation. And well she might, thought Haldean. The only reason Tim's body had been moved late last night was in deference to Lady Harriet's supposed feelings. The least she could do was pretend to have some.

He shared a quick look of resignation with his aunt before turning back to the Robiceuxs. They looked upset, and no wonder. "Don't worry," he said in a low voice. "Lady Harriet's totally self-centred. Do you want to stay on here? If not, I'll take you home in my car and your luggage can be sent on later."

The two girls exchanged looks. "We'd more or less made up our minds to stay," said Squeak eventually. "It seems like running out to go now."

"And we'd only have to come back for the inquest," added Bubble. "If only I knew why he did it, Jack. We were having such a good time last night and we'd made plans and . . . and . . ." She blinked very rapidly. Isabelle exchanged glances with Haldean, before taking her friend's arm and leading her firmly out of the hall, passing Alfred Charnock as he came in.

"What's up with the girl?" Charnock asked Lady Rivers. "The one that's weeping all over the place, I mean. Didn't she like the vicar's sermon or something?"

Lady Rivers looked at him in exasperation. "Don't be flippant, Alfred. She's upset about Mr Preston."

"Mr Preston?" repeated Charnock, puzzled. "Who's . . . Oh yes, the one who topped himself, you mean. I hope she's not going to sob through lunch about it. Speaking of which, when is it? Lunch, I mean?"

Sir Philip gave him a hostile glare. "As always, Alfred, lunch is at one o'clock." He was about to say more but stopped as Lawson, the footman, walked into the hall and, approaching Sir Philip, coughed respectfully.

"May I have a word, sir?"

"What is it?"

"There is a disturbance in Lord Lyvenden's room, sir."

"A disturbance?" repeated Sir Philip, puzzled. "What sort of disturbance?"

"An inharmonious disturbance, sir." Lawson coughed again. "I fear it may become a violent disturbance before long."

Sir Philip's eyebrows shot up. "Who the devil's Lyvenden got in there?"

"The person would not give his name, sir. I believe him to be a Russian and it is possible that he did not understand my question. He waited while I ascertained what Lord Lyvenden desired me to do and Lord Lyvenden, after seeing the person, gave orders that he should be admitted. I may say I was surprised, sir, as he struck me as an unlikely caller for Lord Lyvenden to entertain, but his lordship's instructions were unequivocal, sir."

Alfred Charnock grinned. "Maybe Bertie the Bolshie's come to complain that his last bomb didn't go off."

"Be quiet, Alfred," Sir Philip said absently. He looked at Lawson in bewilderment. "A *Russian*? And they're having a quarrel, you say?" Lawson bowed his head in agreement. "What the devil's Lyvenden doing, seeing Russians in my house?"

"Perhaps it would be as well to go and find out, Philip," put in his wife.

"I shall most certainly do so," he said grimly. "Damn me, as if there wasn't enough going on to worry about without Russians disturbing the peace. Well, I'll soon set the feller to rights." He braced himself and shot his cuffs in a determined way.

58

"I'll come with you, Uncle," said Haldean. A Russian? That was the second one in the space of two days and he didn't sound the sort of character whom his uncle should tackle alone. In fact, the more help he had the better. He certainly didn't want Charnock along, but he inclined his head towards Stanton.

"I'll come too, Jack," said Stanton, taking the hint, and together they walked off down the corridor, following the fuming Sir Philip.

They hadn't gone far before they heard shouting. "That's not Lyvenden," said Haldean, listening. "It must be the other chap. My word, there he goes again! He's pretty shirty about something, isn't he?"

"I'll teach him a trick worth two of that," said Sir Philip. He strode on and knocked sharply on the door. "Hey! Lyvenden! What's going on in there?"

The door was flung open by Lord Lyvenden who, when he saw them, nearly collapsed in relief. "Rivers, my dear chap. Thank God you're here." He stepped back to let them enter.

A dark, thickset man with a seamed face and a wisp of beard was standing by the french windows. Well, thought Haldean, it's not the same bloke as last night, but he's a nasty piece of work, all the same. Unconsciously his hands curled into fists.

The Russian was smoking a thin black cigar and, as they entered, turned to look at them with raised eyebrows. "So, *my lord*." There was a wealth of sarcasm in the title. "These are your friends, are they?"

"Don't you take that tone of voice with me," said Sir Philip pugnaciously. "Who the devil are you?"

59

The man smiled, revealing yellowing teeth. "A business associate of the lordship here. We were just discussing matters. Private matters." He put his head to one side, looking at Lyvenden. "And the business has just been concluded, yes?"

"I . . . I think so," said Lord Lyvenden, weakly. "You really shouldn't have come down, my good man. I would much prefer all this to be settled in Town. Look, for God's sake, will you go!"

The Russian casually dropped his cigar on the rug and ground it out with his heel.

Sir Philip looked at the rug, looked at the Russian and, with eyes blazing, stalked across to him. "Out! Now!"

The man spread his hands wide. "I am going. I do not wish to spend more time here than I have to."

Haldean dropped a hand on his uncle's arm. If Uncle Philip really lost his temper, the Russian looked as if he could be vicious. Who on earth was this chap? That could wait. The main thing was to get him out of here, before Uncle Phil got hurt. "The door's this way," he said pleasantly. "After you."

They walked out of the room together, Sir Philip pausing only to jerk his head at his guest. "Lyvenden! I'd like a word with you."

Their progress back to the hall was punctuated by Lyvenden's attempts at an apology. He scurried after them, his flabby face pale and working with emotion. "Terribly sorry . . . wouldn't have had it happen for worlds . . . just a little matter of business . . . most unfortunate . . . very sorry for this unfortunate incident . . ." The Russian stopped dead and turned to glare at Lyvenden, who cringed like a kicked dog.

"Come on," growled Sir Philip, putting his hand on the man's shoulders. "The sooner you're out of here the better."

The Russian threw off Sir Philip's hand with a contemptuous shrug and strode into the hall. Here curiosity had evidently been too much for everyone, for no one had left. The Russian glanced round at the silent group in obvious disdain before striding to the door, his feet ringing in the silence on the marble floor. Egerton opened the door in his stiffest manner, waiting for the unwelcome visitor to go.

Haldean breathed a sigh of relief. That bloke could have been very nasty indeed. He looked swiftly at Alfred Charnock, pleased if rather surprised that Charnock hadn't started something. His pleasure was short-lived.

Charnock unpropped himself from the pillar of the door where he had been leaning and said, "Just a minute, old sport. I can't possibly let you pop off without any sort of explanation. What are you doing here?" His tone was deliberately offensive.

The Russian didn't answer, but stood with his arms folded across his chest. Charnock stuck his hands in his pockets and lounged back against the pillar.

The two men were oddly alike, trading arrogant stare for arrogant stare. Charnock laughed. "Well?"

"This is a business associate of Lyvenden's, Alfred," said Sir Philip rigidly. "He is just leaving."

Charnock grinned, and walked to the front door, barring the exit with his body. "Not so fast, Philip. I want to know who this chap is." Then, head to one side, he asked a question in what was, presumably, Russian.

The man started, unfolded his arms and slowly nodded a reply.

"Well, well," drawled Charnock. He shot a glance at Lord Lyvenden, who had sunk on to a chair, before snapping out another question. The man nodded again.

Charnock, who was obviously enjoying himself hugely, stepped back, his weight balanced on one foot.

"Alfred, don't," said Lady Rivers, quickly.

Charnock ignored her. With a lift of his eyebrows, he asked another question.

The man gazed at Charnock as if not believing what he had heard. Charnock repeated himself, and, with a yell, the man lunged out. He grasped at Charnock, there was a flurry of movement, a yelp, and the Russian was left nursing his arm.

Charnock laughed once more. That was a mistake. The Russian fumbled at his waist with his good hand and drew out a long-bladed knife. The crowd in the hall gasped and Mrs Strachan gave a little scream.

Charnock backed off warily, and the Russian pounced.

Haldean, Stanton and the other men leapt forward but Charnock was quicker. Like a striking cobra, he shot out his hand, seized the man's wrist and twisted it upwards, the knife gleaming between them. For a few brief seconds they stood eye to eye, before Charnock, with a grunt, slammed the Russian's arm behind his back, sending the knife clattering to the floor.

"Shall I break your arm?" asked Charnock, a dangerous glint in his eye.

The man stared at him, then came an interruption. The stairs out of the hall curved up to the corridor and from the corridor Malcolm Smith-Fennimore's voice broke loudly into the tension.

"I don't know, Lady Harriet," he was saying, "but there's an awful rumpus going on. The funny thing is I thought I heard someone speaking in Russian. Good God!" Preceded by Lady Harriet he rounded the stairs and they both stopped dead as they took in what was happening in the hall.

"Victor," called Lady Harriet, in a voice with an edge to it. "Who is that peculiar person?"

Lyvenden stood up with an odd little bob and shuffle. "Just business, my dear, nothing but business. Nothing for you to worry about. I've got it all under control. It's all under control. Totally under control."

The Russian stood absolutely still, staring up the stairs, then looked round with a triumphant smile. "So," he said eventually. "I learn something today. That alone was worth coming for." Still smiling, he walked over to where his knife lay and bent to pick it up. Charnock stuck his foot out and pinned it to the floor.

The Russian straightened up and Charnock smiled back.

"Mine, I believe. I'd like a little souvenir of our meeting. Now, if you don't mind, old man — or should that be comrade? — I really do think you've outstayed your welcome." He grasped the Russian's shoulder and steered him firmly to the door, shutting it behind him.

It was like a dam bursting. Everyone spoke at once. Unregarded, Smith-Fennimore came down the stairs into the hall and picked up the knife, turning it over in his hands. As Charnock came back from the door, he handed it over with a few words that were not English.

Charnock took the knife with a look of surprise. "I didn't know you spoke Russian."

Smith-Fennimore nodded. "Why did you ask him if he was one of the Chërnye Sotni? That's a pretty deadly insult. You might have known it would stir him up."

Charnock straightened his cuffs. "Yes, it did rather, didn't it?" he drawled.

Haldean looked at Aunt Alice's white face. "You deliberately provoked him. How could you?"

"What the devil's a Churny whatever it was?" demanded Sir Philip.

"They were thugs," said Smith-Fennimore quietly. "Thugs and murderers."

Charnock spared him a glance of lazy unconcern. He didn't bother to look at his sister. "They were enthusiastic supporters of the Tsar. Perhaps a bit over-enthusiastic at times. I had a fancy to find out which side he was on and I did. It made him see red, in every sense of the word." He glanced at his watch and raised his voice so he could be clearly heard, revelling in being the centre of attention. "How early it still is. Far too long to wait for lunch. I'm going to the pub to celebrate. I haven't enjoyed myself so much since I came here." His eyes flicked over to Lord Lyvenden.

"You've got some more interesting associates than I gave you credit for. How come you're on visiting terms with a Bolshie?"

"A Bolshevik!" exploded Sir Philip. "Lyvenden, what the devil's going on?"

Lyvenden, who had been sagging quietly in a corner, bristled. Haldean caught Stanton's eye. Lyvenden was brave enough now any danger was past. "The Bolsheviks are no friends of mine, Rivers. I think I may say without fear of contradiction —" he was gaining confidence with every word he spoke — "that you have known me long enough to concur with that remark. But any commercial enterprise, my dear fellow, especially one as fraught with difficulties as mine, renders one liable to contact with some very strange company indeed." He was nearly back to his old verbose self. "It would be foolishly indiscreet of me to say more, as the affair is not mine to discuss. What I can say is that the Government are fully cognizant of the man who has so unfortunately intruded on the peace of this Sabbath morning and see eye to eye with me in my treatment of the matter. I have their complete confidence, Rivers, I am happy to say." The cringing, frightened figure of a few moments ago had vanished as if he had never been. "Complete confidence."

Haldean was glad to see that his uncle, although soothed, wasn't entirely won over.

"The Government agree with you?" said Sir Philip, incredulously. His expression left no one in any doubt as to his opinion of the Government. "Well, all I can say," he added, "is that if being in business means that you have to deal with that sort of gentry, thank God I'm not in business."

Lunch was a strained meal, which, after the tragedy of the night before and the melodrama of the morning, was hardly a surprise. As was usual in the summer months, coffee was served on the terrace afterwards, where things were more relaxed but far from smooth.

Haldean felt a stab of sympathy for his aunt, who was trying to make conversation against the odds. Lord Lyvenden still had the jumps from his fright that morning (and he had been very badly frightened — what *had* that bloke wanted?), his wife, when she spoke at all, was bitterly sardonic, Mrs Strachan (was she Lyvenden's mistress?) gushed, Malcolm Smith-Fennimore was wrapped in introspection, as, uncharacteristically, were the two Robiceux girls, and as for Isabelle . . . Well, at that moment he could have happily taken a sandbag to Isabelle.

For Isabelle was being very, very nice to Arthur, and he, poor fool, was drinking it in. What the hell was she trying to do to him? *Leave him alone*, he begged, trying to indicate his thoughts with his expression, but Isabelle wouldn't switch it off. She was being breathtakingly pleasant. Smith-Fennimore looked at the pair of them with a puzzled frown and, under the guise of refilling his coffee cup, moved closer. Isabelle suddenly became aware of him and faltered, before carrying on her conversation with Arthur, her glance flickering between the two men. If she was using Arthur to spur on Smith-Fennimore . . . But it sounded so *real*. Haldean suddenly worked out what was going on. Now Isabelle had finally turned Arthur down, she was wondering what she'd lost. He'd always thought Stanton had been the one who counted. Maybe, just maybe, Isabelle might start to think so too.

"More coffee, Isabelle?" said Smith-Fennimore. He took her cup and filled it, then planted himself firmly between Isabelle and Arthur. "You missed all the excitement in the hall this morning."

"I heard about it though," she said. "I can't think what Uncle Alfred was playing at."

There was a very succinct answer to that but in deference to the present company, Haldean decided not to make it.

Sir Philip cleared his throat and looked at Smith-Fennimore. "There's something I want to ask you, Commander. I was wondering how it was you spoke Russian. You weren't there in the war, were you?"

Smith-Fennimore laughed. "No, unfortunately. I did ask to be sent there, because I know the country — or bits of it at least — quite well, but, on the grounds that you're always posted where you can be of the least use, I never made it. No, it goes back to when I was a kid. I used to spend my holidays in Russia and the Baltic. The bank had a strong Russian connection and my father saw to it that I grew up speaking both Russian and French."

"All Russians speak French, don't they?" said Isabelle, intelligently.

Smith-Fennimore grinned. "All the educated ones used to. Goodness knows if they still do. I imagine all that stopped after the revolution in '17. Naturally that was the end of the bank's connection with the place, but fortunately my father had seen the writing on the wall and started to pull out before then. Things went downhill for a couple of years but I'm glad to say we had sufficient interests in both this country and the Argentine to cover the loss."

"I'm glad to hear it," said Sir Philip, finishing his coffee. "About the bank being able to recover, I mean. There were plenty of poor devils who were ruined when Russia went up in flames." He put down his cup with unnecessary force. "Bolsheviks!"

"Talking of Bolsheviks," said Lady Harriet, with a glance at her husband, "I'm still waiting to hear an adequate explanation of what that peculiar man wanted, Victor."

Lord Lyvenden winced. "Business, my dear, business." Lady Harriet raised an ironic eyebrow, piercing his pomposity like a pin in a balloon. He faltered, recovered himself and blustered on. "Talking of business, I find I am most gravely inconvenienced by the lack of a secretary."

There was a collective intake of breath round the terrace at this monumental display of callousness.

"I sent a telegram to his uncle, Mr Urqhart, this morning," put in Lady Rivers, who had seen the frankly hostile stares of Haldean, Stanton and Smith-Fennimore. "I have to thank you, Lord Lyvenden, for giving me his address."

The hostess in her made her stress the words "thank you". It wasn't her fault it seemed sarcastic. "Obviously we want to do the best we can in the circumstances, and I've assured Mr Urqhart that we shall do everything possible. It will be a terrible blow to him, I'm sure."

"To all of us, dear lady," said Lord Lyvenden, with a funereal expression. "And to voice my own concerns, it is especially hard to be deprived of Mr Preston's services at a time when I can ill spare them."

Lady Rivers sighed and gave up.

"I am afraid I must go up to Town tomorrow to begin the search for a replacement."

"That won't be very hard, will it?" asked Sir Philip, with distaste. If Lyvenden doesn't have the hide of an elephant, thought Haldean, he'll drop this now. "With all this dreadful unemployment I'd have thought you'd be able to find someone easily enough."

Lord Lyvenden might be impervious to hints, but he could be shocked. "You can hardly suppose I would select my personal secretary from the ranks of the unemployed, Rivers." He dabbed his mouth with a handkerchief. "This is excellent coffee, excellent, by the way. All this talk of unemployment is grossly exaggerated. There would be no unemployment if the men concerned were not, in fact, unemployable."

Smith-Fennimore stirred, looked daggers, but said nothing.

"As an employer of labour I am in the position to speak assertively on this topic. The men who badger, absolutely *badger*, both my Birmingham factories and the bank are, without exception, incapable of maintaining any sort of paid position, even at the lowest level. They are, Rivers, not a type of man you have ever encountered."

"I've encountered a fair variety of types in my time, Lyvenden," said Sir Philip. "I haven't lived in the country all my life, you know."

Lyvenden smiled dismissively. "I hardly think you have had much to do with the sort of men I have in mind. Why, only the other day one had the impudence to actually accost me in the street." He glanced at Smith-Fennimore. "You remember the incident, Commander? I had to leave you to deal with the fellow. My doctor insists that I avoid any unnecessary stress. I trust you dealt with him effectively."

There was a dangerous light in Smith-Fennimore's eyes. "Oh, I dealt with him all right," he said softly. "I gave the poor devil a job as a messenger."

Lord Lyvenden gaped at him. "You did *what?*" Haldean felt like cheering. "No good will come of it," spluttered Lyvenden. "Mark my words, Commander. The engagement of the lower grades of staff should properly be left to the managers of the departments concerned, but if you do feel moved to take such an intimate interest in the minutiae of the bank's affairs, why not go to one of the properly recognized agencies? Such rash impulsiveness will lead to nothing but trouble. Look at that poor dead boy whose untimely decease has done so much to mar what should have been the happiest of occasions. I took him on, much against my better judgement, as a personal favour to his uncle, Andrew Urqhart, who thought it would steady the lad."

70

And I bet you got something in return, thought Haldean, viciously. Anyone but Lyvenden, seeing the disapproval on the faces round him, would have drawn a halt there, but he rolled on like a juggernaut, crushing the feelings of those in his path.

"However," continued Lyvenden, "as in all these cases where the heart rules the head, it turned out to have been an injudicious decision." His face lengthened. "Although I have no wish to speak ill of the dead, I fear Mr Preston's heart was not always in his work. I had to upbraid him several times for some very elementary errors and I fear he mistook my attempts at constructive correction for petty fault-finding. Those who knew him best will agree that his end was, I'm afraid, marked by the same characteristics as his life; rash impulsiveness, small thought to the effect of his actions on others and an imprudent disregard for consequences. Is that not so, Commander?"

Smith-Fennimore drew a deep breath and flexed his jaw.

Sir Philip, who had been listening to Lord Lyvenden with mounting unease, uncharacteristically rushed into speech, seizing the first topic to hand. "Er . . . the weather. Yes, the weather. Nice day, isn't it? We're being awfully lucky with the weather, aren't we?"

"Absolutely we are, Dad," said Isabelle quickly. "Don't you think so, Malcolm?"

"I think . . ." began Smith-Fennimore, then stopped. He paused for a moment then his shoulders relaxed. "Terribly lucky," he agreed politely. Then, catching Isabelle's eye, he made a visible effort. "I think we're

71

due for a change though," he continued. "Look at those clouds. They're mares' tails. There's a storm brewing somewhere."

Isabelle looked at her cousin, willing him to help the conversation along.

Haldean was only too willing to play his part in steering it away from the emotionally fraught subject of Tim Preston. If for no other reason, the sight of Bubble Robiceux's stricken face would have spurred him on. She was usually a happy, light-hearted girl but she'd had a rotten blow and he was damned if that fatuous swine Lyvenden was going to make it any worse for her. Besides that, if Smith-Fennimore could make an effort, so could he. "D'you know," said Haldean, stirring his coffee, "I believe I could have told you were either a sailor or an airman just from the way you looked at the sky."

"You'd be right on both counts," agreed Smith-Fennimore. His voice changed. He was no longer simply making conversation. "I started off in the navy, got bitten with the flying bug, and transferred to the Air Service."

"I think Jack was born with the flying bug," said Isabelle, affectionately. "He lied about his age to join the RFC and he's still crazy about it."

"Stretched the truth slightly," corrected Haldean with a smile. "Everyone was doing it. Do you still fly, Fennimore? The newspapers always talk of you as a racing driver."

"No, I still fly. I'd hate to live without it. Where d'you park your bus?"

72

Haldean smile faded slightly. "I haven't got one."

"Why not? If you came up to Brooklands you'd be handy for London."

"Because . . ." Despite himself, Haldean was suddenly irritated. Smith-Fennimore might find money no object but he had to be *careful* with money and it annoyed him to spell it out. "It's a bit beyond my reach, I'm afraid. I did wonder about it." He broke off. Why shouldn't he say it? Why not come down to raw figures? "It's a hundred quid a year to rent a hangar at Brooklands, to say nothing of the fitting and rigging charges, and that's just the start of it." That had been a bit sharp. He softened it with a laugh. "The reading public will have to be a sight more gullible before I fly again. If I did, Brooklands would be my first choice. That's where I trained and I was seconded back there to a Home Defence Squadron to have a crack at the bombers." He laughed again, a genuine laugh this time. "That's before I disgraced myself by being silly round Members' Bridge."

"What!" Smith-Fennimore sat upright in his chair. "Jack Haldean! I knew I'd heard the name when I met you. Apart from your books, that is. You're the one who looped the loop through Members' Bridge! It was a Sopwith Pup in '16." He gave Haldean a look of unqualified admiration. "You're a legend, man."

Haldean grinned. "Hardly that. It all ended in tears. I frightened a Staff Colonel into fits — the poor devil was on the bridge at the time — and wound up being sent back to France with my tail between my legs. It was a pretty goofy stunt."

"Oh no, it wasn't." Smith-Fennimore leaned forward in his chair. "I wish I'd known who you were before. Look, about this Brooklands thing. Why don't you share my hangar? I'm sure I can fix you up with something worth flying and I've got my own fitter and rigger."

Haldean looked at him. "I couldn't do that."

"Well, let's halve the fees, then. Besides that, I've got a flying project in mind that I wouldn't mind talking over with you." He raised an eyebrow. "Interested?"

"I . . ." It had been downright sensitive of Fennimore to guess why he'd hesitated. He couldn't take it as a free gift, but a halved cost would be just about manageable and the thought of flying again sent a tingle down his spine. "I'd love to," he said.

"Excellent," said Smith-Fennimore, his temper well and truly restored. "I'll look forward to it, Haldean." He got to his feet and smiled down at Isabelle. "You promised to show me something of the grounds. Shall we go for a walk?"

She slipped her arm into his. "Let's."

Stanton watched them go before he, too, pushed his chair back.

"Are you off, Arthur?" asked Haldean.

"I thought I might have a stroll by the river."

"I'll tool along with you." Haldean winced as he stood up. "This wretched leg of mine is horribly stiff. I've been sitting for far too long."

Stanton didn't answer. He didn't, in fact, say anything until they had crossed the lawn to where a line of trees marked the course of the river. He was,

74

apparently, completely absorbed in reaming out his pipe.

Haldean, whose leg was really throbbing, found the pace Stanton was setting too much. "Hang on, Arthur. I'll need my stick if you're going to crack along at this rate."

Stanton stopped. "I'm sorry, Jack. Would you mind letting me go off by myself for a while? I don't think I'm very good company at the moment." He looked across the lawn to where Smith-Fennimore and Isabelle were still in sight. "I don't suppose I have to tell you why."

"Why . . ." Haldean broke off as the pain in his leg flared.

Stanton, his eyes fixed on Isabelle, took it as a question and flared. "Why? Hellfire, Jack, you know why."

"I —"

"It's bad enough listening to that unctuous creep Lyvenden making remarks about Tim without you asking *why*.'

"I didn't mean —"

"To say nothing of having to watch that Fennimore character swipe the only girl I've ever given tuppence about before wrapping you round his little finger. I didn't think you'd be interested in running with the Brooklands crowd but as soon as he mentioned flying, you were eating out of his hand."

"I wasn't!" said Haldean indignantly. "But when a man makes an offer like that, you don't throw it back at him."

"No, you roll over when he says so."

"Well, you'd better get used to it, because it looks as if he's going to be around Belle for a long time."

There was a charged silence. Haldean looked at Stanton's white face and twisted inside. "Arthur . . ." He sighed. "I'm sorry." He'd reached for and used a shameful weapon, deadly in effect. "It was a really rotten thing to say. That was below the belt. If you'll accept an apology, I'm sorry."

Stanton breathed again. "It's all right," he said quietly. "It's only the truth, after all. And I'm sorry too, Jack. I went over the top there. I'm finding this all very difficult and my temper's gone to pieces. I suppose part of it's me being a bad loser but I'm unhappy at the thought of you getting in with that crowd, especially after what happened to Tim. I know damn well you haven't the money to throw around that they have and I'd hate to see you get in over your head." He paused. "As I say, it's . . . difficult."

Difficult? Yes, it was certainly that, thought Haldean, genuinely touched by Stanton's concern for him. He hesitated before he spoke. "I'll be all right, Arthur. I know only too well that I haven't got money to burn. And I'm really sorry that things aren't working out."

Stanton gave a humourless smile. "Not working out? That's a bit of an understatement, isn't it?" He concentrated on his empty pipe once more. "I can't blame Isabelle," he said distantly. "I can't even blame Smith-Fennimore. Not much, anyway." He attempted a smile. "Now I can blame Lyvenden. I don't think I've ever disliked anyone more."

"He's putrid," said Haldean, delicately accepting the olive branch.

"The funny thing is," added Stanton, clearly willing the wounded friendship back to full health, "I keep on thinking I should know something about Lyvenden. Something nasty, I mean."

"Something to do with Tim?"

Stanton shook his head. "No. Something personal. And I can't place what it is."

CHAPTER
FOUR

Haldean left Stanton and half climbed, half slid down the grassy bank to the river with a feeling of relief. He was consciously hunting for a retreat. There were some very messy emotions kicking around, his own included. He'd hardly ever had so much as a disagreement with Stanton before and the argument had shaken him more than he cared to admit. They had been really close friends and at times it still seemed as if they were, but it wasn't like it used to be.

He ducked under the leafy curtain of a weeping willow and found a gentle depression in the earth beside the massive trunk which could have been made for him. Here, with the sound of the river and where dappled sunlight flecked the water under the shade of the trees, was a place which soothed his spirit, a place where he could put things in their proper order.

Stanton; what was it? It could be nothing more than that their paths had diverged. It could . . . But Haldean refused to follow his thoughts to their logical conclusion. Mind you, what with Isabelle on the one hand and Tim on the other, Stanton couldn't be expected to behave like the resident ray of sunshine.

He snuggled down with his back to the tree, and lit his pipe, the smoke curling bluely upwards. What about Tim? Yes, he could have been alone in Lyvenden's room with a gun to hand and been overwhelmed by sudden despair. That really could be the answer. Neither Stanton nor Smith-Fennimore had guessed what he had guessed, which could mean that he had guessed wrong. Isabelle; he needed to talk to Isabelle. And he really wanted to talk to Superintendent Ashley.

A flash of blue in the spotted, rippling shade brought a stab of unexpected delight as he realized it was a kingfisher. Halcyon days. That's what the Greeks called the time when the kingfisher flew. Halcyon? He smiled cynically and yawned. Being so damn tired didn't help. He hadn't been able to sleep last night.

The kingfisher flew unheeded, the languid drone of insects washed over his senses and the well-behaved river flowed placidly on. The pipe fell from his hand and he slumped, fast asleep.

He awoke to the sound of voices very near by, aware that he had been hearing them for some time. The shadows were longer and he realized, with drowsy surprise, that he must have slept for a couple of hours. A woman laughed and he peered round the tree. His heart sank.

Lord Lyvenden and Mrs Strachan were standing on the bank of the river, outside the veil of willow leaves, kissing each other. Haldean drew back against the ridged bark of the tree. Bloody *hell*! If Lord Lyvenden absolutely had to carry out a senile intrigue, why on earth did he have to do it here? The worst of it was, he was completely stuck until Lyvenden decided to move.

"Now, now, Victor," giggled Mrs Strachan with ghastly coquettishness, slapping Lyvenden playfully. "Don't be greedy."

Haldean dug his hands into the soft earth in frustration. Their voices on the other side of the curtain of willow were only too clear. If he tried to escape up the bank they'd be bound to see him.

"I'm always greedy for you, little woman," said Lord Lyvenden with elephantine playfulness.

This was simply revolting. He couldn't move, he couldn't escape, he simply had to endure this appalling pair and their antics. He couldn't see them but he could hear every sound they made and Lyvenden's breath was coming faster.

"I think my precious Victor is being a wee bit naughty," cooed Mrs Strachan. Some of the most disagreeably suggestive sounds Haldean had ever heard indicated that Precious Victor was being naughty again.

More than anything in the world he wanted to get away but even if he ducked under the far side of the tree out of their line of sight there was a solid clump of bulrushes in the way. In the marshy ground he'd sound like a herd of water buffalo.

A wheezing breath indicated that Lord Lyvenden was coming up for air. "Let me come to your room tonight, Valerie. I haven't been near you all weekend."

She giggled playfully. "It's been difficult, darling." She gave a simpering laugh. "Stop it. No, Victor, no. Stop it. Perhaps you can visit me tonight but only if you're good. And perhaps, Victor, you shouldn't be so secretive. You've been keeping things from me, haven't you? I don't like secrets, Victor."

Now the words meant nothing but it was the sudden and startled hush which followed them that put Haldean on the alert.

Very cautiously, he risked a glance through the leaves. Lord Lyvenden was holding Mrs Strachan tightly by the shoulders, his red, angry face close to hers.

"What d'you mean by that, woman?"

Mrs Strachan tried to get away. She looked frightened, so frightened that Haldean suddenly felt sorry for her. She wriggled helplessly under his large, strong hands. "You're hurting me, Victor. Let me go."

"I'll let you go when you tell me what you mean." His voice was very low and very threatening.

She put her arm up against his chest, trying to force herself free. "Please, Victor. I don't mean anything really. Let me go. It's only those silly papers. I couldn't help seeing them. You'd left them in your bedroom. They didn't mean anything, it's just that you made such a fuss about me not seeing them and I couldn't help looking. That's all."

For a moment Haldean thought Lyvenden was going to hit her.

Mrs Strachan shrank away, her hand to her mouth. "I thought there was another woman. I thought it was something to do with me. Please, Victor, let me go! I know it's nothing like that. I couldn't understand them, I really couldn't."

Lyvenden slackened his grip, still looking intently into her face. Then he stepped back and dropped his hands. "Papers?" he said with a coarse chuckle. Mrs Strachan nodded timidly. Lyvenden rubbed his hands together with an unpleasant expression. "You've been snooping, my dear, into matters that don't concern you. I don't like that."

Out of that ferocious grip Mrs Strachan recovered some of her self-possession. "You haven't been very generous lately," she said in a feeble attempt at her earlier manner.

Lord Lyvenden slowly smiled. "And so you thought you'd see what you could find out, eh? That was very ill advised, Valerie. Blackmail's not a game you should play. Now, if I come to your room tonight, I hope I can be sure of a welcome."

"If you could be a little more generous, Victor, we'll say nothing about it."

Lyvenden took her by the shoulders once more, shaking her as he spoke. "You won't say anything about it anyway, my dear, will you? That would be most unwise." Mrs Strachan looked terrified. The way he said the last word made Haldean feel cold. "I'll be there, with enough to make sure that our little secret stays between just the two of us." He dragged her to him and kissed her. She broke away, her hand to her mouth. Lyvenden looked at her in satisfaction. "Don't ever snoop in my things again." She shook her head slightly, unable, at a guess, to speak. "Now off you go, my little pet. It wouldn't do for the two of us to leave here together."

82

She walked up the bank, her hand still to her mouth.

Lyvenden took a deep breath and, taking out his cigarette case, lit a cigarette.

Haldean, waiting for him to go, sighed in frustration as footsteps sounded on the river bank above. A low, penetrating voice broke the silence.

"Victor? I know you're there, Victor. I've just seen that bloody woman come up the bank." It was the well-bred but furious voice of Lady Harriet.

Lord Lyvenden looked as if he had suddenly shrunk. "Harriet? How nice to see you." He held his cigarette with shaky fingers. "Which woman would that be?"

Lady Harriet gave him a look that cut like a whip. "You know who I mean, Victor. Have you no sense of shame? Chorus girls in London are one thing but to bring that . . . that *street walker* into a decent house is going too far."

"Mrs Strachan is not a street walker!"

"Maybe not," agreed Lady Harriet, icily. "I lack your vast experience in these matters. But I know she is your mistress and I know you pay her. That is an ugly combination with an ugly word to describe it."

Lord Lyvenden took a deep draught on his cigarette. "I never knew you cared so much," he said with a feeble attempt at insouciance. His voice cracked. "Perhaps if you were a little more accommodating I wouldn't be tempted."

With narrowed eyes Lady Harriet stepped back and half drew a small pistol from her bag. With a shock Haldean recognized it as the twin of the one that had killed Tim. "If you dare to approach my room, Victor, I will shoot you with the greatest of pleasure."

Lord Lyvenden stepped back in alarm. "Put that thing away, Harriet! Damn it, woman, why shouldn't I come to your room?"

"You know exactly why not."

"But you're my wife, aren't you? Not that you've ever acted like one."

"You never wanted me to. Ever. You never even had the grace to pretend."

"I couldn't pretend about the amount of money you cost me. That was real enough. What about that, eh? I wanted you enough to pay for you. Don't you remember how generous I had to be to your father?"

"And haven't I earned it?" asked Lady Harriet, passionately. "God knows, Victor, I've earned every penny. You didn't want me, you wanted who I was. People received you because of who I was, you know that. In public, I have been the perfect wife. In private, I have endured your fatuities and your whoring, but I will not endure very much more." Her voice was very low and very urgent and Haldean had no doubt she meant every word she said. "I can make things so unpleasant for you, Victor, that you would be forced to give me a divorce. And that, let me remind you, would hurt you far more than it would hurt me. As long as you leave me alone, I am perfectly happy for things to continue as they are. But I will not stand for being made a fool of. If you dare to bring your mistress to a house party once more, I will arrange matters so you can never show your face in decent society again."

Without another look at her husband she turned and walked away.

Lord Lyvenden, breathing deeply, threw his cigarette in the river and followed her.

Haldean gave Lord Lyvenden plenty of time to get away before he climbed back up the river bank. That had been an unpleasant little scene. Two unpleasant little scenes, he corrected himself. That Lady Harriet didn't care for her husband was apparent but he'd had no idea of the depth of passion in that rigidly controlled woman. If Lyvenden did try anything on, he could very easily credit that Lady Harriet would indeed shoot him. He returned thoughtfully across the lawn to the house.

As he walked through the open door to the hall, Stanton came out of the morning room. "Jack? There you are. We couldn't think where you'd got to. We've been looking everywhere. There's a policeman in the library taking statements from everybody. He needs to speak to you."

"It's not Superintendent Ashley, is it?" asked Haldean, hopefully.

Stanton shook his head. "It's not a Superintendent anyone. He's a sergeant, I think. We've all spoken to him. He's interviewing the servants now." He paused. "Look . . . about what I said earlier. I know I apologized but I'd like to do it again. I know I was wrong, but it's difficult to keep on an even keel with all this going on." He shrugged. "All I can say is that I'm sorry."

So completely had Haldean been caught up with Lord Lyvenden and his affairs, it took him a moment to understand that Stanton was apologizing for their argument. He grasped his friend's arm. "Forget it. I'd better go and face the Law, but I want to talk to you and I really want to talk to Isabelle about Tim."

Stanton gave a rueful smile. "Haven't we talked enough? Isabelle's in the garden with Smith-Fennimore. I suppose I could go and get them but I feel a bit awkward about butting in." He looked at his friend. "Okay. I'll do it."

"Thanks, Arthur," said Haldean. "I know this isn't particularly easy for you but I'd be very grateful. Can you meet me here in about half an hour? I don't think I'll be much longer."

Leaving Stanton by the morning room, Haldean went along to the library where there was a little knot of servants outside the door, contentedly grumbling about this break from routine. Amongst them was Lady Harriet's maid, Yvette, who was perfectly happy to speak to Monsieur le Commandant 'Aldean and tell him all about her emotions, her horror, her lacerated feelings on discovering that the crack she had heard from the room of milor' was not, as she had supposed, a *feu d'artifice*, a how-do-you-say? — a firework, but that so-'andsome young man, Monsieur Preston, in the act of self-annihilation.

Monsieur le Commandant went thoughtfully into the library to give his statement. As it was a purely factual account of Tim's apparent suicide, it didn't take long. He took the opportunity to ask when Ashley would return and was delighted to find out that he should be back on Tuesday. He had met Ashley, said Haldean, the previous year, and had promised to look him up again. Once established as the Superintendent's friend, Haldean was able to learn one other thing. The gun used had been one of a pair. Lady Harriet had one and Lord Lyvenden the other.

He walked back to the morning room where Stanton, Isabelle and Smith-Fennimore were waiting for him.

Isabelle looked at him with a worried smile. "Hello, Jack. Arthur tells me you've got some notion that Tim didn't shoot himself, and Malcolm said you'd all had a good look round Lord Lyvenden's room this morning while we were at church. Are you sure? That it really isn't suicide, I mean?"

Haldean shut the door carefully behind him. "No, I'm not, Isabelle. I thought I was on the right lines but I'm not nearly so certain now." He draped himself across an armchair, stretched out his long legs, lit a cigarette and sighed. "How d'you feel about murder, Belle?" he asked. "About the idea that Tim was murdered?"

She wrinkled her nose in concentration. "To be honest I was shocked at first, but now I've got used to the idea I think it makes sense. You see, I couldn't understand why Tim had done it. I saw quite a bit of him last night and he was really looking forward to all the things that he and Bubble were going to do next week, such as taking a picnic on the river, playing tennis and going dancing and so on." She looked at

Smith-Fennimore beside her. "He talked about you, Malcolm, and the Isle of Man race, and Bubble said she'd come and watch the race and, well . . . it seemed so odd that with all that in mind he should suddenly decide to end it all. It just seemed so out of character, somehow."

Haldean nodded. "That's virtually what I said to Stanton and Fennimore earlier."

Stanton shifted in his chair. "I still think you're wrong, though, Jack. He really had been stuck for money, don't forget."

Isabelle wriggled impatiently. "But you explained all that to me, Arthur. He wasn't stuck now."

"And I would have helped," said Smith-Fennimore quietly. "He must have known I would have helped."

"The only trouble is, Belle," said Haldean, "that if Tim was murdered, that presupposes a murderer."

She looked at him alertly. "Yes." She drew her breath in. "I see what you mean. Pass me a cigarette, will you?" Smith-Fennimore lit her cigarette and she smoked it thoughtfully. "So you're saying that someone here, someone we know, is a murderer?"

"That's about the size of it, yes," replied Haldean quietly.

"But who, Jack?"

Haldean ran his thumb round the angle of his jaw. "That's the interesting question. You see, I thought I knew." They all looked at him, startled. "The trouble is, my favourite candidate is out of it. He can't possibly have done it so now I'm back to square one."

"Are you going to tell us who your favourite candidate was?" asked Smith-Fennimore.

Haldean hesitated. "I wouldn't have said anything before I was a great deal more certain but it can't do any harm now, I suppose. I'd settled on Lord Lyvenden."

Smith-Fennimore looked bewildered. "Why?"

"All sorts of reasons, but I'm wrong. The man's got a rock-solid alibi. Yvette, Lady Harriet's maid, the one who was sent upstairs for Lady Harriet's shawl, heard the shot. She thought it was a firework and was a bit fed up to think she was missing the show."

"How d'you know it wasn't a firework she heard?" asked Isabelle.

"Because when she got back with the shawl, the show proper hadn't started."

"But those wretched fireworks were going off all evening," said Stanton.

Haldean shook his head. "Not then, they weren't. Lyvenden was building up to his big moment. When Yvette came back into the ballroom, Lord Lyvenden was still gassing about what a wonderful occasion it was and that fixes the time at about ten to ten. I remember looking at my watch and wondering how long he was going to spout on for. And, although he was my first choice, he can't possibly have been boring us all rigid and murdering people at the same time."

"No," said Isabelle after a pause. "No, he can't have been. So who is it, Jack?"

Haldean put his hands wide. "Search me. And, as Arthur reminded us, Tim might have committed suicide after all."

"That's silly," she said decisively. "You can't get us all thinking about murder and then just bow out like that." She stubbed out her cigarette and put her hands round her knees, silent for a few moments. "Look," she said eventually. "You write detective stories, don't you?"

"It has been known," muttered Haldean. "I've got to earn a crust somehow."

"Can't we think of it as a story? Every time I remember it's Tim I feel sort of crushed and can't think straight, but this way we might be able to come up with some ideas. I know it's a bit off to play Pin The Tail On The Murderer, so to speak, but I can't do it any other way. Actually, Jack, if this was a story then I wouldn't suspect Lord Lyvenden for a moment."

"Why not?" asked Stanton. "Don't tell me you like the man."

"Of course I don't. He's horrible and I wish Uncle Alfred hadn't introduced him to Dad, but that's just it. He's so obnoxious that he's the obvious red herring that I always discount. I'd be right, too, wouldn't I? I mean, if he's got an alibi he's out of it."

"As a matter of fact," said Haldean, "if this was a story, then his alibi would make him very suspicious indeed."

"This is nonsense," said Stanton. "For one thing I don't believe it was murder and for another I just can't see it. I mean, I can't stand Lyvenden but I'm blowed if I'm accusing him or anyone else of murder, especially as you've just proved he can't be guilty. I mean, you haven't got any evidence, have you? Anyone can make a guess. You might as well say the butler or the Chief Constable or Mr Charnock did it."

"Uncle Alfred?" asked Isabelle in bewilderment. "Uncle Alfred can't have done it. Why on earth should he? Besides that, he wasn't here last night. I suppose that means you find him suspicious too, Jack."

"Deeply suspicious," he said gravely.

"Are you serious?" demanded Isabelle.

"Not really," he said with a grin. "I wanted to see how you'd react."

"Jack!" She threw a cushion at him, which, to her irritation, he caught. "If we carry on like this, I'm going to decide you did it. Actually, you'd make a very satisfactory murderer. You're dark and sinister."

Smith-Fennimore grinned. "If Haldean had done it, I don't suppose you'd be too anxious to try and convince us it was murder, would you, old man?"

"If it was one of his stories he might," chipped in Isabelle before Haldean could answer. "He could be dying to boast about how clever he'd been and sort of daring us to catch him out. I remember reading one where you did just that. But what made you think of Lord Lyvenden, Jack? There must be more to it than the fact he's easily one of the most unpleasant guests we've ever had."

"He's a bit much, isn't he?" agreed Haldean. "But no, Belle, it wasn't his lack of charm and want of ready tact that made me pick him out, it was the circumstances. Lyvenden's got the breeze up about some papers he has with him. Tim told me last night he'd been strafed by Lyvenden for looking in the wrong

91

file. Apparently the noble lord really went over the top about it. So, I thought intelligently, that could be a motive. I believed that Lyvenden had the opportunity to bump off Tim by following him upstairs after he'd sent him to get the cigarette case — and, although it's unimportant, Lyvenden didn't half look flushed when he came into the ballroom to start his speech before the fireworks — and, of course, the fact that it was Lyvenden's room and Lyvenden's gun that was used all seemed to point to Lyvenden, but I'm wrong."

Stanton scratched his chin. "Of course you're wrong, Jack. Even if this was a story I'd think you were wrong. What about the note Tim left? It'd be easy enough to scrawl a message like — oh, I don't know — *Sorry*, I suppose, but I can't see Lord Lyvenden or anyone else sitting down and writing reams about how broke he was and so on."

"That's very well spotted, Arthur," said Isabelle admiringly. "Unless the murderer's a master forger then the whole case goes up the spout."

"No, it doesn't," said Haldean with weary patience. "And he hardly wrote reams. Look, Fennimore, you saw the note. Describe it for Belle, will you?"

Smith-Fennimore wrinkled his brow. "The note? It was Tim's writing, all right. I'd swear to it. That throws a spanner in your murder theory, wouldn't you say?"

"Go on with your description," said Haldean without heat.

Smith-Fennimore shrugged. "All right. It was written in ink on a half-sheet of cream notepaper and the words were at the top of the sheet. He said that he was sorry and that the cause was money."

Haldean nodded. "That's pretty good." He stretched his legs out, put his hands behind his head and half closed his eyes. "The actual words ran, as far as I remember, *I am sorry for what I have been forced to do* — no, hang on — *course of action I have been forced to undertake and for any distress that might ensue. The motive is purely financial.* The note itself is still upstairs and we can check it if it's necessary but that's about the gist of it. Now, does anything strike you as odd about that note?"

Isabelle cupped her chin in her hands thoughtfully. "Not really. It sounds a bit stilted, but so what?"

"But that's it," said Haldean. "It was far too stilted to be an ordinary note. It sounds much more like a business letter, doesn't it?"

"Hold on there, Jack," objected Stanton. "It's all very well to talk about the language being stilted but most people write far more formally than they speak. I know I do. It takes quite a bit of skill to write something so it sounds natural. You manage it. I think you must be quite a good writer, really."

Haldean grinned. "Thank you for that glowing tribute, said the blushing author. Signed copies of all my works will be available at the back of the hall after the meeting. What I think happened is that the murderer found part of a business letter and used that. Any more comments, anyone?"

"Well, yes," said Isabelle. "If the note was taken from a business letter, then where's the rest of it?"

"The murderer took it with him, of course," said Haldean, witheringly. "He wouldn't leave a dead give-away like that lying around. And that's something else fishy, too. The waste-paper basket was empty, and it shouldn't have been. Tim was working in there yesterday and he told me some of the letters he wrote were duds, so there should have been something in it. None of the servants emptied it. I've asked. So who did empty it? The murderer, obviously, to get rid of any incriminating evidence."

Isabelle pulled a face. "Come on. I bet one of the servants emptied it, realized they shouldn't have done and won't own up. That's a much simpler explanation than yours."

Smith-Fennimore coughed. "I think we're straying from the point. Was Tim murdered or wasn't he? And granted that Lyvenden can't be guilty, who else could it be?"

"I've been thinking about it," said Haldean. "If the shot was heard at ten to ten, that rules out everyone who was in the ballroom. Who do we know wasn't there?"

"Lady Harriet's maid," said Isabelle, promptly. "She could have killed him when she went up for Lady Harriet's shawl."

"Whatever for?" asked Stanton.

"Goodness knows, but she was away from the room at the right time. Who else was missing?"

"There's your Uncle Alfred," said Haldean. "He wasn't at the ball but he could have crept back in."

94

"You've got a thing about Uncle Alfred," said Isabelle. "You've never liked him."

"How shatteringly perceptive of you. You're right, of course."

"I think it's colouring your judgement, Jack. It can't be Uncle Alfred. You know the doctor gave me something to help me sleep? I was out like a light but woke up at about four in the morning because the boards outside my room had creaked. They do when someone walks along there. I looked out and Uncle Alfred was creeping along the corridor, shoes in hand. If he'd been out until four, he can't have had anything to do with what happened to Tim, can he? The odd thing was that he was dripping wet."

"Dripping wet?"

"Absolutely soaking. I heard him squelching and this morning there were wet patches on the carpet. I don't know what he did with his wet things."

"I wonder what the dickens he'd been up to? I wouldn't have thought your Uncle Alfred would have gone in for midnight bathing, especially wearing full evening dress." Haldean clicked his tongue. "As you say, it's odd, Belle, but it doesn't let him out. He could have come back much earlier and then gone out again."

"He could, I suppose," agreed Isabelle reluctantly. "But if we're throwing suspicion around, what about Lady Harriet? She'd make a wonderful murderer. I don't know why she'd murder Tim but I can imagine her murdering her husband. You should see how she looks at him when she thinks nobody's watching."

Haldean was silent. After the scene on the river bank, he too could imagine Lady Harriet murdering her husband without any compunction whatsoever. Not only that but she carried a gun.

"No, hang on," continued Isabelle. "She was watching the fireworks, of course. That's a pity. How about Mrs Strachan? She seems completely brainless but she might have hidden depths. I can't remember if she was watching the fireworks or not. If this was really a story then she'd be my favourite suspect because, although we all know her, we haven't paid much attention to her. Tim might have found her rifling through Lord Lyvenden's secret papers and she could have snatched up a gun and shot him."

Haldean sat upright. "D'you know, Belle, that's not a bad idea. Tim being shot by accident, I mean. That would work."

Smith-Fennimore gave a dismissive snort. "Can you honestly see that twitty woman having the brains to do something like this?"

"Why not?" Haldean stubbed out his cigarette. "You see, Mrs Strachan certainly has been snooping in Lord Lyvenden's papers. I heard the pair of them discussing it, if I can put it like that, earlier on. They didn't know I was there, of course. He . . . well, he wasn't happy and she was in a blue funk. It was a nasty little episode altogether. Say Tim did surprise her. She'd have the gun close to hand and if there was a letter lying on the desk even Mrs Strachan would be able to see how it could be used as a suicide note, no matter how dim she seems."

Smith-Fennimore was silent for a few moments. "You could be right," he said eventually. He looked at Isabelle. "Well done. Have you any more suggestions? This idea of yours of treating it as a story has more going for it than I thought."

"Well, there is another possibility," she said with a smile. "This really is a solution from a story. I read it the other day in *Modern Thriller*. This young man was going to come into a fortune when he was twenty-one but his solicitor had made away with all his money and then killed him so he wouldn't be discovered. The thing was, that the room where the body was found was locked up and no one could work out how the murder had been done. Tim was going to get his money next year. His uncle holds the funds and paid him an allowance. What if his uncle had embezzled the money? He could have come here secretly, lain in wait, shot Tim, then slipped away."

"Hold on," said Stanton. "I read that one too. It was brilliant. I see what you're getting at, Isabelle. It could be Tim's uncle, couldn't it? No one suspects him, because no one knows he was here. I say, Isabelle, that really could work."

Haldean looked at his friend disbelievingly. "What d'you mean, it could work? It's goofy. How did this bloke get into the house? There were servants swarming all over the place."

"Not when the fireworks were going off," argued Stanton. "Besides that, there was soot in the hearth."

"So?"

"So don't you see? It could have happened like it did in the story. The chap who was the solicitor got on the roof and climbed down the chimney."

Haldean shook his head and sighed. "Isabelle, if you think this is a probable solution you must be loopy. Look, Arthur, old fruit, about this story. It wouldn't be by Edgar Wallace, would it?"

"It might have been," said Stanton defensively.

"Yes. Not actually terribly feasible, I would have thought."

"Well, why not?" argued Stanton. He grinned. "If you're determined to make it a murder, this idea's as good as any other. Besides, who's to say I'm not right? Some of the chimneys here are massive. It'd be perfectly possible to climb down them."

"Look, you prune, I don't care if they're as big as barn doors. Let's take it that Uncle Andrew did shin down the chimney — although why I'm having this conversation, God only knows — what the dickens was Tim meant to be doing while his uncle played at Father Christmas? I know he wasn't the most observant of souls, but even he'd have noticed someone come down the chimney and prance across the carpet, gun in hand. He'd stand out a bit, don't you think? Apart from anything else, he'd be as black as the ace of spades."

"He could have climbed down beforehand and lain in wait," countered Stanton. "Besides that, the solicitor didn't shoot this chap I was telling you about. He stabbed him with a hat-pin loaded with snake poison so everyone was looking for a snake and —"

"It was by Edgar Wallace, wasn't it?"

"Well, so what? It worked in the story and Isabelle said to treat it as a story and that's what you've been doing."

Haldean picked up the cushion Isabelle had thrown at him and hurled it at his friend. "I agreed to treat it as a story to try and get some ideas, not to listen to you talk unadulterated mashed potato. For heaven's sake, bury your face in that so I can't hear you . . ."

He suddenly broke off and stared sightlessly into the empty fireplace. "The soot," he whispered. "Of course. The soot explains it." He turned to the others, suddenly completely serious. "The soot explains the alibi. Everyone's alibi. The death didn't occur at ten to ten. It could have occurred at any time between the limits the doctor gave. Twenty to ten to ten o'clock, give or take ten minutes or so either side."

They all stared at him. "How does the soot explain the alibi?" asked Isabelle sharply.

Haldean waved her quiet with an imperious gesture. "Don't you see? The house was full of fireworks yesterday. *Anyone* could have pinched a banger and a piece of fuse and put it in the fireplace. Depending on the length of fuse and what type it was, it'd be easy enough to make it explode at any time you wanted it to. Ten to ten, say. And then we come along, find out there's been a bang heard in Lord Lyvenden's room and brightly inform each other that's the time of the shot. But fireworks come in a cardboard tube." He got up, strode to the fireplace and drummed his fingers on the mantelpiece. "We didn't find the cardboard tube. Why didn't we find the cardboard tube, Belle?"

"Because the murderer took the gunpowder out of the tube so it wouldn't be discovered later," Isabelle said slowly.

Haldean smacked his hand down on the mantelpiece. "That's it! Damn it, the maid even told me it sounded like a firework! It was only afterwards she assumed it must have been the gun."

"Just a minute, Haldean," said Smith-Fennimore. "You couldn't simply tip gunpowder into the grate and put a fuse in it. The charge would have to be contained in something. An old cartridge case or a cigar tube would do the trick."

Haldean looked at Stanton. "Was there anything in the grate? A container of any sort?"

"Hang on a mo," said Stanton doubtfully, trying to remember. "There was a cigarette packet. It was all burnt and charred at one end. I think it was a packet of Goldflake. I assumed it had been tossed into the fire and got burnt."

"But the fire wasn't lit. We don't have fires at this time of year. So how did the cigarette packet get burnt?" He felt in his pocket. "I've got my room key and I know it fits Lyvenden's old room. Let's go and have a look."

All four went upstairs to Lord Lyvenden's room where, after some coaxing with his key, Haldean opened the door. They lifted the fire screen to one side and looked in the grate. The soot was there but no cigarette packet.

Haldean felt the hairs on the back of his neck prickle. "Someone's moved it. Look, you can see a patch where

100

the packet was. Someone's moved it who knew what it was used for. We're on to something. It really is true. And unless someone can prove an alibi between half past nine and ten past ten, then it could be anyone. Anyone at all."

There was a long pause. "There's another possibility," said Smith-Fennimore, eventually. "It was something you said, Isabelle, about Lady Harriet looking daggers at Lord Lyvenden that's made me think of it. Tim might not have been the intended victim after all. It was Lyvenden's gun and Lyvenden's room. Couldn't Lyvenden have been the one who should have been killed? After all, the light was very dim and if someone came in and saw a figure sitting at the desk they might have assumed it was Lyvenden."

"If that's the case, then it can't have been originally intended to look like suicide, though," said Haldean, thoughtfully. "I mean, that would imply Lyvenden had dictated a suicide note to his secretary. That argues a remarkable degree of foresight, to say nothing of the lack of ordinary feeling on the supposed victim's part."

Smith-Fennimore shook his head. "Maybe when the murderer found they'd killed the wrong person, they found part of a business letter, as you said, and used that."

Isabelle drew her breath in. "Malcolm, I wonder if that's it. It seems so unlikely someone would kill Tim but I can easily imagine someone wanting to kill Lyvenden. It needn't be Lady Harriet, though. Has he ever done someone down in business, say?"

"He certainly has," said Smith-Fennimore. "He's got a pretty ruthless reputation. He's always been a good boy with the bank and I can't question his expertise but there's plenty of people who wouldn't be sorry if our Mr Todd bought it. I only found out some of the things he'd done after he became a director. There's been a few times I've regretted the fact that we did appoint him, but I haven't any real grounds to suggest he moves on."

Stanton gazed at Smith-Fennimore. "What? What did you say he was called?"

"Victor Todd," repeated Smith-Fennimore, clearly puzzled by the intensity of Stanton's voice. "It was his name before he got the peerage."

Stanton stared at him open-mouthed. "Lyvenden's Victor Todd?" He turned urgently to Haldean. "You remember I said I knew something nasty about him, Jack? This is it. He ran the Colonial and Oriental Mining Conglomerate. It was nothing more than a fraud. They sold my father a pack of useless shares and when they crashed he lost nearly everything. The shock killed him. My mother had to sell up to make ends meet. She had a rotten time of it. My sisters and I did the best we could, but I was in the army and they were doing VAD work, so we had no money to help. She was so hard up and she missed my father so much she literally worried herself to death. My grandfather's money was tied up in a trust and I couldn't get hold of it until after she'd died. My God, when I think what he put us through . . ." He drew a ragged, angry breath. "The absolute swine. There he is, strutting around

102

calling himself Lord Lyvenden and all the time it's my father's money and other poor devils like him who paid for his precious title." He ran a trembling hand though his brown hair. "I don't know if someone tried to kill him but he deserves it. I could throttle him myself." His white face left no doubt he meant what he said.

In all the time he'd known him, Haldean had never seen his friend so angry. "I'm not surprised," he said quietly. "I knew your family had had a lousy time. To find Lyvenden was behind it must be unbelievable."

Stanton shook his head, unable to reply.

"Arthur," said Isabelle. Her voice was urgent. "Please don't do anything rash. I know it's awful but you can't bring back your parents whatever you do. Please, Arthur, don't do anything. I know it's a lot to ask but please, if you can, don't say anything, either. My mother was looking forward to her silver wedding and it's been ruined. Don't make it worse. Lyvenden's staying until Friday morning. As soon as he's gone I'll tell my parents exactly what sort of man he is. He'll never be invited here again."

Stanton was silent for a few moments. "All right," he said. "All right, Isabelle. Don't worry." He drew a deep breath. "After all, I suppose you could say it's all water under the bridge. My father was always far too trusting. He didn't have to buy the shares but he was so honest, he wouldn't dream there were crooks like Victor Todd in the world." He bit his lip. "There's one thing," he said, making an obvious effort to recover himself. "I think you've solved your mystery, Jack. Someone killed

Tim in mistake for Lyvenden. Maybe one of these days he'll get what's coming to him."

"Perhaps," said Haldean, looking at Stanton's strained face. "Perhaps."

CHAPTER
FIVE

It was a sober group who left Lord Lyvenden's room. Isabelle walked down the stairs, sunk in thought. Jack had taken Arthur off for a whisky and soda in the billiard room and Malcolm had politely absented himself. She guessed that all of them, herself included, needed some time to think about what they'd discovered. The cigarette packet had been removed and the only person who would have moved it was, as Jack said, someone who was covering up murder. Had Tim been killed in mistake for Lord Lyvenden? There was no doubt that Arthur thought so.

Arthur; she'd always known there was some misfortune in his family's past — her mother, who had known the Stantons as distant neighbours, always referred to "poor Jane Stanton" without ever spelling out why Arthur's mother should be commiserated with — but the depth of his feeling had shocked her.

She stopped at the foot of the stairs, looking at the homely grandeur of the hall. The sun laid sharp-edged paths of light across the black-and-white marble floor, catching the pillared doorways and bringing out the warm richness of the oak panels. Above it all, the painted roof showed a sailing ship battered by a storm while an oddly smug Neptune, complete with trident and attendant goddesses, looked on from a becalmed and sunlit rock. She'd known this place all her life. She loved it; it was home. Arthur's home had been wrenched from him by greed and she'd asked him to say nothing and do nothing to the man responsible. She didn't know if she'd be capable of such self-control.

Arthur; she liked Arthur. He was attractive, with his obstinately curly hair, his shy, rather hesitant manner and his thoughtful hazel eyes. She could make him happy and, what's more, she enjoyed making him happy. So why hadn't she said yes last night when he asked her to marry him?

Because of Malcolm. When she had first met Malcolm he had struck her as ridiculously glamorous. Her first suspicion, that he was too handsome for words and knew it, simply wasn't true. He wasn't remotely vain. Instead he was serious, thoughtful and rather intense. She guessed he felt things far more deeply than it was fashionable to admit. And he was very good-looking.

She went out to the gardens with the idea of finding either Bubble or Squeak and, after a half-hearted and fruitless search, ended up wandering down to the stables. Sixpence, the stable cat, had had kittens, and she spent quarter of an hour watching them chase each other on unsteady legs.

She was feeling much more cheerful when she heard footsteps. She looked up and saw Malcolm Smith-Fennimore.

106

His rather solemn face brightened at the sight of her. "Hello, what have you been doing? Playing with the kittens?" He crouched down beside her. "Jolly little things, aren't they?" He screwed up a few wisps of straw into a ball, smiling as the kittens chased after it. "I'm going for a drive," he said, nodding towards the big green Bentley. Part of the stables had been converted into garages and the Bentley stood at one end. A kitten patted his hand and he flicked a piece of straw for it to play with. "Do you want to come? Last night at the ball I promised to teach you how to drive, remember?"

She hesitated. For some reason he made her feel slightly nervous. "I was going to try and find Bubble and Squeak. I haven't seen them since lunch. Could they come with us?"

He stood up and gently took her arm, ushering her towards the car. "I'd rather they didn't. It's hard enough trying to cut you loose from your cousin and that Stanton chap, without bringing the Robiceuxs along. Four would very definitely be a crowd." He turned the engine over, climbed in beside her, and drove the car out into the sunshine. "I like driving," he said, negotiating the stable yard and bringing the car out on to the drive. "It helps me think."

"I wish I could stop thinking," said Isabelle.

"Why?" he asked, giving her a quick glance.

She sighed. "Because it all seems so incredible." She indicated the park with a wave of her hand. "Out here, in the sunshine, it's hard to believe any of it really happened."

"It happened all right," he said, keeping his eyes on the road. "And quite apart from Tim, there's something damned funny going on. Who was that visitor your uncle had last night? Haldean told me about him and he sounded downright peculiar. And then there was that Russian who turned up this morning. I tell you, Isabelle, I don't like it. I can smell danger. So much so, I picked up this from my room." He took one hand off the wheel and half pulled an automatic pistol from his jacket pocket. Her startled gasp made him glance round momentarily. His face softened at her expression. "Don't look so scared. It's my old navy Colt. It won't go off by itself, you know."

If Arthur had produced a gun and talked about smelling danger — or Jack, come to that — it would have seemed ridiculously melodramatic. She'd have probably laughed. She wasn't in the least tempted to laugh at Malcolm. "Why have you got a gun?"

"To protect . . . well, anyone who needs protecting. You, for instance."

Isabelle looked at him. He meant it. "I'm not in any danger."

"And I intend to keep it that way," he said, with a rather grim smile. "It looks as if we've got a murderer among us. Haven't you thought that he or she might not like us playing detectives? We might come too close."

They turned out of the gates of Hesperus and up the road, away from the village. The lane took them between high hedges, flashing in and out of patches of sunlight where a gate gave on to open fields and on into the woods, where the road was a tunnel between the trees. The tall beeches and squat oaks met overhead in a rustling canopy, filtering the light on to the narrow road. Blinding shafts of white sun stabbed through the green shade. It gave Isabelle the oddest sensation that they were travelling along the bed of a river, with the tops of the trees breaking through like vast water plants to the surface. Down here, amongst the ivy-entwined trunks, was a place that was hidden, unexplored and alone. She rather liked the idea.

They came out of the trees to a crossroads. Smith-Fennimore chose a road at random and drove a short distance before pulling into the side and stopping. With the noise of the engine gone, silence flooded round them, followed by all the little Sunday in summer sounds. A train chugged far away, the noise taking on a musical note in the distance. It was the sole indication that they were not the only people in the world. Although they hadn't driven far, it felt as if they'd come a long way from Hesperus. Isabelle found herself growing more light-hearted by the minute.

Smith-Fennimore climbed out of the car and opened Isabelle's door. "Slide across. I need to get in. There's no door on the driver's side. This is the perfect spot. A longish straight road with no sharp bends. We can see anything coming in plenty of time." He grinned at her puzzled expression. "Well, if you're going to have a crack at driving, you've got to sit behind the wheel. That's what we're here for."

Isabelle slid across the front seat and tentatively held the huge, corded steering wheel, listening to his detailed explanations.

"Have you got that?" he finished.

"I think so," she said doubtfully. "I'll try, anyway."

The first couple of attempts were not a success.

With admirable patience, Smith-Fennimore ran through the array of switches and levers on the dashboard and steering wheel once more. "It's all quite simple, really. Retard the ignition — that's the lever on the top of the steering column — and turn the throttle switch to the slow running position — that's right — and then turn the mixture control to the rich position. Not too much, she's already quite warm. The pressure feed on the tank looks about right. That's about it. Now press in the twin magneto switches — that's it — and press the self-starter firmly."

"This one that looks like a mushroom?"

"That's the one."

Isabelle pressed down hard and was rewarded by a burbling thrum from the engine.

"Now dab the accelerator with your foot." Isabelle yelped as the accelerator kicked back at her. "Try again, and if she kicks back, turn the ignition down until the engine fires in the right direction. There, you've done it. I told you you could. You've just got to be firm. She's ticking over nicely. Now advance the ignition and dip the clutch — hard down — put her in first gear — that's the lever beside your right leg — and release the handbrake — that's the lever on the outside of the car — *keep your foot on the clutch!* — and press down on the accelerator as you bring your other foot slowly away."

Malcolm Smith-Fennimore winced in almost physical pain as one thousand, three hundred and forty-two pounds' worth of the most elegant machinery in the world kangarooed down the road. The engine screamed a protest, then stalled.

"Oh dear," said Isabelle mournfully. "I hope I haven't damaged the car."

"Don't worry," said Smith-Fennimore, with rather a forced smile. "It's got a five-year guarantee."

"How do I change gear?" she asked.

"I think we'll cover that later. Let's try again."

They tried again. "Perhaps," he said, after two more false starts, "you'd have a better idea if you knew what was happening under the bonnet when you started her up."

Which was a very tactful way of saving his precious Bentley from her mistreatment, thought Isabelle. It might even be true.

Climbing out, Smith-Fennimore took his jacket off, rolled his sleeves up, and undid the leather straps over the long, aristocratic nose of the car. She stood beside him to peer into the mysterious depths of the engine bay. "Now, when you press the self-starter, the magnetos fire a spark which is amplified . . ."

Isabelle's education had been varied and expensive, but weak on electricity and its application to the internal combustion engine. She summoned up a memory of Jack and her brother playing with magnets and copper wire in the barn long ago, and nodded intelligently.

"This is the fly-wheel which conducts the power . . ."

She watched the muscles flex on his arms. She was suddenly intensely aware of his physical presence. Strong arms, with strong, capable hands. She swallowed. It was as if she'd developed another sense. He bent his head closer into the engine and she noticed how his fair hair swept back behind his ears. Fair hair on tanned skin . . .

"And the distributor carries the current . . ."

She reached out to touch the shining magneto and he caught her hand.

"Hey, don't touch that. The engine's hot." Still holding her hand he continued, "And then it goes to . . ." He stumbled over his words and seemed to be finding it difficult to speak. She looked straight into his eyes, the bluest eyes she'd ever seen. He was an incredibly attractive man. *Why not?*

"And then it goes to . . . goes to the spark plugs . . ." He gulped, and reached out for her, gathering her blindly in his arms. He paused momentarily, then kissed her passionately, one hand round her waist. She arched her back under the pressure of his fingers and sensed his delight in her response. She leaned her head on his shoulder, feeling the hard muscle under his shirt, listening to his quick breathing.

"I've been so unsure how you felt about me," he said in a whisper.

"I love you, Malcolm," she said simply. She relaxed against him, totally happy as he kissed her forehead and her hair.

He held the palm of his hand to her face and gazed into her eyes. "You're going to marry me, aren't you? You will marry me? Soon. It has to be soon."

She kissed his hand. "Of course I will."

He held her tightly. "I'm going to love you until I die." He sounded oddly solemn and she shivered. "Here," he said gently. "You're cold. Come and sit down in the sun."

"It's not that," she protested, but let him lead her to the grassy bank at the side of the road. He spread his jacket out and sat beside her, leaning back on his elbow. He reached out and stroked her hair.

Isabelle looked up at him with a pensive smile. "Malcolm, tell me about yourself. There's so much I don't know."

"There's not much to tell, really," he said with a smile. "All the usual things. School, Oxford. I spent my holidays in Russia. I loved it out there. I went to the Argentine for two years with the bank and learned a lot. When the war started I came back home and joined the navy. I've always been good with mechanical things and I fell in love with flying. After the war I took up racing."

Isabelle smiled. "Everyone knows you as a racer."

"Yes, I suppose they do." His smile faded. "What happened to Tim has taken the shine off that a bit. Tim was a brilliant driver, you know. When I think of him really stuck for money — desperately stuck — I can't believe I didn't know. I should have known something was wrong."

She covered his hand with hers. "You did try to find out, Malcolm."

"I should have tried harder. That Stanton chap knew all about it. And now Tim's dead. I . . . I was really turned over by it, Isabelle. He was alive this time yesterday. My God, I wish I'd known. I could have stopped it somehow." His eyes clouded and Isabelle knew he was no longer thinking of her. "I said it'd never happen again," he muttered, more to himself than her.

"Happen again?" she asked gently. "What do you mean?"

He recalled himself with a start. "Nothing." He spoke quickly then hesitated, looking at her. "At least . . . You want to know, don't you? I've never told anyone before but I'd like to tell you."

He sat up and brushed some grass off his sleeve. Taking out his cigarette case he offered her one and for a few moments he smoked thoughtfully. "In some ways it's a very commonplace story. That's probably the worst thing about it. There was a man in my squadron, a James Chilton. Anyway, we hit it off but we lost touch when he got invalided home. I meant to look him up but never got round to it. It was the winter after the war — it was a beastly cold winter if you recall — when I came across him. He was absolutely broke. I mean really broke. You've seen the poor devils sleeping on the Embankment, haven't you? Jimmy Chilton was there. Jimmy Chilton MC."

114

Isabelle drew her breath in, her eyes fixed on his face.

His mouth trembled for a moment, then he continued. "I gave him some money, all I had on me, but it wasn't much. God knows why I didn't do more. All I can think of was that I was so shocked I couldn't think straight. I gave him my address and told him to look me up. He never came. After a few days I went to find him, determined to see he had a job and a proper place to sleep and so on, but I was too late. It was the police who found him in the end." His voice was so quiet Isabelle had to strain to catch the words. "He'd been admitted to hospital suffering from pneumonia and he died. I should have helped him."

"You tried, Malcolm," she said. "You did try."

He looked at her with haunted eyes. "Yes. And I could have tried a damn sight harder. Just as I could have got through Tim's assurances that everything was all right when I knew damn well it wasn't."

"But you can't blame yourself, Malcolm," she said earnestly. "You simply can't. I don't know about your friend, this James Chilton, but it was Tim's own fault he was stuck for money, you know. He had enough to live on."

Smith-Fennimore gave a pensive smile. "But not enough to race on. That was the problem, wasn't it? Your pal Arthur Stanton pointed that out and he's right, damn him. Money! I spend my life moving money about. Funnily enough, I love it. You'd expect Tim to have remembered that, wouldn't you? There was no need for him to go to Stanton."

Isabelle thought Stanton was a subject they'd better not explore. "Do you really enjoy the bank?" she asked, wrinkling her nose. "It sounds a bit dull."

Smith-Fennimore laughed. "Not the way I do it. Money means influence, you know. I like having the influence to back schemes I think are worthwhile such as bridges, roads, new factories. It's mainly abroad, worse luck. I wish there was more I could do in this country and help the poor devils with no work, but there isn't. It's all got to make a profit, of course, but it's worth doing." He grinned. "Besides, I can afford the things I really like."

"Such as?"

"Well, motor racing, obviously. Parties. I like parties. Flying, too. I'd love to have a crack at flying over the Himalayas. I did wonder, if Haldean takes me up on my idea of sharing a hangar, whether he'd consider being my co-pilot for the Himalayan flight. I've been looking for someone for a while."

Isabelle laughed. "I don't think you have to wonder for very long. He'd jump at the chance. I'm glad you get on with Jack. He means an awful lot to me."

"How much?" There was a chill note of worry behind the question.

Isabelle shot him a reassuring glance. "Nothing, in the way you mean. I've known him all my life. I don't think you fall for people you know as well as that, do you? He's always been happy with us. At home, if you understand what I mean."

"At home." The phrase seemed to strike him with unusual force. He took her hand again. "D'you know, of all the women I've ever had anything to do with, there's never been one I wanted to share a home with before?" He looked at her with great tenderness. "Isabelle, I want a home."

She pressed his hand to her cheek. "Yes. Malcolm . . ." Something he had just said bothered her slightly. She could never imagine Arthur, for instance, saying anything of the sort. "Have there been many other women? I mean," she added hurriedly as a slight frown crossed his face, "it sounds as if there have been."

He looked rather hunted. "Why do women always want to know the full ghastly details of Bluebeard's chamber?" He sat up and gathered her into his arms again. "My dear girl, I'm a grown man. It'd be odd if there hadn't been 'others'." He held her tightly once more and kissed her slowly. "But none of them mattered," he whispered. "None of them. There's never been anyone like you. Emeralds," he added after a pause.

"Emeralds?" asked Isabelle, puzzled.

He grinned. "For your engagement ring, of course. Emeralds, to go with your eyes. You know, you've got beautiful eyes. In fact . . ."

Isabelle shut her eyes as he kissed her again.

"I think," he said eventually, "we'd better be getting back." He stood up and reached down a hand to her with a very happy smile. "I suppose I should have a word with your father."

She smiled back. "I suppose you should."

He helped her into the car. "Is there anything wrong? You look very serious all of a sudden."

She sighed. "Arthur."

"Never mind him," he said impatiently, climbing into the car.

"But I do mind him, Malcolm," she said. "I like him. Jack thinks the world of him and I . . . well, I like him. He could be a really good friend but it's difficult. He asked me to marry him last night."

"Did he, by Jove?" He sat thoughtfully for a few moments. "I didn't realize that. How did he take it when you refused?"

Isabelle raised her hands and let them drop helplessly. "I could tell he was hurt. All I can hope is that he'll get over it."

He started the engine. "I don't know if I would," he murmured.

They drove back and, as they approached the house, Isabelle caught sight of Stanton walking up the front steps. "Drop me here, Malcolm. I'll see you later. If you do want to speak to Dad, he's usually in the library with the newspaper at this time of day."

She got out of the car but, before she went, Smith-Fennimore caught hold of her hand and kissed it. "Remember I love you," he said with curious earnestness.

"Don't worry," she said. "I love you, too."

She caught up with Stanton in the hall. He looked so happy at the sight of her that she felt suddenly mean, as

118

if she were planning to kick a trusting dog. This was going to be harder than she thought.

"Arthur," she said, and her voice wasn't quite level, "can we go somewhere quieter? I've got something to tell you. I'm sorry, but I don't think you'll like it very much."

His smile faded. Without a word he opened the door of the dining room and stood aside for her to enter.

She shut the door and stood with her back to it. "I wanted to tell you before you heard it from anyone else. I owe you that much." She twisted the belt of her dress round her fingers. "It's Malcolm and me," she said in a rush, wanting to get it over with. "We're engaged."

For a moment she thought he hadn't heard her, then he drew a long, jagged breath. "Engaged?" he repeated dully.

She nodded. "I'm sorry, Arthur."

"Sorry!" He turned and, walking to the table, gripped the back of a chair. "Why him?" he said sharply.

"Why not?" she said brusquely, annoyed by his tone. "It's not everyone who has to wait for months to find out they care for someone." That was unkind and she immediately regretted saying it.

He was staring at her with an intense, fixed expression. "I loved you the first moment I saw you," he said softly. "It was at the Stuckleys' ball. You came with Jack. You were the loveliest girl I'd ever seen. Perhaps I can explain what you meant to me."

She shifted uncomfortably. "Is there any point?" She met his eyes and suddenly knew — knew beyond argument — how deep his feelings were and how badly he was hurt. "I'm sorry, Arthur," she repeated in a softer voice. "I wish things could have been different."

There was a long silence. He swallowed and tried to manage a smile. "I hope you'll be happy. I mean it. I really hope you'll be happy."

Impulsively she moved towards him, but he shook his head and went to stand with his back to her by the window. She nearly called his name, but thought better of it. She opened the door quietly, but, before she left, looked once more at his tense figure, standing ramrod straight. Something wrenched inside.

Smith-Fennimore was in the hall. "I've told your father. He's delighted," he began and then stopped, looking at Isabelle's face. "What's the matter?"

She took a handkerchief out of her pocket and blew her nose. "It's Arthur," she said in a muffled voice. "I feel so mean, Malcolm. I don't know what to do about him."

He took her arm firmly. "There's nothing you can do. He'll just have to live with it. Did he take it hard?"

She nodded. "It's his own fault. He took so *long* about things. If he hadn't, then it might have been very different."

Smith-Fennimore's eyebrows crawled upwards. "Perhaps it's just as well you met me, then. Would you really have married him? He seems so . . . well, ineffective."

Isabelle blew her nose once more and put her handkerchief away. "It doesn't matter now, does it?" She slipped her hand through his arm and gave him a consciously bright look. "Come on. We've got plenty of other people to tell."

It was over breakfast the next morning that the visit to London was arranged. Lord Lyvenden had departed on the early train in search of a secretary but he was merely the first of many. Haldean was meeting his godfather for lunch, Isabelle had a fitting for a dress and wanted to do some shopping, and Bubble and Squeak decided they'd like to come as well. Alfred Charnock, who came in on the tail end of the conversation, coolly invited himself along. He too, it seemed, wanted to go to London. Without actually asking him, Isabelle decided that Malcolm could drive her up to London and Jack could take everyone else. Malcolm, she said, had told her last night that he could do with going up to Town.

Haldean parked his car at the front of the house and ran lightly up the steps into the hall. "Bubble, Squeak, the car's ready . . ."

He broke off. At the bottom of the staircase, Isabelle and Smith-Fennimore were discussing something in low voices.

Isabelle looked cross. "But why won't you take me, Malcolm?" she said, her voice rising. "As we're both going to Town it seems silly not to go together."

"Because I've got some private business that I don't want you to know about yet. You'll find out soon enough."

"But all I want you to do is to drop me at the dressmaker's. I've got a fitting that's going to take ages,

121

so you'll be free the rest of the time. We can meet at the Savoy Grill for supper and come back together." She saw the indecisiveness in his face and said, "If you really don't want to take me, I can go with Jack." There was a tread on the stairs above her and she glanced up. "And Arthur, of course," she added, slyly, as Stanton and Sir Philip came down the stairs towards them.

Smith-Fennimore frowned. "I'll take you, if you're so set on it," he said quickly. "But I really can't get roped into carrying parcels whilst you go shopping, Isabelle."

"You won't," she said, glad to have got her own way. "If you'll get the car, I'll meet you by the front door." She turned to her father as Smith-Fennimore left. "What is it, Dad?"

Sir Philip tapped the newspaper under his arm. He looked worried. "I don't know if I'm very happy about you going to London, Isabelle. It was different when I thought you'd be with Smith-Fennimore all day. There's been more trouble with these wretched Communists and apparently there's some sort of march planned for today. Are you sure you can't stay with the girls, Jack?"

Haldean shook his head regretfully. "I'm sorry, sir, but, as I said, I'm meeting my godfather for lunch." He looked at Stanton. "Do you fancy a run up to Town, Arthur? You're welcome to join us."

Stanton pulled a face. "No thanks, Jack. I thought I might go and see if there was anything worth catching in the lower pool. Either that or a walk. I feel a bit aimless."

122

"Just as you like." Arthur seemed positively washed out and Haldean hoped a quiet day would do him some good. He turned back to his uncle. "I'm sure Isabelle will be fine, sir. She's going to meet Bubble and Squeak in Regent Street after she's been for her fitting and they'll be together for the rest of the day."

A horn sounded from the front of the house. Isabelle kissed her father quickly. "That'll be Malcolm. Don't worry, Dad. We'll stick to the West End. See you all in Town." She ran out to the waiting car.

"Are we going to London this morning or this afternoon?" asked Alfred Charnock.

Haldean wasn't going to be drawn. "Just as soon as you're ready, Mr Charnock." He turned to Bubble and Squeak. "Shall we go?"

Archie Wilde KC settled back amongst the solidly Victorian comforts of the Garrick Club. "What d'you fancy next, Jack? You're pretty safe here if you stick to what they know how to do. Steak and kidney pudding? They can't go far wrong with that." He picked up his soup spoon. "How's things at Hesperus? It's a pity I couldn't get down for the ball. It was a nasty business about that young feller shooting himself." Something in Haldean's expression made him pause. "He did shoot himself, didn't he?"

"It's certainly meant to look that way," agreed Haldean quietly. "I know you'll keep this to yourself, sir, but I'm not at all happy that's what happened."

Archie Wilde looked at him sharply. "Murder? At *Hesperus*?"

Haldean nodded. "I tried to contact Ashley — you remember I told you about Superintendent Ashley? — but he's been away. He's back tomorrow, thank goodness. I haven't got anything I'd like to go to the police with officially, but Ashley will listen to me. Until then . . ." He reached for a bread roll. "Until then I think it'd better remain as suicide."

Archie Wilde drew his breath in. "Be careful who you speak to," he said quietly. "This isn't a game, Jack. I know you can look after yourself, but if you're right it'd be far too easy for you to come off worse." He glanced round the dining room. "There are too many people here for this sort of conversation. You can tell me all about it when we get back to my rooms. Until then —" his voice rose to its normal pitch — "you can fill me in on the rest of the news. Is Alice's brother still making a nuisance of himself?"

"Mr Charnock, you mean? Yes, he's still there."

"Dreadful feller," grunted Archie Wilde, between spoonfuls of Brown Windsor soup. "I can't think why Philip puts up with him."

"I think he more or less has to, doesn't he? Didn't he come a cropper in the City earlier in the year? I gather, without it having actually been spelt out, that he's at Hesperus because he's on his beam ends."

Wilde grunted. "That's as maybe, but he was chucking money about at the Derby and at that gaming club, the Ultima Thule. They play very high there. Too high for my pocket. You steer clear of him, Jack. I wouldn't say as much to Alice, but he's not a nice man. He was in the Ukraine in the war. I don't say he wasn't

124

useful, but I couldn't stomach how he got his results. He's a ruthless beggar and arrogant as the devil. Still, it's not my problem." He buttered a bread roll. "Has anyone else proposed to Isabelle?"

"She's got engaged," said Haldean with a grin.

"Good Lord." He stopped with the roll in his hand. "Who to? That boy of Jane Moorcroft's? That's been on the cards for some time. What's he called now? He got the DSO. Nice lad. Stanton. Arthur Stanton."

Haldean shook his head. "No, 'fraid not. That didn't come off. No, it's Smith-Fennimore, the racing driver."

"Him, eh?"

"I didn't know you knew him," said Haldean.

"Oh, yes," said Archie Wilde, finishing the last of his soup. "I don't know him well, but I know him. Mind you, I don't mix with the speed crowd. I can never see the damn point of tearing round a race track. After all, however fast you go, you only end up where you started from. That bank of his seems pretty sound, though. All I know about his private life is that he has a very expensive mistress who I've seen him out and about with. She says she's a connection of the Romanovs. Aren't they all!" He laughed. "For heaven's sake, don't look so shocked, boy."

"I'm not shocked," said Haldean, piqued. "It's just that . . . well, you know. It'd be rotten for Belle if he's got someone else. Still, I daresay he'll give her up if he's going to get married."

"If he's got any sense he will." Wilde turned in his seat to summon the waiter. "Did you want boiled potatoes with your pudding, Jack? If it worries you,

you'd better tackle him about it. It's not something I'd like to ask Philip to do, but you should be able to manage. It's a pity Gregory's not around as it's more a brother's job, but you're close enough."

"Tackle Smith-Fennimore?" Haldean shifted unhappily. "I suppose I've got to, haven't I?"

The Countess Drubetskaya might, thought Malcolm Smith-Fennimore, be apparently giving him the benefit of her whole-hearted attention, but he was willing to bet that what she was actually thinking of was the dark blue jewellery case he had placed on the table. He looked dispassionately at the beautiful woman in front of him. Whatever had he seen in her? She *was* beautiful and intensely sophisticated. Those were the qualities which had first attracted him. Now she seemed artificial and slightly overdone.

Compared to Isabelle . . . He stopped. He didn't want to compare Isabelle to anyone, especially to this hothouse flower. It wasn't just her looks, although Isabelle's looks thrilled him. All the women he'd ever known were beautiful enough. That was, in a way, taken for granted. But Isabelle . . . He could talk to Isabelle properly. She was interested in him, not merely the things he could give her. He'd never told anyone that story about Jimmy Chilton. She'd understood. The only fly in the ointment was Stanton. Stanton was in love with Isabelle. Everyone had expected Isabelle to marry Stanton. He'd heard the Robiceux girls yesterday, discussing it. *What a catch! Yes, but will it last? I honestly thought she'd marry Arthur. Maybe she will in* the end. *She thinks the world of him* . . . It would be fine. Everything was going to be fine. He'd make it work. Yes, it'd work all right.

He'd never trusted a woman before. He'd never — this was a shocking thing to admit — known any love he hadn't had to pay for. In a way it was inevitable; Oxford, the navy, the bank, the track . . . all men. That was how it was. Men were friends, women were desirable, expensive commodities. But it didn't have to be like that. He wanted, with a stomach-churning intensity, to love someone who would love — really love — him in return. And why the blazes shouldn't he? The clerks at the bank, the stewards at the club, the mechanics at the track; they were married. They didn't spell love with a pound sign for an L. He was tired of "arrangements". He wanted to say, openly, honestly, "This is my wife . . . This is Isabelle, my wife . . ." Isabelle. It was going to work.

The Countess was still talking. He sighed inwardly, trying to cut off the drone of words. He wanted to carry on thinking about Isabelle. Well, if he was going to make the break, he'd better get on with it. He hoped there wouldn't be too much of a scene. The Countess thrived on them. He'd found that exciting at first. He smiled, cynically. The jewels should ease his passing.

He held out the case towards her. "I called at Garrard's before coming here. These are for you." He saw the greed in her face.

The Countess stopped in mid-sentence and took the case eagerly, her eyes widening as she saw the diamond necklace and ear-rings nestling on the dark blue velvet inside the box. "But Malcolm, they are exquisite!"

"They are to say goodbye," he said, rather more abruptly than he had intended.

She looked up, her attention momentarily diverted. "But why is this, Malcolm?"

The accent on "Malcolm" intrigued him no longer. "Because I am going to get married."

She threw up her hands and laughed. "Married! Not you, chéri. No, wait. It is that little English Miss with the so-proper Mama and Papa we saw at the Savoy? You will be bored within the week."

Her black eyes sparkled and he had a sudden, vivid picture of her as she had been that night at the Savoy, the night he had met Isabelle. He had ushered her into the Delage Salamanca and she had reclined back, her face framed by her white fur stole, the silver fittings and the silk braided cushions of the Salamanca surrounding her as if by right. He tried to imagine the Countess at the wheel of the Bentley while he instructed her in the gentle art of driving. The picture was so incongruous that he nearly laughed out loud. He would sell the Delage now; it wouldn't suit Isabelle and he had no further use for it.

The Countess whirled on him angrily. "You find me funny? Yes?"

"No, no," he apologized. "Something just struck me, that's all. I think I'd better be going." She was gearing up for a fight, another orgy of throbbing, insincere emotion.

"I throw these diamonds back at you." She carefully didn't suit action to words. "You think you can go? You will leave me? Alone?"

He'd had enough of this. "Well, there's always the others." He knew perfectly well that he wasn't the only man the Countess saw, but she had no idea he'd guessed.

"Others? What others, Malcolm?"

"Well, there's that asinine young idiot, Fraylingham, for instance, and your fat Italian friend." That should take the wind out of her sails.

It did. "But they are no fun," she protested, in a lightning change of mood, her white teeth parting in a smile. "And the Italian snores!"

The crisis had passed. He bent over her hand and kissed it. "Goodbye, my dear. Thank you."

Vargen Yashin, well dressed, well fed but very far from well contented, strolled into Soho Square, turned down Sutton Row and into Lacey Street. He was thinking about Victor, Lord Lyvenden. He had walked back from the Café Royal because he wanted time to think. What he had heard there made him want to think very carefully indeed.

The Café Royal had been a good choice. The personality he had so carefully built up fitted into that artistic, bohemian atmosphere. It was fashionable, too. The right people went there. He made no secret of his Bolshevik sympathies. He could, when called upon, talk mournfully of life under the Tsars. And society, London society, or certain sections of it at least, loved it. They flirted with Communism as embodied by Yashin. He was a Good Bloke, Not Bad For A Russian, a Decent Sort. And as for his politics, what did you expect? You should hear his stories . . . I tell you, there's a lot more to this Communism business than you think. You can't believe what you read in the papers. That's just propaganda. Listen to Yashin; he'll tell you what it's really like. Of course he's nothing *official*. And there London society was wrong.

For Vargen Yashin was the head of the English section of the Third International and if Yusif Dolokhov, his chief and leading light of the Central Committee of the Russian Communist Party — Yashin winced slightly at the name — found out how close Yashin's section had come to wrecking his plans for a revolution in England, he could look forward to a firing squad at the best. If it wasn't preceded by painful hours in a cellar, he'd be lucky.

For Lyvenden had been visited at Hesperus. Lyvenden had been badly frightened at Hesperus. And if Lyvenden turned awkward or if Lyvenden said too much . . . Yashin sighed. Lord Lyvenden's visitor — he had recognized the description — was Youri Gerasimov. His lip curled. It was typical of Gerasimov to try and frighten Lyvenden into speeding things up. Then — for he knew Gerasimov's mind as clearly as he knew his own — Gerasimov would be hailed in triumph, he, Yashin, would be deposed and Gerasimov would be the new leader. Fool! Great, blundering fool! He had no idea of the people he would be dealing with. They had to be coaxed, cajoled, fed a mixture of flattery, self-interest and ideals. Once the revolution had been won was the time for education by terror. He looked forward to teaching these innocents that particular lesson. Yashin bit his lip thoughtfully. The revolution: the English — his English — took it as a joke. "After the revolution" was a joke. That suited his purpose, but it annoyed him, all the same. Even the most earnest of his English followers seemed to have no idea of what actually happened after a revolution. They honestly thought it would be sweetness, happiness and light. But people had to be educated. They never dreamed it could really happen. Yashin suspected that if they ever thought it could, they would be horrified. In spite of all the Central Committee had announced about spreading revolution abroad, they persisted in believing it could never happen here. Yashin shook his head. It could. But if Dolokhov ever found out that Gerasimov, a man supposed to be under his control, had threatened his plans, then he, Yashin, would pay the price.

Gerasimov was doubtless feeling very pleased with himself. He'd got a couple of little nuggets of information on his visit to Hesperus, which he would look forward to using. Yashin smiled in anticipation. He would enjoy dealing with Gerasimov.

He paused by the entrance to the Paradise Club. It was his club and he was proud of it. His name wasn't on any deed or document, of course, but it was his all the same. Gerasimov would never have been able to think of a place like this. A magnet for the wealthy who enjoyed a frisson of real life (real life!) with their drinking and dancing. *I know a most wonderful place in Soho.* He'd heard it said lots of times. *It's just too thrilling.* A wonderful place meant excitement; it meant mixing with carefully cultivated guests like Belayaev, whose pictures had shocked half of fashionable London whilst baffling the other half. It meant the tantalizing prospect of seeing a real fight. Only two nights ago Konstantine had given Savchuk a black eye. The Paradise Club smelt of kippers, had a dance floor like gravel and sold wine they'd throw back in any West End restaurant. These things added up to real life. For some of these fools a wonderful place meant a few words in the right ear which produced enough white powder to make the Paradise Club live up to its name.

But no one at all guessed that the real purpose of the club was to hide an attic room from which he could carry out his plans. Looking for somewhere secret, the likes of Gerasimov would never have dreamt of the Paradise Club. It was too open, too loud in its support for the new Soviet state. And that was precisely why Yashin had carefully made it so. He knew how the English mind worked. The Paradise Club? Nothing really goes on there, old boy. We know all about the Paradise Club. He gave a very thin smile. Even in the eyes of the English authorities, the Paradise Club was known and discounted. The real power, they cleverly told each other, must lie elsewhere.

Vargen Yashin went into the cloakroom and up the small staircase leading from the back, along the bare and filthy corridor, and entered the attic overlooking Clarkson's Rents.

132

There was a meeting in progress. Yashin's heart sank as he looked at them. There were eight men in the room and all of them, even the native English and Scots, looked exactly what they were; rough, uneducated, mindless slum dwellers and peasants who thought violence was the answer to all questions. Not one of them was subtle enough to see that violence had to be used sparingly and correctly. Not one of them realized that fear was the best weapon of all. And none of them had a hope of moving, as he did, between the world of the rich and gullible to the world of the avaricious and dispossessed, adding them together and making the answer to the sum equal power.

Tanswell, a small, underfed, red-headed Cockney with a bandage round his head, was holding forth. He lit another cigarette, adding to the pall of smoke that sat over the room like a rain cloud. "A waste of bleeding time," he was saying. He looked up anxiously, then relaxed. "Oh, it's you, boss. I was just making my report, if you can call it that. That march today. Well, I ask you, where did it get us? *Really* get us, I mean? A lot of smashed windows and a couple of dented coppers. I tell you, as I've told you before, we need money. If I had a thousand quid I could have the Pool of London banged up so tight no bugger could move. What's the point of pouring money into Ireland? We need it here. Here's the heart of the bleeding British Empire. This is where it'll hurt them."

Gerasimov, at the head of the table, smiled smugly. "Money, eh?"

Yashin cut in. "Money, Gerasimov. Money which, by your stupidity, you have imperilled." He pulled off his gloves. "You are in the wrong place, by the way. That is my seat. Move."

Gerasimov thought about it, then, with a sulky insolence, moved.

"Very good. Youri Gerasimov, you acted without orders. You were clever, yes? You found out who a certain person was and where a certain person was and paid him a visit. He did not enjoy that visit. I am unhappy that he was troubled. You found out other things as well which I do not wish you to know." Gerasimov, he was glad to see, was beginning to look frightened. He would enjoy spinning this out, but regretfully decided against it. His authority had been questioned recently. There were a couple of these . . . these *peasants* who thought they would make a better leader. Let them watch.

Vargen Yashin looked at the man sitting across from Gerasimov. "Boris. Boris Paputin, I have sometimes wondered about your loyalty to us. You are a friend of Gerasimov's."

Paputin licked dry lips and nodded nervously.

Yashin sounded, if anything, slightly bored. "You have in your right-hand pocket a loaded Mauser pistol. Take it out and shoot Gerasimov."

Paputin, Yashin noted, didn't flinch. This was his chance to prove his loyalty. He drew out the gun and held it in a steady hand.

"No!" cried Gerasimov. "Boris, no!" He jumped to his feet, kicking his chair over. Paputin steadied his aim and fired.

The report of the gun was deafening in the small room. Gerasimov slumped down, clutching at the table, blood pumping sluggishly from his chest.

The men round the table sat, heads bowed, afraid to catch the eye of either their neighbour or their leader.

Yashin nodded in satisfaction. His authority was restored. "Boris, Michael, dispose of the body in the usual way." He spoke quietly but the two men leapt to do his bidding as if stung. They were afraid. Good. He pulled out a chair and sat down. "This meeting is over. You may leave." He watched as his men silently filed past, then, once he was alone, drew out his silver cigarette case and lit a cigarette thoughtfully.

Hesperus. There was a lot for him to be interested in at Hesperus. He didn't understand all of it and that worried him. How much had Lyvenden let slip? That worried him, too. It wasn't so much what he'd said but what could be worked out and inferred by a clever man. There was a very clever man at Hesperus. Major Haldean, a police spy. He frowned in concentration. Just at the moment, Major Haldean was a latent, undeveloped threat. But he, Yashin, didn't like threats. He was safe because he didn't like threats. He shrugged. To take action now would be stupid. But, if the opportunity arose, he would make sure he dealt with Major Haldean.

CHAPTER
SIX

Haldean put down the phone in the hall with a feeling of satisfaction. Yes, said the sergeant at Stanmore Parry police station, Superintendent Ashley was back from his holiday, and yes, he, the sergeant, would certainly pass on Major Haldean's message. Good. That meant, if it all worked out as he hoped, an early evening pint and an interesting conversation in the Wheatsheaf.

And after that, he was going to have a quiet night in. He yawned. It had been three o'clock before they had got back from London after a very jolly evening in the Savoy Grill. Malcolm Smith-Fennimore had presented Isabelle with an enormous emerald engagement ring, and that could, of course, only be celebrated with champagne, then they had run into Mark Stuckley and his crowd, which called for more champagne, so, what with one thing and another, everyone had been very merry indeed.

It had been so merry it had been a real effort to get up for the golf party which Uncle Philip, a lifelong early riser, had organized for that morning but he'd managed it, and so had everyone else. The only one who wasn't on time was Stanton, who didn't even have a late night as an excuse. Haldean, who knew all about his uncle's views on punctuality, had winced as Stanton ambled into the hall, a good ten minutes after the cars were at the door. "I can't find my cuff-links," he announced. "I've looked everywhere."

"Do you want to borrow some of mine?" Haldean asked, hearing his uncle snort like a leaky radiator in the background.

Stanton had heard the radiator impression too. "No thanks, Jack," he said hastily. "I don't want to hold everybody up any longer. I'll play with my sleeves rolled up. It's a blinking nuisance, though. I can't think where they've got to."

"The same place as your tie-clips, your shirt studs and the blue tie which you were sure you'd brought with you and then decided you'd left in London?" suggested Haldean.

Stanton smiled sheepishly. "I suppose so." He looked round the assembled group. "Are we going, then?"

Sir Philip turned up the heat on the radiator and led the way out of the hall at a very military quick march.

Not that the standard of play when they'd got to the links had been very high. Sir Philip, a twelve handicap man, had won easily by playing a succession of fair-to-medium balls, which improved his mood enormously. Haldean had the occasional flash of brilliance in a very average game but even Bubble and Squeak had played like things inspired compared to Lord Lyvenden whose awful golf was only matched by his still more awful plus-fours. Smith-Fennimore, who said he had a handicap of nine, was definitely off his form.

Malcolm Smith-Fennimore. Haldean bit his lip. He'd have to tackle the man sometime, especially as Fennimore had said he didn't want a long engagement. That conversation with his godfather had left him no choice in the matter but he couldn't pretend he was looking forward to it.

He glanced at the grandfather clock. Just after half past one. The side door from the garden opened and Smith-Fennimore came into the hall. Haldean looked up. "Hello, Fennimore. I wondered if I could have a word, old man."

Smith-Fennimore rubbed the side of his chin with his hand and yawned discreetly. "Of course. I'm not late, am I? I've just been out to my car."

Haldean shook his head. "No, we've got a few minutes yet. My aunt put back lunch for us. She knows what my uncle's like once you get him on the links."

"He enjoys his game, doesn't he? So do I as a general rule." Smith-Fennimore was obviously making an effort to talk. He looked stale, and scrubbed his eyes with the heel of his hands. "Was there anything in particular you wanted to talk to me about?"

Haldean glanced up and down the hall. There was no one else around. He drew closer. "There was, as a matter of fact." He plunged in. "It's about you and Isabelle."

Smith-Fennimore drew back. He suddenly looked very awake indeed. "What is it?"

"Well, naturally I hope you'll be very happy. Isabelle means an awful lot to me, as you can imagine."

"She means an awful lot to me, too." Smith-Fennimore looked puzzled. "For heaven's sake, Haldean, get to the point. What do you want to say?"

This was it. "I had lunch with my godfather, Archie Wilde, yesterday. He said . . . well, he said it's common knowledge you've been linked with a very beautiful woman. A Countess Drubetskaya."

Smith-Fennimore drew back abruptly. "And exactly what concern of yours is this common knowledge?" he said icily.

"Of mine personally, none whatever. Don't think I'm enjoying having to ask you about this, because I'm not. What you do is your own affair. But don't you see? Isabelle thinks the world of you and I care enormously about what happens to her. She'd be terribly cut up about it if there's anyone else on the scene."

"I still don't see why it's your concern," Smith-Fennimore repeated.

Haldean smacked his fist into the palm of his hand in frustration. "Because I'm the only one of the family who knows! Her brother's in Malaya and I can hardly tell Uncle Philip. I certainly don't want to tell Uncle Philip. I've got to ask you."

Smith-Fennimore thought about it for a long moment and then his frown cleared. Impulsively he thrust out his hand. "I suppose you did. The affair's over."

Haldean took the outstretched hand with relief. "I'm glad to hear it. I wasn't looking forward to that conversation."

Smith-Fennimore half smiled. "No, I can see you wouldn't be. Look, Haldean, I told Isabelle last night that the reason I didn't want her around yesterday is because I wanted to buy the engagement ring. That was perfectly true. But the other reason I needed to be alone was that I had to see . . ." He hesitated. "I had to see the lady in question. I wanted it finished and as quickly as possible. I didn't want there to be any doubt, and you can take it from me that there isn't. I could hardly tell Isabelle that's what I was going to do, but it's over." He paused and added in a softer tone. "I think an awful lot of your cousin, you know. I would never do anything to hurt her."

Haldean smiled. "Thanks for being so decent about it." He broke off suddenly as footsteps sounded on the stairs and became apparently transfixed by the portrait of Claudia, first Lady Rivers, which hung above their heads. Isabelle and Alfred Charnock joined them.

"Whatever are you gazing at that picture so raptly for, Jack?" asked Isabelle. "Hello, Malcolm."

"We were wondering if it was by anyone famous," said Haldean, mendaciously. "Reynolds or someone."

"I wouldn't have thought so," said Isabelle, frowning at the portrait. "It looks very ordinary to me."

Charnock looked at Claudia, first Lady Rivers, critically. "I think she should have been painted by Stubbs. She looks exactly like a horse. I suppose one can comprehend why she had her portrait painted, but one can't possibly condone it."

Isabelle giggled. "You mustn't be rude about her, Uncle."

Charnock raised an eyebrow. "Why ever not?"

"She was a terrific business woman. She's why Hesperus is called Hesperus. She was married to Gregory Rivers who went off with Captain Cook to watch the transit of Venus across the face of the sun, and he was away for years."

"I can see why," said Charnock, softly.

"And when he came back he built her this house, as an apology, I suppose, and they called it Hesperus — you know, Latin for Evening Star or Venus. Anyway, soon after they'd built it, he went off again and was drowned at sea so she flung herself into business and made lots of money and increased the estate no end."

"So," said Alfred Charnock. "A happy ending all round, eh?"

The hall started to fill up. As if to avoid the crowd, Smith-Fennimore moved edgily to one side.

Isabelle followed him. "Are you all right, Malcolm?" she asked softly. "You don't seem quite yourself, somehow. You've been off colour all morning."

He managed a smile. "I'm all right. I'm just feeling a bit stifled." He made an obvious effort. "The late night didn't help but I think it's the change in the weather. There's a storm brewing. Have you seen the clouds racking up? I bet we have thunder this afternoon and it always gives me a headache."

Charnock glanced at Egerton, who, after looking at the grandfather clock, sounded the dinner gong with a practised crescendo. "I'm going out for lunch. I must be off. I've got an appointment in Brighton. Let me have your car, Jack. Philip always gets agitated when I use the Rolls."

Given the casual way in which Charnock drove, Haldean's sympathies were entirely with his uncle, but he couldn't think of a socially acceptable way to refuse. "I suppose so," he said reluctantly. "Careful with the clutch, though. It's a bit sticky."

"Malcolm's giving me driving lessons," said Isabelle, brightly.

Haldean grinned. "Brave man. I wish someone had taught your Uncle Alfred," he added, watching Charnock's departing back. "I know for a fact he's wrecked at least one car."

"That was an accident."

"That was rotten careless driving. Talking of wrecks, it's an odd thing, but I'd not heard that story about Hesperus before. I always associated it with that poem we used to be bullied into reciting as kids — you know, 'The Wreck of the Hesperus'."

"*It was the schooner Hesperus that sailed the wintry sea,*" quoted Isabelle. "It makes me giggle like mad, now. The captain comes to grief because he won't believe there's a storm on the way."

"I used to have to recite that too," said Smith-Fennimore. "Talking of captains, where's Stanton?"

Isabelle looked around the hall. "I don't know. I hope he's not going to be late again. I thought Dad was going to go pop this morning. Lord Lyvenden's missing, too."

142

"I hope he's changed out of his golf things," said Haldean. "Lord Lyvenden, I mean. I've never seen more gruesome plus-fours."

"Horrible, weren't they?" said Isabelle. She looked at the clock impatiently. "I wish they'd hurry up. Arthur certainly knew what time lunch was. Dad gets so agitated when people are late for meals. Can you go and get them, Malcolm? They might not have heard the gong."

"Right-oh," said Smith-Fennimore obligingly. "You coming, Haldean?" he said with a discreet jerk of his head. "You go in, Isabelle. We won't be long. We'll get Stanton first and then go on for Lord Lyvenden." Haldean and Smith-Fennimore walked up the stairs together. "I just wanted to repeat what I said earlier," said Smith-Fennimore in a low voice. "You really needn't worry about Isabelle. And as for you tackling me about it, don't worry about that, either. I see you had no choice."

"Thanks, Fennimore," said Haldean with a smile. "I wonder what the dickens is keeping Arthur?" he added.

"Whatever does keep him on these occasions. He's a bit scatty, isn't he? As far as I can tell he's been late for virtually every meal."

"Yes. He's between valets at the moment which is probably why. He'll have lost his braces or something," said Haldean. "By the way, talking about losing things, d'you know that Russian who was here on Sunday? I wondered if you'd seen anything of the knife Mr Charnock took off him after their set-to. Apparently it's gone missing. He was sounding off about it at breakfast."

"No, I haven't seen it. It's bound to turn up. He can't lose a knife like that. Apart from anything else, it must be unique."

"Unique?" Haldean shook his head. "Not really, although he said he'd put his initials on it. But you can get those big sheath knives anywhere."

"Can you?" Smith-Fennimore shrugged. "I haven't come across them. Mr Charnock must have left it lying around somewhere."

They knocked on the door of Stanton's room and a distracted voice shouted, "Come in!"

"Oh, it's you, Jack," said Stanton as they entered. "And you, Smith-Fennimore," he added in slightly less welcoming tones. Although he had put on a fresh shirt and was wearing his braces, his collar was undone and he hadn't put on either his jacket or tie. "Do you know, I still can't find any of my cuff-links," he said in a distracted way. "It's one thing playing golf, but I can't go down to lunch with my sleeves flapping. They're in a long brown leather box and I always keep them on my dressing table, but they've completely vanished. I can't think where I've put them."

"Honestly, Arthur, you need a nurse maid," said Haldean indulgently, starting to move the clutter on the dressing table. "If you can't find them, I'll lend you a pair of mine. You'll have to get a move on. I don't suppose they've slipped into your top drawer, have they?" He opened the drawer and, taking out a heap of socks, started to search.

"Here they are," said Smith-Fennimore, stooping down beside the chest of drawers. "They must have got knocked off."

"Oh, thanks," said Stanton, taking the box and quickly doing up his cuffs. "I thought I'd looked there." He glanced at Haldean who had stopped dead, staring into the drawer. "What are you gazing at, Jack? I can't think there's anything so exciting in there. Put those socks back, will you? I don't want to lose them as well."

Haldean reached into the drawer and took out a long-bladed sheath knife. He held it up. "What's this doing here? It's Alfred Charnock's knife." He turned it over in his hands. It was Alfred Charnock's knife, all right. Scratched into the leather binding of the hilt were the initials A.C. and Sunday's date.

Stanton froze, cuff-link in hand. "How on earth did that get there?"

"Let me see it," said Smith-Fennimore, holding out his hand.

Haldean passed it across, handle first. Smith-Fennimore tested the blade on his thumb with a grimace. "It's some weapon. How did you come by it, Stanton?"

"I haven't a clue," protested Stanton. "Let me have a look at it."

As Smith-Fennimore passed it over, Stanton reached out for it. The knife fell and Smith-Fennimore reached out to catch it.

The knife clattered to the floor. Smith-Fennimore drew his breath in sharply, looking at the line of blood across the palm of his hand. "That was pretty stupid of me," he said. He pressed his thumb into his palm. "Give me a handkerchief, someone," he said tightly.

"Here, have one of mine," said Stanton, reaching into a drawer.

They watched as the cloth turned red. "You'd better get some iodine on that," said Haldean. "It looks a nasty cut."

"It stings, that's for sure," said Smith-Fennimore. "I won't be able to use this hand for a bit. It's my right one, worse luck." He drew a little jagged breath. "Look, Haldean, there's no point in us all being late. I know what your uncle's like. Stanton can help me put some sort of bandage on my hand. You get along and tell the others we're coming."

"All right. Shall I collect Lord Lyvenden on the way?"

"Leave him to us."

"All right. Good Lord, look at the time! Hurry up, won't you, Arthur. My uncle really does hate people being late. Your tie's on the back of the chair in case you didn't see it and your jacket's there as well."

He hurried through the door as Smith-Fennimore said, "Have you got another handkerchief, Stanton? I'll need some help to tie the knot properly."

Lunch was past the soup stage and a dish of lamb cutlets was being served by the time Smith-Fennimore joined them with a makeshift bandage round his hand. "Sorry I'm late, Lady Rivers," he apologized, sitting down. "I had a bit of an accident."

"Jack told us," said Isabelle, adding sympathetically, "You look a bit shaken."

146

"I'll be fine. It was my own fault."

Haldean helped himself to spinach from the dish Egerton was offering. "Where's Arthur?"

"He went to root out Lyvenden while I went to the bathroom. I hoped I'd find some iodine in the cupboard." He drank some water, wincing slightly as the movement hurt him. "I see we're without Lady Harriet and Mrs Strachan as well."

"They're both out for lunch," said Sir Philip. "As far as Mrs Strachan goes, I can't say I'm sorry." He hunched his shoulders. "That was a disgraceful scene last night, Alice. What on earth the silly woman was doing with all that cash in the first place, I don't know."

"Whatever happened?" asked Isabelle, all agog.

"Mrs Strachan apparently had about fifty pounds in her bedroom," explained Sir Philip, "and, of course, she mislaid it. Instead of looking for it properly, she immediately accused Lady Harriet's maid, that little French girl, of taking it. Pretty bit of a thing," he said absently, then caught his wife's eye. "Not that that's anything to do with it," he added hastily. "Anyway, they were screaming at each other, Lady Harriet joined in, Lyvenden tried to intervene and made matters much worse, the house was in an uproar and we eventually found the money tucked in a drawer. Mrs Strachan gave the girl five pounds to make up, the maid stopped screeching and everyone was happy. Apart from me. It was a shocking fuss. Where *is* Lyvenden? If the man's not going to come to lunch, why doesn't he say so?"

At this point, Lawson, the footman, approached and said something quietly to Sir Philip who responded by flinging down his napkin and getting up from the table.

"Apparently Lyvenden's at it now," he announced to the whole table. "He's kicking up a row, I mean. He's having an argument in his room. God knows who with. I suppose it's his valet or someone but I'd better go and sort it out. We can't have this sort of thing going on."

Smith-Fennimore glanced up. "It's not his valet. My man, Sotherby, has gone out with Lyvenden's man for the afternoon." He paused and looked at Haldean. "You don't think that Russian has come back, do you?"

Haldean got to his feet. "I'll go and find out." If the Russian had come back then the last thing he wanted was his uncle, in his present mood, to meet him.

"You can come with me," said Sir Philip pugnaciously. "But my word, if that Russian's here I'll have a thing or two to say to him. And Lyvenden, come to that."

Haldean inclined his head towards Smith-Fennimore who pushed his chair away from the table and stood up.

Isabelle stood up too.

"There's no need for you to come, my girl," said her father.

"Do let me, Dad. After all, I missed out on the fun last time."

Sir Philip would have normally argued the point but he was anxious to go. "Fun!" he said in a way that left no one in any doubt about his feelings, and marched out of the room towards the garden suite. Both the Robiceuxs got up, determined to be in on the action.

148

Sir Philip could hardly forbid them, but it didn't improve his temper when he looked over his shoulder and saw his retinue.

They heard the noise from the far end of the corridor. Although they couldn't distinguish the words, they clearly heard shouts followed by a series of bangs, as if the furniture was being savagely kicked. Sir Philip increased his pace.

"What's going on? It sounds as if someone was being murdered in there," said Haldean to Smith-Fennimore. "I say . . ."

Smith-Fennimore looked at him. "Come on."

The two men exchanged worried glances, and ran to catch up with Sir Philip, arriving slightly before him.

Sir Philip banged on the door. "Open this door immediately!" he shouted. There was sudden silence.

Smith-Fennimore knelt down and put his eye to the keyhole. His injured hand caught on the handle and he winced away, falling sideways. Sprawled on the floor against the door, he looked up at Sir Philip anxiously. "I think we'd better break it down, sir." He hastily scrambled clear as Haldean prepared to charge.

"Shoot the lock off, Malcolm!" called Isabelle.

All the householder rose in Sir Philip. He caught hold of Haldean and looked in horror at the gun Smith-Fennimore was brandishing. "Put that thing away, man. You'll kill someone with it. As for you, Jack, you can run at that door until you're blue in the face. This door opens outwards, as you should well know."

"Oh. Sorry, Uncle. I say," said Haldean, his impetuous rush halted. "I suppose the door is locked, is it?"

Sir Philip rattled the handle and the door swung open towards them. They all rapidly went in and then stopped short.

In the middle of the room, huddled by the desk, his arms flung wide, lay the body of Lord Lyvenden. A dark and sinister lake surrounded him. The rich salty smell of blood hit them like a clenched fist. A long-bladed knife stuck out grotesquely from Lord Lyvenden's chest and beside the body, his shirt stained and his hands covered in blood, knelt Arthur Stanton.

Haldean looked from the sprawled body of Lord Lyvenden to his friend's white, nervous face in horror. "Arthur? Arthur, what happened?"

Stanton looked at him with wide, frightened eyes. "I didn't do anything. Anything at all. I didn't do it. I don't know how it happened. Honestly, I didn't do it."

He struggled to his feet and walked towards them. His hands were red and slimy with blood. Bubble Robiceux screamed and Stanton turned to her. "I tell you, I haven't done anything." He glanced behind him at Lyvenden's body. "I didn't do it. I know what it looks like but I didn't do it." He turned to Haldean, hands outstretched. "Tell them, Jack. You know I wouldn't do it." Stanton put a bloodstained hand on Haldean's arm. "You know I didn't do it."

Haldean stared at his friend, then at the hand on his sleeve. "Arthur?" he said in a whisper. "What did you do?"

150

"Nothing!" There was rising hysteria in Stanton's voice. "Nothing!"

"We'll let the police decide that," said Smith-Fennimore curtly. He had his gun in his hand. "Back against the wall, man."

Stanton shook his head. "You don't understand. I didn't do it. I haven't done anything."

"Back against the wall," repeated Smith-Fennimore, walking slowly towards him, his gun pointed at Stanton's chest.

Stanton raised his arms as if to fend him off, walked backwards and stumbled over the body. Lord Lyvenden had evidently been lighting a cigarette when he was struck down, for his ornate cigarette case lay flung open on the rug, the cigarettes covered in blood. On his knees, Stanton picked it up. He started to laugh, a horrible, hysterical sound. "He wanted a cigarette. Look." He covered his face with his hands. "He wanted a cigarette."

"Stop it, Arthur!" said Haldean urgently. "Stop it."

Stanton had his hand to his mouth, gasping for breath. "I know. I know. It's not funny. I know. It's just that —"

"Get up and back against the wall," said Smith-Fennimore again.

Stanton got up unsteadily. "You know I've not done anything."

"Arthur," said Haldean quietly. "What happened?"

Stanton looked at the body beside him and at the faces in front of him. "Isabelle," he cried. "You don't believe I did it, do you?"

She shook her head, unable to make sense of what she saw.

"Back against the wall," said Smith-Fennimore once more. "You can't get away."

Stanton shook his head, bewildered. He looked at them in despair, then saw one chance of escape. Gathering himself for a spring, he put his shoulder down and rushed at the french windows, splintering his way through them with a crash.

At the same moment Smith-Fennimore fired. The bullet went wide. "Stop, man!" he roared, and, striding to the wreckage of the window, levelled the gun again.

Isabelle shouted, flinging herself at him as the gun exploded once more. On the lawn, halfway between the house and the shrubbery, Stanton stumbled, fell to his knees, picked himself up and carried on running.

Smith-Fennimore whirled round on Isabelle. "You fool!" he snarled. "You nearly made me kill him!"

Isabelle shrank back from the fury in his face. "You ... you ..." she faltered and, snatching off her engagement ring, flung it at him. The emerald scraped his cheek then clattered to the floor, the noise suddenly loud in the silence.

Like someone moving in a trance, Smith-Fennimore put his hand to his face where the emerald had struck him.

Isabelle put her hand across her eyes and burst into tears. Smith-Fennimore stood like a statue, gun lowered, gazing at Isabelle.

152

"I say," said Haldean, his voice sounding utterly unnatural in his own ears. "Hadn't someone better get after Arthur?"

CHAPTER
SEVEN

Sir Philip Rivers escorted Superintendent Ashley to Lord Lyvenden's room. "It's all in here, my dear feller." Sir Philip was sincerely glad to see the Superintendent, a solid, dependable-looking man in his middle forties who radiated a steady calm. Apparently Superintendent Ashley had actually been on his way to Stanmore Parry police station when Sir Philip had telephoned. Much to Sir Philip's relief, Ashley had arrived less than an hour after they'd found Lord Lyvenden's body. "I never believed that this sort of thing could happen at Hesperus," continued Sir Philip. "It's been a very difficult few days. Very difficult."

Sir Philip, Ashley decided, looked as if he'd been having a rough time. When he had met Sir Philip the previous year his impression had been of a self-confident, vigorous man, very well contented with his lot, with an outdoor face and humorous eyes. Now he moved like a man at least fifteen years older and his face was mottled with care. He looks worried to death, poor beggar, thought Ashley.

"Is Haldean here, Sir Philip?" Although he had the bare facts recorded in his notebook, Haldean, he knew, would give him the sort of detail he needed to make

154

sense of the case. Because the bare facts as recorded didn't make any sense at all. Why should an ex-army captain, late of the Royal Sussex, a man with an excellent record and, apparently, a close friend of Jack Haldean's, suddenly take it into his head to stab a Birmingham arms manufacturer?

"Jack?" Sir Philip shook his head. "He's taken his car out looking for Stanton. Isabelle's gone with him and the two Robiceux girls. I don't know when they'll be back." He paused with his hand on the door of Lyvenden's room. "Prepare yourself, my dear chap. It's a ghastly sight."

It certainly was. Ashley's first impression was of biting cold. The storm, which had been threatening since lunchtime, had broken in earnest. The rain drove in through the shattered windows and the curtains flapped wildly in the wind. He shivered as he looked at the body on the rug.

"This is nasty," he said to Sir Philip, raising his voice above the noise of the wind. He crouched down beside the unlovely remains of Lord Lyvenden. Lyvenden had always been stout, and now, robbed by death of any movement, he seemed flabby, like a part-deflated balloon. The killer had struck three times before his last blow had found a vital spot, the ripped shirt and gashed skin underneath testifying to the viciousness of the attack.

"It's ghastly," repeated Sir Philip. "And the worst of it is, his wife, Lady Harriet, doesn't know a thing about it. She was out this morning and she hasn't come back yet." He rubbed his hand across his forehead. "I'm not looking forward to breaking the news to her, I must say."

Ashley briefly shifted his attention from the knife buried in Lyvenden's chest. "Don't worry about that, Sir Philip. I'll talk to her." He opened his briefcase and, taking out an insufflator, gently puffed a film of grey powder over the hilt of the knife. "Gloves, by the look of it," he murmured, more to himself than Sir Philip. "Definitely gloves. And what looks like initials and a date scratched on to the hilt." He returned the insufflator to its box. "No, I'll talk to Lady Harriet. It's not something I like doing but it's my responsibility." He snapped his briefcase shut and stood up. "It's going to be dreadful for the poor woman, seeing him like this. Was she very close to her husband?"

Sir Philip raised his hands in frustration. "I don't know. I suppose she was, but I found her a bit of a cold fish. You could never tell what she was thinking. But whatever she thought of him, Ashley, it's bound to be a shock."

"Yes, we can't wrap it up, I'm afraid." Ashley stared once more at the body. "Do you recognize this knife?"

Sir Philip looked at the knife in a dissatisfied way. "I think it's the one Charnock took from the Russian I told you about. Damn it, Ashley, what's happened to the world? When I met Captain Stanton he seemed a likeable young feller. He came from a good family, too, only twenty miles or so from here. Jack told me he suffered from shell shock, but he was supposed to be cured. Every damn bit of nonsense in the world seems

156

to be put down to shell shock these days." He chewed his moustache. "We've had a lucky escape."

"A lucky escape?" Ashley looked at him enquiringly. "How? That Captain Stanton could have murdered you all, you mean? Did he ever strike you as violent or not in control of himself?"

Sir Philip looked surprised. "No, it wasn't that. It never crossed my mind. To be honest, as I say, I rather liked Captain Stanton." He chewed his moustache once more. "No, it was that the feller was keen on my daughter. She's seen a lot of him in London, although this is the first time he's been down here. Alice liked him, I know, and we wondered if they'd make a match of it. Then, thank God, things cooled off and she got engaged to this other chap I told you about, Commander Smith-Fennimore. Maybe Isabelle knew or guessed something we didn't. Anyway, it was all over before this awful tragedy. I can hardly believe it, Ashley. A suicide and a murder in my house and Isabelle involved." There was a plaintive note on the word "my". "I suppose it'll be in all the papers."

Ashley nodded. "We can scarcely keep it out, I'm afraid. However, I don't see why we should bring Miss Rivers' name into it. She'd never been engaged to him, had she?"

Sir Philip shook his head. "No, thank goodness."

"Then let's just hope we can clear it up quickly, sir, before the Press find out there was any connection between them."

Sir Philip, unable to stand still, strode impatiently round the room. "There's not a lot to clear up from your point of view, is there? We know who did the murder. We virtually saw him. All you need to do is lay hands on the man and you're there. It's an open and shut case." He broke off as footsteps sounded in the hallway outside, nodding a greeting as Smith-Fennimore came into the room. He turned to the Superintendent. "This is Commander Smith-Fennimore, Ashley."

"Superintendent Ashley?" asked Smith-Fennimore. "Haldean's mentioned you. Pleased to meet you. I came to tell you that my valet, Sotherby, has arrived together with Lord Lyvenden's man, Adamson. They know all about what's happened. They were in the pub. Apparently everyone in the village is talking about it."

Sir Philip's face fell. "How on earth does anyone know?"

"The servants will have told the postman or the butcher's boy or something," said Ashley. "This sort of news spreads like wildfire. I particularly want to see Lord Lyvenden's man. I'm hoping he'll be a valuable witness." He looked at the bloodstained handkerchief tied round Smith-Fennimore's hand. "That looks nasty, sir. What happened?"

Smith-Fennimore cradled his right hand in his left and nodded towards Lord Lyvenden's body. "I cut myself on that knife. It was stupid of me."

"Cut yourself on the knife?" repeated Ashley.

Smith-Fennimore grimaced. "Before Lyvenden was murdered, obviously." He looked tired and there were lines etched round his mouth. "It's a real nuisance. It means I can't drive. I wanted to go out and look for

158

Captain Stanton but I simply can't manage the car. I did try. I had a scout round on foot but couldn't see any sign of him."

"We should pick him up soon," said Ashley. "It's bad luck about your hand, sir. As you're here though, can I ask you to make a statement?"

Smith-Fennimore nodded. "Of course."

"But before that, Commander, can you tell me if you recognize the knife?"

Smith-Fennimore nodded again. "I recognize it, all right. I've handled it twice. Once on Sunday morning . . ." He broke off and glanced at Sir Philip.

"I've told the Superintendent about our Russian friend," said Sir Philip.

"And I also handled it earlier on today. That's when I injured myself." He bit his lip. "And then, of course, I looked at it after we discovered all this."

"Would you mind having another look, sir?" asked Ashley. "Don't touch it, if you don't mind."

He stood aside to allow him to approach the body. Smith-Fennimore hunched down beside Lord Lyvenden with some reluctance. "Haldean told me these knives were fairly commonplace but I've never seen one before." He looked at the A.C. on the hilt. "Yes, it's the same knife that Mr Charnock took from the Russian."

"Thank you, sir," said Ashley. "It's important to be as certain as possible in these cases, as I'm sure you'll appreciate." He walked to the window, looking carefully at the broken frame. "Captain Stanton made a pretty mess here. Did you notice if he cut himself?"

159

Sir Philip shrugged. "I couldn't tell you. The feller streaked off like a bullet from a gun."

A sudden gust of icy wind through the wreckage of the window made them shiver. There was a peal of thunder and more rain splattered in. Sir Philip stepped back. "I'd like to get this boarded up. I suppose I can do that, can I, or do you need the room to be left as it is? I don't know much about police matters but Jack always seems to want things left well alone."

Ashley shook his head. "No, you can get it seen to. Have your men work from the outside, though, don't let them come in here. I'd like this room locked up for the time being, Sir Philip. I've sent for the doctor and the photographer should arrive soon. When they've been, we'll be able to remove the body. I'll arrange all that, of course. What I will have to do is take statements from anyone who was a witness, starting with the Commander here. Is there a room I can use?"

"You'd better have the gun room," said Sir Philip after a few moments' thought. "I'll show you where it is." They left the room and Sir Philip locked the door behind him with a sigh of relief. "I'm glad to be out of there. I'll send Jack, Isabelle and the girls along to you when they arrive. Naturally, they'll want to change and so on after having been out in this weather. They'll get their deaths of cold otherwise." He sighed once more. "A suicide and a murder. In *my* house. Unbelievable!"

Ashley liked the gun room. It was a room that would be easy to relax in and he found witnesses talked more if they were at their ease. There were comfortable chairs and a table with cigarettes, and the pleasantly

160

masculine odour of whisky and cigars mingled with the light metallic smell of gun-oil. The guns themselves, ranged in glass-fronted cases round the wall, spoke not of violence and sudden death but of days in the long grass and heather with a spaniel at your heels. All these things helped to dispel the hard fact that this was a murder inquiry and that a sergeant with a notebook was sitting at the table writing down every word which was said.

Smith-Fennimore gave a few brief details about himself, then looked ruefully at the rain streaming down the windows. "I can't say I envy old Haldean and the girls out in that." He rubbed his thumb gingerly over his injured palm. "It's rotten not being able to drive, though."

"It must be very trying, especially for you, sir," said Ashley, pulling his chair closer to the table. "Sir Philip told me who you were. I saw you race at Brooklands last month. My son's very keen on motor-racing. He's twelve and thinks of precious little else. I took him along for a birthday treat."

"Did you?" Smith-Fennimore settled himself in one of the old leather armchairs and lit a cigarette. "Next time you come, drop me a line care of the track and if you arrive early enough I can show him the car. I don't mind kids."

Ashley was touched. "That's very generous of you, sir. Now, about this business. You played golf this morning, I believe."

Smith-Fennimore nodded. "That's right. We got back from the links about quarter to one."

"And how was Captain Stanton? Was he nervous or apprehensive at all?"

Smith-Fennimore frowned, trying to remember. "Not especially, I don't think. He always did strike me as a bit nervy. I believe he suffered from shell shock but he was supposed to be cured."

"So I believe, sir," said Ashley. His eyes crinkled, inviting a confidence. "I know Sir Philip thinks Captain Stanton simply went off his head, but is that your opinion? Or do you think there's another reason?"

Ashley knew immediately he'd struck gold. Smith-Fennimore looked horribly uncomfortable but said nothing. "This is a very serious matter, sir," prompted Ashley eventually. "You must understand that we need you to be as accurate as you possibly can."

"Well, yes." Smith-Fennimore scratched his chin. "I can see that." He frowned. "I don't suppose there's any big secret about it. Haldean certainly knows and so does Miss Rivers. Lord Lyvenden was a colleague of mine but we didn't always agree. As a matter of fact, the more I got to know about him, the unhappier I became, but I couldn't honestly complain about the work he did for the bank. He was a very acute — some would say ruthless — businessman. During the war he was the promoter of the Colonial and Oriental Mining Conglomerate. This was before he got the peerage and was still plain Mr Todd. Lyvenden got out before the crash, but Stanton's father was ruined. It gave Captain Stanton a real shock when he found out Victor Todd and Lord Lyvenden were one and the same person. He attributed the deaths of both his parents to the collapse of the Colonial and Oriental."

Ashley whistled. "I see. Was this the first time since his parents died that Captain Stanton had met Lord Lyvenden?"

"As far as I know, yes."

Ashley was silent for a moment. A motive, a proper motive, the thing which had puzzled him, had emerged. It was very early days, but the case was taking shape. "To return to your own affairs, sir. What did you do when you got back from playing golf?"

"I went up to my room to change."

"And was your valet there?"

Smith-Fennimore shook his head. "No. Tuesday is his afternoon off. I don't think he'll be able to help you much, but ask him, by all means. After I changed I had some time in hand so I started to look through some business papers. There's been a particular problem I've been trying to crack and I had a few ideas about it this morning. I hadn't got very far before I saw I needed to discuss it with Lyvenden. So I went along to his room — that would be about ten past one at a guess — to see him. When I arrived, he had just finished dressing. It was rather awkward in a way." Smith-Fennimore paused. "You see, the matter was highly confidential, and his valet, Adamson, was still there. I was surprised to see him, because I knew my man, Sotherby, had planned to go out with him this afternoon. I explained things as best I could in the presence of a third party and Lord Lyvenden promised to look into it right away. I left the papers with him. I hadn't been long. Certainly less than ten minutes. What did I do then?" He thought for a moment, then his face cleared. "I went out to my car. That was it. I'd left my lighter in it. Then, when I came back into the house, I spoke to Major Haldean. Like me, he was waiting in the hall before we went into lunch."

"Who else was in the hall, sir?"

"Only myself and Major Haldean to start with, then the place filled up. There was my fiancée, Miss Rivers, and her uncle, Mr Charnock. Mr Charnock went out for lunch. When the lunch gong sounded, neither Lord Lyvenden nor Captain Stanton had arrived and the custom is, as everyone knows, to be in the hall beforehand. Sir Philip is very keen on punctuality at mealtimes. Major Haldean and I went to hurry up Captain Stanton. He'd lost his cuff-links and was searching for them. We found them easily enough, down beside his dressing table."

"Why didn't Captain Stanton use the cuff-links from his golf shirt?"

"He'd lost them, too." Smith-Fennimore smiled at Ashley's expression. "He was always losing things. He's been late for nearly every meal so far because of losing his tie-clip or his collar-studs, or something of that sort. On the links this morning he had to play with rolled-up sleeves. The thing is, while we were searching for them, Major Haldean looked in Captain Stanton's chest of drawers. He found the sheath knife that the Russian had left on Sunday. It was buried under Captain Stanton's socks."

Ashley sat up. "You found the knife in Captain Stanton's drawer?"

"Major Haldean found the knife," corrected Smith-Fennimore.

"But what did Captain Stanton say? How did he account for the knife being there?"

Smith-Fennimore spread out his hands in a puzzled gesture. "He didn't. He appeared to be as surprised as we were. Haldean had mentioned that Mr Charnock had said the knife was missing but we never dreamed it would turn up in Captain Stanton's drawer."

Ashley sucked his cheeks in. "Can you suggest how it got into Captain Stanton's drawer?"

Smith-Fennimore shrugged. "Obviously someone put it there. As I say, Captain Stanton seemed as surprised as Major Haldean and myself, so surprised I wondered if someone had put it there as a sort of joke."

"Can you think of anyone who would be likely to play that sort of joke? One of the young ladies, for instance?"

Smith-Fennimore looked startled. "I wouldn't have thought so for a minute. I mean, it's not like making an apple-pie bed or anything, which they might do. It's not very funny."

"Could Mr Charnock himself have put it there?"

"He could have done," said Smith-Fennimore dubiously. "If he did, he wouldn't intend it as a joke, though. He's not that sort of person."

"So really, although you talked of it as a joke, you believe that Captain Stanton himself hid it there?"

Smith-Fennimore shifted in his chair. "It's hard to think of any other explanation, but all I can say is that at the time it never crossed my mind. Captain Stanton seemed stunned by the sight of it and it never occurred to me he was telling anything but the truth when he said he didn't know how it had got there. We passed it around between the three of us, and, I'm sorry to say, I managed to cut myself on it. Major Haldean went downstairs as there was no point in us all being late, and Captain Stanton helped me tie a handkerchief round my hand. Then . . ." Smith-Fennimore hesitated.

"What is it, sir?" asked Ashley.

Smith-Fennimore didn't answer.

Ashley waited but Smith-Fennimore didn't speak. "I must remind you once again that this is a very serious matter."

"I didn't like Stanton's manner," said Smith-Fennimore reluctantly. "I don't know the man well, as I said, but he'd always been amiable enough, even if he was nervy. He seemed really rattled. He must have told me a dozen times he didn't know how the knife had got into his chest of drawers. To be honest, I didn't pay much attention. My hand was hurting like the dickens and I wanted to find some iodine. I knew the longer I was the more irritated Sir Philip would be. Stanton was utterly distracted by the knife and didn't seem to realize that we were already late. So I asked him to go and roust out Lyvenden and join us when he was ready."

"So you left Captain Stanton in his room with the knife?"

"That's right. I went into lunch and very shortly after that, Lawson, the footman, told Sir Philip that there was some sort of row going on in Lord Lyvenden's room. I suppose I should have thought of Captain Stanton right away, but I didn't. He'd always seemed such a harmless sort of chap that it never crossed my mind he'd do such a thing."

"Even though you hadn't liked his manner?"

"I ask you, man," said Smith-Fennimore with some irritation, "is it a likely thing to think? Two men can be late for lunch without our jumping to the conclusion that one's murdered the other. When I heard there was a row in Lyvenden's room, I thought the Russian who'd been here on Sunday had come back and so did everybody else. He was a nasty piece of work and no mistake. Sir Philip asked Major Haldean and myself to accompany him. Miss Rivers and the two Robiceux girls came as well." He smiled tightly. "They said they didn't want to miss out on the fun."

"What happened then, sir?"

"Well, there was a dickens of a kick-up going on. You could hear the noise from a long way off. Sir Philip banged on the door and demanded to be let in. I peered through the keyhole and could just see an outstretched arm. Our first thought was to break the door down, but when we tried the handle we found it wasn't actually locked."

"You're sure about that, sir? That the door wasn't locked, I mean?"

Smith-Fennimore nodded. "I'm certain. Sir Philip turned the handle and the door opened right away. We went into the room and found Captain Stanton kneeling by the body, his hands covered in blood. It was a pretty awful sight, I can tell you. The Robiceux girls started crying, and Stanton kept on saying he hadn't done it. I had my gun with me and told him to get back against the wall. My idea was to keep him under cover until the police arrived. I had no idea of what he was going to do next. He made a spring, crashed through the french windows, and ran for it. I fired to warn him to stop, but he kept on running. I went to fire again, but Miss Rivers grabbed my arm and I nearly hit him. I might have actually winged him. He certainly stumbled, but he picked himself up and carried on running." Smith-Fennimore paused, biting his lip.

"What happened next, sir?" asked Ashley quietly.

The pause lengthened. Ashley knew that Smith-Fennimore was strapping down some strong emotion. Anger? No. Although his face was devoid of emotion, his hands were trembling. With an odd shock, Ashley realized that the big, confident man in front of him was close to tears. The rain hissed down against the windows and the gun-room clock ticked its seconds into the silence for a full half-minute.

Ashley looked at Smith-Fennimore's impassive face and decided not to probe that particular wound any further. Not only would it be close to cruelty, he could always ask Haldean about it afterwards. He changed the subject. "Your gun, sir. May I see it?"

Smith-Fennimore's shoulders relaxed. He produced the pistol from his pocket and passed it to the

Superintendent, who held it briefly. He noticed there were smears of blood on the butt.

"This is an impressive weapon, sir. Where did you get it?"

"It's my navy Colt. I bought it from Harrods in the war. I've got a licence for it."

"Didn't it hurt your injured hand to use it?"

Smith-Fennimore nodded ruefully. "It hurt like sin. I didn't notice until afterwards that it had reopened the cut. You must remember, Superintendent, that we were all pretty wound up and even though my hand was giving me gyp, it didn't seem to be as important as trying to stop Stanton."

Ashley handed back the Colt. "Why do you carry it, sir?"

"Because," said Smith-Fennimore, putting the gun back in his jacket pocket, "there have been some peculiar things happening in this house and I wanted to be sure of protection. You know about Mr Preston's suicide? Well, Major Haldean believes there was more to that than met the eye, and I am inclined to agree with him."

Ashley sat upright. "Another murder, you mean, sir?"

"Another murder," agreed Smith-Fennimore. "Major Haldean can tell you more about that than I can. He's full of ideas."

Ashley grinned, despite himself. "Yes, he usually is."

There was a tap on the door and a police constable entered. "Sorry to interrupt, sir, but the doctor and the photographer have arrived."

169

"Thank you, Bevan. I'll be along right away. We've just about finished." Ashley rose to his feet. "Thank you, Commander. I'll get your statement typed up and ask you to sign it later. You've been a great help." He paused, noticing the way Smith-Fennimore was cradling his hand. "Why don't you come along and get the doctor to look at that?"

Smith-Fennimore got up. "Good idea."

Dr Speldhurst was, Ashley realized when he and Smith-Fennimore got back to Lord Lyvenden's room, in no very happy mood. Sir Philip Rivers stood by the body with a faintly proprietorial air while the doctor fussed round.

Speldhurst looked up as they entered. "You're Superintendent Ashley, eh? I was saying to Sir Philip that this was getting to be a habit. I'd rather see people while they were still alive than keep on inspecting corpses in his bedrooms. Don't worry, I haven't touched the knife. I suppose you want me to tell you how long he's been dead and so on?"

Ashley smiled placidly. "We will need that information, Doctor, of course, but first of all I'd be glad if you'd look at Commander Smith-Fennimore's hand."

Speldhurst tutted as he saw the clumsy, blood-soaked handkerchief round Smith-Fennimore's palm. He didn't attempt to untie it but cut it off with scissors. "By jingo, I bet that hurts," he said, looking at the wound. "No permanent damage, I'm glad to say." He started to clean off the dried blood. "What is it? A knife cut?"

"Yes," said Smith-Fennimore tightly. "It was my own fault."

"Well, it doesn't hurt less for that." He picked up a bottle of iodine. "This is going to sting, I'm afraid."

Smith-Fennimore endured the doctor's attentions with gritted teeth, flexing the fingers of his rebandaged hand with relief. "Thank you."

The doctor grinned. "You almost sound as if you mean it, man. Get that bandage changed every day and it should be much better in a week or so."

Ashley looked down at the body. "Have you had a chance to come to any conclusions, Doctor?"

Dr Speldhurst turned away from Smith-Fennimore and glared at Ashley over the top of his pince-nez. "My conclusion is that he was stabbed, but you hardly need me to tell you that. There's no doubt how he died but it'd take a good strong push to get the knife in like that. I imagine the killer — Captain Stanton, did you say, Sir Philip? — held his shoulders while he struck. It couldn't really be done in any other way. The knife glanced off the ribs twice before it punctured the aorta, which accounts for all the blood. It's a wicked-looking weapon."

"It certainly is," said Ashley thoughtfully. "Where's the photographer, by the way? I expected to find him here."

The doctor grinned once more. "He's being sick in the scullery. He's that weedy-looking fellow from the village. I don't suppose he's ever photographed anything more exciting than a wedding in his life. Now for the time of death. Let me see . . ." Dr Speldhurst took his watch from his pocket. "It's five o'clock now. I'd say he's been dead about four hours, which makes the time of death somewhere around one o'clock or thereabouts, give or take twenty minutes on either side."

"Is that as close as you can get?" asked Ashley.

"Damn it, man, I'm not a clairvoyant!" exploded Dr Speldhurst. "Besides that, why d'you need me to tell you when he died? According to Sir Philip you saw the chap do it, didn't you?"

"Not quite," began Sir Philip when he was interrupted by voices in the hallway.

Lady Harriet, followed by a protesting police constable, came into the room. "Sir Philip!" she cried. "This man tells me some stupid story about my husband."

Sir Philip gave Ashley an agonized look. "This is Lady Harriet, Lyvenden's wife," he said in a low voice.

Ashley stepped forward. "I'm sorry, Lady Harriet, but this is going to be a terrible shock. Would you like to come with me? I'd rather you weren't in this room."

He'd hoped to get her away, but she was staring past him at the body on the floor. She turned white and swallowed. "I see it's true," she said faintly. "No. No, I don't want to stay in here."

Smith-Fennimore looked at the doctor. "I'll be off," he said quietly. "There's nothing much I can do."

Ashley took Lady Harriet's arm and escorted her out of the room and into the hall to where there were a table and two chairs set against the wall. She sank into a chair and sat with her hands rigidly folded across her

172

handbag, staring in front of her. Sir Philip, Dr Speldhurst and Smith-Fennimore followed.

"Lady Harriet," said Sir Philip gruffly, "we know what a shock this is for you. Would you like to retire to your room?"

She gave a little shudder, shaking off the suggestion irritably. "No, please don't fuss. I shall be perfectly all right." She sighed and drew a cigarette out of her case with shaky hands. Sir Philip lit it for her. "Poor Victor," she said eventually. "That it should end like this. Still, he had it coming to him." The men exchanged surprised looks.

"Did your husband have any enemies, Lady Harriet?" asked Superintendent Ashley.

"Oh, absolutely heaps, officer. I presume that is what you are. Yes, poor old Victor did everyone down in the end. You never had any business dealings with him, did you, Sir Philip? That's probably why you were still friendly with him. He was always impressed by people who didn't have to buy a title. He was very keen that Mr Charnock should introduce you to him. Do you know who did it?"

"Captain Stanton, Lady Harriet," said Sir Philip.

She raised a carefully plucked eyebrow. "Captain Stanton? That boy? But that's absurd. There are stacks of people with a better motive — and here's one now," she added viciously.

Mrs Strachan came into the hall. Her face was stained with tears. She gestured down the corridor towards the garden suite. "Is . . . is it in there?"

"Yes," said Lady Harriet flatly. "Victor's dead body is in his room. He's been stabbed."

Mrs Strachan gave a little scream and burst into renewed sobs. "Oh, Victor, Victor," she cried. "And dear Lady Harriet. So brave. I can't bear it!" She dabbed her tears with a wet handkerchief.

"Oh, do stop it," said Lady Harriet in disgust. "Stop it, woman, or I'll tell them exactly what you were doing here."

A shrewd eye peeped above the handkerchief. "You wouldn't . . ." stammered Mrs Strachan. "You couldn't."

"I could," said Lady Harriet firmly. "Now, gentlemen, I think I will go to my room."

"Just one moment, Lady Harriet," said Superintendent Ashley, courteously. "Perhaps you would care to explain what you have just said?"

Lady Harriet spared him an uninterested glance. "No."

"We'll need a statement from you," persisted the Superintendent in a firmer voice.

She looked at him coolly. "My good man, you'll get a statement when and if I choose to make one. I shall be in my room. It's next to the one that had the other dead body in it." She got up and swept up the stairs, leaving a stunned group of men behind her.

"Whew!" said Ashley at last. "She's a cool customer and no mistake. What did she mean by that?"

"Perhaps Mrs Strachan would elucidate matters for us?" asked Sir Philip.

Mrs Strachan sniffed and put down the handkerchief. "It's just Lady Harriet's way, Sir Philip. She always resented my friendship with poor Victor. She never did understand that we were simply friends. Yes, friends."

"Friends?" repeated Sir Philip in a dangerous voice.

"Friends. We were only ever friends."

"Friends?" ground out Sir Philip in a glacial tone. "What sort of friends?"

Mrs Strachan buried herself in the handkerchief once more. "Don't be hor-hor-horrible. How can you dream of such a thing?"

Superintendent Ashley took one look at his incandescent host and decided to intervene. He put a kindly hand on the sobbing woman's shoulder. "Now, now, Mrs Strachan, why don't you come along to the gun room with me? We can have a cup of tea and you can tell me all about it." He steered the still sniffing Mrs Strachan down the hall, pausing to speak to his constable at the door of the garden suite. "Organize some tea for us, Bevan."

The Superintendent escorted Mrs Strachan to the gun room, chatting of strictly neutral topics until the tea arrived. Helping her to sugar, he judged the moment right to start asking questions. "Perhaps you can tell me what you were doing this morning?"

"This morning?" she quavered. "Nothing. I decided to go into Stanmore Parry and have lunch there. I don't know this part of the country very well, and I decided to have a look round. And . . . and . . ."

"Yes?" asked Ashley, sympathetically.

"I had some money with me, rather a lot of money. I'd mislaid it last night. I thought Lady Harriet's maid had taken it. She's French, you know, and in my opinion she is not at all trustworthy. One thing led to another and there was a bit of a fuss about it."

Superintendent Ashley thought that "a bit of a fuss" was a magnificent understatement contrasted with the screaming row detailed at some length by Sir Philip to him earlier in the day. His face showed nothing but polite interest and, emboldened, Mrs Strachan continued.

"She does take things, that girl. She's fundamentally dishonest. I never have trusted foreigners. I'm sure she'd moved the money from where it was. Anyway, I thought the best thing to do would be to pay it into the bank."

"Where did the money come from, Mrs Strachan?" asked Ashley, gently.

She licked her lips, nervously. "I brought it with me."

He smiled. "No. Now where did it really come from?"

She dissolved into sobs again. "Victor gave it to me. He was always so kind and generous. And Lady Harriet thought ... Lady Harriet thought ..." She was overwhelmed by tears.

Ashley cleared his throat. "Did Lady Harriet think you were having an affair?"

There was silence, broken only by the sound of tears. "Yes," Mrs Strachan whispered eventually. "She was silly and jealous, but Victor and I were only friends."

Ashley reserved his opinion about the nature of the friendship and pressed on. "What did you do after you'd been to the bank?"

"I walked round the village, before going to a little tea shop for lunch. It was called the Oasis. I had cod in parsley sauce and a gooseberry tart with custard. After lunch I called into the chemist's for a new toothbrush and some aspirin. I didn't like the look of the weather so I went into another tea shop for an early tea, hoping the rain would blow over. It was quite a nice place. It's called the Golden Rose. It has golden roses on the wallpaper. I had Welsh rarebit and a pot of Ceylon tea and a plate of mixed cakes. Then I got a cab back. I instructed the driver to drop me at the far side of the park because I wanted to walk."

Ashley's face expressed polite incredulity. "You wanted to walk? In this weather?"

"I had my umbrella. I thought a walk would be nice. And then when I got back in I heard the terrible news and I can't bear it!" The handkerchief was pressed into service once more, but Ashley wasn't being fobbed off.

"Mrs Strachan, you can't honestly expect me to believe that you fancied a stroll in the worst thunderstorm we've had in months. You were going to meet someone, weren't you? Who was it? Lord Lyvenden?"

"No, no, it wasn't. I'd rather not say, officer. Why won't you believe me?"

"Because I . . ."

There was a noise in the corridor outside and he heard one of the constables say, "Miss! Stop, miss! You can't go in there!" The door was flung open and Isabelle Rivers, followed by two other girls and Jack

Haldean, came into the room. Malcolm Smith-Fennimore brought up the rear like a blond and gloomy sheepdog.

Haldean gave Ashley an apologetic glance and shrugged. If he had said, "It would take more than me to stop her," his meaning couldn't have been clearer.

"Mr Ashley!" proclaimed Isabelle in ringing tones. "You've got this all wrong. Dad says you think Arthur killed him, but he didn't. I know he didn't!"

Superintendent Ashley had risen to his feet. "Miss Rivers, please —"

She brushed her hair back from her face impatiently. "But can't you see, Superintendent? You've got to believe that Arthur's innocent. He couldn't have committed a murder, he just couldn't. You've got it all wrong!"

CHAPTER
EIGHT

Superintendent Ashley pulled out a chair for Isabelle, but she waved it aside. "You've got it all wrong," she repeated. "Tell him, Jack. Tell him Arthur couldn't have done it. He'll believe you. Mr Ashley, you'll believe Jack, won't you? You've got to." She glanced at Haldean impatiently. "Tell him, Jack."

Haldean felt and looked wretchedly indecisive. "I'm sorry, Belle. I don't know if I can."

She rounded on him furiously. "I thought he was your friend!"

Haldean flinched. "Isabelle! For heaven's sake." He looked at Ashley with a lift of his eyebrows. "Hello. Nice to see you again, even if this isn't the meeting I had in mind."

"Jack," broke in Isabelle, "will you please tell Mr Ashley how wrong everyone is? Arthur's not guilty. He can't be."

Haldean remained silent. Isabelle bridled with impatience and turned to Bubble and Squeak Robiceux for support. "You'll tell him, won't you? It doesn't matter what we saw. It doesn't *mean* anything. You don't believe Arthur's guilty, do you?"

Bubble Robiceux shook her head. "It was horrible, absolutely horrible, but I don't believe Arthur killed Lord Lyvenden. He couldn't be a murderer."

Isabelle looked at her with gratitude. "Thanks, Bubble." She gave the Superintendent a defiant glare. "You see, that's two of us who believe he's innocent."

"Unfortunately, Miss Rivers, we don't find out if someone's guilty by taking votes. Unless you're on a jury," he amended, conscientiously. "You know how we work. We take statements, examine the evidence, and come to a conclusion that way."

"Then take my statement," said Isabelle, forcefully. "Please, Mr Ashley."

Ashley looked at her thoughtfully. He remembered Isabelle Rivers perfectly well and had seen her worried and anxious before now, but he had never seen her quite as strung up as she was at the moment. She was crackling with tension. He made a mental note to refer the puzzle to Haldean but for the moment he had Isabelle herself to deal with. "Don't you want to go and get changed, miss?" he asked. "In fact," he added, looking at the little group, "doesn't everyone want to go and get changed? That was a pretty nasty bit of weather to be out in."

"I want you to take my statement," repeated Isabelle vehemently. "And Bubble and Squeak's." She flicked her wet hair out of her eyes with a nervous twitch of her hand. "The sooner we can convince you of the truth, the better."

180

Ashley glanced round the crowded room. "We usually take statements singly. I was going to ask you to make a statement of what you'd seen, but —"

"Do it now!" demanded Isabelle.

Ashley gave an almost imperceptible gesture in Haldean's direction. "I suppose now's as good a time as any."

Haldean got the hint. "We'd all better push off. We'll be close at hand should you want us."

"Bubble, you stay," said Isabelle, quickly. "And you, Squeak. Now I know who Arthur's real friends are," she added meaningfully, glaring at her cousin.

"Shall I stay, Isabelle?" asked Smith-Fennimore.

Isabelle gave him a withering look. "You!" It was like a whip crack.

Smith-Fennimore shrugged in a depressed way and held the door open for the still sniffing Mrs Strachan to leave.

"Now," said Ashley, when they had the room to themselves. "Perhaps you ladies can tell me what you know. When did you get back from playing golf?"

Haldean stood in the open doorway looking across the terrace to where the distant line of trees shielded the river. The fury of the storm had subsided into low, far-off grumbles of thunder and the rain had lost its slashing, tropical force. Arthur was out there, somewhere. He leaned his forehead on the cool stone of the door frame, absorbing the smell of hot, wet earth. He was aware that Smith-Fennimore was near by but couldn't think of anything to say.

There was a movement by his elbow. "Cigarette?"

He half turned. Smith-Fennimore was offering him his open case. "Thanks." He glanced at the man's face and felt a twist of compassion. He was about to speak when Smith-Fennimore broke in.

"I can't understand it! Why the hell has Isabelle reacted like this? Can you tell me what I'm supposed to have done?"

The obvious answer was probably the best. "Shot Arthur."

"But . . ." He drew heavily on his cigarette. "I didn't shoot him. Not as she means. I was trying to stop him. You saw that. What is it about Stanton? I know everyone assumed he cared about Isabelle but he did damn all about it if he did. I've done everything by the book. Everything."

And Smith-Fennimore *had* done everything by the book, thought Haldean. He had courted Isabelle — the word "courted" was exactly right — openly and . . . well, courteously. He'd met Aunt Alice and Uncle Philip, he'd been respectful, polite and touchingly tender. Yes, the man had a mistress, but so what? He was rich, handsome and a man of the world. It was almost inevitable he'd have a mistress, for God's sake. Smith-Fennimore had assured him that Countess Whatnot was a thing of the past and he believed him. There wasn't any doubt about Smith-Fennimore's feelings for Isabelle. As for Arthur . . .

Haldean sighed inwardly. How on earth could he think of Arthur without seeing once again the scene in Lord Lyvenden's room? And yet this was Arthur he was thinking about, his oldest friend whom he'd known, trusted and liked for years. He'd wanted him to marry Isabelle, for heaven's sake. If the man had a fault, it was his slowness in getting off the mark, the way he goofed around looking like a lost sheep, not going off the deep end and knifing some wretched munitions manufacturer, no matter how appalling he'd been. The whole thing was nuts. Was Arthur nuts too? He'd had shell shock, yes, but that had left him shaken and ill. Diffident, if anything. That was why he'd taken so much time to come to the point with Isabelle. All that made sense. What didn't make sense was that Arthur should suddenly turn into a homicidal maniac. Yes, he'd been angry, really angry when he'd found out Lyvenden was Victor Todd. Isabelle had begged him not to do anything. Maybe the effort of keeping his feelings bottled up had got too much. Maybe Lyvenden had taunted him. Maybe . . .

Smith-Fennimore smoked his cigarette down to the butt, threw the end out of the door and tried to light another one. He swore under his breath as his lighter failed to work.

"Here," said Haldean, throwing him a box of matches. Smith-Fennimore tried to catch them in his bandaged hand, fumbled it, and swore again. "Sorry," said Haldean, picking up the matches and giving them to him. "Here you are. Keep them." He was a bit ham-fisted with his left hand, thought Haldean, struck by his uncharacteristically clumsy movements. He noticed how Smith-Fennimore's fingers holding his cigarette trembled. Perhaps it wasn't just his hand that was making him clumsy.

"Haldean, you saw what happened. Isabelle seems to think Stanton's innocent, that it's all a ghastly mistake. Can she possibly be right? I'm racking my brains to try and come up with some other explanation for what we saw."

"I'm blowed if I can think of one." Haldean broke off as, down the corridor, the door to the gun room opened. Isabelle, Bubble and Squeak came into the hall.

"Superintendent Ashley wants to see you now, Jack," said Isabelle, coldly. "Off you go. I just hope you remember who your friends are. I'm going to my room."

"Damn that," broke in Smith-Fennimore quickly. "I need to talk to you, Isabelle. We're engaged, remember?"

Isabelle drew herself up. "Jack, I would be obliged if you would inform Commander Smith-Fennimore that I have no desire to speak to him."

"Inform him yourself, Belle," said Haldean. "Don't drag me into it." He was stung by her attitude and moved by the emotion on Smith-Fennimore's face. "I think you're being rotten. And get off your high horse. It doesn't suit you."

"Isabelle," said Smith-Fennimore firmly. "You're going to speak to me. I couldn't care less about Stanton."

"I could!"

184

"Well, I don't! I don't care if Stanton murdered fifty Lord Lyvendens. What I care about is us." He caught hold of her hand. "Us, do you understand? We're engaged."

She shook her hand free. "We were engaged. If I thought Arthur had . . ." She swallowed and for a moment looked close to tears.

Smith-Fennimore looked earnestly into her face. "Do you love him? Is that it?"

Haldean suddenly arrived at the point where he couldn't take any more. "I'm off." He pushed past Bubble and Squeak Robiceux who were gazing at Isabelle and Smith-Fennimore and went into the gun room, slamming the door behind him.

Ashley looked up, startled. "What's wrong?"

"Isabelle," said Haldean succinctly. He flung himself into an armchair.

Ashley turned to his sergeant. "I know Major Haldean. He'll make a proper statement later. You take yourself off for the time being, my lad. Now then," he said when the sergeant had gathered up his notebook and gone, "what's the problem with Miss Rivers?"

"Miss Rivers," said Haldean, "bit my head off and is in the middle of a huge scene with Smith-Fennimore. Anyone who says a word against Arthur is in the doghouse. Smith-Fennimore's getting the worst of it with me as reserve."

"But why?" asked Ashley. "I don't really like saying this, but from the way Miss Rivers is reacting, you'd think it was Captain Stanton she was engaged to, not the Commander."

"You're telling me," said Haldean with feeling. "I knew she liked Arthur but when he asked her to marry him, she turned him down. God knows how this is all going to end up. Although I could shake her at the moment, I think the world of Isabelle and I've known Arthur for years. As for that poor devil Smith-Fennimore, she's putting him through the wringer and no mistake."

He stood up and walked to the mantelpiece and rested his hands against it, stretching his arms. "I don't know if I'm going to be much use to you, Ashley," he said eventually. "I'm too involved. I can't get my ideas straight and I don't know if I ever will." He stared into the empty fireplace. "If only it wasn't Arthur."

"Well, it is," said Ashley practically.

Haldean didn't react for a couple of moments, then he turned, leaning his back against the mantelpiece. Ashley was pleased to see the ghost of a smile. "And that being the case, old fruit, I'd better stop having forty thousand fits and get on with it, eh?"

"That's about the size of it," agreed Ashley.

Haldean was very still for a moment, then he relaxed and laughed. "Okay. Fit over. So, Superintendent Ashley, sir, what do you think?"

"I think," said Ashley, aware that Haldean's mood was still fragile, "that there's a dickens of a case against your friend, Arthur Stanton. I think that on the facts alone it looks as clear a case of caught in the act as I've ever come across. There really doesn't seem to be any doubt about it. Just let me run through the facts with

186

you. Lord Lyvenden ruined Captain Stanton's family. Is that right?"

"That's what Arthur said. He's certain his father and mother died as a result."

Ashley nodded. "So that's a motive. Captain Stanton mysteriously found a knife in his drawer. Yes?"

"Actually, I found the knife. Arthur seemed bewildered by it."

"So I've heard. That's his means. Then, complete with knife, he goes to Lord Lyvenden's room while everyone else is at lunch. That's his opportunity. The next thing we know is that Arthur Stanton is discovered in Lord Lyvenden's room beside the dead body of Lord Lyvenden who now has the knife in his chest. So far from offering any explanation, Stanton ups and crashes through the french windows and scarpers. It doesn't look good."

"It looks bloody awful, Ashley," said Haldean. "I couldn't agree more. On the one hand I don't see how he can be guilty, on the other I don't see how he can't be. Not only can't I see it, I can't make any guesses, either."

Ashley raised his eyebrows. "Now, that is a first. To be honest, Haldean, I haven't much doubt, but Miss Rivers was so very positive, to say nothing of the two Robiceux ladies, that I caught myself wondering if there was any other explanation."

Haldean shrugged. "If you think of one, let me know, won't you?" He shook his head. "We've had a really peculiar few days, what with Tim Preston and those Russian blokes . . ."

"Blokes?" asked Ashley. "I've only heard about one."

"No, there were two. I don't know why either of them came here. Perhaps," he said, seeing Ashley's inquisitive face, "I'd better wise you up, as the Yanks say." He perched himself on the arm of a chair and, as quickly as he could, ran through the events of the past few days.

Ashley listened intently. "So there's not one Russian but two?" he said when Haldean had finished. "One on the night of the ball and the one who visited Lord Lyvenden." He scratched the side of his chin thoughtfully. "And it was Captain Stanton who discovered that the cigarette packet was missing from the grate in Lord Lyvenden's bedroom?"

Haldean nodded. "Nobody but Arthur saw it, so you may think that particular cigarette packet has a Cheshire Cat quality about it, but it had been there, Ashley. The depression in the soot was perfectly visible. And that means that somebody was fixing up an alibi and that means, O Sleuth, that poor old Tim didn't top himself as we were expected to believe."

Ashley sucked his cheeks in. "Can we stick to Lord Lyvenden's murder for the time being? At least we know for certain that *was* murder. Miss Rivers tried to tell me that Captain Stanton simply walked in on Lord Lyvenden after he was dead."

"In that case, why didn't the idiot walk straight out again?" Haldean put his hands wide in frustration. "The door wasn't locked. All we had to do was turn the handle and it opened. He could have got out any time. Say he did walk into the room. You'd think the first thing anyone would do when finding themselves with a punctured corpse would be to mention it to someone. I know I would. And you've seen the remains. I've never seen such a punctured corpse in all my born days. There was gubbins all over the place. You pointed that out to Belle, I suppose?"

"Yes, and she says he must have been overwhelmed by horror and didn't know what to do. I understand he suffered from shell shock," added Ashley tentatively.

Haldean clicked his tongue irritably. "Yes, he did. He had a perfectly foul time in the war and if he's caught and sent for trial that'll probably be his best defence. But damn it, Ashley, you know and I know that even if the sight of Lyvenden pushed him over the edge, he'd crumple. He'd be wiped out, unable to move. He'd be hiding in a corner, not standing there bellowing the house down and kicking the furniture."

"So what was his reaction when he saw you all? I mean, was he insane?"

Haldean thought for a moment, tapping his fingers on the arm of the chair. "He obviously wasn't himself, so to speak. He was very upset and I'd say he was a bit hysterical. Having said that, I didn't think he'd lost his marbles. He wasn't very coherent, but I doubt many people would be very coherent in those circumstances." Haldean leaned forward and took a cigarette from the box on the table. "But I keep coming back to the fact that this is my old friend Arthur I'm talking about." He tapped the cigarette on the back of his hand before lighting it. "If you knew him, you'd understand how simply incredible it all seems. Did you check the knife for fingerprints, by the way?"

"Yes, I did, but the results were inconclusive. It looked as if the killer had been wearing gloves."

Haldean frowned. "Arthur certainly wasn't wearing gloves. Not when we saw him, anyway." He glanced up. "Ashley, I don't like those gloves. I mean, why on earth should he wear gloves and then hang about in the room, unless he really has gone doolally tap? Were there any other prints on the knife?"

"Some, but they were smudged by the glove marks."

"It just doesn't add up," muttered Haldean. He stretched his legs out and put his arm over the back of the chair. "Look, forget Arthur for a moment. Who else is there in the house who's capable of murder?"

"You know who's in the house. Whether they're capable of murder or not is something I wouldn't like to say."

Haldean grinned. "I'm not nearly so timid in my judgements. You've got a list of residents there, have you? Who's on it?"

"Well, there's Miss Rivers . . ."

"Isabelle? You know Isabelle. Not a chance."

"And Sir Philip and Lady Rivers . . ."

"Not a chance with knobs on. Besides that, they were at lunch."

Ashley looked at his list. "There are the servants, of course."

Haldean shook his head. "I don't somehow think the butler did it. All the Hesperus servants are local people. Aunt Alice knows their families and so on. There's

190

Lady Harriet's French maid, but she's only a little bit of a thing. From what Tim Preston told me, it seems likely that Lyvenden would have made a pass at her, but even if she was suffering from an excess of outraged virtue, I can't see her having the strength to grab hold of a man like Lyvenden and stab him three times. Maybe if the knife had gone in right away, but it glanced off his ribs twice. Unless he was being held pretty firmly, he'd have fought back good and hard. Not only would she probably look as if she'd been in a scrap, I don't think she'd be able to land the final blow. Smith-Fennimore's got a valet. I don't know anything about him. Lyvenden's got a valet too, of course. His name's Adamson."

"I haven't spoken to either of them yet. I particularly want to see Adamson."

"Let's leave them out of it for the time being. Who else have you got?"

Ashley ran his finger down the paper he was holding. "Miss Celia and Miss Cynthia Robiceux, who backed up Miss Rivers in her claim that the Captain was innocent."

"And who are familiarly known as Bubble and Squeak." Haldean tapped the ash of his cigarette. "They were at lunch, too. They're great friends of Isabelle's and I've known them for ages. Not," he added with a grin, "that that's any defence against the baser passions, but you know what I mean. Also, everything I said about the French maid, Yvette, not having the strength to do it applies to them as well."

"Alfred Charnock?"

Haldean sat forward. "Now he wasn't at lunch. He borrowed my car and went out. You'll have to see for yourself, Ashley, but I think there's something dodgy about him. He's Aunt Alice's stepbrother and he's milked the relationship for all it's worth. He's been living here scot-free for ages and I'd like to know why. Uncle Philip can't stand him."

"I haven't seen him yet," said Ashley. "I'll bear your comments in mind. Commander Smith-Fennimore. I realize he was Lord Lyvenden's business partner and goodness knows what sort of motive that could throw up, but he's injured." He screwed up his eyes in a frown. "He's right-handed, isn't he? Mind you, he'd need both to do this particular murder."

"It sounds like it," said Haldean. "He's fairly clumsy with his left, too," he added, remembering the box of matches Smith-Fennimore had dropped. He clicked his tongue. "He was late for lunch, but not very. He'd have had to move like greased lightning to murder Lyvenden and clean himself up so he was in a fit state to tackle a lamb cutlet. I can't see it. Who's next?"

"Lady Harriet," said Ashley.

Haldean cocked his head to one side. "Who wasn't tackling cutlets either. She was out. And, as we know, when a husband's killed the first person you think of is his other half and vice versa. And, not to be unduly gossipy, they weren't exactly on Tristan and Isolde terms. She couldn't stand him. Not that you can blame her for that." He ran his thumb round the side of his chin. "Lady Harriet's a strong woman. She's got that wiry sort of nervous energy. I think she'd be strong enough, you know."

"I certainly thought she had a very odd reaction to her husband's death," said Ashley. "She said he had it coming to him."

"She wasn't exactly distraught, then? Mind you, that would be downright hypocritical."

"Hypocritical or not, I still think it was an odd reaction. She refused to say where she was this morning. I didn't like her attitude at all."

"She's a bit hard to take," agreed Haldean. "Mind you, by all accounts, Lord Lyvenden's private life was exotic. Maybe it got to her."

"And then there's Mrs Strachan," continued Ashley.

Haldean grinned. "Mrs Strachan was Lord Lyvenden's private life, as I've told you, or part of it at least. And she was also out for lunch. But honestly, Ashley, you've met her. She's a spineless sort of female, or at least that's how she appears. I can't imagine her sticking a knife into anyone. She might stir arsenic into the tea, perhaps. Having said that, Lord Lyvenden definitely threatened her and she was very frightened."

"A frightened woman can be very dangerous." Ashley frowned. "I'm not at all sure about Mrs Strachan, despite the impression she makes. Her statement was very circumstantial but vague about times." He boxed his notes together. "I don't know, Haldean. It's been useful getting the background to the case and your insights into the house party, and I do take your point about the gloves, but I honestly can't see I'm much further forward." He broke off as a knock sounded on the door.

Constable Bevan entered. "Excuse me, sir, but the photographer's finished and Mr Charnock is waiting for you in the library."

"Well, ask Mr Charnock to come in here."

Bevan coughed. "I did ask him, sir, but he said you could come to him. He was quite rude about it, sir."

Ashley shrugged and rose to his feet. "I'd better go to the library, then. Far be it from me to inconvenience Mr Charnock."

"God forbid," muttered Haldean. "That would never do. I'll leave you to it, Ashley."

"Thanks, Haldean. As for Mr Charnock, I suppose I can talk to him in the library just as easily as I can here. Any news of Captain Stanton yet, Bevan?"

"None, sir," replied Bevan, holding the door open. "I expect he'll be holed up somewhere. Apart from anything else, it's nasty weather to be out."

Ashley collected Sergeant Ingleton and walked into the library. It might have been Haldean's opinion of Charnock that had put him on his guard, but when Ashley saw Alfred Charnock sprawled in an armchair, he felt his hackles rise. The man was darkly handsome with the worn charm of an ageing roué, and, thought Ashley, dangerous.

Charnock flicked the ash off his cigarette on to the carpet. "Ah, Superintendent, do come in. I understand I missed all the excitement."

"If you want to call it that, sir," said Ashley, knowing he sounded at his most wooden. Perhaps that wasn't a bad thing. It never did to underestimate an opponent and Charnock obviously thought himself superior to any mere policeman. Ashley wasn't given to coarse language but the words "cynical bastard" framed themselves in his mind and stayed there. "Can I ask you where you were this afternoon?"

Charnock looked at him from under drooped eyelids. "Oh, Superintendent," he said softly, "I do wish I had something exciting to tell you, but I haven't. I started off in Brighton and then I went to the pub."

Ashley looked at him appraisingly. "Just what are you doing here, sir? Don't you find it dull?"

Charnock yawned. "Deadly." He gave a sudden, attractive smile which lit up his face. The smile took Ashley by surprise. He's got real charm, Ashley reluctantly acknowledged to himself, even though it is a bit shop-worn. "Do you remember the story of my famous namesake who burnt the cakes?" said Alfred Charnock. "Well, I burnt my fingers. I was caught out in the City and have retired to bucolic bliss in the bosom of my family. Tough on the family, but there! Think how happy they'll be when I leave. Philip loathes me and I derive a good deal of innocent amusement from seeing how far I can push him before his veneer of horribly correct good manners cracks."

Ashley's sympathies were strictly with Sir Philip, but his attention was alerted. Lady Harriet had told him Charnock had introduced Lord Lyvenden to Sir Philip, which meant there was a connection between the two men. Lyvenden's reputation, so he knew from both Haldean and Smith-Fennimore, was that of a financial shark. A clever enough shark to have caught Alfred Charnock? He drew a bow at a venture. "Before you answer the next question, sir, I'd like you to bear in mind that these things can be checked. This financial loss of yours. It wouldn't be connected with Lord Lyvenden, would it?" He was pleased to note a flicker of irritation in Charnock's eyes. The arrow had hit home.

"Got it in one, Superintendent. I suppose you now think I have a motive for killing the wretched man. That should make it easier for you to blame me if you fail to catch Captain Stanton."

Ashley reverted to wood. "We've not got to the stage of blaming anyone yet, sir. We're simply collecting information."

"An admirably uninformative reply. What information do you want to collect?"

"I would like to know what you were doing around one to one thirty today, sir."

"Before lunch?" Charnock frowned. "Oh yes, I was in the hall. I talked to my niece and that rather solid young man she's going to marry. Jack Haldean was there as well. We discussed Art, if you can call that ghastly daub of a portrait of Claudia Rivers Art. I suppose people have to have ancestors, but why they want to look at them beats me. Then I borrowed Haldean's car and went on my merry way. Have I said enough for you to arrest me yet?"

"Not really, sir," replied Ashley, stolidly. "I take it it wasn't a local pub you went to."

196

"Wrong, actually." Charnock stubbed out his cigarette and stretched his arms. "The pub's one of my local haunts. It has the great virtue of being the sort of place none of my family would be seen dead in. You can't imagine the relief."

"Who did you see in Brighton?"

Charnock raised an eyebrow. He looked highly amused. "I don't believe I caught the lady's name. Careless of me, but you know how it is." He laughed. "Or perhaps you don't."

"Can you be more specific, sir?" said Ashley without heat.

Charnock laughed once more. "Certainly not. Use your imagination, Superintendent. She was a lively girl, but we didn't have much in the way of conversation." Ashley would have given a good deal to have wiped the smile off Charnock's face, but he sat without speaking, waiting for Charnock to say something else. Charnock, however, was silent.

"What is the name of the pub you went to, sir?" asked Ashley eventually.

"Are you arresting me?" asked Charnock, softly, lighting another cigarette. The Superintendent shook his head. "Then I don't believe I have any obligation to answer your questions. Any other points you wish to bring up?"

"Yes, sir. Who was the Russian who came on the night of the ball?"

"An old friend."

"I think not, sir. He didn't recognize you."

Charnock gave him a swift glance. That rattled him, thought Ashley with satisfaction. "You mean young Haldean says he didn't recognize me," said Charnock, smoothly enough. "His grasp of the situation was not all it might have been."

"Where did you go on the night of the ball, sir?"

"I went out." Charnock rose to his feet. "Where I am going now, rather than waste any more time answering irrelevant questions. I would suggest your time might be better spent in searching for Captain Stanton rather than intruding into my personal affairs. Goodbye, officer. Pleasure to meet you." He wafted out of the room in a cloud of cigarette smoke.

And the devil of it is, thought Ashley wrathfully, that he's probably right. He glared after Charnock's departing back and was rewarded by a sight which made him draw his breath in.

The library led out on to the hall and in the hall stood a massive oak sideboard with a mirror split into three parts. Its purpose was to enable the ladies of the house to check that their hats were on correctly before venturing into the outside world. Ashley could see Charnock reflected in one of the side mirrors.

Charnock leaned against the wall, drew heavily on his cigarette and momentarily put his hand to his forehead in a gesture of relief before walking away.

Standing by the library table, Ashley smiled grimly to himself. If that arrogant devil hadn't insisted on being interviewed in the library but had had the humility, to say nothing of the common courtesy, to come to the

198

gun room like everyone else, he'd have been all right. There wasn't a mirror outside the gun-room door.

He thinks he's got away with it, thought Ashley, his heart lightening. He tried to put one over on me and he thinks he got away with it. He really does have something to hide.

CHAPTER
NINE

Arthur Stanton stared at his hands. They didn't seem like his hands. They were slimy with blood. Lots of blood. Blood from that . . . that *thing* on the rug.

"Back against the wall!"

The voice seemed to come from the end of a long tunnel. He didn't know who said it. It was imperious, commanding. It reminded him of a voice in hospital. His stomach knotted in fear. He thrust his arms out in front of him, fending off that voice, that harsh hospital voice. He instinctively shrank backwards, caught his foot and fell, fell over that *thing* on the rug. He was on his knees beside the *thing*.

He tried hard not to scream. Someone was laughing. Why were they laughing? *He* was laughing. He'd tried not to scream because officers and gentlemen are never frightened and have to set a good example and don't scream, but he'd laughed instead. He had to stop laughing, he knew that. He tried hard to look away from the *thing*. Still on his knees, he saw a cigarette case. It seemed massive, as if it covered the whole floor. He picked it up, watching it shrink back into focus. He blinked. Even the cigarette case was covered in blood. "Look. He wanted a cigarette."

The cigarette case was slimy. He thrust it away, into his pocket. Instinct, that. He covered his face with his hands, trying to catch his breath so he could explain what he'd done, but all he could do was laugh.

"Stop it, Arthur! Stop it!"

And that, too, was a hospital voice. Worse, even. He'd known that voice in hospital.

He had to get control of himself. He managed to stop laughing, took a deep breath and tried to explain. "I know . . ." *I shouldn't have laughed.* "I know . . ." *I really didn't mean to laugh.* "It's not funny." *I know it's not funny. I was trying so hard and it came out wrong.* "It's just that . . ."

And then that other voice came again, stopping him. A hospital voice. He had to get off his knees. He had to get away from that *thing*. Isabelle? Isabelle would understand. Isabelle wouldn't blame him.

He'd never seen her look like that. She was afraid. Afraid of *him*.

They were all afraid of him but that was stupid because they had the gun and they were talking to him in hospital voices and they were going to take him away and lock him up in a hospital and he couldn't let them do that because it would be dark and he would be frightened and officers and gentlemen are never frightened and he had to *get away*.

The window, the french window, was the only way out. *Run, Arthur, run! Cover your face and run!*

The glass splintered and hurt, but he was outside. The gun roared, a terrifying noise. Then he was on the grass, running for the shelter of the shrubbery. The gun cracked out again and a searing pain shot through his head. He lost his footing, falling on to grass, scrambling back up, ignoring the pain in his head, putting one foot in front of another, falling once more. He'd fallen amongst twigs and leaves. Bushes. Lots of bushes. Crawl into the bushes. Crumbled earth under the bushes. Dead leaves. Fallen twigs. Dry, crumbled earth where the rain never fell. He dug his fingers into the earth and pulled himself further in, under the thick shrubs. The leaves whirled and kaleidoscoped before his eyes and he fell forward in a dead faint.

When he awoke it was to the sound of slashing rain. His head throbbed and he wiped his forehead with his hands, before he stopped, horrified. Where had all that blood come from? He frantically rubbed his hands on the earth. He had scratches on his wrists and the backs of his hands, but not nearly enough to account for all this blood. He had blood on his palms and all over his shirt, too. His head sang as he tried to remember.

He mustn't stay here. They would be after him soon. He knew they were after him. He parted the bushes on the side away from the house and tried to run across the lawn to the river. He couldn't run but could only manage a plod, his footsteps squelching into the soggy ground. He missed his footing on the bank and slid down the grassy slope to the bulrushes. It was swampy and the clinging black mud between the reeds came over his knees. It was horribly difficult to walk. The river lay before him, churning with brown, ugly, yellow-tipped water in the whipping rain.

They were after him.

He plunged in, fighting for his footing against the current, the water pulling at his legs like iron hands. Weeds streamed out, blocking his way, and he had to thrust them aside as they tangled round him, drawing him down. The cold bit into him.

He fell rather than climbed on to the far bank, the water still growling past him. He forced his legs up out of the river and lay exhausted on the slippery mud and stones, his breath coming in great gulps.

His head ached and he touched his temple lightly, wincing. More blood. That must have been the gun. He could remember the gun, but why had they fired at him? He frowned, and that hurt too, as the muscles of his forehead tightened. He couldn't remember who *they* were. They were going to do something that he was afraid of. Really, cripplingly, afraid of. The fear was a hard, physical knot in his stomach. He had to get away but for a long time all he could do was lie on the stones and mud, the pebbles so close they filled his entire world, looking at the rain washing the earth over the tiny stones and rivulet away.

They were after him.

He raised himself unsteadily to his feet, lurching forward off the bank to the grass beyond. A clump of trees stood blackly in front of him. Underfoot was grass in clumps, churned up into countless shallow muddy hollows. The tussocks were hard to walk on and he had to thread his way through using the little muddy paths of the hollows. He was near the woods now and the ground was changing. It banked up, a rim of dirty chalk and earth, about two foot high, edging the field. He crawled over the chalky rim and found himself on firm, springy grass.

Hemming in the trees was a barbed wire fence.

For the first time he was aware of an emotion other than fear. Call that a fence? It was useless. There should be barbed wire in rolls, lots of barbed wire, with picket stakes at intervals. What was the wiring party thinking of? They'd get a rocket, an absolute rocket from their sergeant. Come to think of it, why hadn't he been stopped? Where the blazes was everyone? And where the blazes was he?

He'd come over no man's land. He knew that. The earth had been churned by bullets. That's why it was difficult to walk on and now he'd reached the wire. Why weren't there any snipers? Why wasn't there *anybody*? There was something happening here he didn't understand.

The Germans must be behind him; that was obvious. Only the Germans would have fired at him and he knew he'd been shot at. Then he'd run for it . . . Yes, he'd run for it, but where had he run to? Was that pathetic piece of barbed wire ours or theirs? He was puzzled to find he didn't know.

Great columns of beeches arched overhead. No sound of artillery fire. He must be miles away from the lines. Every tree at the front had been blasted and the ground ripped by shells but there was no sign of war here amongst the trees. He could almost believe he'd died and slipped through to another world, but his head was hurting. Dead men couldn't feel pain, could they? Besides, this — wherever *this* was — was real. He walked cautiously forward, listening for any noise, but apart from the wet drip of rain from the branches, the place was utterly silent. The stand of trees came to an abrupt end, hemmed in by another inadequate fence. Below him lay a country lane that looked as if it belonged at home, but he knew he was far away from home. Surely he was in Flanders? He couldn't remember. He stopped and let his breath out in a sigh of relief. There, far in the distance, he'd heard the deep rumble of the guns. Flanders.

He was about to scramble down on to the road when he stopped with a feeling of sick despair. He wasn't wearing his uniform! What on earth had he been doing? Dear God, he thought, with the taste of panic rising in his throat, if they catch me I'll be shot as a spy.

He dropped down on to the road. His feet were heavy and his whole body ached but he had to find his regiment. His men, his company, needed him. The rain slashed into his face but from far away came the comforting growl of the guns.

The last thing he could definitely remember was the order for his company to advance up the Menin Road for the assault on Poelcapelle and then on to Passchendaele Ridge. So where was he? There had been some talk of sending him up to join the Staff. Had that happened? Was he in Intelligence? Surely, even in Intelligence, he'd have his uniform. Yes, of course, a uniform with green tabs. So why wasn't he wearing it?

Was he a spy? He shuddered. He loathed the idea of spying. It was one thing for the French. It was their country and he had nothing but respect for the men who worked undercover on the other side of the lines, but it was quite another thing that he should be one of them. He shook his head and instantly regretted it as his headache flamed. The guns seemed to be getting nearer and he welcomed the sound. He wished, passionately, he was back with his company.

Half blinded by the rain, he could make out a crossroads ahead and slipped into the shallow trench at the side of the road. Heedless of the mud, he crept up to where the road divided. A blue and silver car, with its hood closed, was parked on the other side of the road. It looked like a Staff car. German? It wasn't a British car, that was for sure. Steam was rising from the bonnet. A cart creaked up the road behind him. The carter had draped a sack over his shoulders and head as a makeshift coat.

A man, collar turned up and hat pulled down, got out of the car and hailed the cart. "Hey, driver! Have you seen a man? He's wearing a brown flannel suit and he's got no hat. We're looking for him." His stomach turned over. It was a hospital voice.

They were after him.

He shrank further back into the mud of the trench.

The driver shook his head. "No, sir. Haven't seen a soul. Nasty weather to be out."

The man nodded. "Thanks anyway." He turned back to the car, climbed in and drove off.

He huddled down into the mud of the shallow trench. Why on earth had the men spoken in English? Fantastic thoughts chased round his head. Which side of the lines was he on? He had to be behind German lines, surely, otherwise why would anyone shoot at him? Were the motorist and the carter traitors? There must be some explanation. He rested his forehead against the cold mud of the trench, trying to think, but his headache flared again.

They were after him and one of the men who was after him was in that car. The guns thundered, louder than ever, sending a golden wire of hope through his thoughts. If he could just get back to the lines he could get across somehow, find his company and, if he had done something wrong, take his punishment. Anything was better than not knowing where he was and what he had done.

The cart creaked away, its wheels sending up fountains of spray. He waited until he was sure it had gone, then crawled up to the top of the trench. He had a choice of four roads. He couldn't go the same way as the Staff car and the cart. The road across from him looked little used. There was no sentry posted. There wasn't anyone. Maybe that road would take him away from the enemy, back to his company.

He climbed out of the trench and got across to the road he'd pinned his hopes on. He couldn't understand it. The road turned into little more than a muddy track with grass growing high in the centre but he could swear the guns were getting closer. High hedges flanked him in, cutting off his view of the countryside, but at least the hedges sheltered him from the worst of the weather. The rain gullied down the sides of the lane, turning it into little more than a stream.

The guns were definitely closer now. He'd chosen the right road. Mixed in with the guns was another noise, a low, roaring sound that seemed oddly familiar. The grassy track was coming to an end. Through the rain he could just make out where it ran down to join a proper road, a metalled road. Once on the road he might even see the Lines. He stepped out to the road and, with a shriek and a wail like a thousand lost souls, the wind assaulted him. He staggered back, feeling the wind like a blow to his chest, and gazed in astonishment at the grey, white-flecked sea.

He was on the coast road, flanked by a sea wall. The waves crashed over the top, contemptuous of such puny defences. He crept along the road, stopping many times to hold on to the hedge that bounded the landward side. The way led up, following the contours of the cliff, but still he kept on. The sky grew darker, turning from grey to black, and he huddled into the hedge, awed by the violence of the storm. Then, with a crash that seemed to tear the clouds apart, lightning forked down and hit a post on the summit of the hill. There was a dreadful pause before the guns roared out again and with a ghastly movement the cliff ahead of him collapsed into the sea. Shrinking back, he saw the road rear like an angry horse and in that instant knew that the familiar sound of guns was merely the impersonal noise of thunder; and that he was totally and utterly lost.

Wearily he carried on until he found a gate. A track led into the field beyond. Little dancing sparks flitted across his eyes and he shook his head

208

impatiently. At the top of the field ran another road, picked out by the lights of houses. He half walked, half crawled up the slope towards the lights. Even if they were German, he'd rather be near other people than lost in this cauldron of loneliness and noise. He staggered the last few feet on to the road and found himself across from a large building behind an imposing wall with gateposts. The gateposts had pineapples on the top and for some reason that made him laugh. He was still laughing when he read the brass sign on the wall. Cranston Cottage Hospital.

He sobered instantly, the sick taste of fear filling his mouth. A hospital! *They* were the ones who were hunting him. But . . . but a hospital? He forced himself to think. A real hospital, not a casualty clearing station. Why? And what had he done? Perhaps, just perhaps, if he went back by himself it wouldn't be too bad. Perhaps . . . He opened the gate and walked down the drive to the lighted porch of the house, hardly able to lift his feet.

He had run away from hospital. That must be it. He'd done it once before and they'd caught him. And now he was beaten again. He couldn't run any longer because out here were guns and danger and his head was full of constant, crashing noise. He rang the bell and heard it jangle far away. A nurse was standing in front of him and he tried to raise his hat, but he didn't have one. The nurse's mouth was opening and shutting, talking to him, but he couldn't hear her because the noise had got worse, cutting out all other sound in a swelling roar. "I'm sorry," he managed to say, and fell forward as the lights in his eyes split up and faded to black.

He awoke in a comfortable bed in a brightly lit room. A voice was speaking and he gradually made out the words.

"I think he's coming round now, Doctor."

He blinked and saw a starched-aproned nurse and a blue-suited doctor standing by his bed. The doctor leaned over him and smiled. "Well, young man, what have you been doing to yourself?"

The doctor seemed friendly but Stanton was on his guard. The doctor sounded English enough, but so had the motorist and the carter. He mustn't tell them anything, he knew that, but he was incredibly thirsty. "Water," he managed to say, and the doctor nodded to the nurse who poured a glass of water from a jug at his bedside and held it to his lips.

"Now then," said the doctor. "What happened?"

What on earth had happened? There had been a gun. He didn't want to talk about the gun. They were entitled to his name and rank, but that was all. "An accident," he said slowly.

"I see," said the doctor thoughtfully. "What sort of accident? Can you remember?"

He couldn't, not really, and he wasn't going to mention the gun. He shook his head.

"Very well. Don't worry. It'll probably come back to you later. What's your name?"

He felt on safer ground here. His name was . . . what? He searched his memory but came up against a blank. He hazarded a guess. "Rivers?"

"And your Christian name?"

Again, that awful feeling of blankness. He tried hard and the name Tim came to him from somewhere. Both names carried a tinge of sadness.

"Timothy Rivers. Well, Mr Rivers, we've put a few stitches in your head and I think you'd better rest until the morning."

He couldn't do that. He tried to get out of bed but the doctor stopped him. "Now, Mr Rivers, just stay where you are. Can I have your address? Your family may be worried about you."

"I haven't a family," said Stanton. "Are you keeping me a prisoner?"

The doctor laughed. "Of course not, Mr Rivers. This is a hospital."

Hospital. He'd been caught once more. Very deliberately he raised himself up in bed, then swung his legs out. The floor rose up giddily to meet him and he gripped hard on the bed rail until the room steadied. He felt the doctor's hand on his shoulder and a voice telling him to lie down. Stanton swallowed. "Am I free to go?"

The doctor dropped his hand and looked worried. "Mr Rivers, if you are determined to leave there is nothing I can do to stop you, but I really cannot advise it. You have four stitches in your head and you may be suffering from concussion, if nothing else."

"But you can't stop me."

"No, of course I can't, man," said the doctor with a frown. "But you need rest."

Stanton gripped his arm. "Please let me go. I want to go. I can't stop here."

The doctor shrugged and turned to the nurse. "Can you bring Mr Rivers' clothes please?"

The nurse left the room in stiff disapproval. The doctor turned back to Stanton. "Now look, old man, for your own sake you should spend the night here. You'll feel better in the morning and then you can go wherever you please."

Stanton didn't answer and the doctor sighed. "Very well. It's up to you. Don't say I haven't warned you. Keep those stitches dry and if you have any giddiness or double vision, for heaven's sake see a doctor right away. Have you any idea where you're going?"

Stanton tried to make his voice convincing. "Oh, yes. I've got some friends near by."

"I'm glad to hear it." The doctor sounded unconvinced. "I can only give my medical opinion and that is, you should stay here." Stanton looked at him mulishly and the doctor shrugged once more. "Well, the nurse should be back with your clothes soon. If you change your mind, you're welcome to stay."

He left the room. Stanton sank back on the bed, feeling he had won a significant victory. To his surprise the nurse arrived back promptly with his things. So they really were going to let him go.

"Are you still determined to leave, Mr Rivers?" she asked frostily. Stanton nodded and immediately wished he hadn't. "It is never wise," she said coldly, "to ignore the doctor's advice. Still, that is your choice. When you have finished, I would be grateful if you would come to my office. We need you to sign the book and there is the small matter of your bill. Unless you have an existing arrangement with the hospital there is a fee of ten shillings."

She shook her head censoriously and rustled out of the room, leaving Stanton contemplating the wreck of his clothes. They were dry, that was something, but he had seen scarecrows in smarter rigs. Grimacing, he slowly dressed in his filthy suit, adjusted his tie and walked gingerly to the door.

He found the nurse's office easily enough and signed the book. The nurse was cold and formal, but he didn't care. They were letting him go. She handed him a small cardboard box containing his watch, his notecase, a small silver matchbox and two cigarette cases. One case was of gunmetal grey and seemed familiar enough. The other was of heavy gold and bore a coat of arms picked out in diamonds and rubies. He could have sworn he'd never seen it before. "Are you sure this is mine?" he asked.

"It was in your pocket," snapped the nurse. "Here is your bill." She handed him the bill and Stanton gave her a ten-shilling note. He had a few coins in his pocket, but no other money. Registering disapproval in every line of her starched body, the nurse showed him to the door.

Hardly daring to believe his luck, Stanton stepped outside. He was free. The storm had died down, leaving a thin rack of gusty clouds. To his surprise, there was still some daylight left.

Stanton trudged wearily down the drive. His watch had stopped and he didn't have a clue what the time was. He supposed he'd better find some shelter for the night.

Where was he? It felt like England but how could he be in England? And what had he done wrong that people were hunting for him — shooting at him even? Had he deserted? The thought was so horrific that he stopped walking for a moment before pushing it sternly away. And yet it would explain so much. He could have deserted and got back over to England and . . . and then what? It still didn't make any sense. A church clock started to chime and he half hoped it would call someone out on to the empty village street. No one came. There was just a row of cottages with light glinting through red blinds and wood smoke curling up from their chimneys. In the clearing sky a group of bats began to perform their jerky little dance, like puppets on wires. He longed for his company with a yearning hunger. But where that was and who he was, he had no more idea than if he had fallen from the moon.

The dusk had turned to night when he smelt cooking. He had long since left the village behind and was walking along a lane, black with overhanging trees. A farm track led off the lane and peering into the gloom he could make out the glow of a camp fire and hear the low murmur of voices. The smell was wonderful. Until that moment he'd had no idea how hungry he was. He started towards the fire. Two men were huddled under a tree, cooking something in an open pan. Tramps. They looked up as he approached. Not a friendly look, but the smell of the food drew him on. "Hello," he said, with a hesitant smile. "I don't suppose you could let me have some of that, could you?"

A burly man spat into the fire. "You're right. We can't. Bugger off."

"I can pay for it," said Stanton, feeling the coins in his pocket.

"Oh, you can, can you?" The man got to his feet and looked Stanton's lean form up and down. "I'll be havin' some of that." His fist shot out.

Stanton feinted instinctively, guarded with his right and landed a neat upper-cut on the point of the man's jaw. Although there was little strength behind the blow, the man sprawled backwards.

"Nice hit," said the little man on the far side of the fire. "I can see you've done a bit of boxing in your time." He caught hold of the burly man, who was scrambling to his feet, fists raised. "Cut it out, Spiky. You hit him first." He squinted through the wood smoke towards Stanton. "You talk like a gent. How come you want to eat with us?"

"I'm hungry," said Stanton simply.

The little man started. "I know you!" He got to his feet, pulled a burning stick from the fire and looked at Stanton by the flickering light. "It's me, sir. Corporal Miller." He looked delighted. "I'm Dusty Miller. You remember me, don't you, sir?"

"Miller?" Stanton was puzzled. "Is this your section?"

"All present and correct, sir," said Miller with a laugh. "Not much to look at, are we?"

So this was his company. These were his men.

"Come and sit down, sir," said Miller. "I just wish I had something better to give you. And you," he added to Spiky who was muttering beside him, "can like it or lump it. The Captain's eating with us and no nonsense about paying for it."

Miller spooned some stew out of the pan and put it on a tin plate for Stanton. It tasted delicious. Spiky had his own plate but Miller ate out of the pan.

"I'm sorry to see you've fallen on hard times, sir," said Miller after they'd finished. "We all thought happy times were coming after the Armistice, but you never can tell, can you? Lots of gents came off worse, I know."

Armistice? What was the man talking about? "What Armistice?" asked Stanton, puzzled.

Miller laughed. "The one when the war stopped, of course," he said. "I don't know about any others."

Stanton was desperately tired. The Armistice was too complicated to think about. Perhaps it would all make sense in the morning. He lay down beside the fire and the last thing he knew was Miller putting a coat over him before he drifted away to sleep.

It was a long time before Miller went to sleep. He didn't trust Spiky. Spiky would rob his own grandmother and nobody was going to touch the Captain.

216

The Captain. Miller looked affectionately at the sleeping man. He'd been one of the best officers in the Royal Sussex, and that was saying something, thought Miller, with a surge of loyalty to his old regiment. He pulled an apple out of his pocket and looked at it doubtfully. He'd never really liked apples since the war. The smell reminded him of gas. He stuck the apple on a stick and put it in the fire. They weren't too bad roasted. Gas! He remembered the Captain shouting "Gas!" Very keen on gas drill, the Captain was, and quite right, too. There'd been a lad at Hell's Corner who couldn't manage the straps on his mask. He'd ended up with eyes like ping-pong balls. Dead, of course. Just as well, poor kid.

He rooted in his pockets once more and pulled out a stub of cigarette, lighting it with a twig from the fire. The Captain. He'd always wondered what had happened to the Captain. They'd been given the order to advance on Passchendaele Ridge. It had been miserable weather, nearly as bad as today. But at Passchendaele there was mud, mud and more mud and shell-holes deep enough to drown in. Miller smoked his cigarette thoughtfully, remembering the scene. The machine-gun bullet had hit him in his leg and he'd gone down. That should have been it. On the Somme a bullet in the leg meant a nice Blighty one but at Passchendaele he knew he'd drown before anyone could get to him. He had always hated the thought of drowning. And now he was going to drown in mud. He'd seen enough bodies floating in shell-holes to know what was in store. They all swelled up. Disgusting, it was. He didn't want to drown.

If he'd been with his section he'd have put a brave face on it. That's what an NCO did. Don't let the men down, Corporal Miller. Drilled into you, that was. But there were no men. Just himself, a wounded leg, the rain drenching the sodden ground, and that terrible fear as the mud grew deeper round him hour by hour.

There was no chance of a stretcher-bearer. Fritz had taken nasty and were machine-gunning the Red Cross lads. Bloody Fritz. Bloody war. Bloody mud.

And then the Captain had arrived. Miller wiped the back of his hand across his eyes. It always got to him like this. Remembering what it was like to wait helplessly for that horrible mud to fill his mouth and his lungs and then to hear the Captain's voice always made his eyes smart. He'd learnt the full story afterwards. The Captain had called for volunteers and taken them out himself. Braving the raking machine-gun fire he'd made three trips, bringing in the wounded. Miller would never forget his gratitude at the sight of the Captain's long, determined face as he pulled him out of that mud and on to a stretcher. When they got back to the lines, he could see the Captain had organized fresh men and was going out again. He had to be stopped. Talk about the pitcher going too often to the well . . .

From his stretcher, Miller had grabbed the Captain's hand. "Please sir, don't go. They're all playing harps by now."

218

The Captain had grinned. "Don't be bloody silly, Miller. I heard someone call out. I can't leave him."

And that was that. He hadn't come back, of course.

Miller heard the story in a hospital behind the lines the next day. Fritz arranged a truce at long last to clear the wounded and amongst them was the Captain. Apparently he wasn't right in the head any more. He'd found his injured man, been wounded himself, and spent the entire night in a shell-hole, holding up the injured Tommy so he wouldn't drown. The Tommy was dead by the time they found him but the Captain had to be forced to let him go. He'd got the DSO and a bad dose of shell shock. A night out there would drive anyone barmy. Passchendaele.

Miller threw away his cigarette and ate his roasted apple, looking affectionately at the man beside him. Shell shock. It didn't seem like the poor beggar was right yet, not the way he was talking about the Armistice. The fire was dying down. Spiky was dead to the world. He wouldn't give the Captain any more trouble. Miller lay down and, although he missed his coat, was soon fast asleep.

Stanton awoke in the early morning, feeling stiff and bruised. Drifting in and out of sleep, he lay for a little while, his eyes still closed, hearing the sound of men speaking in low voices. Then the voices went away and the only noises were those of the birds and of someone walking round as if they were trying to be quiet. He sat up, saw Miller, and the events of the previous night came flooding back to him.

"Morning, sir," called Miller cheerfully. "Spiky's gone. There's free bread and soup being given out at Great Syston if you get there before twelve o'clock and he wants some." He was frying something in a pan. "Eggs, sir," he said in answer to Stanton's enquiring look. "The lock on the hen-run up the way isn't all it might be. There's some bread, too. It's only a couple of days old. It'd be wasted on the pigs, that would." He scooped some on a plate and gave it to Stanton. "Tuck in, sir, while it's hot."

Stanton tried a tentative spoonful and found it surprisingly good. "This reminds me of the army," he said between mouthfuls.

Miller laughed. "What I wouldn't give for a cup of army tea right now. By the way, sir, who's Jack? You were saying his name in your sleep."

"Jack?" The name brought mixed feelings but it had an oddly sinister overtone. The memory stayed frustratingly elusive. "I don't know. Miller — you keep calling me 'sir'. Who am I?" Miller looked startled at the question. Stanton smiled and touched the bandage on his head. "I've had a bit of a knock and I can't seem to remember anything. Who am I?"

Miller wiped out the dirty plate with a tuft of grass. "Captain Stanton, sir. I don't recollect your Christian name. You lived in Upper Ranworth, the next village to me."

"That's right." The words were like a candle in the dark. "That's where I live. Upper Ranworth. My house is there. Home." Miller packed his pan and plate into an old knapsack. "Where are you going?"

"I'm off, sir. You get home. You don't want the likes of me tagging along. No, you can't stop me, I'm off." He looked for a moment at the outstretched hand Stanton offered him and blinked. "Please don't thank me, sir. You got me out of that shell-hole. I'll never forget it." He broke into a sudden, delighted grin. "And you hit old Spiky. I've been wanting to do that for a month of Sundays."

Stanton watched him go, then shook himself. He'd better be going too. Home? Apparently home was a place called Upper Ranworth, wherever that was. Maybe they'd be able to tell him what he'd done. But who were *they*? His parents were dead. He did remember that. Other odd flashes of memory came to him as he walked along in the rain-fresh summer morning. Miller had mentioned Jack. Jack? Of course, he'd known a Jack at school. He had a vivid picture of a crowd of cheering boys sitting round a boxing-ring, while a dark, foreign-looking type stood over him. "I say, did I wallop you a bit hard? I didn't mean to go for the KO." Concern in the black eyes, followed by relief as Stanton got up and the odd realization that they were friends. But who was this other Jack? The one who'd done something so terrible that he shrank at the name — where did he fit in? And what was he was running away from?

CHAPTER
TEN

Haldean folded up the last of the newspapers and put them back on the hall table. His uncle always took a good selection of newspapers which were left in the hall for the benefit of anyone who wished to inform or entertain themselves over breakfast. He opened the front door, went down the steps and, with his pipe drawing nicely, strolled down to the knot of men waiting by the gates of Hesperus.

There wasn't, he thought, anyone at Hesperus who would be informed, still less entertained, by that morning's papers. Despite Uncle Philip's urgent wish that it could all be kept quiet, there wasn't the slightest chance that Fleet Street would allow the murder of Lord Lyvenden to go unremarked. Even if Lyvenden had been a mere nobody, the *Sensational Slaughter*, as the *Daily Messenger* put it, would have made the front page. When the headline writer could add, as he gleefully had done, *Of Peer*, Hesperus was well and truly in the news. *Diabolical Crime* thundered *The Times. Appalling Tragedy* said the *Express*, adding that Victor, Lord Lyvenden, had succumbed to *ferocious blows.* The *Morning Post*, catering to a more restrained readership, had contented itself with *Death*

Of Lord Lyvenden but it was a lone voice of sobriety amongst front pages peppered with adjectives such as *Grim, Gruesome* and *Ghastly*. The *Messenger* had something of a scoop in that, in addition to a photograph of Lord Lyvenden, it also had photographs of Stanton and, Haldean was pained to see, of himself.

It hadn't improved Sir Philip's temper when he saw that, in addition to his other worries, Hesperus was under a state of virtual siege by Fleet Street's finest. The fact that his nephew, from whom he had looked for better things, knew a good few of the reporters personally didn't alter his opinion that they were a pack of scurrilous knaves and vagabonds. "Riff-raff" and "Jackals" were the kindest terms he had used.

"Haldean!" called Ernest Stanhope of the *Messenger*, pressing up to the barred gate. "Give us some news, old man. We can't get a thing out of anyone in the house and the lodge-keeper won't let us into the grounds."

Haldean grinned. "He's under orders, I'm afraid. I can't do anything about it. The trouble is, Stanhope, that nobody knows very much to tell you, apart from the bare facts that Lord Lyvenden was murdered yesterday and Stanton's still on the run. Where did you get the photo of Stanton from, by the way?"

"One of our bright lads looked up his address in London and had a word with the porter of the flats where he lives. It cost a few quid, but it was worth it. What did you think of seeing yourself in the news this morning?"

"Not much."

Stanhope laughed. "Pull the other one. It'll probably sell a few more books for you. Have you any idea where Stanton could have got to?"

Haldean shook his head. "I know how he got out of the grounds, but that's all. He ran across the lawn, waded through the river, carried on through the far field where there's usually cows pastured, and then, I imagine, through the woods and on to the Breedenbrook road. I was able to follow his traces some of the way and guessed the rest. Goodness knows where he is now."

"Thanks, Haldean," said Stanhope, scribbling in his notebook. "That's something, anyway."

A shout came from the back of the group, announcing that Superintendent Ashley had arrived. Stanhope abruptly left Haldean and raced to where Ashley was holding court. Ashley, who knew the importance of keeping the Press satisfied, made a brief, polite and uninformative statement before battling his way though to where Haldean was standing by the lodge-keeper's gate ready to let him in.

"Thanks for coming down to meet me," he said as they walked up the drive towards the house. "I got your message about the gates being locked." He jerked a thumb backwards. "I had no idea all this crowd would be here. They're a damn nuisance."

"The poor devils have to earn a living," said Haldean tolerantly. "Uncle Phil's up in arms about them hanging around, but what can he possibly expect? I know quite a few of them through working for *On the Town*. Not that newspaper men and mere monthly

224

magazine types, such as me, have much in common, but Stanhope's all right, for instance, and so's Morgan of the *Sentinel* and some of the others. By the way, if you want to come and go without running the gauntlet all the time, I'll show you the entrance from the Home Farm on to the grounds. They haven't discovered that one yet."

"Let's hope that state of affairs continues," said Ashley with feeling. "Now, what was it you said on the telephone about looking for a key? What key? The key to Lord Lyvenden's room was on his dressing table. Sir Philip's got it now."

"As a matter of fact, it's in the lock of the door," said Haldean. "I asked Uncle Phil for it earlier and he told me to leave it there. The garden suite's one of the very few rooms I can't get into with my room-key. I suppose the lock's better than most of the others because it's a fairly new addition to the house. Anyway, what I was looking for was the key to the french windows." Haldean led the way up the steps and into the hall. "I can't find it. Aunt Alice said it was always left in the lock, but it's not there now. I suppose it could have been swept up by the men who cleared away and boarded up the window yesterday afternoon, but I asked Grafton, the head gardener, who supervised the clearing up, and he was certain no one came across it."

"Is it important?" asked Ashley.

Haldean tapped out his pipe on the heel of his shoe. "It might be. I'm not sure. It just seems odd it's gone missing. By the way, could Aunt Alice have a word with you? She's in the conservatory."

Lady Rivers was standing by the conservatory door, looking out on to the lawn. She turned to them with a tired smile. "Thank you for coming to see me, Mr Ashley. Are those wretched reporters still at the gates, Jack?"

"They are, Aunt Alice. We'll have to think of something to say to them. If Uncle Philip, Ashley and I can work out a proper statement, I'll try and do a deal so that they'll leave us in peace."

Her shoulders relaxed. "If you could do that, Jack, it would be a great help." She sat down and looked helplessly at Ashley. "It was bad enough when Mr Preston shot himself, without having this to cope with as well. Poor Philip really does hate all the fuss." She shook her head briskly. "Still, Mr Ashley, you don't want to hear about our domestic concerns. I wanted to ask if you have had any news of Captain Stanton?"

"Yes, we have, Lady Rivers," said Ashley.

Haldean looked at him sharply. "What? You didn't tell me that."

"I was going to," said Ashley pacifically. "We've had over a dozen sightings of Captain Stanton, most of which I've discounted, but out of all the possibles, I think there's two probables. It seems that the Captain was treated for a head wound in Cranston Cottage Hospital. A man answering his description turned up on the doorstep in the late afternoon. He was in a pretty poor state and needed four stitches for a head wound. The doctor isn't a particular expert on gunshot wounds, but when I asked him if the injury could have been caused by a bullet, he agreed it was possible. I'd have preferred him to have been more definite, but he wouldn't commit himself. After Captain Stanton received treatment, he insisted on paying his bill and leaving and, of course, there was nothing the hospital could do to stop him. Not that they suspected he was a wanted man at that stage, you understand, but the doctor thought he should stay the night for his own sake. He seemed very vague, which is, of course, what you'd expect. He seemed frightened, too, the doctor said."

"Frightened of being caught?" asked Lady Rivers.

Haldean shook his head. "That wouldn't be it. He'd be frightened of the hospital. It goes back to when he was treated for shell shock," he explained in answer to Ashley's enquiring look. "I don't know exactly what happened to him, because he could never bear to tell me, but I don't think the treatment was as sympathetic as it might have been."

"Perhaps," said Ashley, clearly unmoved. "Be that as it may, he got out as soon as he could. He must have known we were after him, Haldean, no matter how vague he appeared. He didn't give his own name, which tells you something, but evidently said the first name that came into his head. He called himself Timothy Rivers."

"He used our name?" said Lady Rivers indignantly.

Haldean moved uneasily. "Look, Aunt Alice, don't be too hard on him. If you think of the state he was in yesterday, it's likely he didn't know what he was doing." He caught her look, realized his plea had fallen on stony ground, and moved on. "What about the other sighting?"

"It was a report from a tramp in Great Syston. Apparently Captain Stanton camped with them overnight on the road between Melling Bridge and Caynor. The man says that Captain Stanton, if it was him, didn't seem quite right in the head, so we're warning people not to approach him."

"Arthur wouldn't be a danger to anyone," said Haldean.

"How on earth can you say that after yesterday?" said Lady Rivers in exasperation. "You're as bad as . . ." She broke off. "Can you give me a few minutes with Jack, Superintendent?"

"Of course, Lady Rivers." Ashley stood up. "I'll wait for you outside, Haldean."

After he had gone, Lady Rivers didn't say anything for some time, but sat looking at her hands entwined tightly together in her lap.

"Aunt Alice?" prompted Haldean. "What is it?"

"What," she said, clearly holding her temper in check with difficulty, "are you playing at, Jack? You evidently still have some affection for this Arthur Stanton and I suppose I can hardly blame you for that. However, don't you realize what effect even a casual remark from you in support of Captain Stanton will have on Isabelle? She is behaving in a disgraceful way to Commander Smith-Fennimore. After becoming engaged to him — an engagement which both I and your Uncle Philip thoroughly approved of — she threw him over in the most public and distressing way. She refuses to speak to him and is acting as if Captain Stanton was the man she had agreed to marry. What's behind it?"

Haldean shifted uneasily. "Well, you know, Aunt Alice, she was fairly keen on old Arthur before Smith-Fennimore turned up. He was goofy about her."

Lady Rivers shuddered. "His feelings are immaterial. As for Isabelle, I hardly know what to say. Despite the fact that she was, apparently, fond of Arthur Stanton, she became formally engaged to another man. And now, now Captain Stanton has clearly gone off his head, committed a brutal crime and thrown us all into chaos, now she decides she prefers *him*?"

"I don't know that she does prefer him," said Haldean helplessly. "I think she's sorry for him, that's all. Smith-Fennimore's been sort of caught up in the machinery. It's a bit tough on him, I must say."

"A bit tough on him?" repeated his aunt in a dazed voice. "Tough? It's appalling for him, Jack. Simply because of some ridiculous feeling of totally unmerited pity, Isabelle is behaving like an idiot. She won't talk to either your uncle or me and I gather she won't talk to Commander Smith-Fennimore either."

"She bit my head off too."

Lady Rivers sighed dangerously. "Jack, go and talk to Isabelle. Find some way, some method, of pointing out the stupidity of what she is doing. I want a reconciliation between her and the Commander and I want it to happen soon. Naturally if, after reflection, she finds she has made a hasty decision and cannot marry Commander Smith-Fennimore, then I will support her. But this childish behaviour has to stop.

Get her to see sense. Get her to speak to the Commander, for heaven's sake. She obviously liked him well enough before. What's made the difference?"

Haldean shrugged. "You've got me there. Look, what if I suggest running down to Brighton or somewhere? If Belle agrees, then we could go out for the evening with Fennimore and Bubble and Squeak. Safety in numbers and all that. I don't know why she won't speak to the man, but maybe if we got away from here it would do her good. Things have been a bit intense, don't you know? Perhaps she needs to step away from it all."

"I wish I could step away from it all," said Lady Rivers bitterly. "Brighton sounds like a very good idea. See if you can get her to agree, Jack, because I honestly cannot tolerate this situation." She stood up. "And now you'd better go and find Mr Ashley. You don't want to keep him waiting longer than necessary."

"Right-ho. By the way," added Haldean, reaching for the door handle, "I know you tried to get in touch with Tim Preston's uncle. Did you have any luck?"

"We got a telegram this morning," said Lady Rivers shortly. "Apparently his uncle, Mr Urqhart, is in India and won't be back for at least six weeks. I've also heard from his sister, a Mrs Carhew, in Scotland. She won't be able to attend the inquest either and, quite frankly, I'm not sorry. Things are complicated enough without having to see to yet more people. The inquest will have to go ahead without any of Mr Preston's family in attendance, but that's not really important." She gave him an exasperated look. "The important thing is to talk some sense into Isabelle."

"Okay, Aunt Alice," promised Haldean. "I'll do my best."

Ashley was waiting for him in the hall. "Is Lady Rivers all right?" he asked as they walked along to the garden suite. "She seemed a bit put out about something."

Haldean grinned. "I think she's a bit put out, to use that incredibly mild expression, that the house has filled up with corpses. Isabelle isn't helping, either. Smith-Fennimore was the dickens of a catch and she used to go all wobbly at the sight of him, but he's in the doghouse at the moment, and no mistake. God knows why."

"No, I can't understand it either," agreed Ashley. "By the way, I spoke to Lady Harriet's maid, Yvette Charbonneau, and Sotherby, Commander Smith-Fennimore's valet. They were both in the servants' hall from twelve o'clock on Tuesday and couldn't tell me anything. I also spoke to Adamson, Lord Lyvenden's man, and he was very helpful."

"In what way?"

"He's been through Lord Lyvenden's room for me. He was also able to tell me what Lord Lyvenden was doing before lunch. Despite it being Adamson's half-day, he was stuck in the room until after one. Apparently Lord Lyvenden was a bit shirty with clock-watchers. If he was getting dressed, he wanted his valet there, half-day or no half-day. Adamson says the Commander brought his master some papers in a large briefcase and they had a discussion in low voices. That,

I may say, chimes in with Commander Smith-Fennimore's own story. It was obviously something confidential. The Commander stayed for about five minutes or so before leaving the papers with Lord Lyvenden. Lord Lyvenden set to work and dismissed Adamson right away, much to his relief. Incidentally, he's got very little strength in his left arm. He got a bullet through it in the war, and it's affected the muscle. So not only can he not have done it, the only result, as far as I can see, is that he's out of a perfectly good situation."

Ashley opened the door to what had been Lord Lyvenden's room and stopped.

Malcolm Smith-Fennimore was sitting at the desk, a stack of files in front of him. He looked up as they came in.

"What are you doing in here, sir?" asked Ashley politely. "I'd prefer this room to be left alone."

Smith-Fennimore stood up. "I'm sorry, Superintendent. I didn't realize. The key was in the lock." He indicated the scattered papers on the desk. "There's a document that Lyvenden signed — at least I hope he signed it — and I can't find it anywhere."

"I would prefer that nothing was touched, sir."

"But it's vital," said Smith-Fennimore wearily, rubbing his hand across his face. "There's a whole raft of business in the Argentine depending on this one document and I can't find it. Please let me look for it, Superintendent. If necessary you can examine it, but I simply have to find it."

"Well, what is it, sir?"

232

Smith-Fennimore hesitated before replying. "It's confidential. I know it sounds hard-hearted," he added, "but I could wish Lyvenden had kept this stuff in better order. It's a single sheet on ordinary foolscap paper in my handwriting and headed *Señor Ignacio Fauró: Argentine Railways* and, quite frankly, it could be anywhere."

"And what's it about, sir?" asked Ashley, picking up some of the cardboard files.

Smith-Fennimore lit a cigarette. "It's about the bank not checking properly before we lend money. I could be ruined if this gets out."

"That sounds serious," said Haldean.

Smith-Fennimore grimaced. "I mean it. Oh, I'd pull it back somehow, but it would be damned hard. I've got enough to cope with without saving Smith, Wilson and Fennimore from going under. You know how things are in the City. One hint that we're not rock-solid and the gossip gets going, share prices tumble and the speculators move in."

"That sounds really serious," said Haldean. "Er . . . what's the problem?"

Smith-Fennimore pulled on his cigarette nervously, and came to a decision. "Not a word," he warned. "Last year we joined forces with this Ignacio Fauró. He imports rolling stock for the railways from Britain. Railways in the Argentine are booming and it seemed a solid proposition. However, I then found out, through our agents in Buenos Aires and Bahia Blanca, that Fauró has a string of other businesses and they're all rotten. There's an amber mine, some building projects and an electricity company. They're all broke. The profits on the railway fell off and my suspicion — well founded as it turned out — was that our man was using our railway money to prop up his ailing interests."

Smith-Fennimore put his hands on the desk, leaning on his arms. "You see the problem? We had a gentlemen's agreement which would be considered a Joint Venture. If the railway failed, then we would not only be liable for the railway's debts, but lose the money lent, so to speak, to his other concerns. We'd invested so much I didn't want to pull out. That way we'd lose the whole amount. I've been thinking about this all week. It was when we were playing golf, Haldean, that the solution came to me. If it wasn't for everything else which has happened, with Tim and so on, I'd have worked it out before. If we put the railway into a Joint Stock Company, we'd limit our liabilities to that company alone. We'd hold fifty-one per cent of the shares, thereby turning the money Fauró borrowed, so to speak, into our shares. Fauró couldn't refuse. We knew too much and I was going to make sure one of our agents acted as the manager to keep tabs on him. That's what I had to discuss with Lord Lyvenden. I needed his signed consent before I could go ahead with getting a final agreement drawn up and it's that signed consent I've been looking for. It has to be kept secret, though. If it ever got out that such a major investment had been so badly mishandled, it would really put the cat amongst the pigeons."

Haldean whistled. "I can see why you want it kept shtoom. But what happens now Lyvenden's dead?"

"To be quite honest, I don't know. I don't want to seem callous, but I'm hoping that Lyvenden signed my proposal before he died, otherwise I'll have to go to old Wilson." He shook his head. "He's about ninety and uses an ear-trumpet. He's only still on the board because my two nephews bought it in the war. I'm the only one of the younger generation left. That's why I needed Lyvenden in the first place. It'll take Wilson weeks to appreciate what I'm talking about and we haven't got the time." He looked at Haldean. "The bank's going to be fine if we can keep it quiet, but there's going to be so much work involved if Lyvenden didn't sign that document." He looked at Ashley. "You see why I need it, Superintendent."

"I do, sir. I don't want to harm your business interests. Shall we help you look?"

Smith-Fennimore stood up straight. "Thanks. It could be anywhere. Lyvenden was hopelessly disorganized."

The three men hunted through the stack of files. "By the way, Fennimore," said Haldean, "I don't suppose you've come across anything that could be these coded papers Tim talked about?"

Smith-Fennimore shook his head. "No, I haven't, but I'd like to know what it was all about, I must say. If they were that sensitive perhaps Lyvenden took them with him when he went up to London on Monday."

Haldean clicked his tongue. "D'you know, I bet he did. Damn. I was hoping to find them. Any sign of your Argentine paper yet?"

"No." They searched for a few more minutes in silence, then Smith-Fennimore gave a sigh of relief. "I've found it. Thank goodness for that."

Haldean looked at the single sheet of paper Smith-Fennimore was holding. It was covered with small, neat writing and at the bottom was written *Agreed*, with Lord Lyvenden's flamboyant signature followed by yesterday's date.

"Thank God he's signed it," said Smith-Fennimore. He sat down and lit another cigarette. "That's one problem out of the way, at all events. Haldean, have you talked to Isabelle?"

"Not yet, but I intend to. I think she needs to get away from here. I did wonder if we ran down to Brighton or somewhere tonight — you, me, Isabelle and Bubble and Squeak — she might see sense. We can all go in my car."

Smith-Fennimore thought for a moment. "If she'll agree, then it's a good idea. I'd like the drive, if nothing else." He looked round the room and shuddered. "It's hard to believe it's only yesterday it all happened. Have you heard anything of Stanton?"

Haldean glanced towards Ashley and received an almost imperceptible nod in reply. "He's been seen twice. Once in Cranston and once between Melling Bridge and Caynor. It's not that far from where he used to live."

"Well, I hope you catch him soon." He looked round the room once more, this time with a thoughtful frown. "Why do you want this room left alone? I mean, we all know what happened."

"It's just procedure, sir," replied Ashley. "We have to make sure we're not overlooking any clues."

Smith-Fennimore half smiled. "It looks a mess to me, with the windows boarded up. I suppose Sir Philip will be able to get those reglazed, will he?"

"As soon as possible, sir. We don't want to cause any more disruption than necessary."

Smith-Fennimore smiled again. "Yes, there's been enough disruption to keep us all going for quite some time. What clues can there be, though? In the stories I read the murderer always seems to leave a glove or a handkerchief which gives the whole show away. I've never really followed that. I mean, look at all the things in here. How could you possibly say if the murderer dropped anything?"

Haldean glanced at Ashley. "Was there anything here that shouldn't have been?"

Ashley shook his head. "I had Adamson, Lord Lyvenden's valet, go through the room. He didn't touch the papers, of course, but everything else belonged either to the house or to his master." Ashley paused. "There was something missing, though. I was going to ask round about it. Adamson can't find Lord Lyvenden's cigarette case. It was a gold one, apparently, with jewels on it."

"His cigarette case?" repeated Smith-Fennimore. "I didn't know that was missing. It's pretty valuable, I would have thought."

Haldean grinned. "It's pretty horrible, I would have thought. I wouldn't be seen dead in a ditch with it. No, you won't find that in here. Arthur ran off with it."

"Did he?" asked Smith-Fennimore in surprise. "Are you sure? I didn't see that."

Haldean nodded. "It was when you were hovering over him with the gun. He walked backwards, stumbled, picked it up, waved it round a bit, then shoved it in his pocket."

"That's worth knowing," said Ashley. "Thanks, Haldean." He looked towards Smith-Fennimore. "I don't want to hurry you, sir, but I really must ask you to leave. And now," he said, when Smith-Fennimore had gone, "let's have a look for that key to the french windows, shall we?"

They didn't find it.

It was later that morning when Haldean ran Isabelle to earth in the summerhouse.

She looked at him defensively. "Has my mother sent you?"

He sat down beside her. "In a manner of speaking, yes. She's worried about you. I'm worried about you, if you must know. You seemed to react so . . . well, so oddly."

Isabelle sat upright, a spot of colour flaring in her cheeks. "I like that. This is Arthur we're talking about — Arthur! You're supposed to be his best friend. You must know he's innocent. All you have to do is get at the truth and everything'll be all right. You can do it, Jack, you know you can."

Haldean took out his pipe and penknife and cleaned the bowl out thoughtfully. "Why've you suddenly

238

decided to loathe Smith-Fennimore? You must have a reason."

Isabelle drew her knees up on to the seat and clasped her arms round them. "He shot Arthur." She stared straight ahead, avoiding his eyes.

It was as if she was closing herself off, thought Haldean. "Look at me, Isabelle," he said gently, taking her hand. "Fennimore says he was trying to stop him."

She shuddered. "He wasn't. I know he wasn't. I saw Malcolm's face, Jack. It frightened me. Really frightened me, I mean." She paused. "Look, I know you think I'm being rotten to Malcolm, but I'd swear he was trying to kill Arthur. Once I'd seen that look on his face, I was scared to be near him."

Haldean sat back with his arms folded. "Don't you think you might be mistaken?" he said eventually, taking out his tobacco pouch. "After all, we were all pretty wound up and Fennimore's hand must have been giving him hell. It's easy to mistake an expression, particularly when we were as tense as we were yesterday. Fennimore really does care for you, you know. We're going to run down to Brighton for the evening with Bubble and Squeak. If you come with us, you don't have to be alone with him but I think you could be civil and hear his side of it. He's wretched about all of this."

She looked at him with worried eyes. "Let me think about it. Jack, I've been wrong about lots of things, but I'm not wrong about Arthur, I know I'm not. I mean, look how he was with Tim. You told me how he gave Tim all that money. He's a good man, Jack."

Haldean didn't contradict her. He liked Arthur tremendously and had done for years. And Isabelle was right; Arthur was a good man. But . . . there was always a but. Granted that Arthur had knifed Lyvenden, it was because of what Lyvenden had done to his family. Was Arthur capable of nursing such resentment? *He resents you*, said a voice at the back of his mind.

For the first time ever, he faced the matter squarely. He knew perfectly well that Arthur blamed him for taking him back to hospital after that incident in the Euston Road. It had been then their paths had diverged. When they'd had their flare-up on Sunday afternoon he'd known it was lurking beneath the surface. But what else could he have done? A car had backfired, Arthur had crumpled and the poor devil had been ill for months afterwards.

They'd papered over the cracks but they'd never talked about it. It wasn't something that could be talked about, but it had been there for years, an unspoken barrier between them. And it was so damned unfair. He'd devoted a whole precious Short Leave to meeting Arthur. It wasn't his fault that it had all turned out so very badly.

He shook himself. Arthur associated him with one of the ghastliest times in his life. That was all there was to it. The poor devil couldn't help himself. Having said that, it still rankled.

And there was another thing. Although Isabelle hadn't doubted it, they only had Arthur's word for it that he had given Tim the money. That's rubbish, he told himself sternly. If Arthur said he'd shelled out, he had. You couldn't analyse what a friend said as if it was evidence in a court of law where nothing could be believed unless it was backed up by a witness. Good God, what a state of affairs that would be. Arthur told the truth. It was as simple as that. If he said he helped Tim, he helped Tim. *Tim . . .*

"I wouldn't mind talking about Tim," he said, putting a match to his pipe. "Ashley listened to me, but it's Lyvenden's murder he's concentrating on. I don't think he's convinced Tim was murdered, you know."

"Well, you can't blame Arthur for Tim's death," said Isabelle.

"No, although he did keep insisting that Tim committed suicide. He had the opportunity, I think, but he discovered the empty Goldflake packet."

Isabelle wriggled. "I hate talking about people we know as if they're specimens in an experiment," she said crossly.

Haldean grinned. "Play along, old thing. If we can't do it like they do it in detective stories, I wouldn't know where to start."

"If you were writing this, who would be guilty?"

"That's easy," said Haldean. He broke off impatiently. "Look, old prune, stop twitching. Why don't you stop wriggling, put your ankles on my knees and get comfortable?" Isabelle grinned and swung herself round. "That's better," said Haldean. "If I was writing this I'd be the mysterious villain."

Isabelle giggled. "Don't." She reached out. "Give me a cigarette, Jack. Now — you'd just decided Arthur didn't kill Tim." She leaned forward as he struck a match. "And, to be fair to him, Malcolm didn't either. He thought the world of Tim. He wasn't putting that on. Besides that, he was in the ballroom all the evening. If he wasn't talking to Dad he was with me."

"I can't see Bubble or Squeak in the role of First Murderer, either. As it happens, I'm not guilty, so that leaves, apart from Uncle Philip and Aunt Alice, whom I refuse to consider, your Uncle Alfred, Mrs Strachan and Lady Harriet."

"What about the Russian who was here on Sunday? He could have murdered Tim by mistake on Saturday night."

Haldean raised an eyebrow at her. "How d'you mean?"

Isabelle frowned. "He sounded, from what I heard, a murderous sort. He clearly had something going on with Lord Lyvenden. What if his visit on Sunday wasn't his first? He could have sneaked in on Saturday night and up to Lyvenden's room. When Tim came in, he mistook him for Lyvenden and shot him."

"I think we're back to Arthur and his ideas about chaps popping down the chimney," said Haldean drily. He held up placatory hands. "All right. I'll grant you it's just about within the bounds of possibility that the Russian saw Tim off on Saturday, but how would he have been able to get to Lord Lyvenden yesterday? He certainly didn't come through the front door and the side door's out as well. We were all milling around in the hall before lunch and someone would have seen him. I can't think that Lyvenden would have opened the french windows for him. He'd have been scared stiff."

"I don't know, Jack. The Russian may have threatened him with a gun through the window, or he could have broken in beforehand and lain in wait."

"True, O Moon of my Delight. And since Arthur's bust the window, we can't have a dekko to see if the lock's been tinkered with. I wish we could find the key to those ruddy windows."

"Let's say that the Russian had come back," said Isabelle thoughtfully. "He'd be quarrelling with Lyvenden and Arthur walked in on them. The Russian snatches up the knife that Arthur's holding, stabs Lyvenden and then gets out of the window. Poor Arthur would be so horrified he couldn't do anything."

"Maybe," said Haldean doubtfully. "I can't say I really believe it, but maybe. That Russian bothers me, though. There's no doubt Lyvenden was scared stiff of him. I've asked Ashley to check the local telephone exchange. If the Russian was part of a gang of the sort so beloved by the newspapers, then he might have rung up for instructions. I'm not sure he's our man, though. He struck me as the melodramatic type who'd want to write *Death To All Imperialists!* on the wall in blood after doing the deed. There was enough blood in that room to have written a novel."

Isabelle clicked her tongue. "It's difficult, isn't it? What about Lady Harriet? I can't see why she'd kill Tim but she might have a reason. After all, Tim was part of the household and he could have known all sorts of things about her. I certainly think she could have killed Lord Lyvenden. I think she hated him and she could have slipped out of the ball on Saturday night. Where does she say she was yesterday morning?"

"That's just it," said Haldean in frustration. "She won't say, and while the police are convinced that Arthur's the criminal, they aren't pressing her. She might just be being obstinate, or she might be up to something. After all, if she refuses to talk, she can't be proved wrong. I'll tell you something funny about her, though. Do you remember when that Russian chap on Sunday said that it was worth his while coming, because he'd learnt something? God knows what he meant, but he was gazing at the stairs where she was standing when he said it."

"But what on earth could he know about her?" Isabelle frowned impatiently. "Never mind. You mentioned Mrs Strachan but I can't see her stabbing Lord Lyvenden. What about poor Uncle Alfred?"

"Your poor Uncle Alfred has some explaining to do," said Haldean, rather grimly. "He went out with that weird Russian on Saturday night and he was out yesterday just before lunch. And, although he's here because he's meant to be broke, he was throwing money about at the Derby and at a very exclusive and highly expensive card club called the Ultima Thule. What d'you think of that?"

"Not much. He might have had a lucky streak at Epsom. That could happen to anyone. I don't know about the card club, but the same could apply, I suppose. And as for Saturday night, if he was supposed

244

to be out all evening, why should he bother to plant a squib?"

"He might have wanted to cover his exit in case anyone saw him leave Lyvenden's room." He broke off disconsolately. All their reasoning was so much hot air. Not only did Arthur have the knife, if he had merely witnessed the murder or simply discovered the body why hadn't he gone for help? Haldean had written a few locked room mysteries in his time but he'd never done an unlocked room story, and neither, as far as he knew, had anyone else. The blasted door was unlocked. He couldn't get away from it.

Isabelle put her hand on his arm. "Don't worry, Jack. To be honest I can't understand it either but Arthur's bound to turn up again. When he does we'll know exactly what happened."

And, thought Haldean, in the interests of family relations he'd leave it there.

Out of Stanmore Parry proper, on the lane down to the beach, the village straggled to an end in a row of run-down fishermen's cottages and a pub with dirty windows, flaking paint and a sign which was so faded Ashley could hardly make it out.

"It's called the Pig and Whistle, sir," said Sergeant Ingleton quietly.

It had been Sergeant Ingleton who had alerted Ashley to the fact that Alfred Charnock had, without drawing any attention to the fact, left Hesperus. On the grounds that anything Alfred Charnock did was suspicious, Superintendent Ashley and Sergeant Ingleton had followed him across the park, through the Home Farm and now to this seedy pub. Charnock had admitted, Ashley remembered, going to a pub yesterday.

"It's got a bad reputation," continued Ingleton. "It's owned by a man called Burrows. He's a rough customer, all right. He's been behind bars a couple of times for assault. I'd like to see this place closed down. We've done him a few times for after-hours drinking, gambling and so on. We think he receives stolen goods, but we've never been able to pin it on him. It's a rum place for a gentleman like Mr Charnock to come, I must say. I'd have thought if he wanted a drink he'd go to the Wheatsheaf. Nice, respectable place, that is."

"I don't think he's here because he's thirsty, man," said Ashley. "I don't suppose he can get out the back, can he? You're the one with the local knowledge."

"No, sir. The back leads round on to this lane. We'd see him. Why don't we just go in the pub, sir, if you want to see what he's doing?"

Ashley shook his head. "No. I don't want to let him know we're here."

They stood patiently in the shelter of the trees across the road from the Pig and Whistle for nearly half an hour. Ashley was beginning to think he was wasting his time, when he felt a firm tap between his shoulder blades.

He spun round and found himself looking into the cynically smiling face of Alfred Charnock.

"Hello," said Charnock in a well-bred drawl. "Looking for me?"

246

"How did you get here?" said Sergeant Ingleton with an indignant gasp.

"I'm good at that sort of thing," said Charnock. "I could give you a few tips. You might find them useful. Are you out for a stroll or are you keeping tabs on me?"

"Just a matter of routine, sir," said Ashley, falling back on the well-tried formula.

Charnock's eyebrows rose. "Is it a matter of routine to check on my visits to the pub? You'll never catch your murderer that way."

"We have our own method of doing things, sir," replied Ashley, woodenly. "We usually find it works in the end. May I ask what you were doing in there, sir?"

"Having a drink, of course. What else? Now do excuse me." Charnock repressed a yawn with a slim but powerful hand. "It's been too charming speaking to you, but I must dash."

"Are you going back to Hesperus now, sir?"

"To Hesperus?" Charnock looked highly amused. "To the bosom of my loving family? I can't face them for at least another hour. I have a hip-flask with me which I intend to take to the beach. You're about to ask me why, aren't you? To reflect, to think. Why don't you try it? You might find your work improved if you lavished some thought on it." With a little bow, Charnock walked away, leaving Ashley fuming in the road.

"Whew," breathed Sergeant Ingleton. "He's a cool one and no mistake. Nasty, sneering manner he has with him, too. I hate people like that. You know they're doing you down but you can't catch them at it. It's not what he says so much as his manner, isn't it, sir?"

"He's up to something, Ingleton. I want to know what it is. It's something to do with that pub. For all his talk, he made a mistake when he led us here."

"It's not an offence to go for a drink, sir. You can't stop him doing that."

Ashley clenched his fists in frustration. "He's not just having a drink. I want a man in there, watching the place."

Ingleton shook his head. "We can't do that, sir, not without Burrows knowing all about it. They've got their own regulars and a stranger would stand out like a sore thumb. Besides that, Burrows can spot a policeman a mile off. I told you he'd done time. He knows what's what."

"In that case," said Ashley tightly, "I want a round-the-clock watch kept on that pub and I don't want our men to be seen."

"But we can't do that, sir," protested Ingleton. "We haven't got the men. We're stretched as it is, looking for Captain Stanton."

"Then we'll have to be stretched a bit further," snapped Ashley. "I'm going to nail that sarcastic swine's hide if it's the last thing I do."

CHAPTER
ELEVEN

Haldean geared down as he took the Spyker round the corner, stretching his arms and straightening his back as a length of straight road opened up in front of him. He could do with getting to bed. Despite the rush of the cool night air and the growl of the engine, he felt very tired. Smith-Fennimore in the passenger seat beside him seemed to be half asleep and he was sure that the girls in the back had dozed off.

Brighton had been a very qualified success. So qualified, Haldean thought, that as an evening of entertainment it could be described as, variously, a flop, a frost, and a complete damp squib. They had gone to the Grand Hotel where there were soft lights, champagne, good music and dancing. In amongst the groups of cheerful pleasure-seekers the Hesperus party must have looked as if they'd set off to go to a funeral and taken the wrong turning.

Smith-Fennimore had tried to conceal his wounded feelings but couldn't quite manage it. Every so often he'd attempt to start a conversation, Isabelle would answer with stiff politeness, and then the silence would close over them once more. He'd been edgy and unusually ill at ease in Isabelle's company, lost so much in his own thoughts that he often didn't hear what was said to him, staring at Isabelle with a hungry intensity. Then, as if unable to stand it any longer, he would leave the table for unexplained and lengthening absences.

Isabelle, for her part, spent most of the evening gazing past him, avoiding that intense stare. Every so often she'd make an effort and talk to Bubble and Squeak, but then she, too, would relapse into her own thoughts. Bubble and Squeak were, thank goodness, Bubble and Squeak, but even they couldn't make much headway against Smith-Fennimore's and Isabelle's impenetrable gloom and ended up spending most of the evening with Bunny, Lance and Sue Cotterell and their friends whom they'd chanced upon a few tables away.

Haldean, who liked the Cotterells, wished he could join them but he'd promised Isabelle he wouldn't leave her alone with Smith-Fennimore.

"For heaven's sake, Belle," he said as they foxtrotted round the dance floor, "will you cheer up a bit? We're all sitting there as if we'd been translated from a Russian tragedy. Much more of this and I'll go and hang myself in the Old Barn."

She'd smiled thinly. "I can't do much if all he does is stare at me, can I?"

Haldean was frankly relieved when it was time to go.

They hadn't far to go now. They turned off the main Brighton road, drove through the sleeping Stanmore Parry, out of the village and up the deserted road to Hesperus.

Haldean braked as he approached the gates, then accelerated as he saw they had been left open. Although the newspaper men had now gone, bought off by statements from Ashley, Sir Philip and Haldean and a promise that they would be kept in touch, the gates should have been closed. Haldean idly registered the fact as unusual. It was the first note of warning.

Gravel crunched under the tyres and all the leaves of the bushes and trees were picked out in black-edged relief in the passing gleam of the headlights. Haldean, his mind on his bed, saw the tangled branches just in time. He slammed on the brakes and slewed the car to a juddering halt. It was the second note.

Smith-Fennimore sat up and rubbed his eyes. "What's the matter?"

"There's a tree across the drive," said Haldean. "We nearly ran into it. Let's have a look, Fennimore. We may need some help to shift it."

They climbed out of the car. It wasn't really a tree that had stopped them. Some branches had broken off in yesterday's storm and the gardeners had piled them neatly to one side of the drive. Now the orderly stack had been roughly scattered across the road as if by a mischievous giant hand.

Smith-Fennimore whistled. "I'm glad you saw that little lot in time. It would have made a nasty mess of the car. Who on earth could have put all that stuff there?"

Haldean slipped off his hat and ran a hand through his hair. "I don't know. It's a rotten sort of trick." He yawned and glanced at Smith-Fennimore. "It's too late to do anything about it now. Let's get the girls and walk up to the house. I could drive the car over the lawn but I don't think Uncle Phil would be very happy. I'll put the hood up and leave it here overnight."

They strolled back to the Spyker and ... it happened.

An engine roared into life, headlights blazed out, and a car raced across the grass straight for them. Haldean leapt to one side, flinging up his arm to shield his eyes. The car jerked to a halt, missing him by inches. Figures bundled out, his shoulders were seized by strong hands and a blinding torch was shone in his face.

There was a confusion of sounds: a woman screaming, an engine revving, Smith-Fennimore shouting and, mixed in with it all, a sound as if someone was banging a stick along a line of iron railings very loudly and very quickly, a sound which Haldean incredulously identified as machine-gun fire.

He struck out, driving his fist into the dark face behind the light, and was rewarded with a sharp yelp. He was flung to the ground and writhed to one side as bullets tore into the ground beside him, sending up a spray of earth. He raised his head and saw Smith-Fennimore being seized by two black shapes, outlined in the glare of the headlights. A third man stood near them holding a machine gun and a fourth stood with his foot negligently on the front suspension, a machine gun slung across his knee. Haldean half rose, staggering to his feet as Isabelle ran past him towards Smith-Fennimore. The man by the car levelled the gun at her. Haldean leapt forward and forced her to the

252

ground as bullets spat overhead, covering her with his body.

Smith-Fennimore fought like a man possessed. "Isabelle!" he screamed, then crumpled across the car bonnet as the gun butt smashed into the side of his head.

Isabelle threw off Haldean and the gun fired again. She heard Haldean yell out, then he jerked convulsively and lay silently beside her, eyes closed and arms flung wide.

Smith-Fennimore's limp body was flung into the back of the car, tyres squealed, and the car raced off down the drive, swerving wildly to avoid the Spyker. The night and silence closed in on them once more.

Isabelle was on her knees beside Haldean as Bubble and Squeak ran up. "I think they've killed him," she said in a voice which didn't work properly. "I don't know what to do." She shook him helplessly. "Jack, please don't die. Jack, don't die."

"Let me see him," said Squeak Robiceux quickly, and knelt down beside him, taking his wrist in her hands.

"Is he dead?" gulped Isabelle. "Bubble, go and get the lodge-keeper. Please. We need some help. Is he dead?"

Squeak had undone the stiff cuff and found the pulse with relief. "No, thank God. He needs a doctor, quickly. I'll stay with him. Isabelle, run and get your father. We'll need someone to go for the doctor and we have to tell the police. They may be able to stop the car and rescue Malcolm."

Isabelle ran. Painfully hampered by her evening shoes, she tore them off and, heart racing, she saw lights flare as she panted up to the house. The front door was flung open by her father, flanked by two menservants, who had been awakened by the noise. Sir Philip listened to her story and promptly barked out a set of instructions to the men: fetch the car, telephone the doctor, telephone the police. Then he ran down the drive, Isabelle following.

Haldean still lay unmoving on the grass, Squeak Robiceux kneeling beside him. It seemed to be hours before she saw the headlights of a car come down the drive from the house but she knew it was minutes at most. Sykes, the chauffeur, still dressed in his dressing gown and pyjamas, was driving the Rolls. Sir Philip quickly took command.

"Lift him gently. You'll have to carry him round these branches. Lie him down on the back seat. Gently with him, there." He turned to the chauffeur, pointing to the Spyker. "Take that car and go and get the doctor. We need him here as fast as possible." He swung himself into the driver's seat of the Rolls and revved the engine.

Isabelle scrambled into the back, cradling Haldean's head on her knee. He was horribly pale and there was blood on his coat. "Jack," she breathed. "Jack, please live. I don't want you to die, Jack."

To her unspeakable relief, his eyelids flickered open. "That's nice," he said in a nearly inaudible voice, then fainted again as the car moved forward. He groaned as they got him out of the car and carried him up the front steps. His eyes opened briefly and he looked for her.

254

"Don't worry, Belle," he whispered. "I'll be all right. Fennimore. They got Fennimore . . ." His head sank forward again and he was carried away.

"That," said Dr Speldhurst, accepting the whisky and soda Sir Philip offered him, "is a very lucky young man. He's got a bullet through the fleshy part of his arm and a nasty crack on the back of the head. I've strapped him up and I'll be round to see him again tomorrow." He sipped his whisky. "What on earth's going on, Sir Philip? There's been a suicide, a murder and now this. It sounds like something out of the pictures. Your daughter tells me she thinks the men were Russians. She couldn't understand what they were saying."

Sir Philip looked haggard. "I keep thinking about Isabelle. If they had got to her . . ." He broke off and shuddered. "She tells me that Smith-Fennimore fought like a demon to stop them. It sounds as if Jack saved her from being shot. Are you sure he'll be all right, Speldhurst? Alice and I are damned fond of the boy."

"He'll live," said the doctor, finishing his whisky. "Lady Rivers is with him now and I've given him an injection which should keep him quiet. I've given your daughter and the two other girls a sleeping draught and made sure they took it, too. I've done the same for the lodge-keeper and his wife. They're suffering from shock."

"I bet they are," said Sir Philip grimly. They had found out what had happened at the lodge when Bubble Robiceux arrived at the house. She'd gone to the lodge-keeper's cottage for help and found both

Berwick, the lodge-keeper, and his wife tied up. Apparently they'd gone to bed to be woken up to find four armed men looking at them.

"I've told the police they mustn't ask them any questions tonight," said Dr Speldhurst. "The pair of them were in a real state. From what they told me, I don't think they'll be able to say anything very helpful, anyway." He picked up his bag. "If your chauffeur can run me home, I'll be off now but I'll call first thing. Let's just hope that the police have managed to find Commander Smith-Fennimore by then. I hate to think of anyone being at the mercy of those swine."

In the morning, however, there was still no news of Smith-Fennimore. It was the first question Haldean asked Ashley when he called. He was having a very late breakfast of tea and toast in the morning room with Squeak Robiceux. "Poor devil," said Haldean. "Smith-Fennimore, I mean. I hoped you'd have found him by now, or got on his trail at least. He went down like a log when that bloke bashed him on the head with the gun butt. Sit down, Ashley. There's coffee in the pot, or tea if you'd prefer. Would you like anything to eat?"

Ashley shook his head. "No, I've had breakfast, thank you, but I'll have some coffee." Squeak Robiceux poured a cup and handed it to him. "Thank you, miss. I expected you to be in bed, Haldean. How are you managing with that arm?"

Haldean shrugged, wincing as the movement caught him. "It's not too bad. I've seen the doctor and he was pleased with how it was getting on. I can move my arm

256

and fingers, but it's a bit stiff. Uncle Phil lent me his valet this morning so I could get dressed and have a shave and so on, and that made me feel a bit more like it. It'll be a while before I can do any more boxing though," he added with a rueful smile. "Did you hear I managed to thump the character who'd grabbed hold of me?"

"Yes, I did," said Ashley, stirring sugar into his coffee. "All I can say is that I hope you hurt the beggar." Haldean looked, thought Ashley, a great deal better than he expected anyone to look who'd had a bullet through them only hours previously. His left arm was in a sling, his face was pale and tired, but his eyes were as bright as ever.

"Did you get anything useful out of the lodge-keeper?" asked Haldean, finishing his toast.

Ashley shook his head. "Nothing to speak of. There were four men, all wearing scarves pulled over their faces. He thinks two of the men had beards, and his wife says that the one who tied her up had frightening eyes, which isn't much to go on. The only information of much use is that there was at least one Englishman with the Russians, if that's what they were. He was a short, red-headed man and the lodge-keeper had the impression he was in charge. Can you add anything to that?"

Haldean frowned. "I'm sorry, I can't. I didn't even know one of the men was English. I think one had an ear-ring, but that's about all I can tell you. They had a biggish sort of car, a Wolseley, I think. I didn't get the number, I'm afraid. Did you see anything, Squeak?"

"I didn't, Jack. I couldn't have even guessed it was a Wolseley. I'd been half asleep in the back of the car and then it all happened so quickly I could scarcely take it in."

"That's understandable in the circumstances," said Ashley. "What about the guns they were carrying?"

Haldean picked up his teacup, trying to visualize the scene once more. "I think they must have been Bergman MP 18s. That's my guess, anyway, from what I remember from the war. They were rotten shots, all of them. I can't imagine they'd had any training. They had no idea of keeping the barrel deflected while they fired, which is the first thing any machine-gun instructor teaches you. They just went blazing away like fun. Fortunately for us," he added.

"And you think they were looking for the Commander in particular? I mean, they kidnapped him on purpose, they weren't just scooping up a hostage?"

"I think so. Did you get that impression, Squeak?"

"Yes, I did." She marmaladed her toast thoughtfully. "They were certainly looking for Malcolm, but there's more than that to it. I'm convinced they were after you as well, Jack. I'm certain they tried to kill you. Do you remember? One of the men shone a torch in your face as if to be sure of who you were. You hit him, which made him let go, and then at least one of them fired a whole stream of machine-gun bullets at you."

"They tried to kill me?" Haldean stopped with his cup of tea halfway to his mouth. "Why on earth should they single me out? You must be mistaken, surely."

"I'm not."

Haldean shook his head with a puzzled frown. "I don't see what I've done to merit that sort of attention. They certainly went for Smith-Fennimore, though. He was struggling and fighting, but when they fired at Belle, he went crackers. That's when they swiped him with the gun butt. It was all over so quickly, Ashley. It was weird, like something from a film."

"Russians," said Ashley drumming his fingers on the table. "There's too many Russians in this for my liking. I'd like to know what the devil the connection is between these ruddy Russians and Hesperus. By the way, you know you asked me to check the telephone exchange? There was a call put through at two thirty or so yesterday afternoon from the public call-box outside the post office to a place called the Paradise Club in London. Apparently Scotland Yard keeps a weather eye on it as it's a favourite haunt for Russian émigrés, but they believed it was safe enough. I rang the Yard this morning to check all the London numbers that the operator could remember putting through and the Paradise Club was the only one they knew anything about."

"Did the operator hear anything?"

Ashley shook his head. "Not in the way you mean. The only reason the girl noticed the call at all was because it was to a London number and she thought the Paradise Club sounded nice."

"Nice, eh?" Haldean grinned. "No, I wouldn't call the Paradise Club nice. I've been there once or twice. It's full of hairy blokes shouting about the Revolution and the wine's like engine oil."

"It's very fashionable though, Jack," said Squeak. "I've been there."

"What would your mother say?" he murmured. He cocked an eyebrow at Ashley. "Do we take that as a definite link between the attack last night and Stanmore Parry?"

"Perhaps," said Ashley, cautiously. "It might be someone booking a table."

"I don't think you do anything as conventional as book tables at the Paradise Club. People just seem to turn up and elbow their way in. Did anyone in the post office see who made the call?"

Ashley shook his head. "I asked the woman behind the counter if she'd seen anyone who looked like a Russian, and she asked me what did a Russian look like?"

"She's got a point there," admitted Haldean. He finished his tea and pushed his chair back from the table. "D'you know, I feel absolutely dumb. I haven't got a clue what's going on. I thought I had a glimmer of an idea about the key to the french windows, but that simply won't hang together with anything else. And in the meantime Tim's dead, Lyvenden's dead, Arthur's gone AWOL and that poor devil Smith-Fennimore could be anywhere. Why the dickens should a bunch of hairy Russians kidnap him?"

"Scotland Yard had an idea about that," said Ashley. "You know your friend, Inspector Rackham?"

Haldean looked at him alertly. "Bill Rackham? Yes."

"I spoke to him this morning. I'd had a brief word with him first thing to tell him what I was after and he rang me back after he'd done a bit of digging around. To be honest the Chief's wondering if all this has got beyond me and we should call in the Yard. I've begged a couple of days' grace, but I thought as Commander Smith-Fennimore is a London man and these Russians obviously aren't local, Inspector Rackham might be able to give me a couple of hints without becoming officially involved. He sends his regards, by the way, and says he hopes your arm's soon better."

"That's very nice of him," said Haldean impatiently. "What did he say about Smith-Fennimore?"

"He said that the Commander's bank, Smith, Wilson and Fennimore, holds a large deposit of Russian gold."

Haldean's eyebrows rose. "Does it, by jingo?"

"Yes. It's Tsarist gold, apparently, from before the Revolution. Apparently lots of the London private banks have Russian gold in them and it's a bit of a problem. Most of the real owners are dead, either killed in the war or murdered by the Bolsheviks. That bunch who are running the show over there claim the gold as their own, but you can't call that crowd of thugs a government, so the banks aren't parting with it."

"So what's Bill Rackham's idea? That these Russians kidnapped Fennimore to make him cough up the dosh?"

"That's about the size of it," agreed Ashley.

Haldean stroked his chin. "It's a bit more dramatic than writing a cheque." He frowned. "I dunno. It's a link of some sort, I suppose. They might be dopey enough to think it'll work, but I can't see it somehow." He looked at Ashley with a wry smile. "But why ask me? I told you I wouldn't be much use. It's all too close to home for me to see it properly."

Ashley finished his coffee and got up. "If I were you I wouldn't bother trying to work it out. You concentrate on getting better. That bullet was too close for comfort. I'll be along later to see how you are. I want another look outside. We've examined the lawn already, but I want to see if there's anything we've overlooked."

Haldean stood up. "I'll come to the door with you."

Leaving Squeak Robiceux, the two men walked down the hall. After seeing Ashley out of the house, Haldean picked up the *Daily Messenger* from the hall table and took it into the library. He took a cigarette from the box and settled down in an armchair, the newspaper on the table beside him. He lit the cigarette, his eyes abstracted.

Somewhere was a common thread which tied together his arm, Arthur, Tim, last night's attack, a telephone call to the Paradise Club and the appalling sight of the sheath knife in Lord Lyvenden's chest. The Tsar's gold; did that fit in? And where was the key to the french windows? *If I was writing this* . . . But he wasn't writing it. Writing this sort of stuff was easy. Trying to make head or tail of it when he was plunged in the middle of it was another thing entirely. He reached out for the paper, biting his lip as his arm twinged. By all accounts Squeak Robiceux had done well last night. She'd been a nurse in the war, of course. She was a useful sort of person. She knew what she was doing. Unlike me, he thought gloomily, irritated by how foggy his thoughts seemed.

262

His eyes flicked to the columns of newsprint. Lyvenden's murder still held the front page. He recognized the words he had used to Ernest Stanhope yesterday morning. There was a photograph of Ashley, radiating placid reliability, a snapshot of Uncle Phil looking worried to death and a picture of the house taken through the bars of the front gate. There'll be yet more pictures of Hesperus in the news once Stanhope and his merry men get on to what happened last night, he thought, with a brief stab of sympathy for his harried Uncle Phil.

Searching for other news he turned the page. *MP Found In Soho Love Nest.* That held no appeal. *Mysterious Wreckage From Storm.* The name Stanmore Parry caught his attention. He grinned. This was Ernest Stanhope at his best. Having run out of things to say about Lyvenden — and there had been a heartbreaking and entirely fictitious account of Lady Harriet's reaction — he'd gone on to the weather.

Tomorrow, of course, he expected to see Smith-Fennimore's name and perhaps his own in *Kidnapping At Hesperus: Further Development In Lyvenden Case* but as far as this morning's paper was concerned, today's news from Stanmore Parry was the *Mysterious Wreckage From Storm*. There was a stirring description of the storm, with a lovingly written depiction of mountainous seas and howling winds pounding the coast. The sea wall had been breached, branches and some whole trees had been toppled, chimneys were down and the coast road had suffered a landslip. The mysterious wreckage on Stanmore Parry beach turned out to be five sets of false teeth, a wooden leg, a sewing machine, its needle still miraculously attached, and *a good quality full-length leather coat whose owner will bemoan its loss.*

The door opened and Isabelle came in. She looked dreadful. Haldean glanced at her unhappy face and promptly put down the newspaper. "Come on," he said softly.

Isabelle sat down on the arm of his chair and turned a pale face to his. "Where's it going to end, Jack? I thought you were dead last night."

Haldean reached out a hand to her. "I'm not. Punctured, not perished, as the man said about the car tyre."

She didn't smile. "It's all very well joking about it," she said fretfully, "but anything could be happening to Malcolm, and as for Arthur . . ." She gave a deep sigh. "I've been rotten to Malcolm. I was rotten to Arthur, too. I wish I knew where they were. I wish I knew what was behind it all. I can't understand anything. Who were those horrible men? I'm sure they tried to kill you, Jack." His hand tightened on hers. "I don't know how I feel any longer. I'm numb. It's hard to feel anything. I've been lying awake since goodness knows when this morning trying to work it out, and all I keep coming back to is the sight of Arthur's face and his hands all covered in blood. I keep thinking how much he wanted me to trust him and I wouldn't. Then I see Malcolm again, with the gun butt smashing down on his head and you, falling back as if you were dead, and that

264

awful noise from the guns which seemed to go on and on for hours."

"Come on, Belle," he said gently. "Don't give in to it. I'm all right, if that's any consolation, and you're wrong about how long it went on for. The whole thing must have only taken a couple of minutes, if that."

"Well, it seemed to last for hours," she said, niggled at the contradiction. "It was as if time had stopped working properly."

"I've had that feeling," said Haldean. "I used to get it when I was flying, particularly if there was a fight on. It's as if you split into two people, one looking on, saying what you should do next, and the other person — your real self — actually doing it. And there's always a choice, you know? The two selves can argue about what you're doing, then you do it, and time flips back to normal. I don't know whether it lasts for seconds or only part of a second, but it's as if all the clocks have been stopped."

She looked at him gratefully. "I'm glad you see that. It's exactly how I felt last night. It made it more like a nightmare than something that was really happening, and the most nightmarish bit of all was how the time stretched out."

He stared at her, his mind racing. *Time stretched out . . . Time. That's it! Two people. One person split into two. And there's a choice. There's always a choice.*

"Jack, what is it?" asked Isabelle. Her voice seemed to come from far away.

Not much time left . . .

"Jack, what is it?" asked Isabelle again.

"I think I know the truth," he said in a strained voice.

"What?" she said in astonishment.

He hardly heard her. "There are some bits which don't fit, but I'm sure they will if I keep hammering away at them." He tried to sit up and winced in annoyance. "I've got to check something with Ashley. Give me a hand, will you? I'm stuck with this blasted arm."

With Isabelle behind him, he strode into the hall and down the front steps. On the lawn, Ashley was talking to Sergeant Ingleton. "Don't say anything," he hissed as they approached.

"Did you want me?" asked Ashley, looking up. "I say, Haldean, what is it?"

"I want to check something," said Haldean, forcing the excitement out of his voice. "I need to see Adamson's statement."

"*Adamson's* statement? Well, of course. All the paperwork's in the gun room."

He led the way into the gun room and searched out the file. Watched closely by the others, Haldean ran his finger down Adamson's statement, and sighed.

"I'm right. I wish I wasn't, but I am." He closed the file and got up.

"Hold on a minute," said Ashley. "You've cracked it, haven't you? What is it?"

Haldean looked horribly uncomfortable. "I've got an inkling of what might have happened, but I really don't want to say what it is. Not yet. I'm sorry, Ashley. You know I won't keep you in the dark for a moment longer than I have to, but I'm simply not sure yet and I want to be sure. This may all be nonsense."

"I'd like to hear it though, nonsense or not. Come on," said Ashley, his eyes on Haldean's tense face. "You must be able to tell me something. I haven't got much longer on this case. If I don't get somewhere soon, the Chief'll have to give it to the Yard. Even an idea would be helpful."

"No. I can't tell you anything." That was too harsh. Ashley looked affronted, as well he might. Haldean tried to explain himself. "Ashley, I'm sorry. I want to tell you what I've got in mind, but it's a question of friendship, you see? He deserves that much, at least. I need to make absolutely sure."

"Is the friend Captain Stanton?" Ashley asked shrewdly.

Haldean nodded. "Give me a day, Ashley. Maybe a day and a night. That's all I want. Please."

Ashley drew a deep breath. "All right." He half smiled. "Not that I can stand in your way. But remember, Haldean, this is murder you're talking about. You can't ignore the law just because Captain Stanton's a friend of yours."

Haldean bit his lip. "No. I couldn't do that." He turned and walked quickly out of the gun room and up the stairs from the hall.

Isabelle caught up with him at the doorway to his room. "What's going on, Jack?" demanded Isabelle. "You might not be able to tell Mr Ashley but you've got to tell me."

He looked at her with a twisted face. "Oh, my dear, what if I'm wrong? I hope I'm wrong. Look, will you help me get this sling off my wretched arm? And you'll have to help me on with my coat. I can't quite manage it. And pass me that leather case, will you? It's got all my maps in it."

Still firing questions at him, she followed him round the room, but Haldean refused to answer. "I may be the biggest idiot in England, but I think I've got it," was the most she got out of him. When he'd finally got his coat on, he scooped up the money from his dressing table and turned to Isabelle, taking her hand in his. "Belle," he said seriously. "My dear Belle. For what I've done, and for what I have to do — sorry to sound so churchy — I really am very sorry. If you fancy praying, pray that I'm wrong."

"But *why?*" she said impatiently. "And where are you going?"

A very small smile lifted the corners of his mouth. "That's easy enough to answer, at any rate. I'm going to get Arthur."

"What!" She drew back. "Do you know where he is?"

Haldean nodded. "Well, if he was between Melling Bridge and Caynor the night before last, he should be there by now. Don't tell anyone, though, just in case I'm not right. It'd cause a fearful stink and it wouldn't be fair." He walked to the door. "I should be back today but it might be tomorrow. I'm going in my car."

"Jack! What will the doctor say?"

He grinned. "Tell him I've made a miracle recovery. After all, I've got another arm."

"I wish you'd tell me what was happening."

"Oh, dash it all, Belle, work it out for yourself," said Haldean with a return to his normal manner. "There's a coat on the beach, Arthur hared off with Lyvenden's cigarette case and Smith-Fennimore got kidnapped."

"Don't give me that," said Isabelle. "You know perfectly well it doesn't make any sense. You can tell me one thing. Was Tim murdered by mistake?"

Haldean shuddered. "No. The person who murdered Tim knew exactly what they were doing. I'm not going to say another word." And with that, he clattered down the stairs and was gone.

CHAPTER
TWELVE

Haldean drew the car into the side of the road, switched off the engine and leant his forehead on the steering wheel with relief. Although he had confidently told Isabelle that he could manage the drive, he had found the twenty-two miles from Hesperus rough in places and agonizing in others. The landlord of the pub where he had stopped for a break had looked at his white face critically before consenting to serve him with a double brandy. The last four miles over unmetalled roads had made his left arm feel on fire every time the car had jolted. After a few minutes' rest he wearily climbed out of the Spyker and, leaving the car under the shelter of a tree, walked up the overgrown lane which ran off the main road.

With the ache in his arm reduced to a dull throb, he pushed open the gate which hung on one hinge and walked into the woods beyond.

It was all very quiet. These were the grounds of Arthur's childhood home, choked with brambles, nettles and ivy after the neglect of the war and a succession of tenants. Haldean had never been here but Arthur had described it often enough. If he took the path through the woods he should come to an outcrop of chalky rock with a cave at the base. The cave had, Arthur said, a small opening leading on to a space where a man could stand upright.

He knew Arthur had been thinking a lot about his old home recently. He'd said as much at lunch the other day.

Aunt Alice had started the conversation, one of those ice-breaking conversations good hostesses do start when the talk is flagging, along the lines of "Where in the world would you like to be most?" Haldean, who knew his aunt loved Hesperus, thought it showed something of the strain she was under when she picked Egypt where she and Uncle Phil had been stationed years ago. After all, in Egypt there had been no daughter Isabelle or son Greg — and more to the point, no Lord Lyvenden, Lady Harriet or Alfred Charnock.

Malcolm Smith-Fennimore wanted to be by a river in the Baltic where he'd spent youthful summers; Isabelle chose Paris with references to hats and shoes, but Arthur had remained quiet. "Home," he said, when Haldean had prompted him. "My old home when I was a kid." Hesperus reminded him of The Priory, with its high rooms and winding stairs, but what really stuck in his mind was the cave. "I loved it," he said. "I played endless games of shipwrecked sailors, pirates, and Robin Hood there. It was my big secret. I always holed out there when things weren't going right or I was in trouble."

Haldean thought at the time the remark had a wistful significance. Now it seemed like a prophecy.

He nearly missed the entrance to the cave. An elder sapling, with masses of tiny black berries, had sprung up outside a narrow vertical crack in the rock. A freshly broken twig hung limply from the tree and there were churned footmarks in the mud. Haldean squeezed himself into a gap more suited for a boy than a man and was relieved to find the split in the rocks opened out. It wasn't really a cave, but a damp, moss-covered gap between the rocks, roofed over by earth-packed tree roots. As a place for a boy to play it was excellent, but as a place for a man to stay it was wretched. Haldean shivered. Still, he had slept in far worse places in France and so had Arthur.

He blinked, letting his eyes adjust to the dim, green-filtered light, then smiled and stooped down. On a low spur of rock, away from the wet earth, were the remains of a fire. The embers were still warm. Haldean lit a cigarette, sat down on the earth floor, propped his back against the wall and waited. Tiredness swept over him in an engulfing wave. He blinked himself awake, then relaxed against the chalk wall. Perhaps he could just shut his eyes for a few minutes . . . Seconds later he was fast asleep.

He woke in agony. White stabs of pain lanced through his arm and he jerked his eyes open to see Stanton's furious face close to his. He twisted out from under Stanton's clutching hand and was very nearly sick. "My arm!" he gasped. "Arthur, let go, you're hurting my arm!"

Stanton, his face contorted with anger and fear, dropped his hand and stepped back, fists clenched. Haldean gazed at him in dismay. With two days' growth of beard and filthy clothes, Stanton looked wild.

"You!" Stanton snarled and struck out. Haldean writhed away, sprawling on the ground. He scrambled to his knees. Stanton caught him, hauled him to his feet and slammed him against the wall, his open hand on Haldean's chest.

"I won't let you take me back," said Stanton in a voice that was nearly a sob. "I'm not going back to hospital, I'm not. I'll kill you first. I mean it."

"I'm not taking you back," gasped out Haldean. "Not to hospital, anyway," he added, feeling like Judas.

Stanton lashed out. Haldean flinched away from the blow and Stanton's fist brushed past his jaw and crunched into his shoulder. With an agonized cry, Haldean doubled up, clutching his arm. This time he did retch. Utterly helpless, pressed against the chalk wall, he was violently sick. "Arthur, you bloody idiot," he managed to say after the fit was over. "It's me, Jack. Jack! For God's sake, man, stop it!"

Stanton looked at him in bewilderment, then gave a convulsive shudder and dropped to his knees, covering his face with his arms. "I've dreamt about you," he said in a muffled voice. "Once before I was free and then you took me back. You. You took me in the van and they locked me up. It was a dreadful place. You left me there. You. I'm not going again."

Haldean wearily got to his feet, stumbled the few steps to Stanton, then knelt beside him and put his arm round his shoulders, gentling him cautiously as a man gentles a frightened dog. "I know you hated me for it," he said awkwardly, "but I had to do it. If I hadn't stayed with you, Arthur, they'd have restrained you." Stanton gave another shudder, then was still. "I couldn't let them do that to you, Arthur. Not when I could be there to stop them."

Stanton looked at him with frightened eyes. "What have I done wrong? There are people hunting me. I've had to hide. I didn't think you'd find me here. I thought I was safe. I can't remember what I've done. I can't remember anything."

"Oh, Lord." Haldean, still with his hand on Stanton's arm, collapsed back against the wall of the cave. "Arthur, when you say you can't remember, do you mean it?" He received a scared look in reply. "Isabelle? Smith-Fennimore? Do they mean anything to you?"

"Isabelle?" said Stanton slowly. His breathing steadied and he sat back next to Haldean. The fear gradually faded from his face. "Isabelle?" he repeated. He sank his forehead on to his crooked knees for a few moments and when he looked up, Haldean was relieved to see him look himself again. "Isabelle," he repeated once more. "Is she the girl with the lovely smile?"

Haldean nodded. "That's right."

"The thought of her makes me feel sad," said Stanton in a puzzled voice. "I don't know why it should. There's a man I can remember, too. Tim? Is that right? Something awful happened, didn't it?"

274

Haldean sighed. "Yes. Something awful happened. If you'll listen to me, I'll tell you what I know."

There was a grocer's paper bag on the ground which Stanton had evidently dropped. Haldean reached out and pulled it towards him. "The trouble is, I'd rather hoped you could fill in some gaps for me." He opened the bag. "What have you got in here, old man?" His calm voice and slow movements were having their effect on his friend's nerves. "There's a loaf, a piece of cheese and some beer. Let's have something to eat." Keeping his actions very deliberate, he took out his pocket knife and gave it to Stanton. "You'll have to cut the bread and cheese. I've injured my arm and I'm not up to it."

Stanton took the knife, snapped it open and stared for a moment at the blade in his hand. Then he picked up the loaf and cut off two slices and a hunk of cheese. Despite what he firmly believed, Haldean realized he'd been holding his breath.

"Can you open the bottle, too?" he asked.

He smiled as Stanton took the cork out. "Have a drink, Arthur. You look as if you could do with it. Good man. What's the last thing you can remember?"

Stanton took the bottle and the roughly cut bread and cheese warily. He was obviously trying very hard to strap down his fear. "It's all a muddle, really. Bits of Passchendaele — that's come back to me — and the . . ." He swallowed. "The hospital. After that, it's just odd flashes. You were my friend, weren't you?" He paused. "A good friend. I'm starting to remember that.

Jack." He said the name cautiously, as one remembering old certainties. "Jack, I'm sorry. You are my friend, aren't you?"

"Of course I am, old son," said Haldean quietly.

"I can remember how it really was now. That time you took me back before, I mean." He rested his hand on his forehead. "I think I always resented what you did. Actually, that's not being honest. I know I resented what you did. I also know I shouldn't have done. I remember trying very hard not to blame you for it. After all, you'd helped me. But every time I tried to think about it, I couldn't think about it, if you see what I mean. I've never been able to get that straightened out and it left me feeling bitter. About you, I mean. That's so unfair." He looked up and Haldean was reassured to see a very faint smile. "It's rotten, isn't it? I know you helped me and yet . . ." He shrugged.

"Funny how hard it is to be grateful, isn't it?" said Haldean. "I knew you felt like that."

Stanton looked startled. "Did you?"

Haldean nodded. "Of course I did. Things were never quite the same afterwards and I guessed why. I resented it too, of course. I tried to pretend nothing had happened, but that didn't work. I don't know if you'll believe me, but I only did what I had to do."

Stanton reached out his hand, resting it on Haldean's arm. "I think you did a damn sight more than that. I suppose we've just had the conversation we should have had years ago." This time he did smile. "I'd never intended to throw you round the room, though. Actually . . ." Stanton looked puzzled again. "How come I was able to do that? You were a pretty useful fighter, as I recall. At school I could only ever draw with you on points."

Haldean took a swig of beer. "I had a bullet through my arm last night."

"Good God! Are you all right?"

"I'm better now you've stopped lashing out, I must say."

"Jack!" Stanton looked horrified. "I'm really sorry. I'd never —"

"Relax." Haldean grinned at him. "It's over. Forget about it. Who are these people who are hunting for you?"

"I don't know." Stanton broke off a piece of bread and chewed it thoughtfully. "My God, I'm hungry. I've been steering clear of the police. I had an idea that was a sound move. What the devil have I done, by the way?"

"I'll tell you later," said Haldean. "Go on. Who's hunting you?"

"It was yesterday evening. There's four men. Two have got beards. I think they're foreign, but the other two are English. One's a little red-haired chap, a Cockney, I think, and the other English bloke is bald and looks a real tough. He's called Mick. I'd gone down to the village to try and get something to eat. A car was pulled up in the main street and these men were sitting in it."

"The car wasn't a Wolseley by any chance, was it?"

Stanton looked startled. "Yes, it was. How did you know?"

Haldean tapped his arm. "They were responsible for this. Go on."

"Well, I didn't pay much attention at first, apart from thinking the car looked out of place in such a small village. Then one of the bearded blokes caught sight of me and pointed. He shouted something I couldn't understand, then this red-headed chap yelled, 'Bloody hell, that's him,' or words to that effect. 'Come on, Mick.' They jumped out of the car and came towards me. I ran for it. I got down an alleyway and managed to hop over into someone's back yard and laid low. I could hear them talking on the other side of the wall. That's how I know one's a Cockney. They said my name and they also said that The Boss wouldn't be happy that I'd escaped. I don't know who The Boss is, but they were scared rigid of him. I think one of the foreign blokes is called Boris. They said his name, too. They pushed off eventually. They said something about not wanting to be late for another job."

"I can guess where they were headed," said Haldean. "They came to Hesperus last night."

"Hesperus?" asked Stanton. "What's Hesperus?"

Haldean handed him the rest of the food. "Eat that while I tell you what's happened. Believe me, it's some story."

Stanton ate hungrily, nodding occasionally as parts of Haldean's story chimed in with his memory. He finished the last of the bread and cheese and drained the remains of the beer. "So these Russian devils not only tried to kill you, they've taken this poor Smith-Fennimore chap as well?" he said slowly. "I

278

wonder what they want him for? Perhaps they're after the gold, as your policeman friend said. But who did the murders, Jack? It sounds as if these Russians might have had a hand in that, too. D'you know?"

"Well, the police think it's you," said Haldean, hesitantly. "As I said, I'd hoped you could tell me what happened. You see, I think you're a key to all this. When you ran off after the murder, you took Lord Lyvenden's cigarette case with you. Have you still got it?"

"What, this awful thing?" Stanton drew the gold case out of his pocket and glanced up with the ghost of a smile. "I'm glad to know it's not mine."

"It's too dreadful for words," Haldean agreed, opening and shutting it absently. "Heavy, too. I wonder . . ."

He ran his fingers over the inside of the case and pressed one corner. The plate with the clip for cigarettes flew open, revealing some paper inside. Haldean carefully took out the single sheet, unfolded it and spread it on his knee, smoothing out the creases.

"What is it?" asked Stanton, turning his head to see. "I say, Jack, is it written in code?"

"I don't think so," said Haldean thoughtfully. "At a guess, it's Russian." He tapped the paper thoughtfully. "I'm prepared to bet that this will give us the clue to the entire mystery."

"But you can't read Russian, can you?"

Haldean shook his head. Folding up the paper carefully, he put it in his pocketbook. "We'll have to get it translated but I've got a shrewd idea of what's on it. However, that can keep. I must say what's really bothering me at the moment is the question of what are we going to do with you?"

"Do with me?" Stanton looked scared. "I thought you said you wouldn't take me back. You said so, Jack."

Haldean got up and strolled to the entrance of the cave where he stood, apparently rapt in a study of the damp, rocky walls. "You're being hunted by the police," he said quietly. "They think you committed murder and in the light of the evidence they have, you can't really blame them." A piece of rock was hanging loose where an infant tree had optimistically sent out a root. Haldean started to dislodge it with his finger. "You didn't help matters by running away." He half smiled. "I know why you did it, and in your place I'd have probably done the same, but it looks bad." He turned round suddenly. "You can't remember a thing about this, can you?"

Stanton shook his head. "Not a thing. It's as if I was hearing about someone else. I've got to keep reminding myself you're talking about me."

"Now, if you want to, you can carry on running. I'll give you some money and, with a bit of luck, I can probably get you over to France without being spotted. In the meantime, I'll do my best to clear up this business. However, it'll be a lot easier to work things out if you come back with me. It won't be much fun because you'll be in prison, but at least these other types, the ones in the Wolseley, won't be able to get hold of you. And, just at the moment, Arthur, I can't help thinking they pose the greater threat. If you hadn't managed to give them the slip last night, I think you'd

280

be dead by now. I think I had a very narrow escape from their hands." The rock was nearly loose now.

"I don't know." Stanton's voice was weary with defeat. "I can't keep on running, Jack. It's been awful not knowing who I am or what was happening. It's been cold, too, and I've been jolly hungry as well. I can't go on running and these bloody Russians obviously mean business." He paused. "But I can't get to grips with this idea of a murder. Could I have done it? I don't know what happened or what I might have done. I simply can't remember."

Haldean shook his head. "You're not guilty. If you come back with me I think I can prove it." The rock clattered to the ground and Haldean turned round. "But it's up to you to decide. I can't force you and I wouldn't want to. It must be your decision." He grinned. "I'm damned if I'm having another version of the incident in the Euston Road hanging over me for the rest of my natural."

Stanton smiled fleetingly. "Don't. I can't believe I was ever such a fool as to let that rankle." He sighed. "Part of me says I'm crazy to come with you," he admitted, "but I think it's the right thing to do. And I suppose if I am guilty, then the best thing is to come and face the music. My mother used to say, 'Tell the truth and shame the devil.' If I had the slightest idea of what the truth was," he added unhappily.

"Right," said Haldean briskly. "Let's make a start. I hope I don't let you down."

"You won't." Stanton smiled again. "I'll just have to trust you. You won't let me down, Jack, I know you won't. All sorts of things have come back to me while we've been talking. We've had some good times together, haven't we? You're a damn decent sort and I'm sorry I've been such a fool."

"Don't mention it," said Haldean. It was good to see Arthur smiling again. "Now, to practicalities, as they say. You'll excuse me for bringing the subject up, but you look like something the cat dragged in."

"I'll visit my tailor directly I have the chance."

"You'll scare him into a fit. If you take my coat and hat — you'll have to help me, I can't manage with this ruddy arm — then the worst of the ravages of your costume will be concealed." Haldean gritted his teeth as Stanton helped him off with his coat. "That's better," he said, as Stanton shrugged the coat on. "You very nearly look respectable now. Come on."

They walked to the entrance of the cave, stooping to climb out. Stanton was in front. He suddenly halted.

"What is it?" asked Haldean.

Stanton turned with a finger to his lips. "Jack," he said very softly. "There's a man outside."

As quietly as they could, they retreated back into the cave. "I don't think he knows we're in here," said Stanton in a whisper. "He's one of the Russians. I recognized him. He's standing on the path. I caught sight of him through the trees."

Haldean thought rapidly. It was a real squeeze to get past the elderberry sapling at the front of the cave. They were bound to make some noise and for a few vital minutes they would be helpless as they tried to get out. So that way was blocked . . .

The rear of the cave was a mass of tree roots snaking through the crumbly earth. Stanton had already made a rough hole in the roof to act as a chimney. If the hole could be widened, they might be able to escape that way. The highest part of the roof was a few feet above their heads. If only his damned arm was sound, it would be possible to climb out.

He took his knife out of his pocket and gave it to Stanton, pointing at the hole in the roof. "Can you make that bigger?" he said softly. He crouched down. "You can stand on my shoulders."

Stanton unclasped the knife and, holding on to a tree root for support, climbed on to Haldean's back.

Haldean's eyes widened as he took the strain and he very nearly cried out from the wrenching pain in his arm. After what seemed an unendurable time, Stanton quietly slipped to the ground again. Haldean, doubled up and clutching his arm, felt his stomach heave. He couldn't, absolutely couldn't, be sick. He felt Stanton's supportive hand on his shoulder as he battled against it. Eventually he was able to look up. "I'm okay," he said quietly. He saw the contradiction in Stanton's face. Even in those circumstances, it made him smile.

Stanton pointed upwards. The hole was wide enough for them to get through.

"You first," said Haldean quietly, stooping down once more. He clenched his fists as Stanton's foot ground into his shoulder. There were a few brief moments of agony, then the pressure had gone. Stanton, with his elbows on the outside of the hole, quickly pulled himself through. Then, kneeling on the ground, he reached his arms down for Haldean.

Haldean thought he was going to faint. As Stanton pulled him up, his vision blurred into jagged white lines. He heard Stanton grunt, as if from far away, then — thank God! — he was lying face down and full length on the ground amongst the heaps of fallen leaves, trying to control his ragged breathing.

Stanton put his mouth close to Haldean's ear. "I can still see the Russian," he said. "Wait here. Get your breath back. I'm going to scout round to see where the others are."

If Lenin himself had been after him, there wasn't the slightest chance Haldean could have moved at that moment. He gave a feeble thumbs-up sign, and heard Stanton steal away. Gradually, his breathing steadied and he was able to open his eyes. Very cautiously, he rolled over and got to his knees.

He was on the edge of a chalky cliff, deep with fallen leaves, which rose about fifteen feet above the woods. Crouching behind a tree-trunk he could see the Russian — or most of the Russian, because the trees were in the way — standing on the overgrown path.

Then, from out of the trees on the slope behind him, came the sound of feet. Haldean got up and slipped behind the tree. A small, red-headed man, carrying an automatic pistol, came to the edge of the cliff. "Boris!" he called in a low, carrying voice. "Have you seen anything?"

Boris came into full view. "No," he said, then stared straight past the man. "Look!" he shouted, pointing at Haldean. "Behind you!"

The red-headed man whirled, gun at the ready. Haldean shot out from behind the tree and ran for it, away from the cliff edge and up the slope into the woods. He heard the shots crack past him and saw the bark of a tree explode into splinters.

"Mick! Get him!" called the man from behind him. Haldean glanced ahead and saw a big, black-jacketed man step into his path. The man raised his gun to fire and then Stanton jumped down from the woods behind. He had a branch in his hands and brought it down in a whirling blow.

Mick collapsed at Stanton's feet.

Stanton jerked his thumb towards Haldean. "This way!" They ran up the slope again. Behind them they could hear the red-headed man calling for Boris. Stanton took them up through the woods then back down to the cliff edge. "There's a way out," he gasped as Haldean caught up with him. "Follow me."

As they got back on to the edge, a bullet sang past them. The red-headed man was pounding towards them, firing as he ran. Stanton and Haldean raced along the cliff edge. They'd doubled back on their tracks and were near the cave once more. Stanton skirted round it, but Haldean jumped over the hole. Behind them the thudding feet were getting closer, then came a shriek and an agonized yell.

Haldean glanced round and grinned in triumph. The red-haired man had disappeared down the ready-made man trap of the chimney to the cave. He had hoped that would happen and it had.

However, Boris was still in the woods below and, presumably, another man too. They needed to get off the cliff, through the woods and back to the Spyker. Stanton pointed in front of them. "There are some old steps a little further on that'll bring us to the path. Is the car at the gate?"

Haldean nodded. "If they've got any sense, they'll have left a man on guard beside it."

Stanton bit his lip. "What do we do about that?"

"Let's see how the land lies first," said Haldean.

They got down the steps and, keeping to the trees and paralleling the path, crept down to the gate. Boris was, presumably, still in the woods behind them.

Haldean slipped out of the gate and into the ditch by the side of the road, Stanton at his heels. Very cautiously they risked a glance over the edge of the ditch.

About twenty yards down the road stood the Spyker. The maroon bulk of a Wolseley was drawn in behind it. A bearded man was sitting on the bonnet of the Wolseley, his feet resting on the suspension.

"He must have heard the din in the woods," said Stanton quietly, on his knees in the ditch.

"He'll have been ordered to stay put," said Haldean. "Damn!"

He'd hoped, of course, that the car would be unguarded. They'd just have to think of a way to draw him off. Quickly, too, before the enemy could gather their forces. He smiled slowly as an idea occurred to him. "Arthur," he whispered. "This is what we'll do . . ."

A few minutes later, Haldean was lying in the ditch with the Spyker on the road above him. He had crept that far without being seen. He could hear the guard on the Wolseley shifting his position. He unknotted his tie and took it off, holding it in his hand. That was part of the plan. Now for Arthur to do his thing. Up the road any minute now . . . He heard the man's startled exclamation and a thump as he slid off the bonnet of the car. Looking under the wheels of the Spyker, he could see the man's feet. Haldean knew what had happened: Arthur, about fifty yards away, had run across the road. Shouting, the man raced after him.

Haldean got out of the ditch and ran to the back of the Wolseley. He wanted to make sure that they couldn't be followed. He unscrewed the lid to the petrol tank and stuffed his tie inside, so that it was saturated with petrol. Taking one end out, he trailed it behind the car, leaving the other end in the tank. Quite a lot of petrol spilled on to the road. Good.

Now for the awkward bit. He ran to the Spyker, climbed in and started the engine. On the road ahead, the Russian spun round. He raised his gun and started to shoot. Haldean, crouching low in the seat, drove the car on to the road and slammed it into reverse. When he was level with the petrol tank of the Wolseley, he struck a match and threw it at the end of the tie that was on the road. The match didn't quite land on the tie, but the petrol on the road burst into flame with a whumph.

Without waiting to see what happened, Haldean gunned the Spyker forwards. A massive explosion rocked the car and a cloud of acrid, oily smoke engulfed him. Completely blinded, Haldean kept his foot hard down. Emerging from the smoke, he caught a brief glimpse of the bearded man, standing open-mouthed on the road. The man leapt to one side as the Spyker surged past, his gun forgotten.

Haldean crunched on the brakes as he got to the oak tree which he and Stanton had picked out as a landmark. Stanton hurled himself into the car and they were away. Behind them came the wild crackle of fire and a sound like falling rain as the debris from the Wolseley hit the road. Turning his head, Stanton saw a huge black cloud billowing up from where the Wolseley had been. Choking with exhilaration and laughter, he yelled at Haldean, making his voice carry over the noise. "You've got to see this."

Haldean drove another quarter mile before stopping the car. He got out and looked at the black cloud behind them with enormous satisfaction. "It'll be a long time before they drive anywhere in that."

Stanton shook his head, still laughing. "By jingo, that did me good. I wonder what The Boss will say?"

Haldean grinned. "Let's see. There's a red-headed chap with a broken leg, Mick with a broken head — that was a very well-timed thump with the branch you gave him, Arthur — Boris is undented, worse luck, but if our friend who was guarding the car doesn't get hit by flying debris, then there's no justice in this life." He rubbed his hands together. "And, to top it all, the

Wolseley is in so many bits that it could go through a sieve. I don't think The Boss will be any too cheerful. That'll teach them to come after me with a machine gun, to say nothing of making my friends' lives a total misery." He reached out his hand to the grinning Stanton beside him. "Job done?"

Stanton shook his hand. "Absolutely, job done."

Haldean walked round to the passenger side of the car. "You'll have to drive, Arthur. I'm really not up to it." He glanced at his watch. "Do you know, it's only just gone five o'clock. Can you stop at a telephone box when you see one? I need to speak to Ashley as soon as possible. If he can get some men over here they might be able to pick up the remnants of that bunch of jokers. I want to tell Isabelle we're on our way, too."

"Right you are," said Stanton, climbing into the driver's side of the car. "Where are we going?"

"Stanmore Parry police station."

"Oh," said Stanton, sobered. "Stanmore Parry police station it is."

Haldean made two phone calls, one to Ashley and one to Isabelle. "I told Isabelle we were on our way," he said as he got back into the car. "I've asked her to meet us at the police station with your shaving things and a change of clothes. Once inside the station you'll be safe. In the circumstances, I didn't think we could go up to the house. No one apart from those two knows you're coming." He glanced covertly at Stanton as they drove off. "Isabelle sounded jolly pleased to hear you were all right."

Jolly pleased was the dickens of an understatement. Isabelle had been unable to speak for a few moments and, when she did, she'd left Haldean in no doubt about the welcome Stanton would receive. He mentally shrugged. All he asked of Isabelle was that she wouldn't start the whole sorry business once more of raising Arthur's hopes, then dropping him. Not only did he have more than enough to deal with, but the one good thing about his loss of memory was that it seemed to have taken away the deep unhappiness which Isabelle had caused.

"Isabelle," said Stanton softly. "I remember meeting her for the first time." He smiled. "Other odd bits keep coming back to me. She was wonderful. You introduced us, didn't you?" He broke off. "Anyway, that's all over now. She must be worried sick about her fiancé." He glanced across to his friend. "Jack, it will be all right, won't it?"

"I hope so," said Haldean, suddenly unsure. "But there are some bits that still don't fit, Arthur. I just hope it all comes together."

As he nosed the car through the narrow streets of Stanmore Parry, Stanton felt his spirits sink lower and lower. He must have been insane to return. Prison. Although Jack had avoided the word, a police cell was still prison. But what else could he do? He hated hiding. He couldn't hide any longer. He'd almost rather be hanged and get it over with. He wanted to talk to Jack, but Jack had been asleep for the last few miles and Stanton, glancing at his friend's tired face, didn't have the heart to waken him. He parked the car a little way from the police station and waited for a moment before climbing out. Part of him was screaming *Run!* but he resolutely nerved himself to approach the station steps.

A girl was standing in the entrance to the narrow alleyway beside the police station. "Arthur?" she said. "Arthur?"

It was Isabelle. At the sight of her face and sound of her voice, his heart turned over. Memories flooded back, bringing stabbing unhappiness and a deep longing. But she wasn't his; she never had been his. He swallowed. It was decent of her to come and help him. He could be grateful for that, at least, and the poor girl must be beside herself at the thought of Smith-Fennimore in the hands of those damn Russians. He squared his shoulders and faced her. As she saw him properly, unshaven and dirty, she started back, alarmed. "It's all right," he said gently. "Isabelle, it's only me. I'm sorry if I look a bit the worse for wear."

She drew him up the alleyway a little way. "Please, Arthur, come here. I want to talk to you without everybody looking at us." Her voice broke and she flung herself forward and put her head on his chest. "Arthur, I've been so worried. It's been dreadful."

He put an arm round her awkwardly and lifted her chin up. "It'll be fine, Isabelle, really. We'll get him back for you, don't you worry."

She drew back, puzzled. "Who?"

"Smith-Fennimore."

"Malcolm?"

"Yes," he said, dropping his arm and stepping back. "I know you're engaged. You must be worried about him."

She gave a hiccup of laughter. "I am. Of course I am, but you're here." She broke off, reached up and kissed the angle of his jaw.

Stanton drew back as if he'd been stung, his hand to his face. "Isabelle, don't do that. It's not . . ." He searched for the right words. "It's not kind."

"Don't you understand?" she said softly and kissed him again.

With the touch of her lips on his cheek and the scent of her hair so close, the last rags of his self-control went flying. Shutting his eyes, he caught her in his arms and kissed her lips hungrily. She moved and he held her tightly as the kiss lengthened. Then the realization of what he was doing hit him and he broke away. He dropped his arms to his sides in misery before putting a shaky hand to his mouth. "I'm sorry," he said in heavy despair. "I'm sorry, Isabelle. You needn't worry. I won't do it again."

She looked at him with the faintest of smiles. "But I wanted you to," she said softly. "I love you." She gave him a quick, uncertain glance. "That is . . ." She reached out to him. "Do you still want me?"

It was as if the sun had come out. "Want you?" he repeated in a dazed voice and then, as the full meaning of what she said registered, "Want you?" He took her hands and laughed. "I've never wanted anything more." He brought her hands to his lips and kissed them happily. "I've always wanted you. Oh, my dear," and kissed her again.

"Arthur," she said after an appreciable pause, "you smell terrible."

"I know," he said, "awful," and he laughed. "Actually," he added, sobering up, "it's not funny. This is hard to explain but I can't remember anything. I've lost my memory. Jack told me what's happened. Apparently the police think I'm guilty and, to be quite honest, I suppose I might be."

"No, you're not," she said with a touch of irritation. "Of course you aren't. We'll have to sort it out, yes, but Jack can do it. Where is he, by the way?"

"In the car, fast asleep."

There was an embarrassed cough from the end of the alley. "Well, I'm not, actually, but I didn't want to butt in. You seemed otherwise engaged."

Isabelle glared furiously at him. "You shouldn't have been watching!"

"I couldn't help it," Haldean said with an apologetic smile. "If you will conduct your affairs in the public highway, then it's hard not to watch." He held out his hand to Isabelle. "I take it congratulations are in order?"

"I'm so happy, Jack," she said simply.

Haldean turned to the grinning Stanton. "I hate to break up the party, but I really think we'd better get into the police station. Ashley's waiting for us. You don't know Superintendent Ashley, but he's an excellent bloke. He'll look after you."

They walked up the steps to the station. Ashley was standing by the desk, talking to Sergeant Ingleton. Haldean had been dreading this moment and Ashley, despite his long experience, obviously felt ill at ease. Once the formalities were over, he laid his hand on Stanton's arm. "If you will come with me, Captain Stanton, I'll take you to the cells."

Isabelle gave a convulsive shudder. Ashley smiled at her. "Don't you worry, miss. He'll be safe with us and you can always visit him, you know."

Haldean reached out for Isabelle's hand and squeezed it reassuringly. "It'll be all right." She was clearly making a tremendous effort to hold back her tears. "He's safe. Remember that. He's safe."

Isabelle, her eyes fixed on Stanton's back as he walked away, didn't look at Haldean. "I'm trusting you, Jack," she said with a break in her voice. "We're trusting you. I don't understand what you're doing, but it's got to work."

Haldean suddenly couldn't speak. He had meant to talk to Ashley, to tell him everything that had happened, but he didn't trust his voice. He'd have to catch up with Ashley later. It didn't really matter, anyway. He'd told Ashley about the Wolseley on the telephone and with luck the police should have managed to round up the gang.

He squeezed Isabelle's hand again and led her out of the police station and into the car. He climbed into the driver's seat and sat for a few moments before starting the car. Then, like a man coming up from underwater, he took a deep, shuddering breath. "I'm going to try something," he said briskly. "Now I've got my coat back from Arthur, I can be seen in public again." He gave her a wry smile. "Play along, won't you?"

To Isabelle's surprise, Haldean drove them not to Hesperus, but to the Wheatsheaf. She hesitated at the doorway. Although it was only early in the evening, there was a busy, noisy crowd inside. Haldean slipped his arm through hers. "Come on, Belle. It's a perfectly respectable place and I want to see a man about something."

He guided Isabelle to a table where she sat uncomfortably. It wasn't that there was anything wrong with the Wheatsheaf, it was just that going to the local pub was simply Not Done. Was this part of playing along? Jack was standing at the bar, chatting to the landlord, laughing. He had the drinks, why didn't he hurry up? Oh no, now he'd met someone else and was buying him a drink, too. She smiled artificially as Jack and the stranger came to her table.

"Here's someone I'd like you to meet, Belle," said Haldean, placing a gin and ginger in front of her. "This is Mr Ernest Stanhope of the *Daily Messenger*. He's an old friend of mine." Isabelle and the reporter nodded to each other. "My word," said Haldean, undoing his coat and placing his hat on the seat, "it's busy in here."

"It's nearly all pressmen," said Stanhope, looking round the bar. "It's doing wonders for the landlord's trade." He broke off and stared at Haldean's mud-stained clothes. "What the devil have you been doing to yourself? You look as if you've been rolling round in a farmyard."

"As a matter of fact, I've been rolling round in a ditch," said Haldean, taking a long drink of beer.

"A ditch? Whatever for? You don't look any too lively, either. You seem whacked out."

"I'll tell you about that later," said Haldean, lighting a cigarette.

"I'd like to hear it," said Stanhope. "I was cheesed off when I heard about Smith-Fennimore being abducted. We were caught napping last night when those Russians collared you all, and no mistake. It was the rottenest piece of luck I've ever had. We'd spent ages outside Hesperus, and when something really sensational happened, not one of us was there. I tried to get hold of you today, but there was nothing doing. Still, Haldean, as you were part of it, perhaps I could get you to say a few words?"

"Oh, I can do better than that," said Haldean, sipping his beer. "I've got a scoop."

At the sound of these lovely words, Stanhope switched from mild inebriation to complete sobriety. "Quietly," he hissed, in an agonized voice. "Any minute now some of the crowd'll recognize you. My word, Haldean, you're the goods. What is it?"

Haldean grinned. "Well, as you know, I was attacked last night. This is Miss Isabelle Rivers, my cousin and the fiancé of Commander Smith-Fennimore." He ignored Isabelle's scandalized squeak. "I want to tell you that we've just delivered Captain Stanton to the police station here in the village. What? Yes, he did put up a bit of a fight to start with, but he came quietly enough in the end."

This time Isabelle wouldn't be silenced. "Arthur wouldn't fight you, Jack."

"Oh yes he would," said Haldean. "And he did. He used to be a pretty handy boxer and he's still got the skill."

"So how did you persuade him to come along?" said Stanhope, his pencil poised.

"I won," said Haldean succinctly. "That's partly why I'm not looking my usual suave self. The other reason is that the Russians who attacked us last night turned up, and we had a devil of a job escaping from them. With any luck, the police have arrested them. You can ask Superintendent Ashley for those details."

A muttered "Wow!" escaped Stanhope and his pencil raced.

"But look, Stanhope, I know it might spoil the story, but I'd be glad if you didn't mention I was the person who brought Stanton in. We've got a lot of friends in common and it'd cause no end of a stink if they thought I'd nabbed him."

"If you say so," said Stanhope, doubtfully. "I can't say I like it."

"Come to think of it," continued Haldean, "I'd be awfully obliged if you laid it on a bit thick about the injuries I got last night. If you could say I'm still laid up, that'd let me out, don't you know."

"Perhaps," said Stanhope, even more doubtfully.

"Because if you could see your way to doing that, then I can let you have the dope on Captain Stanton and his fight with the Russians. All right?"

Stanhope wavered, then came to a decision. "How badly injured do you want to be?"

"I'd like a fair degree of dilapidation. Steer clear of permanent mutilation, although this wretched arm is killing me. I'll have to make a miraculous recovery at some time, but suggest any letters should be care of death's door. That should do it."

"As a matter of fact, as I said, you do look a bit washed out," said Stanhope with a grin. "Righty-ho. Consider yourself off the active service list. Now then, what's this dope on Stanton?"

"He's been holed up in a cave at Upper Ranworth, in the grounds of his old childhood home, The Priory, suffering from cold and hunger."

"Cold and hunger," interjected Stanhope. "Great. Lovely copy in that. He's a DSO, isn't he? I could play for a bit of sympathy, especially if he's been fighting Russians."

"But the real news is that he's suffering from amnesia brought on by a head wound sustained while escaping from the scene of the crime and a flare-up of shell shock."

"I say! This is wonderful."

"Now for some reason we don't know, he was hunted by the same Russian gang who attacked us at Hesperus." Haldean smiled. "You'd better say he evaded them. He thumped one with a branch and another fell down a convenient hole. Their car, a red Wolseley, got blown up too." He stifled a yawn. "It had a match in the petrol tank."

Grinning broadly, Stanhope carried on writing. "Anything else?" he said, glancing up. "I could do with a few more details."

"Ashley'll tell you," said Haldean with another yawn. "Or you can make them up. I'm so tired I can hardly see straight. You could point out the obvious fact that as the chief suspect can't remember a damn thing that happened, the full truth of the matter may never be known. Oh, and you'd better mention my book, Stanhope, if you don't mind. I've got *The Secret of the Second Shroud* coming out with Rynox and West next month. You could give the magazine a boost as well. The sales for *On the Town* have dropped off the last couple of months. This should help them along a bit. After all," he said, trying to avoid Isabelle's appalled stare, "business is business."

"It certainly is," agreed Stanhope. "I'll get hold of Mr Ashley and phone this in as soon as I've talked to him. I couldn't get the young lady to say a few words about her fiancé, could I?"

"Certainly not," snapped Isabelle, directing a glare of loathing at Haldean.

"Don't worry, miss," said Stanhope, cheerily. "We'll think of something. You say you're going to keep this to yourself, Haldean? Wonderful!" He walked quickly away, leaving Isabelle alone with her cousin.

"Well," she said in a voice with icicles on it, "at least you've got some publicity for your wretched magazine. I hope you're pleased with yourself."

"Reasonably so," he agreed, finishing his beer. "And, after all, business *is* business."

CHAPTER
THIRTEEN

"I don't think," said Haldean, as he climbed out of the car in the old stable yard at Hesperus, "that you should say anything about getting engaged to Arthur." He was so tired he was slurring his words. "It'll be difficult, you know? For you, I mean. And him. Got enough to cope with."

"All right," said Isabelle. She looked at him slumped against the car, his face paper-white. "Come on, Jack," she said softly, putting her hand through his arm. "We're nearly home now." He leaned on her as they walked round the stables to the side door. "Is there anything else I should know?"

Haldean stopped, swaying. "Yes," he said eventually. "Not a word about meeting Stanhope in the pub. That's really important. Vital. Otherwise everything could go wrong."

"All right," said Isabelle again. "Jack . . . did Arthur really hit you?"

Haldean nodded. "He's a useful sort of boxer. Good fighter. Good bloke."

"Can I tell them he's in the police station?"

"Oh, yes. That's the whole point. Tell them that."

Lady Rivers came into the hall to meet them. She took one look at Haldean and packed him off to bed. "Now then," she said to Isabelle after Haldean was safely upstairs, "will you please tell your father and me exactly what's going on?"

When Haldean awoke the next morning, he felt as if someone had gone over him in a steam-roller. His arm still throbbed, but as he gazed at the bedroom ceiling he felt happier than he had for days. He was on the right lines at last and Arthur was safe. That's what he wanted and that's what he'd got.

He picked up his watch but it had stopped. Stiffly he got out of bed and tried to dress, but his shoulder was like a block of wood. There was nothing for it, he'd have to borrow Chapman, Uncle Phil's valet, once more. He had a vague memory of Chapman helping him last night and was mildly surprised that he hadn't appeared this morning. His morning cup of tea hadn't arrived, either.

He pulled his dressing gown round him. The upstairs of the house was deathly quiet, but there were clinking noises from the hall. He walked down the staircase and met Egerton, the butler, carrying a tray of sherry glasses. "I say, Egerton, where is everyone?"

"They're all at the inquest on Mr Preston, sir."

"The inquest?" said Haldean, astonished. "What time is it, for heaven's sake?"

Egerton glanced at the grandfather clock. "It's nearly one o'clock, sir."

"Good God." Haldean sat on the stairs and grinned at the butler. "I suppose that means I've missed breakfast. Judging by those sherry glasses, they'll all be back for a bunfight soon. Why on earth did no one wake me up? I should have gone to the inquest. I've missed it now."

Egerton returned Haldean's smile. "Lady Rivers left strict instructions, Master Jack, that you were not to be disturbed. She said —" Egerton gave an apologetic little cough — "that *if that silly boy* — I am quoting her ladyship, sir — *has no more sense than to go running round the countryside and getting into fights, then someone has to look after him.* If I may be permitted the observation, Master Jack, you look a great deal better than you did last night."

"I could still do with Chapman to give me a hand getting dressed, though." He ran a hand round his chin. "I wouldn't mind a shave, either. It's a pity about the inquest."

"I'll send Chapman to your room, sir. The Superintendent left a note for you." Egerton put down the tray of glasses and brought Haldean the envelope from the hall table.

Haldean ripped it open. *Dear Haldean, Good work in bringing back Captain Stanton. He's fine. Things are hotting up here. Don't worry about missing the inquest because we're going to move for an adjournment. Yours, etc., E. Ashley.* Mollified, Haldean looked at Egerton. "He says they're going to tie a can to it. The inquest, I mean. Egerton, I know everyone's busy, but there wouldn't be any coffee, would there? To say nothing of breakfast?"

"Her ladyship left instructions with the cook that you should have breakfast when you woke up, sir."

"Tell the cook she's a wonderful woman," said Haldean with a smile, walking up the stairs. "I'm starving."

Dressed and shaved and full of eggs, bacon, sausages, kidneys, mushrooms, fried bread and coffee, Haldean amused himself by reading the lurid account of Stanton's arrest and his encounter with the Russian gang in the *Daily Messenger* when the family arrived home. He finished the article, smiling broadly. Stanhope had done him proud. Although carefully admitting the possibility of Arthur's innocence, he had given the impression that all England could breathe easily now that the deranged killer of Lord Lyvenden was safely behind bars. The Russians were being vigorously hunted down and, as for Haldean, it would be a miracle if he saw the day through. According to the *Messenger*, *The Secret of the Second Shroud* was likely to be published posthumously. He winced a bit as he read the heart-rending description of Isabelle, bravely keeping her lonely vigil, waiting for news of her fiancé. She wouldn't thank him for that at all.

She didn't. "Have you seen the paper?" she hissed at him in an undertone when he joined the rest of the family in the hall. "I can't believe what that man wrote about me and Malcolm. I've a good mind to tell everyone about Arthur."

"Don't do that," said Haldean, alarmed. "For one thing, you could wreck everything and for another, you'd cause a fearful stink. Arthur's hardly the blue-eyed boy at the moment."

"All right," she said mutinously. "But I don't like it, Jack. By the way, Mr Ashley came back with us. He wants to see you. I think he's in the gun room."

Haldean went along to the gun room where Ashley was sitting with a tray of coffee.

"You look much more yourself," said Ashley approvingly. "I thought you were going to keel over at one point last night."

"So did I," said Haldean, lighting a cigarette. "Still, at least I've got Arthur safely under lock and key. Did you manage to arrest any of the Russian gang?"

Ashley shook his head. "I'm sorry to say we didn't. I got on to the police at Upper Ranworth as soon as you'd called, and they were on the spot fairly quickly." He grinned. "By jingo, you made a mess of that car, didn't you? Incidentally, we found a number plate that had been blown clear of the wreckage."

Haldean looked up. "Did you?"

"Yes, but don't get too excited. The number was false, as we might have predicted. It's never been issued. Anyway, what we did find were two dead men."

"What?" Haldean stared at Ashley. "But, damn it, Ashley, we didn't kill anyone. Arthur walloped this bloke, Mick, with a branch and the red-headed chap fell into the cave."

Ashley held his hand up. "I didn't suggest that either you or Captain Stanton was responsible, although I couldn't really have blamed you after what you've told me. No, I think both men were murdered by the two remaining gang members before they escaped. They had both been shot, right through the forehead. It was a real executioner's job. This Mick, whose real name is Michael Wilson and who has a long record of violent crime, was laid out on the path and the red-headed man, whose name is Walter Tanswell, was in the cave, as you described. He was involved in that march in London the other day and he was wanted for assaulting two policemen. He's got a record of robbery with violence. It didn't take long to identify either of them."

"But . . ." Haldean smoked for a few moments in appalled silence. "Neither of them can have been that badly hurt, surely. I'd expected the red-headed chap to have broken his leg, but that's all. As for the other bloke, he'd have come round eventually. Why on earth were they murdered?"

"Because they would have held up this Boris and the other man, I suppose." Ashley shrugged. "That's all I can think of."

Haldean felt sick. It was so utterly ruthless. He finished his cigarette without speaking. At least Arthur was safe. He held on to that thought. Arthur was safe. With a shudder he crushed out his cigarette and looked at Ashley. "Is that what you meant in your note about things hotting up?"

"Not exactly." Ashley got up and checked the door was shut. "This may seem like small beer after your adventures, but I've got a line on Alfred Charnock," he said, sitting down once more. "We've been keeping an eye on him and we think it's all going to come off tonight. With any luck we should catch him in the act."

"And the act is?"

Ashley smiled. "Just at the moment I'd rather not say."

"Hold on." Haldean leaned back in his chair. "Now I know he's really up to something dodgy, let's see if I can guess. I've devoted some thought to Uncle Alfred, after all."

"Well, go on then," said Ashley sceptically. "Let's hear the Sherlock stuff. Amaze me."

Haldean grinned. "Listen to me, Watson, and be amazed." He leaned back in his chair, ticking the points off on his fingers. "One, Alfred Charnock needs some money. Two, it's connected with Lyvenden. Three, whatever it is he's doing, he's been doing it for months, so it's not a one-off affair. Four, we're near the coast and when you add his wartime service, the man who came on Saturday night and the fact that Our Alfred sneaked home at four in the morning, soaking wet, it all points one way."

Ashley laughed. "Well done. That's very neat reasoning but it's not evidence. Now I have got some evidence. Burrows, the landlord of the Pig and Whistle, had two new garages erected at the back of the pub round about Christmas. They're big, expensive structures, both of them, and very securely locked. The really interesting thing is that although Burrows owns a horse and wagon, he doesn't keep the wagon in the new garages."

"Have you managed to have a look inside?"

Ashley shook his head. "We didn't want to ring any alarm bells. That's not to say I don't have a very good idea of what's in there, mind."

He looked up as the door opened and Isabelle came in.

"I'm sorry to disturb you," she said with a smile. "Jack, Dr Speldhurst's here. He wants to have a look at your arm."

"Right-ho," said Haldean, standing up. "Ashley, while I'm gone, take a look at this." From his pocket he produced Lord Lyvenden's cigarette case and put it on the table. "Not a word about this, Belle," he warned.

"I'll add it to my list of secrets," she said. "Is that Lord Lyvenden's cigarette case?"

"Yes. Arthur ran off with it. Now, inside that horrible object was this piece of paper." He took out his pocketbook and produced the note, laying it on the table beside the cigarette case.

Ashley picked it up with a frown. "What's it all mean?"

"I bet it's in Russian."

"Have you any idea what it says?"

Haldean gave a very slight warning glance at Isabelle. "I'd rather not say just now. I can guess. Mind you, that's all it is, a guess, but it makes sense. However, there's no point guessing when we can get the thing translated easily enough. Can Scotland Yard do it for us, d'you think?"

"I imagine so," said Ashley.

"Well, why don't you give Bill Rackham a ring? You can use the phone in the library. I'll go and see Dr

Speldhurst and then we can run up to London, if you don't mind driving my car."

"Drive your car?" said Ashley doubtfully. "I can drive, but I've never handled a car like yours."

"It's simple enough."

Ashley came to a decision. "Very well then. I have to be back for this evening, though."

"Jack," said Isabelle as they left the gun room, "what's my mother going to say when she finds out you've gone up to London?"

He grinned. "Break it to her gently, old thing. I'll be back tonight."

Superintendent Ashley buttoned up his coat and climbed into Haldean's Spyker. "I've been on to the Yard and it's all right with them." He grasped the steering wheel with a certain amount of apprehension, looking down the rakish length of the blue-and-silver bonnet. "I've never tackled anything like this before."

"You'll be fine," said Haldean. "Be careful with the gears. It's a four-speed box, but quite simple when you get used to it. She's a bit sticky on the clutch. Off you go. I've turned the engine over so she's quite warm."

Ashley gingerly put the car into gear, released the brake and depressed the accelerator. "God strewth!" Despite his caution, the car leapt forward with alarming speed. "How on earth you can drive round in this without breaking your neck, I don't know. Didn't you tell me you won her in a bet?" he added, carefully bringing the car out of the stable yard. "I never had you pegged as the sort who went in for high stakes."

Haldean grinned. "Not unless you count getting licked to a splinter by Uncle Phil at billiards. Careful, old thing. There's a bit of oversteer until you're used to it. I won her fair and square. The editor and most of the staff of *On the Town* went down with flu and I agreed to write an entire issue from Society Snippets to Answers to Correspondents — plus From the Editor's Office, a twenty-thousand-word thriller and a story of Young Love. I had the thriller tucked away in a drawer, but the rest was real sweat-of-my-brow stuff. The proprietor, who stood to lose a goodish bit if the issue didn't come out, bet me this car I couldn't do it in three days. I did it in just over two and a half and he paid up like a gent."

"Blimey, it takes me that long to write a letter." Ashley hunkered down further in the seat. "Now, tell me what you think is on that piece of paper . . ."

Inspector Rackham stood up as they were shown into his room. "By crikey, Jack," he said, his Lancastrian voice rich with relief, "I thought you'd had it when I read this morning's paper. It sounded as if you were on the way out. I could hardly credit it when Mr Ashley said you were on your way up to London."

Haldean grinned. "Almost everyone I know expects to cough up for a funeral wreath in the very near future. However, reports of my early demise are, I'm glad to say, very much exaggerated. Can you get the translation done for us?"

"There'll be no problem about that. Hand it over."

309

Rackham put the paper in a cardboard file and took it out of the room. He was back within minutes. "It won't take long. I'd warned our Russian expert we had some business for him. Is there anything else we can do for you?"

Haldean sucked his cheeks in. "As you know, I'm interested in the Paradise Club. Somebody from Stanmore Parry telephoned the Paradise Club the day Smith-Fennimore was kidnapped. I'm wondering if the Paradise Club could be connected with the Russians who attacked us at Hesperus and chased Stanton and me round the grounds of The Priory yesterday."

"A sort of gang headquarters, you mean?" Bill Rackham tapped his fingers on the desk. "Not that those two who were killed yesterday were Russian, of course. It's interesting about the Paradise Club, Jack. I'm told it's all right. Keeping an eye on undesirables isn't my department, but they usually know what they're doing. It gets rather boisterous from time to time, that's all. It's a bit of a dive, but it's fashionable. Goodness knows why. Have you been there?"

"I've been a couple of times. You're quite right, it is a dive. But fashionable."

Rackham smiled. "I don't know why you waste your time or money. Now, having said that about the place, I think there might be more to it than we've realized." He opened his desk and took out an envelope. "I was going to get in touch with you anyway this morning, Mr Ashley. Here's a picture of a real beauty." He took a photograph out of the envelope and laid it on the desk. "It's another dead man and he is a Russian. He was fished out of the Thames yesterday morning with a bullet through his chest. It didn't attract much attention, because the papers have been full of the Lyvenden case, but I wondered if you knew anything about him, as you seem to have had quite a lot of Russians on your hands recently." He looked at Haldean. "Do you recognize him?"

Haldean's eyebrows rose. "I'll say I do. It's the man who was at Hesperus on Sunday. You didn't see him, Ashley, but it's him all right. He looks a bit the worse for wear." Haldean handed back the photograph. "Who is he, Bill? Do you know?"

Rackham returned the picture to its envelope. "His name's Youri Gerasimov and he frequents — or frequented — the Paradise Club. That's what made me wonder if there is anything going on there. We've had him for armed assault. He attacked a fellow Russian with a knife about a year ago, but the fight was split up and he ended up with a caution. So that's the man who was at Hesperus, is it?"

"That's right. He terrified the wits out of Lord Lyvenden. Bill, I want to find out a bit more about the knife he had."

"The knife which was used on Lord Lyvenden?" asked Ashley.

"That's right. I'd like to know where it came from. Is there a suitable shop where this bloke could have bought it from? It could come from anywhere, I know, but I wonder if there's anywhere likely near the Paradise Club?"

"There might be." Rackham stood up and took a Kelly's Street Directory from his bookshelf. He spread the book open. "It's off Soho Square, isn't it?"

"That's right," said Haldean. "Lacey Street."

The telephone on his desk rang. "Excuse me," said Rackham briefly, and picked it up.

Haldean and Ashley could see his face change as he listened to the tinny voice on the other end. "Right! I'm on my way. Get some men and the surgeon as fast as you can. Tell them to meet us there. We'll be inside."

He slammed the phone down triumphantly. "We've got Smith-Fennimore! We had a break with an informer. We might've known where he'd be. He's in the Paradise Club."

"Let's go in my car," said Haldean urgently. "I know where the club is. I'll drive."

"What about your arm?" asked Rackham, making for the door.

"Damn my arm. What do you need the surgeon for?" he asked as they hurried downstairs.

"The informer said he's in a bad way."

Haldean shot the Spyker out of Scotland Yard, threading his way in frustration through the London traffic. They arrived in Lacey Street in record time.

Rackham climbed out of the back of the car. "We're first to arrive. I'm not surprised, the way you drove. I say, Jack, look across the road. I think that might be the shop you're looking for."

Across the street stood a small fishing tackle and gun shop. Haldean shook his head impatiently. "Never mind that now. Here's the club. Is it locked, I wonder?"

He put his hand to the door. It swung back.

"Watch yourself," warned Rackham. "We don't know who's inside."

Half expecting to be challenged, the men filed into the building. No sound came from the club. The reek of stale tobacco and the sickly smell of spilled alcohol met them. Like all places that are meant to be seen at night, the Paradise Club seemed unreal in the daylight. It was tawdry enough in the evening, but with a superficial glitter that could pass for glamour. By day the ugliness showed through the cheap and grimy furniture.

"What a dump," said Ashley in disgust.

They were beginning to think the entire club was deserted, when Ashley noticed a door leading from the cloakroom that gave on to an enclosed stairwell. "This looks like the entrance to the attics," he said. "We might have better luck upstairs."

Rackham stopped at the doorway and picked up a little glittering syringe, handling it carefully with a handkerchief.

They turned as the street door opened. Dr Crimmond, the police surgeon, and three constables under the charge of a sergeant came in. Rackham handed the syringe to the doctor. "Have you any idea what that's been used for?"

"Not until it's analysed," said Dr Crimmond. "It's an unpleasantly suggestive thing to find though, isn't it?"

They walked quietly up the stairs, hearing no sounds apart from the traffic in the street outside. The stairs opened on to a landing off which ran four rooms, containing old boxes and various bits of junk: broken lights, decrepit chairs, an antiquated piano. A thick layer of dust, tracked through by footprints, covered the bare floorboards.

At the end of the passage, a door stood partly open. Rackham pushed it back and gave a triumphant cry. "Here he is!"

Malcolm Smith-Fennimore lay unconscious, hands and feet tied, under a window at the far end of the room. His breathing was slow, quiet and shallow and his face was slicked with sweat. The doctor, followed by Haldean, pushed his way through and knelt beside him.

Haldean was appalled as he took in the extent of Smith-Fennimore's injuries. A dark, ugly bruise ran across his dirt-smeared forehead and temple, and his shirt sleeves had been ripped open, exposing ominous marks on his forearms. "What on earth have they done to him, Doctor?"

The doctor glanced up briefly. "Those are cigarette burns from the look of it. The swine really had it in for him." He lifted up Smith-Fennimore's eyelids and nodded. "Pupils contracted. Just as I thought." He glanced at Inspector Rackham. "This man's been poisoned with one of the opiates. Morphine or heroin, I should imagine." He opened his bag and, taking out a little bottle, started to prepare a syringe.

"What's that?" asked Haldean.

"Strychnine," replied the doctor, briefly. "It's a stimulant." He pinched a piece of skin on the inside on Smith-Fennimore's arm and plunged the needle home. "All we can do now is wait." The doctor sat back on his heels. "He's pretty far gone, though. It's going to be touch and go. Let's get him untied."

The rope round Smith-Fennimore's wrists and ankles was too tight to be undone, so they cut him loose with Rackham's penknife. The doctor cleaned the wounds on his forehead and arms. Smith-Fennimore stirred and groaned.

Haldean settled down beside the unconscious man, taking one of the cold hands in his own, seeing where the rope had bitten into the flesh of the wrists. Smith-Fennimore coughed, and, rolling his head to one side, retched. Haldean and the doctor held him until the spasm was over, then sat him up, supporting his back.

"Treat him gently," warned the doctor. "We have to get him on his feet but he mustn't make any sudden movements."

Smith-Fennimore blinked wearily round the room, then focused on Haldean. "Jack! I thought you were dead." He reached out and grasped his arm feebly. "Jack, thank God you're not dead. I didn't want you to die."

"We've been worried about you," said Haldean in a voice that wasn't quite steady.

"Have you?" asked Smith-Fennimore, faintly. He put a hand to his face. "My arms are sore."

"Cigarette burns," said the doctor laconically, pleased with his patient's recovery.

"I remember now. It was pretty beastly."

Dr Crimmond looked up as a noise sounded in the street. "That'll be the ambulance we sent for." He nodded at a policeman standing near the door. "Go down and tell them where we are."

"No," said Smith-Fennimore, weakly. "I want to go to Hesperus. I want to see Isabelle."

"You're going to hospital," said the doctor firmly. "You'll be as right as rain in a couple of days, but I want you to receive some proper treatment and you need to be under observation tonight. And no questions until tomorrow," he told the watching Inspector Rackham.

The ambulance men lifted Smith-Fennimore on to a stretcher and, with Dr Crimmond in attendance, carried him down the stairs and into the ambulance.

"Can I come with you?" asked Haldean.

The doctor shook his head. "There's nothing you can do," said the doctor. "He'll be all right now. We're going to the King Edward's. He's in good hands."

Haldean shook his head irritably, but climbed into the ambulance beside Smith-Fennimore, and took his hand. "I've got to be off now, old man," he said softly. "I'll ring the hospital to see how you are. All the best."

"All the best," repeated Smith-Fennimore, answering Haldean's tentative smile with the ghost of a grin. "Don't worry." His eyelids flickered shut. "Lord, I'm tired."

The ambulance drove off. Rackham heaved a sigh. "I think we got to him just in time. What do you want to do now?" He gestured across the road. "We could go and have a word with your gun-shop man and see if that's where Gerasimov did buy his knife."

Haldean shook his head. The sight of Smith-Fennimore had shocked him so much he was finding it difficult to put his thoughts in order. "No," he said eventually. "You'll have to do that, Bill. You're official. You can ask questions. I can't."

"Fair enough," said Rackham cheerfully. "Buck up, Jack. You heard what the doctor said. He's very sound, Dr Crimmond. Your friend'll be fine. I suppose we'd better get back to the Yard. You need that translation, apart from anything else. After all, that's what you came for."

"Yes," agreed Haldean dully. "Yes, I suppose it is."

It was gone ten o'clock before they finally arrived back in Stanmore Parry, after what, with Ashley at the wheel, seemed like a horribly slow journey.

As he drove the car into the stable yard at Hesperus, Ashley looked at Haldean's strained face with concern. His eyes were haunted and he had said little on the way back. The trip to London had taken it out of him all right. "Are you sure you want to be around tonight?" he asked. "You look as if you'd be better off in bed rather than sitting on the beach in the cold."

"And miss out?" said Haldean with an attempt to summon up his old spirit. "Don't be silly. Besides that, I couldn't sleep. Not now."

"Well, if you're sure." Ashley climbed stiffly out of the car, glad to stretch his arms and legs once more. "I'll walk from here. Nothing much should happen before three or so, but we want to be in position long before then. Meet me at the station at one and we'll walk down to the beach together. I know I can rely on you not to say a word."

Haldean walked into the house. He hoped there was something to eat. He hoped he wouldn't have to face too many questions. The last hope went unanswered.

Haldean lowered himself from the grassy overhang to the sand below, and found a little hollow set into the bank where he could sit unobserved from above. There was a scrambling noise and Ashley joined him.

"I've got the men sorted out," said Ashley in a low voice.

Haldean glanced up and down the dark and apparently deserted beach. "They're well hidden," he whispered. "You'd never guess they were here."

"That's the idea," agreed Ashley. "I think we've got a good hour before anything happens, so we can relax a bit. How was Hesperus?"

Haldean pulled a face. "Mixed. Everyone was glad to hear about Smith-Fennimore. Charnock was twitchy."

Ashley grinned. "I bet he was."

Haldean hugged his knees, watching the moonlight catch the waves in drops of silver before rippling out in surf. "Bubble and Squeak Robiceux have gone home, by the way. Now the inquest is over they haven't got any reason to stick around. Lady Harriet and Mrs Strachan have pushed off too. Lady Harriet announced that now Arthur had been arrested there was no reason for her to stay. Mrs Strachan didn't say an awful lot but folded her tents and stole away."

"Technically they're within their rights, of course," said Ashley. "I hope we've got addresses for all of them."

Haldean nodded. "Aunt Alice has. She didn't say as much, but it was obvious she wasn't sorry to see the back of either Lady Harriet or Mrs Strachan. How's Arthur, by the way?"

"Captain Stanton? I saw him this evening. I couldn't help liking him. He's pinned a lot of faith on you. Look, Haldean, I know what you believe and I'm inclined to agree, but I'd be a lot happier if Captain Stanton could actually tell us what happened. I'd like to think of a way to jog his memory."

Haldean wriggled back in the sand. "It'd help Arthur, certainly. What I'm really interested in is seeing what Bill Rackham turns up about this knife of Gerasimov's. That'd show us whether we're on the right lines."

"And that'd be a relief," said Ashley. "Not that I honestly doubt it."

They sat in silence in the darkness, watching the full moon make a dancing path on the black, lapping water. "The sea's high, isn't it?" said Haldean eventually.

"It's high tide at three. We're coming up to the spring. They'll need it to get the boat in."

Haldean shivered. "I wish they'd get on with it. This waiting's awful."

Ashley grinned and relaxed back against the sandy earth. "That's nine-tenths of proper police work. We've traced the ins and outs of this operation. It's been going on for months now. You can't expect them to hurry just because we're here."

It was nearly an hour later and the moon had moved across the heavens before another sound broke into the rhythmic murmur of the sea. It was the deep chug of a ship's steam engine. Haldean screwed up his eyes as the shape of the headland across the bay seemed to alter. He watched, fascinated, as the dark bulk of a ship loomed close into the shore. The engine was silenced, then there was the rattle of an anchor chain, followed by voices and splashes as two boats were lowered from the ship.

From the road behind came the creak of wheels and the clopping of hooves. Above their heads rose a sudden whisper of voices, quickly hushed, and the noise of footsteps coming down the cliff path. Haldean and Ashley shrank back into the deep shadow of the overhang as a few loose pebbles scattered past them. The two boats drew nearer to the shore, the sound of the oars in the rowlocks and the grunt of the stroke clearly audible across the water.

Two men jumped lightly from the grass on to the sand. Haldean caught sight of their faces in the moonlight. One was the white-haired Slav he had seen on the night of the ball. The other was Alfred Charnock. The men went down to the sea's edge to meet the boats and help pull them on to the sand.

A few yards further along a man led a horse pulling a wagon heavily laden with rectangular boxes down the gentle slope on to the beach. "That's Burrows," muttered Ashley in Haldean's ear.

"We'll get these crates unloaded," Haldean heard Charnock say, "then go back for the rest."

Charnock, the Slav and the boat crews started to unload the boxes from the wagon and pile them on the sand.

Ashley gave a glance at Haldean, drew out his police whistle and gave a piercing blast. At once the beach was full of shouts and men running to surround the wagon. Burrows lashed out and was brought down by a truncheon on his shoulder. The Slav leapt back defensively, was caught by two policemen, struggling as handcuffs were snapped round his wrists. The boat crews, for the most part, stood bewildered by the pile of boxes. Alfred Charnock drew a revolver.

"Now then, my lad, none of that!" Ashley brought his stick crashing down on his arm, sending the gun flying. Charnock nursed his arm, looking at the policeman in disgust. "I suppose I'm meant to say, 'The game's up.'" Then he caught sight of Haldean. "You! My God, I might have known you'd be involved."

Haldean said nothing.

Ashley wasn't having it. "Shut up, Charnock. You can have your say afterwards. Get those boxes open, men."

Charnock went for his jacket pocket. Ashley started forward. "Don't be so edgy, officer," said Charnock smoothly. "I'm only getting a cigarette. And please address me as *Mr* Charnock." He drew out his case and struck a match. "Why don't you ask your friend, Jack the lad there, to tell you what we're shipping?"

"It's my guess the boxes contain arms," said Haldean in a controlled voice. "Ah, I see they do." The lids had been crowbarred off and the inner tarpaulin ripped open, revealing an array of gun barrels, gleaming in the moonlight. He stooped down and picked one out. "And they come from Lyvenden's factory."

"Perhaps you can tell me where they're going?" drawled Charnock, pulling on his cigarette.

"Ireland, at a guess," said Ashley.

"Ireland!" Charnock looked genuinely amused. "No, we're going a little further afield than that. Try Yalta."

Haldean stared at him. "What? In the Black Sea?"

"Congratulations. Ten out ten for geographical knowledge."

"Are you supplying the Reds?" asked Ashley.

"As if," drawled Charnock. "Wrong side, my dear man."

Haldean paused, gun in hand. "You're taking them to the Ukraine, aren't you? Where you were in the war. These are for the White Russians. I bet you're getting a handsome profit."

"Naturally. Well done. I see I can't put anything past you."

"But what the dickens is it all about?" demanded Ashley. "If you want to ship guns to the Ukraine why are you doing it in this hole-in-a-corner way? Why all the secrecy?"

Charnock smiled. "It makes life more exciting?" Ashley snorted. "No, I can see you won't buy that. However, it does raise the interesting question of what I'm actually meant to be guilty of, doesn't it, officer?"

"Damn me, I'll get you under the Firearms Act if I can't get you for anything else," said Ashley pugnaciously.

Charnock's smile flickered for a moment. "Yes, there is that," he said, in the tone of one approving a good stroke by his opponent on the cricket field. "Yes, I must admit you've got me there. I must admit that piece of petty legislation hadn't actually crossed my mind."

"It's going to occupy it extensively soon," said Ashley grimly. "Alfred Charnock — *Mr* Charnock — I arrest you on the charge of holding arms without a licence as prohibited by the provisions of the Firearms Act 1920. You do not need to say anything, but anything you do say may be used in a court of law. In fact, my lad," he added with great satisfaction, "you're nicked."

CHAPTER
FOURTEEN

The next morning, Superintendent Ashley had a long interview with Sir Philip and Lady Rivers. Haldean, waiting in the hall for his telephone call to King Edward's Hospital to be put through, gave him the thumbs-up sign as he walked past. After half an hour Ashley sought out his friend who had migrated to the stone seat on the terrace.

Haldean put down his newspaper, offered Ashley a cigarette and, like a conjuror producing a rabbit from a hat, brought out a quart bottle of beer and two glasses from under the seat. "I thought you might need a spot of something," he said with a grin, "so I laid in supplies."

Ashley poured a beer and took a much-needed drink. "My word, I'm glad that's over. As you know, I've got a great respect for your aunt and, despite what I think of Charnock, he is her stepbrother, after all. You'd told them what had happened, I gather."

"Yes." Haldean sat back thoughtfully. "Aunt Alice took it pretty hard. That's only natural, of course. I broke the news first thing this morning and it wasn't at all nice. She knew Charnock was always on the windy side of the law but this time he could end up in quod."

Ashley pulled a face. "He probably won't, more's the pity. Between you and me, I'd love to see him behind bars for no other reason than to wipe the smile off his face, but a decent barrister could probably get him off, worse luck."

"And I suppose poor old Uncle Phil will have to foot the bill. Still, it should put a crimp in Mr Charnock treating the place like a home from home. Uncle Phil won't stand for that any longer."

"What beats me," said Ashley, finishing his beer, "— is there any more in that bottle, by the way? Thanks — is why Charnock couldn't get the correct licences and do the thing openly instead of all this cloak-and-dagger stuff. I was convinced he was shipping arms to Ireland but those weapons really were destined for the Ukraine, you know. I still can't understand why he needed to shroud himself in so much secrecy."

"Well, he'd have had to apply for a gun licence, of course," said Haldean. "And with his record there's absolutely no guarantee he'd have got one. The Ukrainians probably wanted it kept as much undercover as possible so as not to alert the Moscow authorities. And then again, when you consider who the arms were destined for, I can't see Lyvenden being too anxious to explain things to his associates."

Ashley smacked his knee. "That's it! That'd scuttle the whole show before he'd got it off the ground."

"So come on, Ashley, tell me all the juicy details. What's happened to the ship?"

"That's in our hands. There wasn't any trouble about that, especially as most of the crew were on the beach. No, it all ended fairly tamely and Charnock, Burrows and the crew are all safely in custody in Lewes. To be honest, I imagine we'll end up letting the foreigners go but I'd love to nail Charnock and Burrows. Anyway, this smuggling racket has been going on for months. Charnock was in control of things on this side. He'd order the arms from Lyvenden, and Lyvenden would supply them on the QT. He'd dispatch a lorry-load of arms from Birmingham once a month and they were stored in those garages of Burrows' until they could be shipped across to the Ukraine. Incidentally, listening to your uncle on the subject of Lord Lyvenden was interesting."

"I bet it was," said Haldean with a grin. "I never could make out what he saw in him. Go on."

"How it worked was like this. A large amount of money was paid to Lyvenden in January. That was followed by a regular payment every month. The Birmingham police are checking all this, but that's more or less what happened. That white-haired bloke who came to the ball — his name's Volodymir Ferencz, by the way, if I've pronounced that right — is first mate on the Ukrainian ship. Anyway, there should have been a shipment on Saturday, the night of the ball, but things went badly wrong. There was a fire in the engine room and the captain was injured, so they had to limp round to Newhaven for repairs. Ferencz was sent to tell Charnock, who went to see for himself, which is why he came back here late and wet through. Ferencz has been dividing his time between Newhaven and the Pig and Whistle where he met up with Charnock. We followed him back to the ship, made enquiries and found that the work was due to be finished yesterday. I knew they needed high tide to get the ship in to the beach, so when I looked up my tide-tables and found that high water was at three this morning, I thought we could make a pretty good guess as to when everything was going to happen."

"This is brilliant stuff, Ashley," said Haldean. "How did Charnock come to be involved?"

Ashley filled his pipe reflectively. "He knew the Ukrainian captain, an Andriy Dobryrnin, who was in charge of the other end of the operation. We've got Captain Dobryrnin in hospital and I saw him first thing this morning. I've got a lot of sympathy for him. His wife and children were massacred by the Bolshies and his home destroyed. He was left for dead, but when he eventually recovered, he wanted to start his own private war. They're not exactly pro-Moscow in those parts, so he had a lot of support. He contacted our friend Alfred, who he'd worked with in the war, and, as it happened, came as the answer to Charnock's prayers. Charnock had got badly involved in one of Lyvenden's schemes last year and couldn't pay up. He offered Lyvenden the chance to export arms at a fair old profit and Lyvenden agreed. Charnock, of course, creamed off a handsome take. To give him his due, his part worked like clockwork. They used the Pig and Whistle as a meeting place. It's pretty isolated and no one noticed a thing until our attention was drawn to it, as you might say."

Haldean poured another glass of beer for them both. "It'd be better for Aunt Alice if he could get away with it, I suppose, but I bet he won't dare show his face near my uncle for a long time to come. I'm not surprised you're pleased with yourself. Here's to."

Ashley smiled and raised his glass. "What have you got to tell me? Do you know how Commander Smith-Fennimore is getting on?"

"He's doing fine. I rang the hospital and was able to talk to the doctor who's looking after him. He should be discharged tomorrow morning. I presume he'll be coming back here. In fact, he's almost bound to come back here." He paused. "He nearly went west, you know," he added thoughtfully. "We really did get there just in time. If he'd died . . ." He shook himself. "Anyway, after that, I spoke to Bill Rackham about Gerasimov's knife. He's left an official message for you at the station, but the gist of it is that we were right."

Ashley raised his eyebrows. "You were right, you mean." He rubbed his chin thoughtfully. "That changes things. That changes things quite a bit."

"Yes . . . What d'you think?"

Ashley sat back and didn't say anything for quite a time. "I'm satisfied," he said eventually. "But I know I won't be able to convince the Chief. As I said last night, if only Stanton could remember what actually happened, it'd help."

"It might," said Haldean. "Though I'm not all that convinced it would." He bit his lip. "Look, will you telephone Lady Harriet? She wouldn't talk to me, but she might speak to you. We could do with knowing what she really was doing on the morning Lyvenden was killed. I can guess but I'd like to be sure. After that . . ." He paused. "What we need now is a confession. Anything which backed it up would be a bonus."

"Well, I could have told you that," said Ashley blankly.

Haldean gave a fleeting grin. "Don't worry. I'm not being as dopey as I sound. I've got an idea . . ."

A couple of hours later Haldean walked into the summerhouse. Isabelle was in there, an open book face down on the bench beside her. "Hello," he said. "I didn't know you were in here."

"I was just thinking things through." She watched curiously as her cousin started to poke around under the bench that ran round the wall. "Jack, what are you doing?"

"I was looking for a plant pot or something."

"Why don't you try the potting shed?"

"I can't. It's full of gardeners and so on. Ideally, I want an undisturbed plant pot or a Greek urn or something like that." He stood up and looked round the summerhouse in a dissatisfied way. "The trouble is, on the one hand, this place is perfect. It's far enough from the house so no one need see anyone coming or going but there's a very convenient shrubbery within sight. On the other hand, it's a bit bare."

"There's a table, a bench and an oil lamp. What else do you want?" She stopped. "I know. A plant pot."

"The lamp certainly isn't much use," he said, picking it up. He stepped back and a floorboard creaked under his foot. "Ah!"

He knelt on the floor and took his knife from his pocket. Wincing slightly, he opened the blade. "My arm's improving," he said cheerfully. "I couldn't have done that a couple of days ago." He ran the knife round the floorboard. "This sounded very promising . . . Bingo!" He pressed down on one end of the board. The other end rose and he pulled it loose, revealing an empty space beneath. "Wonderful," he said with deep satisfaction, kneeling down and peering into the hole. "Do you know, it's all matchboarded under here?" he said in a muffled voice. "It makes a very nice space. Excellent." He replaced the board and sat back on his heels.

Isabelle was watching him with amused interest. "Are you going to tell me why you're ripping up the floorboards?"

Haldean scratched his nose. "To be honest, I don't think I'd better. Sorry, old thing. Not yet, anyway. Er . . . there's no need to tell anyone what I've been doing." He stood up and took out his cigarette case, offering it to her.

"Thanks," she said abstractedly. "I'll add it to my list of things I mustn't mention. Have you finished your excavations?"

"Yes," he said, dusting off his knees. He struck a match for her cigarette and she leaned forward thoughtfully.

"Jack, I've been to see Arthur. He says there's some sort of scheme to bring him up here tomorrow."

"That's right. The idea is to try and give his memory a jolt."

Isabelle pulled a face. "There's a whole lot I could do with him forgetting. How I kept him on a string, for instance. I can't believe I treated him like that."

Haldean sat down beside her. "Don't be too hard on yourself," he said gently.

"Too hard on myself!" She rounded on him. "Just at the moment I don't feel as if I could be. You tried to tell me, didn't you? About being rotten to Arthur, I mean, and I wouldn't listen. And then there's Malcolm, as well. We parted on such dreadful terms but since then he's been through the mill and I feel I owe him an explanation. After all, he did try and save my life when those Russians attacked us. Apparently he's coming here tomorrow, too. I hope to goodness he doesn't run into Arthur."

Haldean coughed and rubbed the back of his neck awkwardly. "As a matter of fact, that's the whole point and purpose of it all. To get them to bump into each other, I mean."

She gazed at him. "But why, Jack?"

He shrugged. "To be honest, this is more Ashley's scheme than mine. I'm a bit iffy about the whole thing, but Ashley's frustrated by Arthur's inability to remember what actually happened. He believes his loss of memory is genuine all right, which is more than Major-General Flint, the Chief Constable, does, and he's prepared to let Stanton run into Smith-Fennimore to see if that will do the trick."

"But you don't think it'll do any good?"

"I didn't say that," said Haldean, flicking the ash off his cigarette. "In fact, it might be quite useful." He smiled at her. "But we'll have to wait till tomorrow to see if it comes off."

Sister Agnes Birch smiled brightly at her patient. "I'm glad you passed a good night, Commander. You're due to leave today, aren't you?"

Smith-Fennimore, with a thermometer in his mouth, could only grunt in reply.

Sister Birch extracted the thermometer and held it up to the light. "Excellent," she said and then stopped. "Is everything all right? You look worried about something." She looked at the typewritten envelope he was holding. "I hope it's not bad news."

Smith-Fennimore grimaced. "I've had better. When can I leave?"

"The doctor should be round shortly, Commander. As soon as he says you're free to go, you can. There was a telephone call, by the way, earlier this morning, from a Major Haldean. He rang yesterday, didn't he? He sends his regards and asked if you'd telephone him as soon as you can."

"Thanks. Look . . . can you ask the doctor to hurry up? I really need to leave as soon as possible." His eyes flicked involuntarily back to the letter. "Something's come up. Something urgent."

★ ★ ★

Haldean prised up the loose floorboard in the summerhouse. "What d'you think?"

Ashley peered into the hole. "Yes, that should do it."

Haldean put the board back and the two men walked along the path by the shrubbery to the house. "As we know, five o'clock is the latest things can happen," he said. "If the balloon hasn't gone up by then, we'll have to think it all through again."

"When's Commander Smith-Fennimore due to arrive?"

"From what he said on the telephone this morning, he'll be here round about three. He explained that he had to come by train as his Bentley's here and he wants to take it back. I offered to pick him up from the station but he said he'd get a taxi. When are you bringing Arthur along?"

"I'll have him here just after three." Ashley looked at Haldean keenly. "Are you all right?"

Haldean pulled a face. "I just hope it all comes together. If it doesn't — well, you've got Arthur under lock and key and with General Flint convinced of the case against him, it might be very tricky."

"I think," said Ashley drily, "that it might be very tricky in any event."

It was ten to three. Haldean, who had been waiting on the stone seat at the end of the terrace since before two, looked up as Constable Bevan approached.

"Note for you, sir," said Bevan.

"Thanks." Haldean took the note, read it, sighed, and stuffed it in his pocket. So far the plan had worked.

He heard the doorbell ring as he went back into the house. Going into the hall, he was in time to see Egerton opening the door to Smith-Fennimore.

"Hello, old man," he said, as Egerton took Smith-Fennimore's hat and coat. "My word, you're looking brighter than when I saw you last."

"I feel a bit brighter, too, Jack. How's things?"

"Interesting." Haldean motioned for Smith-Fennimore to follow him across the hall. "Look," he said in a low voice, "I feel I ought to warn you there's something happening. Unless you've seen the papers, you won't know anything about this, but Arthur Stanton's been arrested."

"So I gather," said Smith-Fennimore. "Apparently he's lost his memory, which I thought was rather convenient."

Haldean shook his head. "You don't understand, Fennimore. He really has lost his memory. He can't remember a thing about Lyvenden or being here for the ball or anything. Superintendent Ashley thinks there's a fair chance that if Stanton could see us in Lord Lyvenden's room, something may click."

Smith-Fennimore's eyebrows crawled upwards. "A sort of reconstruction of the crime, you mean?"

Haldean grinned. "Well, I think we'll stop short of actually stabbing anyone but that's the general idea, yes. I know you've only just arrived so I don't know if you'd like a wash and brush-up first, but will you join the merry throng?"

"Count me in. I'll change later. When does it all start?"

"Fairly soon. If we go and park ourselves in Lyvenden's room, we'll be around when Arthur arrives."

"Anything you say, Haldean," said Smith-Fennimore, falling into step beside him as they walked along the hallway to the garden suite. "What I really want to do is to see Isabelle. She must have come to her senses by now."

"She was very concerned, that's for sure," said Haldean tactfully. "I told her what a state you were in when we found you in the Paradise Club. You were very nearly a gonner."

"So I believe. Apparently the police had a tip from an informer. What were you doing there, by the way? According to the papers you were on the way out yourself."

Haldean shook his head. "I had a bullet through my arm and a nasty crack on the head. This arm's still crocked but the papers exaggerated it all. I suppose it made a better story. Anyway, Ashley and I had gone to see Inspector Rackham of Scotland Yard. There's a bit more to all this, but I'll bring you up to date later. You know that Russian bloke who came here last Sunday? Well, he was found dead in the Thames. He'd been shot. I was looking at his photograph when the call came through about you, so I led the way to the club."

Smith-Fennimore looked at him sharply. "He was shot?" He looked oddly shaken. "Do the police think he was connected with the gang who attacked us?"

"He might have been."

"They're a ruthless bunch, all right. It was very lucky for me you were there."

Haldean shook his head. "Don't mention it. Did you find out what was behind it all? I mean, why were you abducted in the first place? Were they after money?"

"Only in a manner of speaking."

They went into the garden suite. Smith-Fennimore paused on the threshold and drew a deep breath before entering.

"It's strange to be in here again," he said. There was a twist in his voice. "And you say Stanton's being brought along?" Haldean nodded. "I don't really like the idea," said Smith-Fennimore. He looked round the room. "And I don't like it in here. There's an atmosphere, somehow. I don't know why but there is."

And there was, thought Haldean. It should have been just a room. The bed had been stripped and a bright blue canvas cover laid over it. The oak dressing table, wardrobe, table and desk, which had been full of Lord Lyvenden's papers and belongings, were bright with polish, the stained rug had been removed and the boards over the windows were gone. The newly glazed french windows were wide open, filling the room with sunshine and all the scents from the garden outside. It should have suggested nothing but cleanliness, fresh air and diligent housework, but there was something else present. Haldean realized with a shock that he knew what it was. He'd known it often enough in the war. It was more like a smell than a sensation, but it set the hairs on the back of his neck tingling. It was fear.

He shuddered involuntarily. "So why were you abducted?" he asked, settling himself on the edge of the table. He was being, he knew, deliberately casual. He pulled the ashtray towards him.

"Influence, I suppose," said Smith-Fennimore, offering him a cigarette. "Have we got long to wait before everyone turns up, Haldean?"

"Not long. How d'you mean, influence?"

Smith-Fennimore prowled restlessly round the room. "The gang — they were Russians, of course — knew I was due to attend the Paris Conference in October." Haldean looked puzzled. "You've got to remember that the Soviets are desperate for international trade, and for that they need credit. I've just found out how desperate they are."

"You mean they want someone to lend them a few quid?"

Smith-Fennimore smiled briefly. "They need more than a few quid. Germany's sympathetic but the Germans are as badly off as the Russians. Do you know one American dollar is worth about four million marks? I think we and the Italians would be more willing to grant Russia credit if they would accept responsibility for Tsarist debts. If they could be persuaded to grant compensation for the foreign assets which were seized after the October Revolution, then they might get somewhere. When you think we loaned the Tsar nearly sixty million you can see there are some readjustments to be made. But they're unwilling to pay anything back, of course, because that means money going out and not coming in. Anyway, they wanted me to support their cause in Paris."

Haldean thoughtfully smoked his excellent Turkish cigarette. "I wondered if it was a bit more personal. Apparently Smith, Wilson and Fennimore have substantial deposits of Tsarist gold. I thought they might be after that."

Smith-Fennimore sighed. "Was that in the newspapers? That blasted gold is nothing but a nuisance. They were, of course. We've got well over a million in our vaults that was invested with us ages ago. Most banks who had any dealing with pre-Revolutionary Russia have some deposits. We can't draw on it, of course, because the owners are no longer alive, but we've got to pay to guard it. To be honest, I'd hand it over like a shot if I could find a way of getting rid of it legally, but as it is, they can whistle for it." He tapped his arm and winced. "And stubbing out cigarette ends on me isn't going to make me change my mind, either. When they saw they were getting nowhere, I suppose they thought they might as well finish the job."

"Why did they choose the Paradise Club?"

"I don't know. The police asked me that yesterday but I was only taken there at the very end before they injected me with that stuff. Apparently the club's owned by an Armenian who knows nothing of the day-to-day running of the place. It's my guess that the men who kidnapped me knew the club would be empty at that time and just dumped me there." He crushed out his cigarette and ran an impatient hand through his hair. "All I really know was that it was a foul experience. Is this reconstruction business going to take long?"

Haldean glanced at the clock. "Ashley should be along soon with Arthur in tow. I imagine Isabelle and Uncle Phil will be with him as well."

Smith-Fennimore brightened. "Isabelle's coming? I wish they'd hurry up. It beats me what there is to reconstruct. After all, what's there to find out? We know who murdered Lyvenden. The police have got Stanton safely behind bars and presumably all they're waiting for is a date for his trial." He drummed his fingers on the mantelpiece. "It strikes me as a waste of time. After all, who else could it be but Stanton?"

Haldean wrinkled his nose. "That's fair enough, but I did wonder about Alfred Charnock. D'you know he's been arrested too?" Smith-Fennimore looked astonished. Haldean smiled. "Not for murder, I have to say. He had a very lucrative deal with Lyvenden, smuggling arms to the Ukraine for the Whites."

Smith-Fennimore stared at him. "Lyvenden was supplying arms to the Ukraine? The devil. The old devil."

"The old devil indeed," agreed Haldean. "Charnock ran the whole show and both he and Lyvenden made a mint out of it. It did strike me that if Tim found out, which, considering how careless Lyvenden seems to have been with his papers, he very well might have done, Charnock could have bumped him off. He says he was on board the Ukrainian ship on the night of the ball — that bloke who called for him was the first mate — and I imagine the ship's crew would give him an

339

alibi. Although it would probably hold up in court, to my mind his story doesn't amount to a hill of beans as I imagine the Ukrainians would say anything Charnock wanted them too."

Smith-Fennimore shook his head. "I can't see it, Haldean. Yes, Charnock could have shot Tim, but why would he murder Lyvenden? That would be killing the goose that laid the golden eggs as far as he was concerned, surely. Stanton's the man. He has to be."

Haldean hitched himself further on to the table. "Perhaps, but I couldn't help wondering about who else could be guilty. I did think about Lady Harriet."

"I can imagine her killing her husband certainly," agreed Smith-Fennimore, lighting another cigarette, "but why on earth would she kill Tim?"

"Tim knew all about Lyvenden's affair with Mrs Strachan. Lady Harriet might have guessed but if she knew Tim had actual knowledge and wouldn't tell her, she could have shot him in frustration."

"Surely she'd have been far more likely to shoot Mrs Strachan if she felt like that," said Smith-Fennimore. "There was obviously no love lost between them."

Haldean nodded. "That's true. I wondered about Mrs Strachan, too. Lyvenden scared her rigid and when she lost fifty quid on Monday night, it didn't take Lady Harriet long to work out where the money had come from. You know Lady Harriet wouldn't say what she was doing on the morning Lyvenden was murdered? She'd arranged to meet Mrs Strachan to demand the money back. I guessed that, as they were both out at the same time, their intention was to meet each other.

Superintendent Ashley telephoned Lady Harriet and she, rather unwillingly, confirmed what we'd known and what we'd guessed and filled in the details for us. The meeting didn't actually take place. By that time Lady Harriet had decided to divorce Lyvenden and a meeting seemed, she said, superfluous. It didn't half look suspicious for both of them at the time, though."

Smith-Fennimore sighed. "Look, Haldean, I don't care who looked suspicious at the time. It's completely academic now. The police haven't got Stanton under lock and key for fun. Damn, we virtually saw him do it."

"Yes, we did, didn't we?" said Haldean. "And, d'you know, despite having tried fairly hard to think of anyone else who could be guilty, I keep coming back to Stanton. It's just that I've known him for so long, I felt obliged to try my best for him."

Smith-Fennimore shrugged. "That's only natural, I suppose."

"However, there are still some details Superintendent Ashley wants to find out. That's why he's so keen to give Stanton every chance to regain his memory."

"If he's lost it at all," said Smith-Fennimore cynically.

Haldean smiled. "I don't think there's much doubt he really has. Have you got your gun on you? That Colt automatic, I mean?"

Smith-Fennimore's hand instinctively went to his jacket pocket. "Yes. Why?"

"Can I have a look?"

"I suppose so." Smith-Fennimore pulled out the gun and handed it over.

"Thanks." Haldean weighed it in his hand. "I imagine this packs quite a punch." He aimed the gun at the open window.

"Steady on," said Smith-Fennimore. "It's loaded."

Haldean squinted down the barrel. "You clipped the side of Stanton's head with one of your bullets. Add that to his previous troubles and yes, I think he's genuinely lost his memory."

He looked up as heavy official footsteps sounded outside the french windows.

Smith-Fennimore stood alertly as Stanton, walking between Sergeant Ingleton and Constable Bevan, came into the room. Superintendent Ashley brought up the rear and behind him, walking with her father, was Isabelle. Stanton wasn't handcuffed but the policemen stood very close to him.

"Hello, Malcolm," said Isabelle in as natural a voice as she could manage. "I'm glad to see you've recovered."

"We all are," said Sir Philip.

"Isabelle . . ." began Smith-Fennimore, then stopped. He shook himself like a man coming up from underwater, strode forward to the door and took her hands, looking intently into her eyes. "Isabelle, I have to know. Are we engaged?"

There was a movement from Stanton and Smith-Fennimore turned on him. "So you remember that much, do you? I wonder just how much else you remember?"

Stanton, standing between the policemen, looked honestly puzzled. "I don't remember you at all," he said. He glanced over to Haldean. "I'm sorry, Jack. This isn't working." He looked round the room and shivered. "I wish I hadn't agreed to this. I don't know why, but this place gives me the creeps."

"The creeps, Arthur?" Haldean twirled the Colt in his hand. "I'm not surprised. After all, this is where this happened." He pointed the gun toward the open window and fired.

The noise in the quiet room was deafening. Isabelle yelped and Stanton made an instinctive jump towards her. The two policemen recovered their prisoner with a very unfriendly glare at Haldean.

"Good God, boy!" exclaimed Sir Philip. "What d'you think you're doing?"

Haldean half smiled. "Sorry, everyone. It's scary, isn't it? Especially when you're on the other end of the bullet as Arthur was that day. I'm reconstructing the crime."

Smith-Fennimore held out his hand for the gun. "I think you'd better give me that before you decide to take this reconstruction business any further." He slipped the gun back in his pocket.

"Well, Arthur?" said Haldean. "Did that stir any memories?"

Stanton shook his head and swallowed. "No. I tell you, I can't remember a thing."

Smith-Fennimore made a dismissive noise. "I bet you remember more than you want to admit."

"And so do I," said Haldean quietly. He met Stanton's startled gaze squarely. "I think it's about time we all knew the truth."

Smith-Fennimore looked from Isabelle to Stanton, shrugged, then settled himself on the edge of the table across the room from Haldean. "We know the truth."

"We know what appears to be the truth," corrected Haldean. "For instance, we know Lyvenden ruined Arthur's parents and as good as killed them. That's a dickens of a motive. I found the murder weapon hidden in his room. That's his means. We all know Arthur was alone with Lyvenden. That's his opportunity. And he was caught, literally, red-handed. He protested very loudly that he hadn't done a thing but how can we possibly believe him? Because an innocent man — any innocent man — who discovered the body would have come for help."

Stanton turned desperate eyes to Haldean. "Jack, please! I can't deny it, because I can't remember a blessed thing about it."

"So even if you were utterly innocent, you wouldn't know."

"That's right. I simply don't know. I can't remember a damn thing."

Ashley made a discontented noise. "It might be to your advantage if you could remember what happened, Captain Stanton. There's a very strong case against you. I can't see it failing."

From somewhere on the edge of hearing, Haldean heard a faint sigh of relief. It was a sound he had been hoping for. "There is a strong case against you,

344

Arthur," said Haldean, taking a cigarette and tapping it on the back of his hand. "There's only one thing wrong with it. It's complete and utter rubbish. You didn't murder Lyvenden and you certainly didn't murder Tim."

"Damn it, boy," said Sir Philip testily. "Nobody did murder Preston."

"Oh yes, they did, Uncle."

"Well, who was it, then? And if the police know who it is, why haven't they arrested him?"

"They can't arrest him," said Haldean softly. "You see Tim's murderer is dead. Tim's murderer was Lord Lyvenden."

"What?" Sir Philip looked stunned.

Smith-Fennimore moved restlessly but said nothing.

"You see," continued Haldean, "Lord Lyvenden knew Tim had found a letter. Tim thought it was written in code. In fact it was written in Russian and what was in the letter could destroy Lyvenden. There were other papers, too, and they very well could have been in English. I don't think Tim saw them, but Lyvenden, the careless, stupid, frightened Lyvenden, probably believed he had." His voice was grim. "It was Lyvenden, the arms manufacturer, who was knowledge-able enough about explosives to plant a squib that would go off at ten to ten. It was Lyvenden who sent the maid on a quite unnecessary errand to fetch Lady Harriet's shawl so she could witness the false gunshot when Lyvenden was surrounded by people. It was Lyvenden who sent Tim running backwards and forwards throughout the ball so his absence wouldn't be noticed. It was Lyvenden who had arranged for fireworks to explode all evening so that one little pop from a tiny pistol wouldn't be noticed. It was Lyvenden — who else? — who was in a position to dictate the business letter which could be used as a suicide note and, finally, it was Lyvenden who followed Tim upstairs when he'd sent him for his cigarette case and used his own gun to commit murder."

"Hold on, Haldean," said Smith-Fennimore. "Aren't you overlooking something? Lyvenden was murdered too. You're not saying he stabbed himself in the chest to convince us of his innocence, I presume?"

Haldean shook his head. "Of course not." He blew out a long mouthful of smoke. "You see, you knew Lyvenden, didn't you, Smith-Fennimore? You knew what he was capable of. After all, you shared his secret. It didn't take you long to work out what had really happened. You knew he'd murdered Tim and you hated him for it. Hated him enough to kill him."

Smith-Fennimore slid off the table and stood upright. He looked at Haldean for a few moments with blazing eyes and then he laughed. "Oh, come on! You told me you wanted to do your best for Stanton but this is going a bit too far. Have you any intention of proving this or are you just going to sling accusations around? I'd like to know exactly what you're basing this fantastic theory on. There's such a thing as slander, you know."

"So there is." Haldean met his eyes challengingly. "Slander means making a false accusation. I haven't done that. Perhaps if I just run through your actions, you can tell me where I've got it wrong?"

"Be my guest, old man." Smith-Fennimore took a cigarette from his case. "If it gives you any pleasure, do go on."

Haldean bowed his head briefly. "Thank you. On Monday, when you were in London, you bought a knife identical to the knife the Russian had left. After you scratched the initials A.C. and Sunday's date on it, your knife was indistinguishable from the original. You bought it from Hawley's fishing tackle and gun shop on Lacey Street. You're a well-known man, Smith-Fennimore, and it was easy to get a picture of you. Mr Hawley picked out your photograph very easily."

"He might be a motor-racing fan," said Smith-Fennimore icily. "Have you thought of that?"

Haldean shrugged once more. "He was very certain about it. However, you needed another knife. You'd already stolen the one Mr Charnock had. They're common enough, those knives. I thought it was odd when you insisted otherwise."

"I don't know anything about knives!" Smith-Fennimore insisted. "This is complete nonsense and you know it."

"Nonsense?" repeated Haldean. "I don't think so. After golf on Tuesday morning you went to Lord Lyvenden's room with a large briefcase containing the Argentine business papers, a motoring coat, some motoring gloves and Gerasimov's knife. You must have been irritated to find Adamson still around. However, by producing the confidential papers and asking

Lyvenden to study them there and then, you more or less ensured that Adamson would be dismissed."

"It's odd I don't remember all this."

Haldean ignored him. "You waited concealed in the corridor until Adamson left. It's dark along there and you managed it easily. Then you went back into Lyvenden's room. I imagine that you explained to Lyvenden whilst you put on your motoring things that you were going out in the car. You could even have told him that you wanted to post the document right away, and waited until he signed it. Then you stabbed him, rather messily, with the Russian's knife. You left the papers, which would provide a useful excuse for a search later on, and, stripping off the bloodstained coat and gloves, packed them back in the bag. I think you left through the french windows and took the key. We never did find the key. You put the bag in your car. We're at the end of the house here, and there was little chance of you being seen. Entering the house through the side door, you ran into me in the hall and proceeded with the rest of the grim charade, the business of framing Arthur Stanton. Arthur worried you, didn't he?"

"If you say so," said Smith-Fennimore. "I can't remember being so very worried myself."

Haldean shook his head. "You were. Despite Isabelle being engaged to you, you knew he was your one real rival. Besides that, you needed someone to blame for the murder. You attempted to shoot him when he ran for it, but when he escaped you were going to leave him to a shameful death on the gallows."

348

Haldean stopped, looking at Smith-Fennimore. "You crossed a barrier there, didn't you?" he said softly. "I don't know, but I'm willing to bet that was the first mean, degraded action of your life. The murder you could excuse; it was revenge. But this? I think it worried you. You couldn't justify yourself."

For a fraction of a second there was an expression in Smith-Fennimore's eyes which Haldean knew would haunt him. Defiance, shame . . . regret? Then, just as quickly, the expression was gone, replaced by wary interest.

Haldean shrugged. "You knew Stanton's reputation for mislaying things and played on it. You took his cuff-link box from his room that morning and planted the second knife in his chest of drawers. If I hadn't been so obliging as to find it, you would have done so. You concocted a very natural reason to be left alone with Stanton. I left you both and went downstairs. You took the knife with you, of course."

Smith-Fennimore held his cigarette with a hand that was trembling slightly. "Don't stop there, Haldean," he said pleasantly. "This is fascinating. I can see why you became a writer of cheap fiction."

Haldean ignored the gibe. "You both went to Lyvenden's room — you probably said it was better if you both arrived for lunch together — and you ushered Arthur in first, shut the door after him and jammed it tight with a door wedge. Then you went off, the picture of innocence, to join the rest of us at lunch. That door's rock solid when you wedge it. I know, I've tried, with the help of the Superintendent here. Things worked out

349

perfectly at first. Lawson brought the news of the dust-up in Lyvenden's room, which was, of course, Arthur shouting to be released. When we went to investigate, you made it your business to be first to the keyhole, fell over, and removed the wedge. There's a wedge in the billiard room which has a handle on it. That would do the job perfectly. Then things started to go badly wrong. Arthur escaped and Isabelle spoiled your aim for the second shot. And — this must have been a bitter blow — so far from Isabelle turning against Arthur, she became passionately convinced of his innocence. But you couldn't draw back, could you? You'd gone too far for that. When you went out alone you were able to throw the coat, gloves, bag and knife into the sea."

"At this point," said Smith-Fennimore, in stinging mockery, "I believe I'm meant to shout 'Oh, God, it was me!' and either make a run for it with the flatties on my tail or, less dramatically, fall to my knees and sob out a confession. Well, you can go making up this hogwash until you're blue in the face, but I'm not about to do either. I'm sorry, Haldean, but you're holding a busted flush."

Haldean moved very slightly and his eyes narrowed. "Wait. You wanted the Russian document. This room was securely locked and the windows boarded up but, as soon as you could, you got in here. You couldn't find the document but knew where it must be after I told you that Arthur had run off with Lord Lyvenden's cigarette case. Well, now you had a problem. Not only was Stanton loose, he had a very incriminating piece of paper on him. The police couldn't find him and your Russians couldn't find him, so you arranged your own kidnapping so you could have a free hand to control the search without having to make dangerously traceable telephone calls. When he turned up, you arranged to be found in circumstances that would allay any suspicion."

Malcolm Smith-Fennimore blew a smoke-ring, crushed out his cigarette and lit another one. "Very interesting," he remarked. "Nicely put together, too. I must read some of your stuff sometime. You haven't got a shred of proof, though."

"Oh, haven't we?" said Haldean. He shifted his weight on to the ball of one foot, like a boxer about to strike. "What about the paper we found in Lyvenden's cigarette case?"

Smith-Fennimore didn't reply.

Haldean held up the original and the translation. "I'll read it, shall I?"

The cigarette which Smith-Fennimore was holding to his mouth trembled, but still he said nothing.

Haldean cleared his throat. "*We, the undersigned, promise to transfer the sum of One Million and Forty Three Thousand Pounds Sterling, currently held by Smith, Wilson and Fennimore, Bankers, London EC3, under the title of 'Russian Investment Holdings: 1904–14' less a commission of Twenty Thousand Pounds Sterling, to be divided between the undersigned, to the Account of Yusif Dolokhov, Bank of Vaud and Fribourg, Geneva, Number RN3426750956YD. Signed: Victor, Lord Lyvenden. Malcolm Smith-Fennimore.*"

Smith-Fennimore ran his tongue over his dry lips. "So you've found out some of the bank's private business, have you? I can't see that's any of your concern."

"Oh, really? Not even when the money's not yours to transfer? That's theft."

"Tell everyone who Yusif Dolokhov is, Haldean," said Ashley, quietly. "That'll explain what's been going on."

"Yusif Dolokhov," said Haldean, looking round the room, "is a prominent member of the Central Committee of the Russian Communist Party. He's also known to be very hot on the Third International, which is behind the Bolshevik uprisings that are making Europe such an interesting place. Soviet Russia is desperate for money. Smith-Fennimore decided to supply some. Smith-Fennimore is funding a revolution. Aren't you?"

Smith-Fennimore licked his lips again. "I can't see why these private details of bank transfers should be read out to all and sundry." His voice was unsteady. "But even if you have been poking around in my affairs, you still haven't proved a damn thing about murder."

"Oddly enough, I thought much the same," said Haldean unexpectedly. "You were safe — you were absolutely safe — as long as no one guessed what you'd done. But what if someone had seen you that day in the corridor? What if someone had seen you usher Arthur into the room and wedge the door tightly shut? And what if that same someone had written to you demanding money *and you paid up?*"

Smith-Fennimore's face turned putty white. "I . . . I . . ." he began, then stopped.

"After all," went on Haldean implacably, "all the letter said was that the writer had seen what you'd done in the corridor outside Lord Lyvenden's room at quarter to two or so on Tuesday. If the answer was nothing, you would not have left two hundred pounds under the floor of the summerhouse."

Ashley drew a large brown envelope from his pocket. "I saw you go into the summerhouse, Commander. You left this envelope concealed under the loose floorboard. It contains two hundred pounds in cash which we will be able to trace to you and a note in your handwriting."

Smith-Fennimore, his face a ghastly colour, tried to summon up his old manner. "I really can't see why I should listen to any more of this." He edged down the room, away from Haldean. "In fact, I'm not going to any longer."

Ashley moved forward to block the french windows but Smith-Fennimore made a sudden leap, not for Haldean, but for Isabelle. Holding her tightly by the throat, he wrestled her round in front of him. Pulling out his gun he clapped it to her head. "One move from anyone and she's for it." Sir Philip started forward and Smith-Fennimore's finger tightened on the trigger. "I mean it," he grated. He started backwards towards the french windows. "Come on, Isabelle. You're coming with me."

Isabelle made a valiant attempt to free the clutching hand from her throat. "Malcolm, stop it! You're hurting me!" Her voice was a gasp. "Malcolm, let go!"

The grip on her throat increased, an ugly caricature of an earlier caress. "To be someone else's wife, my dear? I don't think so."

"You damn swine!" It was Arthur Stanton. He slipped from between the policemen and stood between Smith-Fennimore and the window. "Let her go. Let her go or so help me, I'll kill you."

The gun jerked up to cover Stanton. Stanton, regardless, walked towards him.

Isabelle squirmed desperately in Smith-Fennimore's grasp, then stamped down hard on his foot. Grunting, he slackened his grip and she wriggled free. Smith-Fennimore pulled the trigger as Stanton sprang.

The gun clicked uselessly. Smith-Fennimore fell under Stanton's attack and pulled the trigger twice more. Scrabbling on the floor, he threw off Stanton, evaded Ashley's clutching hands, avoided Sir Philip, cracked his fist into Sergeant Ingleton's stomach and raced for the window.

"Come on!" yelled Haldean. "After him!"

Constable Bevan slapped a hand on Arthur Stanton's shoulder.

"Let him go!" yelled Ashley.

Stanton caught hold of Isabelle as Haldean led the way out of the window at a run. "Are you all right?"

"Of course I am," she said in a croak, clutching her throat. "Come on! After him!"

CHAPTER
FIFTEEN

By the time they got out of the house, Smith-
Fennimore had vanished. "Split up!" roared Ashley.
"We'll take the front of the house." He turned on the
two policemen following Stanton. "You there! Let him
go! Smith-Fennimore's the one we're after."

Haldean set off at a run, Isabelle and Stanton behind
him. He expected Smith-Fennimore to go for his car
and, as he reached the old stables, there was the growl
of an engine and the Bentley shot past them, nearly
clipping the wall of the yard.

Haldean swore and made a leap for his car. By the
time he had started the engine Isabelle had scrambled
into the front seat and Stanton had bundled into the
back. Screaming down the drive in fourth, he was just
in time to see the Bentley turn left through the gates
and lurch wildly out on to the road.

"Where's he going?" yelled Stanton from the back.

"I don't know," called back Haldean, hunched over
the wheel. "Not the village, thank God. It might be the
coast road."

The coast road. There was something about the
name that tugged at Stanton's memory but his mind
remained infuriatingly blank. The road twisted and

curved and for a time they lost sight of the car in front. A cart loomed up in front of them and Haldean swerved, misjudged his distance, and ended up with a wheel on the grass. He revved the engine again and they shot off, desperate for a sight of the Bentley.

"Look down the side roads as we pass!" shouted Haldean. "He might turn off."

"No, there he is, look!" called Isabelle. The road straightened out and they were running along an open stretch with hedges on one side and the sea on the other. The Bentley was just visible as it went over a dip and started to climb the other side.

Stanton suddenly realized he had been this way before. Then, desperate for shelter, he had held on to the hedge while the sea raged over the wall, terrified by the roar of the thunder and the violence of the lightning. The lightning! He had a quick, vivid, terrifying picture of lightning forking down and a road which reared up like an angry horse. "Slow down, Jack!" he yelled. "The road's wrecked!"

Haldean saw a barrier across the road at the top of the hill, a flash of white as Smith-Fennimore turned to look at them, followed by a hideous howling squeal from the brakes of the Bentley as the big car slid sideways through the barrier. For a moment Haldean thought the car was safe. It seemed to settle on the edge of the cliff, then, with a ghastly inevitability, toppled over and with a roaring crash fell lazily end over end down to the beach. Smith-Fennimore was flung free and clung desperately to the cliff edge, hands scrabbling in the chalk. Haldean stood on the brakes and skidded to a halt beside the hedge. He switched off the engine and in the silence came a sound he never wanted to hear again: a scream followed by the repeated thud of a man's body, falling.

Haldean scrambled out of the car and ran as if demons were after him, looking for a way down to the beach. There was just one possible path and he half climbed, half fell down, choking with impatience, utterly heedless of broken nails and bleeding hands. Then he was on the beach, the soft sand clogging his heels, running to the body twisted at the base of the cliffs.

He flung himself down on his knees beside Smith-Fennimore. He had seen too many flying accidents to doubt the outcome. From the way the legs were bent back it looked as if the spinal cord was snapped at the hips. "Malcolm!" he cried. "Malcolm!"

Smith-Fennimore's eyes flickered open. His voice came in little painful gasps. "Jack?" Haldean reached out and grasped his hand. "I haven't long. I know. You were right. I killed Lyvenden. I asked him if he'd taken care of Tim and he boasted about it. He thought I was pleased. He'd never be found out, never, and we were safe. Hated him." His hand tightened and his face contorted. "I wanted to help Russia. I loved Russia so much. They're going to have a perfect world. I wanted to help. But . . . but the things they did . . . and I knew. They were ruthless. I didn't stop them. I went rotten inside." His eyes closed momentarily. "Why you, Jack? I liked you."

Haldean swallowed. "I had to help Arthur."

The hand trembled in Haldean's. "Stanton. Jealous of Stanton. Isabelle loved him. I knew that. Barriers. You're right. I crossed a barrier. Rotten . . . inside. Yashin tried to kill you. I wouldn't let him." His face contorted once more. "He said you were dangerous. You were. You knew, didn't you? I thought I could fool you. Told Yashin I'd fool you. Argued . . . I was so damn pleased when I saw you alive. Didn't want you to die. Thought I'd fooled you."

"You did for a time," said Haldean softly. "Then I realized it had to be you, despite everything, even the cigarette burns."

"Morphine. Took morphine. Didn't hurt. Yashin did it. Thought it'd work."

"It nearly did," said Haldean unsteadily. "But Malcolm, it was a hell of a risk. What if we hadn't got there?"

The ghost of a smile flickered and was gone. "Always liked risk . . . and . . . and it didn't matter. Not after what I'd done." He twisted in agony. "I can't feel my legs." He coughed blood and Haldean held his head.

A voice beside him said softly, "I'm here, Malcolm." It was Isabelle. She knelt down and took the twitching hand from Haldean's grasp. In a convulsive movement Smith-Fennimore held her hand to his cheek and kissed it.

His breathing grew harsher and then, with a judder, his head rolled back and he was still.

Isabelle leaned forward and kissed his forehead. Blindly, she turned to Stanton standing behind her. "Take me home, Arthur. Please take me home."

Haldean remained kneeling by the broken body. Time seemed frozen. The sea creamed in and out behind him, the gentle surge of the waves like the far-off breathing of a living thing; and he grieved for the man who might have been.

Eventually he became vaguely aware of other figures on the beach, looking at him, talking about Malcolm — endless talk — and men cautiously approaching the burnt-out wreck of the Bentley many yards away. Then strong, kind hands lifted him to his feet, a blanket was wrapped round his shoulders and a flask of brandy put to his lips. The sharp, pungent taste made him blink and choke. When he looked, he saw that it was his uncle holding the brandy, smiling at him encouragingly. "It's all right now," he managed to say, his voice sounding like that of a drunken man. "Let's go home. It's over."

It was nine o'clock in the evening the next day. Haldean hadn't wanted to talk at all when he had been brought back from the wrecked Bentley at the foot of the cliffs and, rising early, he'd spent most of the day in London. He'd got back shortly before dinner. Now, dinner over, everyone was in the drawing room. Haldean, Isabelle was relieved to see, had lost that awful haunted look.

The telephone rang in the hall and Isabelle went to answer it. "That was Mr Ashley," she said when she came back into the room. "He wanted to tell us that the last of the gang from the Paradise Club have been arrested."

Haldean gave a sigh of satisfaction. "That was today's task. Ashley and I have spent the day in

Scotland Yard. I hoped they'd get the lot and it sounds as if they have."

"And a good thing, too," said Sir Philip, putting down his newspaper. "Mind you," he added, looking at Haldean and Stanton, "from what you told me, it seems remarkable that there was anyone left to arrest. They seemed to be killing each other off nicely."

"Did they get Vargen Yashin?" asked Haldean. "The one they called The Boss?"

She shook her head. "He shot himself before they could arrest him."

"What did I tell you?" said Sir Philip with quiet triumph. "It's a great pity he didn't shoot himself first. It would have saved us all a good deal of trouble." He shuddered. "My word, when I think of that night they came here . . ."

"Things might have worked out differently for that poor devil, Malcolm, if Yashin hadn't been involved," said Haldean, reflectively.

Sir Philip gazed at him. "*That poor devil?*" he repeated incredulously. "What the deuce d'you mean, Jack?"

Haldean smiled. "Don't you see what a tantalizing prize Malcolm must have been? Not only was he rich and sympathetic to the cause, he had over a million pounds of Tsarist gold in his bank. Apparently this bloke, Yashin, was a very persuasive character. I bet Yashin made a point of cultivating Malcolm."

"I think part of what made Malcolm do what he did went back to his friend, Jimmy Chilton," said Isabelle. "You remember how I told you about that? He said how rotten things were here, that a man like that should be left to die of cold. The Communists say that they want to make life better and fairer for everyone." Sir Philip made an impatient noise and Isabelle turned to him. "I don't know I believe them, Dad, but it can sound very attractive."

Haldean nodded. "It can. And to someone who loved Russia as Malcolm did, it must have been compelling. He felt things very strongly. And to be fair to him, he didn't want to hurt you or me. Anything but."

"He didn't seem to mind what happened to me," said Stanton.

Lady Rivers nodded in vigorous agreement. "I can understand him wanting to revenge his friend. I don't agree with private revenge but it's understandable. What was truly wrong was him throwing the blame on Arthur."

"The whole wretched business was wrong from beginning to end," said Sir Philip. "What beats me, Jack, is how on earth you got to the bottom of it all. I mean, why were you so sure that young Preston hadn't killed himself?"

"That's easy," said Haldean. Walking to the sideboard he poured himself a whisky and soda. "Tim hadn't been depressed or suicidal when I met him and I couldn't see why he should suddenly become so. Then Arthur found the famous disappearing cigarette packet and I overheard Lyvenden and Mrs Strachan going at it hammer and tongs about secret papers and so on, on Sunday afternoon."

"I was convinced Tim had killed himself," Stanton said thoughtfully. "The idea of him being murdered seemed so bizarre." He sat up straight. "I've just remembered it! Really remembered it, I mean. How Tim looked when he was telling me about the money he owed and what I said and everything."

Isabelle put her hand over his. "It'll all come back to you, Arthur. I'm sure it will. Tim told you he'd seen some secret papers, didn't he, Jack?"

Haldean nodded. "That's right. Lyvenden obviously had some sort of Russian connection, because of that bloke, Youri Gerasimov, who turned up on Sunday morning. So whatever these secret papers were, I was willing to bet they had something to do with Russia. I must say that Mr Charnock's Slav, or Ukrainian, to give him his proper nationality, rather obscured the issue, as did Mr Charnock himself. And, by picking a fight with Gerasimov and taking the man's knife, Mr Charnock gave Malcolm a weapon for murder."

He sat down and looked at the light reflected through his glass. "Have you remembered what happened on Tuesday yet, Arthur?"

Stanton shook his head. "I keep getting odd flashes of things. I remember you finding the knife in my drawer, but not much else. I was so bewildered by it. I couldn't think how on earth it had got there."

"It had got there because Malcolm had put it there," said Haldean. "And my word, his plan nearly worked. The sight of you in Lyvenden's room was overwhelming as, of course, it was meant to be." He sipped his whisky thoughtfully. "I'm sorry to have to admit it,

362

Arthur, but I really did wonder if you'd flipped and killed him. I thought the effect of seeing Lyvenden — remember you were meant to have a knife in your hand as well — could have pushed you over the edge. Fennimore was there when you found out that Lyvenden was Victor Todd and, like me, thought you had a compelling motive for murder. I really did have to think about it. Isabelle never doubted you for a moment, though."

"I just knew you could never do anything like that," said Isabelle.

"And you were right, Belle," agreed Haldean, "but things looked very black." He looked at Stanton apologetically. "After all, if you hadn't killed Lyvenden, who had? Had someone tried to frame you, or had you simply blundered on the scene? And why on earth didn't you come and get help? As I said to Belle, it was an unlocked room mystery."

"That's something I don't understand," said Isabelle. "I know why Arthur didn't come and get us, of course, because the door was wedged solid, but how could Malcolm be so sure it would work? He didn't know poor Arthur was going to lose his memory. If we'd opened the door and Arthur had told us Malcolm had trapped him in there, we'd have been very suspicious of Malcolm's part in things."

Haldean sat down again. "We would, certainly, Belle, but how would the police look at it? Arthur had a very strong motive to kill Lyvenden, he'd been seen with what I was prepared to swear was the murder weapon, and he'd had the opportunity. And I don't suppose for a moment Malcolm opened the door and shoved Arthur into the room by main force. He probably said something to the tune of 'After you, old man,' and quietly shut the door once Arthur was inside. But, and this is the clever bit, because it wasn't locked when we all came to see what the fuss was about, it seemed for all the world as if Arthur had slipped his moorings altogether, stabbed Lyvenden, had forty fits and remained keening over the body. And what could Arthur say? That Lyvenden was dead when he found him and the door had stuck? It wasn't stuck when we tried it and the implication is that Arthur is a liar. No. It was a very strong circumstantial case and if it had come to trial, you wouldn't have had a chance, old son. I didn't think it would change a thing if you could remember everything perfectly. I believed Malcolm would have taken care to see it wouldn't. Ashley thought it was worth a shot, though."

He lit a cigarette. "Oddly enough, it was something Malcolm said to me that made me think. He'd said that Mr Charnock's knife was very rare, but I knew that wasn't so. They're very commonplace. What if there were two knives? And if there were two knives, then there were two murderers, if you see what I mean. Arthur, the false one, and, in the background, the real one. And the real murderer had held the knife whilst wearing gloves. Arthur didn't have any gloves and there weren't any bloodstained gloves in the room. It was a very messy murder and the murderer must have got a good deal of blood on him. He would hardly have walked down the hall covered in blood, so that meant

364

he'd gone out by the windows. Ashley and I searched high and low but couldn't find the key. That made me fairly sure that you'd been put on the spot. The key was always left in the lock and there was no reason for the murderer to lock the windows and take the key unless he wanted to stop you escaping through them." Haldean grinned. "You solved that problem very effectively, I must say."

Stanton returned the smile. "D'you know, I'm beginning to remember bits of that, too."

"What made you suspect Malcolm?" asked Isabelle.

"I didn't, at first," said Haldean with a shrug. "Then he staged his own kidnapping. He'd made a phone call to the Paradise Club in the afternoon and could have contacted them again when we were in the Grand in Brighton. However, what he didn't bargain for was that they'd not only try to kill me — I suppose Vargen Yashin must have heard how I worked things out in the Breedenbrook fête business and wasn't leaving anything to chance — but were horribly careless about the possibility of killing you, Isabelle."

Haldean took a long drink. "I wish to God I hadn't *liked* Malcolm so much. He wasn't responsible for some of the things that happened. He went barmy when he saw you were in danger, didn't he, Belle? And judging from the way the Russians cracked him over the head, they couldn't give a damn about him, only what he could do for them. He might have used them, but by God, they used him. Anyway, I wasn't killed, but the knock on the head must have done me some good, because the next morning I tumbled to it. I read a bit in the newspaper about a long leather coat being washed up on the beach and suddenly everything fell into place. Of course, the murderer needed some protection, and a motoring coat was just the thing. Motoring suggested Malcolm, and I realized how he'd managed to fool around with time."

"I remember you looking as if you'd seen a ghost," said Isabelle.

Haldean ran his finger round the top of his glass. "In a way I had. If you assume two knives, the murder could have taken place at any time after Adamson had left his master. Malcolm could have easily done it. But I knew that Malcolm hadn't killed Tim and as soon as I asked the question I knew the answer. Lyvenden had murdered Tim and Malcolm had killed Lyvenden in revenge. Once I guessed how Malcolm could have done it, I sort of saw him do it and it turned me over to think of Arthur being cold-bloodedly framed." He drank his whisky thoughtfully. "However, having the grues was no good to anyone. I needed some evidence. Now Adamson had stated that Malcolm had brought the Argentine papers into Lyvenden's room in a big briefcase and left the case behind."

He leaned forward. "The file was there but the briefcase wasn't. I'd thought earlier it was odd that such a slim file needed a large briefcase, but it had to be large to contain the coat. And if it had contained the coat, it wouldn't be in the room because the murderer would have to take it away with him. The notion it contained gloves as well seemed reasonable. That's when I knew I was on to something. And now I began to get a line on what the secret might be. If both Lyvenden and Malcolm were involved, then the betting was it concerned money. Bring Russia into the picture and you immediately get the idea that these two business partners — bankers — were involved in an illicit scheme to transfer money to Russia. Then I twigged the significance of what Lyvenden's Russian, Gerasimov, said on Sunday about learning something of value. He must have recognized Malcolm, Vargen Yashin's star prize, and for the first time linked him up with Lyvenden. Not that the knowledge did Gerasimov any good. He was shot. Malcolm looked really shaken when I told him Gerasimov's body had been found. It was obvious that Yashin only told Malcolm part of what they did. Anyway, we knew this Russian deal had been referred to in either papers or a paper. Ashley and I came across Malcolm searching Lyvenden's room, ostensibly to find the Argentine document. But if Lyvenden had been working on the Argentine document just before he died, then it would have been on top of the heap. So what had Malcolm been looking for? The Russian paper, obviously, and he didn't find it after Ashley and I came into the room. I think Lyvenden had had other papers with him and I wouldn't be surprised if Malcolm had taken them out of Lyvenden's room on the Sunday morning, Arthur, when the three of us were in there. I don't suppose you remember it, but Malcolm was really disturbed by the files he'd found. I bet one of them at least contained documents about the Russian deal. He said he was going to talk to Lyvenden about it and I imagine one of the things he said was to point out how dangerous it was to leave them lying around. He probably saw Lyvenden put the key document into his cigarette case."

"Didn't you find any of these files and so on afterwards?" asked Isabelle.

Haldean shook his head. "No. Either Lyvenden took them back to London on Monday or Malcolm hid them in his car. I can't tell you how I felt, Arthur, when I remembered telling Malcolm that you'd run off with the cigarette case. The document more or less had to be in it because the only things taken out of the room had been the briefcase and the cigarette case. I also told him that you were near your old home. I'd unwittingly set the hounds on your track and told them where to look."

He interlocked his fingers and stared at the palms of his hands for a few seconds. "I knew that as long as you were free, Arthur, you were in horrible danger. Once I'd got you into the safe hands of the police, I could breathe freely again. However, I thought it was as well to advertise the fact because I was pretty sure that once you were found, Malcolm would show up again."

"Is that why we went to the Wheatsheaf that night?" asked Isabelle.

"That's right. I also took the opportunity to tell any interested parties, through the newspaper, that as far as I was concerned, the attack had been successful and I was *hors de combat*. I had no desire for any Russian thugs to pay me a return visit. That came off. Malcolm was found but in such a dreadful state, I couldn't make

368

it add up. From what he said to me on the beach, I don't think he really cared if he lived or died any more. He'd cold-bloodedly taken an overdose of morphine and gambled he'd be found in time. It was very convincing, but I knew I had to be right, despite appearances. Having the document translated clinched it."

"There's something I don't understand, Jack," said Lady Rivers. "Why, with all that evidence, couldn't Mr Ashley simply arrest him?"

Haldean looked at her. "What evidence, Aunt Alice? We could prove he was planning to steal the bank's funds and illegally transfer them to the Soviets all right, but that didn't prove he'd murdered Lyvenden. As soon as the story about the money got out he'd be ruined, sure enough, because with the details on that document it'd be easy to find supporting evidence of the transfer, but that wasn't what I was after. So he'd bought a knife. So what? That's not a crime. For Arthur's sake I had to try to get Malcolm to admit it. We had nothing like enough evidence for a jury. The sort of lawyer Malcolm could afford would have made mincemeat of our case. It all sounded so hypothetical and airy-fairy compared to the sight of poor old Arthur standing over Lyvenden, covered in blood. I was hoping for a confession, but it all went horribly wrong. I realized, of course, that if he confessed he would be arrested, tried and hanged. If all Malcolm had done was take revenge for Tim, then I might have left it. Lyvenden was no beauty and deserved everything he got. But you, Arthur . . . I couldn't stomach that. We had to get him to admit it. Anything less wouldn't do. Malcolm had been completely safe because no one had seen him wedge Lyvenden's door to and trap Arthur in there. But what if someone had seen him? That would change things dramatically. So, I typed a blackmail letter."

Sir Philip gaped at him. "You did what?"

Haldean grinned. "It was very respectful, as these things go. I signed it 'A friend'. All it said was that the writer had seen what Malcolm had done in the corridor that day. If Malcolm had been innocent, it wouldn't have mattered a bean. I promised no further demands would be made if Malcolm could see his way to leaving two hundred quid — I wasn't doing this on the cheap — under the floor of the summerhouse by five o'clock that afternoon."

"So that's what all that was about," said Isabelle.

"Yes, old thing," said Haldean, getting up and helping himself to another whisky and soda, "that's what all that was about. Ashley and Constable Bevan hid themselves in the shrubbery and watched Malcolm go into the summerhouse. As soon as Malcolm had left, Ashley looked under the loose board and there was an envelope with two hundred quid and a request to meet the writer. Constable Bevan brought me a note to say Malcolm had taken the bait, and next thing the man himself rang the front doorbell, having supposedly just arrived from the station. The trouble was that I didn't know, and Ashley didn't know, if our blackmail wheeze would be acceptable in court. Again, when you think of the lawyer Malcolm would have at his beck and call, we might find that we'd run into tiresome things like

Judges' Rules and the whole blackmail business would be deemed inadmissible. We needed to get Malcolm to the stage where, first having believed he was safe, he was suddenly in the position where he was threatened. And that, with a man like Malcolm, was a dangerous game to play. He was as twitchy as a kitten in any event, so I took the elementary precaution of taking the bullets out of the magazine of his gun. Ashley was outside the french windows and as soon as he heard I'd got the gun, he brought you all into the room. Malcolm was far too interested in you, Belle, coming into the room to notice what I was doing." He grinned. "There was another bullet in the chamber which I discharged as soon as I could."

"So that's what you were up to," said Sir Philip. "Damn me, boy, I thought you'd gone mad when you fired the wretched thing."

"It was just as well I did though, wasn't it?" His smile widened. "Quite honestly, Arthur, I don't know what you thought you were playing at. I knew the gun was empty and Ashley knew it was empty, but you didn't know and you still went for him."

Arthur looked sheepish. "I couldn't let him threaten Isabelle, could I? Besides that, I was hopping mad when I thought what he'd put me through. All I really wanted to do was get Isabelle to safety and wallop him good and hard."

"I wish you had done," said Haldean in a low voice. "It would have been so much better than what happened." He was quiet for a few moments, looking at

371

the palms of his hands. "Anyway, I drove him off the road. God help me."

Stanton moved uneasily. "Come on, Jack."

Haldean took a deep breath. "I won't ever be able to forget the noise he made as he fell. Ever. And I found it a bit tough, you know? I liked him. I'd liked him enormously and having to pretend I was his friend and so on when he came into the house was pretty hard, knowing what I knew." His voice broke abruptly. "Damned hard."

Isabelle took his hands in hers, forcing him to look at her. "Jack, listen to me. Arthur was supposed to hang and you saved him. I'll never be able to thank you enough for that."

"Me neither," added Stanton. "And there's something else, too." He looked at Isabelle affectionately. "Don't take this the wrong way, but after what I've been through, I'm blessed if I'm running the risk of you becoming Mrs Anyone Else." He turned to Sir Philip. "Er . . . it's normally the sort of question you ask in private, sir, but can I have your permission to marry your daughter?"

Sir Philip laughed. "I don't think you can wriggle out of it now, m'boy."

"In that case, Jack," said Stanton, "you will be best man, won't you?"

Haldean squeezed Isabelle's hands. "Try asking anyone else," he said with a grin. "I'll forbid the banns."

372

Also available in ISIS Large Print:

Under Suspicion

The Mulgray Twins

DJ Smith is sent to Tenerife to infiltrate a money-laundering organisation run by Ambrose Vanheusen. DJ knows she is in deadly danger from such a ruthless criminal but luckily he has an Achilles heel: his obsession with his Persian cat, Samarkand Black Prince. DJ's passport into Vanheusen's empire comes in the form of Gorgonzola, a moth-eaten ginger Persian and sniffer cat extraordinaire, acting under the pedigree alias of Persepolis Desert Sandstorm.

With drug dealing, money laundering and murder to contend with, not to mention a cat with attitude, DJ has her hands full. So it's not surprising she doesn't realise that the greatest danger lies in Vanheusen's determination to steal her supposedly pedigree moggy. He's prepared to go to any lengths necessary to get his hands on a mate for his brute of a cat, and only a tooth and claw confrontation will determine who survives . . .

ISBN 978-0-7531-8216-1 (hb)
ISBN 978-0-7531-8217-8 (pb)

A Moment of Silence

Anna Dean

Belsfield Hall, 1805. Whilst dancing at a ball held in celebration of her engagement to Mr Richard Montague, Miss Catherine Kent witnesses a silent communication between her fiancé and a stranger, followed by the disappearance of her betrothed. Distraught with worry, Catherine sends for her beloved spinster aunt, Miss Dido Kent. But on the very day of Dido's arrival, a sinister discovery casts unwelcome suspicion on Richard's sudden absence.

Long-hidden family secrets begin to emerge as Dido attempts to unravel the strange happenings. She uses her logical thinking to carve a swathe through the rumour-mongering, ambitious matchmaking and ulterior motives of the other guests. When she finally arrives at the startling truth, it is to change the lives of those involved forever. But will it be for better or worse, for richer or poorer, in sickness or in health? Only time will tell . . .

ISBN 978-0-7531-8188-1 (hb)
ISBN 978-0-7531-8189-8 (pb)

The Girl in the Cellar

Patricia Wentworth

A young woman regains consciousness and finds herself on some cellar steps. At the bottom of the steps is the corpse of a dead girl. She cannot remember who she is, what has happened or why she is there. Terrified and confused she manages to find a way out and, as she flees, she runs into Miss Silver, who offers to help her.

A letter in her bag is the only clue to her identity. But by investigating what has happened to her will she find herself in danger? Can she trust the letter-writer? And who is the girl in the cellar?

ISBN 978-0-7531-8126-3 (hb)
ISBN 978-0-7531-8127-0 (pb)

Murder at Deviation Junction

Andrew Martin

December, 1909. A train hits a snowdrift in the frozen Cleveland Hills. In the process of clearing the line a body is discovered, and so begins a dangerous case for struggling railway detective Jim Stringer.

His new investigation takes him to the mighty blast furnaces of Ironopolis; to Fleet Street in the company of a cynical reporter from *The Railway Rover*; and to a nightmarish spot in the Highlands. Jim's faltering career in the railway police hangs on whether he can solve the murder — but before long, the pursuer becomes the pursued, and Jim finds himself fighting not just for his job, but for his very life . . .

ISBN 978-0-7531-8130-0 (hb)
ISBN 978-0-7531-8131-7 (pb)

A Fête Worse than Death

Dolores Gordon-Smith

It's 1922, and Jack Haldean, a young crime writer and former Royal Flying Corps pilot, is enjoying the local summer fête. As he remarks to his cousins Isabelle and Greg Rivers, this is the England he dreamed of during his wartime missions.

But the idyll is soon shattered when Jack's fellow officer, Jeremy Boscombe, is found dead in the fortune-teller's tent. When a friend of Boscombe's is also found murdered, Jack soon realises that the roots of the crime go back to an incident during the Battle of the Somme.

Money, love, revenge and blackmail all play their part as Jack inches closer to the truth, putting his life and the lives of those around him in danger. The trail leads inexorably back to the Somme and it is in those silent tunnels that Jack faces his final enemy — one who must kill to survive.

ISBN 978-0-7531-7982-6 (hb)
ISBN 978-0-7531-7983-3 (pb)

ISIS publish a wide range of books in large print, from fiction to biography. Any suggestions for books you would like to see in large print or audio are always welcome. Please send to the Editorial Department at:

ISIS Publishing Limited
7 Centremead
Osney Mead
Oxford OX2 0ES

A full list of titles is available free of charge from:

Ulverscroft Large Print Books Limited

(UK)
The Green
Bradgate Road, Anstey
Leicester LE7 7FU
Tel: (0116) 236 4325

(Australia)
P.O. Box 314
St Leonards
NSW 1590
Tel: (02) 9436 2622

(USA)
P.O. Box 1230
West Seneca
N.Y. 14224-1230
Tel: (716) 674 4270

(Canada)
P.O. Box 80038
Burlington
Ontario L7L 6B1
Tel: (905) 637 8734

(New Zealand)
P.O. Box 456
Feilding
Tel: (06) 323 6828

Details of **ISIS** complete and unabridged audio books are also available from these offices. Alternatively, contact your local library for details of their collection of **ISIS** large print and unabridged audio books.